THE RHETORIC
OF CONFESSION

All fiction is fiction.

George Levine,
"Realism Reconsidered"

Shōsetsu wa shosen shōsetsu de a[ru].

Wada Kingo,
Byōsha no jidai

THE RHETORIC
OF CONFESSION

SHISHŌSETSU IN
EARLY TWENTIETH-CENTURY
JAPANESE FICTION

Edward Fowler

University of California Press

Berkeley · Los Angeles · Oxford

1988

University of California Press
Berkeley and Los Angeles, California

University of California Press, Ltd.
Oxford, England

© 1988 by
The Regents of the University of California
First Paperback Printing 1992

Library of Congress Cataloging-in-Publication Data

Fowler, Edward.
  The rhetoric of confession.

  Bibliography: p.
  Includes index.
  1. Autobiographical fiction, Japanese—History and criti-
cism.   2. Japanese fiction—Taishō period, 1912–1926—
History and criticism.   I. Title.
PL747.63.A85F6   1988   895.6'34'09   87-13879
ISBN 0-520-07883-7

Printed in the United States of America

1 2 3 4 5 6 7 8 9

To my parents

Contents

Preface

Early in the summer of 1985, I sat down at a Tokyo hotel with Irokawa Budai, an award-winning writer, to discuss narrative fiction
and particularly the autobiographical form known as the *shishōsetsu*—often *mis*translated (as I shall argue) as "I-novel." We had
hardly settled into our seats and taken in the view from the lobby
when he blurted out, almost apologetically: "*Shōsetsu* and *shishōsetsu*—they are both very strange. You see, there is no God in the
Japanese tradition, no monolithic ordering authority in narrative—
and that makes all the difference."

Irokawa's words astonished me not only for their directness but
also because they brought home to me a truism too easily ignored:
that different cultures can breed very different kinds of narrative
and that our purpose as readers outside the target culture ought to
be to understand such narratives in terms of their inherent dynam-
ics rather than of what they presumably "lack" from the western
perspective.

That the *shishōsetsu* differs from classical western narrative is
plain for all to see. I wish to stress, however, that the basic "difference" derives from the fact that the *shōsetsu* itself—that Japanese
word we glibly translate as "novel"—also differs fundamentally
from western narrative. Indeed, to translate *shōsetsu* or *shishōsetsu*
as "novel" or "I-novel" at all is to assume, wrongly, I believe, some
easy interchangeability of narrative method between the two cultures. The task as I see it, therefore, is to distance *shōsetsu* from
"novel" while collapsing the perceived distinctions between *shōsetsu* and *shishōsetsu*. The latter differs from the former only in that
it can be more autobiographical, not because it distorts the other in
some essential way, as is so often suggested both here and in Japan. The reasons for the popularity of a patently autobiographical
form are manifold and are discussed in depth in Parts 1 and 2.
Other than this aspect, the *shishōsetsu* has everything in common

with early twentieth-century *shōsetsu*. It is not an anomaly; it is the core. It makes the best linguistic sense, moreover, as the narrating voice merges most easily with that of the narrated subject—a feature of the Japanese language generally. We shall see that the first-person *or* third-person *shishōsetsu*, almost by definition, works most effectively when it has but one center of consciousness, which is at once the narrator's *and* the hero's own.

Without denying a basic commonality between *shōsetsu* and novel, then, this book focuses on the distinctions and suggests why they are not always apparent in translation. Given the obvious limitations presented by an English-language study, we will look as closely as possible throughout at the Japanese language. Each part of the book offers a specific approach to *shishōsetsu*. The Introduction provides a discursive context for the argument that follows. Part 1 traces the *shishōsetsu*'s roots to Chinese and native literary and intellectual traditions as well as to the structure of the Japanese language itself. It also argues that the form's special property is not the oft-touted "sincerity" of its confessional style but the rhetorical *style* of sincerity, which is no more—and no less—than a sophisticated verbal artifact. Part 2 explores the impact that literary tradition, the naturalist movement, and contemporary journalistic realities had on the writing of autobiographical fiction early in this century. Part 3 discusses three writers considered central to the *shishōsetsu* enterprise. My concern is less with autobiography than with textual signification—that is, the modus operandi of "sincerity" and "authenticity" as discourse.

Japan has produced many books on *shishōsetsu* writers, but none primarily on the *shishōsetsu* form itself. The one study to do so comes from Germany, not Japan: Irmela Hijiya-Kirschnereit's *Selbstentblössungsrituale* (Rituals of self-exposé; Wiesbaden: Steiner, 1981). It is an important work that treats the mode of confession as formal convention (as opposed to some ontologically truthful account) and introduces eight authors (including those appearing in this book), most of whom are little known in the west. I believe that a discussion limited to a single work by each author, however, cannot fully explain how a writer actually goes about producing, or how a reader goes about consuming, *shishōsetsu*, given its serial nature and its intertextual focus at the level of both oeuvre and canon. The purpose of this book is to clarify that nature and focus.

None of the texts discussed at length in this study are translated into English, with the exception of Edwin McClellan's fine rendering of Shiga Naoya's *An'ya kōro*. There is a good chance, moreover, that many of them will never be translated. (The question of why they will not of course sheds considerable light on our own cultural expectations of fiction and on the nature of the two languages.) I have chosen them anyway (knowing that I would face the same difficulty regardless of the *shishōsetsu* writers I discussed) in the conviction that only an extended treatment of several writers' textual production would reveal the contours of the *shishōsetsu* form— and, more ambitiously, the landscape of modern Japanese literature—with enough resolution to contrast them legitimately with our own classical narrative tradition.

Even as I refer to "traditional" narrative in the west, I am aware of the plurality of narrative forms in western prose fiction, particularly in the twentieth century. I use it as the basis for comparison nonetheless, because it continues to be the dominant popular mode, not just in literature but also in film, drama, and television. To a great extent, it still both reflects and determines the way we see the world. Whether it uses the omniscient third-person narrator of a nineteenth-century realistic novel reigning confidently over his fictional realm, or the first-person narrator of a twentieth-century novel presiding self-consciously over his metafictional realm, narrative in the west has retained its profound faith in the narrator's creative authority and autonomous voice. I see neither in mainstream Japanese fiction. Nor, obviously, does a writer like Irokawa Budai.

This fact is not necessarily to the detriment of *shōsetsu*. What Japanese offers is a degree of narrator-hero-reader identification that is literally unthinkable in English or in other western languages. No wonder confusion between hero and narrator (and by extension, author) is so prevalent: they can be defined only in relationship to one another. This book will explore, and attempt to make sense out of, that relationship.

It is a pleasure to acknowledge the generous assistance of many individuals and organizations in the writing of this book. I wish first to thank my wife, Hiroko, who has over the years selflessly offered me that most precious of all resources, without which this book could never have been contemplated, much less completed: time. I also wish to thank the many teachers and colleagues who shared their expertise. Masao Miyoshi, who chaired my dissertation committee, has been a guiding light, both during and after my years of study at U.C. Berkeley. Without his instruction, encouragement, and uncompromising criticisms, the tenor of this book would have been very different indeed. Robert N. Bellah and Helen C. McCullough offered numerous suggestions when this study was at the dissertation stage. Irwin Scheiner got me thinking in concrete terms about the "myth" of sincerity in Japanese literature. Chiyuki Kumakura continually pressed me to ever-more-rigorous readings of texts. Edward W. Said's seminar on narrative representation at the Sixth School of Criticism and Theory, held at Northwestern University in the summer of 1982, greatly aided my analysis of narrative. I am grateful to Miriam Cooke, Chiyuki Kumakura, S.-Y. Kuroda, Masao Miyoshi, J. Thomas Rimer, and Nobuko Tsukui for commenting on portions of the manuscript. Richard Okada and Victoria Vernon read the entire manuscript and provided important criticisms. Their scrupulous readings gave rise to much of what I think is of value in this book, and not a little of what has been judiciously excised. In Japan, I was the beneficiary of numerous kindnesses and considerable intellectual stimulation. Saitō Akira first introduced me to the major *shishōsetsu* criticism when I was a student at the Tokyo Inter-University Center. Kikuta Shigeo opened many doors to me and gave of his own time and mind during two separate research trips to Japan. Many other scholars and critics, including Hiraoka Tokuyoshi, Imoto Nōichi, Karatani Kōjin, Murakami Hyōe, Nakajima Kunihiko, Ōmori Sumio, Osanai Tokio, Saeki Shōichi, Sasaki Yasuaki, Sawa Toyohiko, and Tazawa Motohisa, graciously accommodated my research in countless ways. Several writers and editors, including Ibuse Masuji, Irokawa Budai, Maruko Tetsuo, Mura Jirō, Nagata Ryūtarō, and Sakamoto Tadao, provided a contemporary perspective on my Taishō-period research.

I benefited enormously from support provided by the staffs of the following libraries and archives: the Nihon Kindai Bungakukan, the Kokubungaku Kenkyū Shiryōkan, the Meiji Bunko, the Toritsu Chūō Toshokan, and the International House and Japan Foundation libraries, all in Tokyo; and in the United States, the East

Asiatic libraries of the University of California, Berkeley, and the University of Chicago. Research for this book was generously funded at the dissertation stage by the Japan Foundation and the Mabelle McLeod Lewis Memorial Fund, and later by the Duke University Asian/Pacific Studies Institute and the National Endowment for the Humanities. Special thanks go to Mavis Mayer and Gail Woods for handling many typing and other production duties, and to Betsey Scheiner, of the University of California Press, for her creative and meticulous copyediting. Thanks finally to the Duke University Research Council for funding the index. To all go my sincere appreciation for assuring me, at times when I was less certain than they, of the need for undertaking such a study as this.

Abbreviations

CSK   Kōno Toshirō, ed. *Chikamatsu Shūkō kenkyū* [A study of Chikamatsu Shūkō]. Tokyo: Gakushū Kenkyūsha, 1980.

CSS   Hirano Ken, ed. *Chikamatsu Shūkō shū* [Chikamatsu Shūkō: an anthology]. Vol. 14 of *Nihon bungaku zenshū* [Japanese literature: an anthology]. Tokyo: Shūeisha, 1974.

KBHT   Inagaki Tatsurō et al., eds. *Kindai bungaku hyōron taikei* [A collection of critical essays on modern (Japanese) literature]. 10 vols. Tokyo: Kadokawa Shoten, 1971–75.

KKK   *Kokubungaku kaishaku to kanshō.* (Periodical)

KKKK   *Kokubungaku kaishaku to kyōzai no kenkyū.* (Periodical)

KZZ   *Kasai Zenzō zenshū* [Kasai Zenzō: collected works]. Ed. Osanai Tokio. 4 vols. Hirosaki: Tsugaru Shobō, 1974–75.

MBZ   Itō Sei et al., eds. *Meiji bungaku zenshū* [Anthology of Meiji literature]. 99 vols. Tokyo: Chikuma Shobō, 1965–80.

NKBD   Nihon Kindai Bungakukan, ed. *Nihon kindai bungaku daijiten* [Encyclopedia of modern Japanese literature]. 6 vols. Tokyo: Kōdansha, 1977–78.

NKBT   Itō Sei et al., eds. *Nihon kindai bungaku taikei* [Collection of modern Japanese literature]. 60 vols. Tokyo: Kadokawa Shoten, 1969–74.

NKD   Nihon Daijiten Kankōkai, ed. *Nihon kokugo daijiten* [Dictionary of the Japanese national language]. 20 vols. Tokyo: Shōgakukan, 1972–76.

SNZ   *Shiga Naoya zenshū* [Shiga Naoya: collected works]. Ed. Mushanokōji Saneatsu et al. 15 vols. Tokyo: Iwanami Shoten, 1973–74.

Introduction

Presentation and Representation in the Shishōsetsu

Every work is rewritten by its reader, who imposes upon it
a new grid of interpretation for which he is not generally
responsible but which comes to him from his culture, from
his time, in short from another discourse; all comprehension is the encounter of two discourses: a dialogue. It is
futile and silly to try to leave off being oneself in order to
become someone else; were one to succeed, the result
would be of no interest (since it would be a pure reproduction of the initial discourse). By its very existence, the science of ethnology proves to us, if need be, that we *gain* by
being different from what we seek to understand. This interpretation (in the necessary double sense of translation
and comprehension) is the condition of survival of the antecedent text; but no less so, I should say, of contemporary
discourse. Hence interpretation is no longer true or false
but rich or poor, revealing or sterile, stimulating or dull.

Tzvetan Todorov, *Introduction to*
Poetics

Prose fiction [*shōsetsu*] depends for its existence not merely
on its having been written but also on being read creatively.

Itō Sei, *Shōsetsu*
no hōhō

This book examines one culture's view of the place of the author in
his writings and of the place of fiction in literature. It focuses on
the *shishōsetsu* (more formally *watakushi shōsetsu;*[1] commonly trans-

---

1. Both terms are readings of the same compound: 私小説 . The sinified reading of the first character, because of its brevity, is more common. Semantic distinctions that have occasionally been made between the two readings seem unsatisfac-
tory and will be ignored here.

lated as "I-novel"), an autobiographical form that flourished in Taishō Japan (1912–26). The *shishōsetsu*, narrated in the first or third person in such a way as to represent with utter conviction the author's personal experience, is riddled with paradoxes. Supposedly a fictional narrative, it often reads more like a private journal. It has a reputation of being true, to a fault, to "real life"; yet it frequently strays from the author's experience it allegedly portrays so faithfully. Its personal orientation makes it a thoroughly modern form; yet it is the product of an indigenous intellectual tradition quite disparate from western individualism. Progressive critics have ridiculed it over the decades as a failed adaptation of the western novel, while traditionalists have reveled in its difference. The difference lies not so much in its autobiographical "purity" (as the Japanese literary establishment, or *bundan*, would have us believe), however, as in its ultimate distrust of western-style realistic representation from which it has presumably borrowed so heavily. Its critically mixed reception notwithstanding, the *shishōsetsu* has been championed by many important writers and occupies a central position in modern Japanese letters. Coming to terms with it means coming to terms in many ways with the entire literature.

The period under discussion begins roughly with the publication of Tayama Katai's *Futon* (1907), commonly regarded as the prototypical *shishōsetsu*, and ends with the form's clear emergence into the literary world's critical consciousness in the mid-1920s. To comment on every writer affected by the rise of the *shishōsetsu* would have the effect of saying very little about the form, since it was embraced by virtually every literary school. A precise measurement of its influence is perhaps impossible, but the critic Terada Tōru did not exaggerate a great deal when he declared in 1950 that only three major post-Restoration authors (Natsume Sōseki, Kōda Rohan, and Izumi Kyōka) had written no *shishōsetsu*.[2] It is a form, in other words, with which nearly every early twentieth-century Japanese writer experimented at some time in his career; each had to come to terms with its legacy, its attractions, and its pitfalls. Some writers, like Tanizaki Jun'ichirō and Kikuchi Kan, dabbled in the form but moved on to other projects. Others, like

2. "Shinkyō shōsetsu, watakushi shōsetsu," 145. Terada considers Sōseki's *Michikusa* and Kyōka's *Kunisada egaku* to be examples of autobiographical fiction but not of true *shishōsetsu*.

Akutagawa Ryūnosuke, belittled the form only to use it themselves in time. Still others, like Tokuda Shūsei, Shimazaki Tōson, and the authors presented in this study, wrote *shishōsetsu* throughout their careers.

The variety of approaches and the uniformly ambivalent attitude displayed by writers toward the *shishōsetsu* make it difficult if not impossible to single out a "representative" author for close examination. This study features three authors: Chikamatsu Shūkō (1876–1944), Shiga Naoya (1883–1971), and Kasai Zenzō (1887–1928). Shiga is a celebrated writer, while Shūkō and Kasai[3] are relative unknowns here and in Japan. The latter two writers have been selected over some of their more famous contemporaries in the belief that their careers as *shishōsetsu* writers par excellence serve to demonstrate the form's characteristics more readily than less extreme, if better-known, examples. Their minor reputations should not, however, obscure the *shishōsetsu*'s importance in modern Japanese letters.

How we interpret the *shishōsetsu* will depend a great deal on how we interpret Japanese literature and indeed all of Japanese culture. Orthodoxy has it that it is a Japanized version of European naturalism. Our reading of it will suggest, however, that it is most emphatically a product of the native tradition (or more precisely, of traditional ways of thinking about literature) rather than simply a distortion of literary naturalism imported from the west. To the extent that the *shishōsetsu* is in fact traditional and by that measure unique, we must understand how Japanese literature as a whole differs from western literature. But to the extent that it is accessible to a readership other than its intended original audience and has some claim to universality, we must also ask what is involved in the process of reading. Is our grasp of an unfamiliar literature made possible by the coincidental overlapping of our own and the originating culture's assumptions and expectations about writing? Or is it made possible by an unconscious molding of expectations during the course of our study? Or, finally, is it made possible merely

3. This book follows the Japanese practice of referring to a writer by his surname (written first), unless the writer uses a pen name. Thus, Shiga Naoya and Kasai Zenzō are referred to as Shiga and Kasai, and Natsume Sōseki and Shimazaki Tōson as Sōseki and Tōson. Writers whose full names are pen names (e.g., Futabatei Shimei) are referred to by their surnames. Chikamatsu Shūkō (Tokuda Kōji) is an exception, because "Chikamatsu" is easily confused with the well-known Edo-period dramatist. Customary Japanese usage is adhered to in all instances.

through a willful misreading in which certain deeply ingrained hermeneutical practices perform a kind of interpretive aggression on the texts we read? However indeterminate the precise combination of factors that informs our "understanding" of another literature, it is a matter of which we, as readers with notably different intellectual baggage than that of the original audience, should continually be aware. If we develop our discussion on the basis of clearly identifiable properties that western fiction can be said to "have," we must avoid talking about a literature outside that tradition in terms of what it "lacks" and thereby give it a negative cast. At the same time, we must take care that the necessary explication of unfamiliar terms and concepts does not divert attention from issues that concern us as a western audience. Some compromise, however fragile, must be struck between overidentification with and insensitivity to the other literature in order to create the climate for a reading that is at once sympathetic and scrupulously critical.

In short, we can take little for granted in our study. Even the ostensibly simple matter of classification is fraught with difficulties. The literary terms and categories with which we are accustomed to work seem inadequate. Are we to take the *shishōsetsu*'s name literally and read it as fiction (*shōsetsu*)? Or are we to treat it essentially as nonfiction as the majority of Japanese critics do? Each approach has attractions and could conceivably generate its own readings; yet it does not deny ipso facto the possibility of the other.

By far the most common approach to the *shishōsetsu* has been the nonfictional one, for the general critical perception has been that it is resistant by definition to analysis as an autonomous text. Unlike "pure literature" in the west, which calls to mind an author aloof from his writing after the manner of Flaubert or Joyce, "pure literature" in Japan (a category to which the *shishōsetsu* belongs) is considered inherently referential in nature: its meaning derives from an extraliterary source, namely, the author's life. The Japanese as readers of *shishōsetsu* have tended to regard the author's life, and not the written work, as the definitive "text" on which critical judgment ultimately rests and to see the work as meaningful only insofar as it illuminates the life. The Japanese reader constructs a "sign" out of the signifying text and the signified extraliterary life, with no misgivings about this apparent blending of "intrinsic" literary and "extrinsic" biographical data. Literature which is not "pure" (i.e., literature that does not serve as a window on the author's life) is relegated to the realm of "popular" reading and considered less worthy of critical attention.

Such an approach raises a serious question, however. Must we then equate the strongly autobiographical tendencies in the *shishō-setsu* with nonfictionality, as do most Japanese critics? The tradition of autobiographical fiction in the west would seem to indicate otherwise.[4] There is sufficient evidence in the *shishōsetsu* themselves, moreover, to make us skeptical about their presumed non-fictionality. It is quite true that the writings of Chikamatsu Shūkō, Shiga Naoya, and Kasai Zenzō are based on the authors' lives; yet to use the texts, as Japanese critics often do, to "document" the extraliterary lives and see the latter as the "true" object of criticism is at best a risky enterprise. Shūkō, for example, by writing in a series of stories about the same event in "real life" many times over, reveals a strategy of variant "readings" that has the effect of calling into question the validity of any single reading of his life. Shiga, meanwhile, approaches personal experience with the taciturn reserve of a censor intent on cosmetic rewriting. And Kasai openly posits an autobiographical reading of any story only to undermine it during the very course of the story or in subsequent texts. All three examples underscore the necessity of making as vigilant a distinction between author and persona in texts that are ostensibly autobiographical as in those that are not.

If one sets out to do so, then, one can indeed read the *shishōsetsu* as fiction, and it is tempting, in light of this second approach, to conclude that the *shishōsetsu* is more a cultural than a literary phenomenon, the product of a particular critical attitude rather than a viable formal classification. Yet even this latter approach is not entirely satisfactory: even though it denies any special generic classification or claim to uniqueness (and thus argues for a certain universal appeal that potentially transcends cultural bounds), it overlooks the fact that many *shishōsetsu* are indeed impenetrable

4. So would a certain strain of autobiographical fiction in Japanese that is clearly influenced by western models. Tokutomi Roka's *Omoide no ki* (1901), for example, is a fairly successful adaptation of *David Copperfield* into the Japanese context. But as Kenneth Strong notes in the introduction to his translation of the work (as *Footprints in the Snow*), even Roka was too "preoccupied, in a manner . . . characteristically Japanese, with himself and his own close circle of relationships" (30 n. 40), to attempt a broad Dickensian depiction of society.

on first reading. This opacity has less to do with content than with form: a western reader might know a great deal about the life of Chikamatsu Shūkō or Shiga Naoya or Kasai Zenzō and still wonder what the author is getting at in his writings. The *shishōsetsu* is often formally unsatisfying, then, because it does not follow the narrative conventions that have governed western fiction.

It would be hard to exaggerate this point. To the extent that form can be distinguished from content, the mode of presentation in *shishōsetsu* (and probably in other kinds of Japanese literary texts as well), would appear to be more culture-bound than the specific information presented. What distinguishes the *shishōsetsu* from western fiction is not how closely it follows "real life" but how singularly it operates as a mode of discourse. As confession, it usually pales before its western counterparts. The novels of many writers, from Strindberg and Tolstoy to Miller and Mailer, contain "revelations" far more blatant and shocking than any to be found in the *shishōsetsu*. Confessional autobiography, however, like most traditional fiction in the west, is informed by what might be described as a secular teleology whereby personal disclosures are made with a specific formal as well as moral end in mind. Confession in the interest of atonement or self-analysis or even self-aggrandizement is the catalyst for some resolution or action that gives the work its shape and direction. In short, fiction and autobiography in the west have as one of their formal properties a sense of forward movement and purpose.

The literary mechanism by which an author makes the reader sense this movement is, of course, the emplotted narrative (henceforth "narrative" will be used in this particular sense), and it is precisely this mechanism that appears to be so attenuated in *shishōsetsu* and in much of Japanese fiction. It should come as no surprise, then, that Japanese critics are generally uncomfortable calling the *shishōsetsu* fiction at all. Fiction, as in other western modes of discourse, from history and biography to the expository essay, houses a narrative dynamo that generates a linear, forward-moving plot and, like harmony and counterpoint in music, propels the thematic development to its conclusion. Since at least the eighteenth century, narrative in the west has been founded on the belief that process—the growth or development of a hero or institution in fiction, biography, or history—was not only an ontological possibility but could be faithfully represented.[5] Japanese literature, however, has traditionally been more concerned with state than with process, and narrative in the sense defined here has therefore played a limited role. The western author has regarded his hero as an autonomous figure with the power to create his own world; he represents, by means of a plot, the teleological process by which his hero strives toward a humanly achievable end. The Japanese author, meanwhile, has regarded his hero as virtually powerless in the face of society and nature and as more comfortable when keeping aloof from society or when submitting to, rather than confronting, the forces of nature. Mori Atsushi, a contemporary *shishōsetsu* writer, characterizes this yielding to natural forces with the Buddhist phrase *shō-rō-byō-shi*—the four unavoidable trials of birth, aging, sickness, and death that all humans must experience during their life cycles on earth.[6] The result is a literature more attuned to acceptance than to reform.

Moreover, while narrative in the west, according to Noël Burch, is weighted heavily toward "realistic" representation,[7] it has competed in Japan with more self-consciously presentational styles in a variety of literary and performative modes throughout history: *waka, haikai, nikki, zuihitsu, nō, jōruri,* and even *monogatari* and *ukiyo zōshi,* which have commonly but incorrectly been regarded as narrative-centered forms. The linear narrative flow in all these forms is continually intersected by allusion, polysemy, and discursive meditations, which disrupt the reader's focus on the object of narration and redirect it insistently on the narrating subject and/or the very process of narration. Seen from the perspective of Japanese literature, the classical western narrative, regardless of the particular orientation (history, biography, fiction, etc.), is a very homogeneous form next to which the Japanese literary tradition, of which

5. The discussion here is indebted to the work of Edward W. Said. See, for example, his *Beginnings,* esp. the section on narrative fiction (81–94) that introduces chap. 3 ("The Novel as Beginning Intention"); and his essay entitled "The Text, the World, the Critic."

6. Mori Atsushi and Takano Etsuko, "Taidan: bungaku to eiga," 15–16.

7. *To the Distant Observer,* 98. This remarkable book on Japanese cinema has provided an important catalyst to my thinking on Japanese literature. See esp. the preface and part 1, in which Burch discusses the "presentational" orientation of Japanese narrative forms and the traditional unconcern for unbroken linear representation or for such hallowed western values as "creativity" and "originality."

the *shishōsetsu* is most emphatically a part, clearly shows itself to be of an altogether different order.

Yet if Japanese critics are uncomfortable calling the *shishōsetsu* fiction in its narrative-charged sense, they are just as uncomfortable calling it autobiography, for autobiography houses the same narrative dynamo that is so alien to the traditional Japanese aesthetic. The urge to use western literary terminology at all in Japan when it would appear to be inappropriate stems of course from the great prestige that western culture as a whole has enjoyed since the beginning of the Meiji period (1868–1912). After studying western politics, economics, law, science, and society, the Japanese studied literature as well, ever conscious of the standard it provided native writers. Japanese critics soon took to applying the taxonomy of English, French, German, and Russian criticism in particular to indigenous literary forms; when they realized that the fit was less than perfect, they insisted for the most part that the fault lay with Japanese literature rather than with western taxonomy.

From the time it had emerged into the critical consciousness in the 1920s, the *shishōsetsu* was commonly looked upon as something of a mongrel or bastard, born to an evolutionary-conscious literary world in which the apparent goal was the development of genres equivalent to those in the west.[8] Indeed, it is possible to chart the entire history of modern Japanese literature, beginning with Tsubouchi Shōyō's famous tract (*Shōsetsu shinzui*, 1885–86) denouncing Edo fiction and extolling western "realism," in terms of newly developed forms—unmetered verse, the short story, the novel—whose very raison d'être was their hallowed place in the western canon. True, such visible influences are frequently the most superficial; as one historian has pointed out, literary influences are perhaps the easiest of all cross-cultural contacts to allege and the hardest to measure.[9] Both literary "mentor" and "student," however, have until recently rarely doubted their import, and they have generally measured modern Japanese fiction against the standard of its

---

8. A typical example of this perspective can be found in Nakamura Mitsuo's *Fūzoku shōsetsu ron*, esp. chap. 1. See also Takeyama Michio, "Honkaku shōsetsu no umarenu wake," for a succinct application of traditional western novelistic conventions to modern Japanese fiction, to the detriment of the latter. This critical bias is discussed in detail in Chapter 3.

9. George B. Sansom, *The Western World and Japan*, 404.

presumed models, particularly nineteenth-century "realism" (by which is here meant the dominant narrative mode in the west rather than some ontologically absolute entity opposed to "fantasy"). Not surprisingly, both have found it to be a poor imitation, and they have viewed the *shishōsetsu* in particular as an example of literary influences gone awry.

Even while pursuing many of the thematic concerns found in European literature, few Japanese writers strayed from the traditional narrative system, which had a very different orientation from that of the classical western narrative. The latter, as we have seen, was founded on the belief that process could be fully represented and that each action or event was linked to a knowable resolution. Representation was the sum total of the narrative enterprise; and the narrator, a sort of secular god, was endowed with the *autho*rity of an omniscient creator. Supreme in his artistic world, the narrator exercised his creative license, giving birth to fictional situations and characters answerable only to his authority and to the constraints of "realism," a powerfully persuasive but nonetheless illusionist descriptive method that avoided reference to or revelation of the mechanics of representation.[10]

The Japanese writer, on the other hand, never had the faith in the authority of representation that his western counterpart had. Rather than attempt to create a fictional world that transcended his immediate circumstances, he sought to transcribe the world as he had experienced it, with little concern for overall narrative design. Unschooled in the notion of telos, he regarded plot as an unnatural fabrication. He therefore limited the scope of his authority to his personal realm, the depiction of which was dictated by lived expe-

---

10. Although the western artistic tradition has generally assimilated Aristotle's positive view of representation as "imitation" (mimesis), we should recall Plato's negative view of it as "illusion," for the latter reminds us of the artifices employed by poets and painters in depicting "reality" and of the conventions and assumptions that underlie any successful representation. See *The Republic*, esp. part 10, in which Plato presents the example of the bed, one made by God, one by the carpenter, and one by a painter, the latter two being at successively further removes from reality. Parodies of the mimetic view of representation have of course been in existence virtually since the beginning of the novelistic tradition (one thinks immediately of a work like *Tristram Shandy* in English literature); yet the mimetic view has prevailed until well into this century. For a contemporary analysis of the conventions and the persuasion inherent in representation, see, for example, Hayden White, "The Fictions of Factual Representation." White's position is discussed further in Chapter 1 of this study.

rience, and his chief enterprise consisted of recording his own thoughts and actions. He compiled this record less out of a sense of his own self-importance than out of skepticism that experience other than his own could be recorded with complete confidence. (This skepticism was reinforced by a language far more contextual and far more strictly oriented than western languages toward the speaker/narrator's apprehension of the world, as we shall observe in Part 1.) "Complete confidence" was not necessarily synonymous with candor, however—and here of course the critics' argument for the *shishōsetsu* as irrefutable evidence about the author's personal life breaks down. As we shall see, the nature of writing is such that the Japanese writer's project of faithful recording was foredoomed; yet the impulse to record was there nonetheless. "Realism" became a kind of literalism that generated a tension between the contradictory urges of documentation and dramatization. In this war between personal history and the imagination, history usually had the upper hand, although it never won a complete victory.

With "realism" in Japan so intimately associated with personal and specific rather than "universal" experience, it is not surprising that the *shishōsetsu* quickly developed into a closely cropped self-portrait, albeit one reflecting a tradition altogether different from that found in the individualistic west. To authorize a self was no easy task in a society unwilling to acknowledge the individual as a viable social unit. As we shall discover, the self in a *shishōsetsu* is defined typically by its separation and withdrawal from a society that normally demands strict allegiance from members, rather than by its confident confrontation with society—the latter, of course, being the common scenario in classical western fiction.

Embracing such a skeptical attitude even as he emulated western realism, the Japanese writer, perhaps unconsciously, yielded to the influence of a traditional literature that was oriented as much to what we shall call "presentation" as it was to representation.[11] If realism can be defined as the concealment of the mechanics of representation, then presentation is the joyously self-conscious revelation of those mechanics. To be sure, the *shishōsetsu* author did not

---

11. I use this term in the sense employed by Noël Burch in *To the Distant Observer* (see esp. 68–70, where he applies the concept to the Kabuki theater). The discussion here is indebted to Burch's analysis.

think of his writing as a highly stylized form; indeed, he was intent on stripping it of what he saw as stylistic excesses in the writing of the Edo (1600–1867) and early Meiji periods. Like the modern Japanese writer in general, he was clearly less involved in the poetics of presentation than his traditional counterpart was. He rarely indulged, for example, in the kind of polysemic verbal play that permeates the literature from pre-Heian *waka* to Edo-period *ukiyo zō-shi*, nor was he particularly steeped in the allusive imagery and subtle intertextual associations generated over the centuries by a community of knowledge surrounding the classical canon. But he was highly conscious of a third aspect of presentation, which might best be described as the actor-audience relationship. Classical poetry and drama, for example, especially in the centuries immediately preceding the modern period, are noted for their strong tradition of audience participation in the reading—one almost wants to say mutual production—of a text. Haiku artists like Bashō and Issa filled their poetic stages with their presence in a way that made every observation, however grounded in experience or in nature, a virtuoso linguistic performance. Readers were attracted to the persona as much as to the poem and read each verse or sketch against the larger image of the poet that they had constructed from the corpus. The Kabuki theater audience, meanwhile, hailed its favorite actors by their stage names at important entrées and at climactic moments, never forgetting that they were actors. This rapport between actor and audience differs notably from that attempted in realistic western theater, which admits of no theatricality and tries to convince the audience that actors are real-life characters and that the stage is a true-to-life setting.

The *shishōsetsu*, too, thrived on an intimate actor-audience rapport made possible by the audience's homogeneity and limited size. Readers of the *shishōsetsu* in its heyday (the second and third decades of this century) numbered only in the thousands. They would recognize the authorial persona in any story regardless of the main character's (or narrator's) name or situation. The convention of the author as an actor who played himself had the effect of drawing the reader closer to the narrator-hero and creating a bond that was often stronger than the reader's affection for any single text. Out of this relationship emerged the institution of the *bundan*, which means, simply, literary circle(s) but which in the Taishō period referred specifically to that close alliance of writers, critics, and interested readers who had an emotional or intellectual stake in the equation between art and private life. Neither author nor reader took seriously the realistic convention of an anonymous, omniscient narrator who remained hidden behind the characters he created. For both, reality in literature stemmed largely from the narrator's ability to speak in literally the same voice as his hero and thereby invite reader identification.

All parties in the *bundan* triad sensed the conventionality of representation, yet they were typically blind to the equal conventionality of presentation. Thus, the myths of sincerity and authorial presence were born. Given the *bundan's* faith in the ability of the writer to apprehend and portray brute reality and to present himself without mediation, the distinctions between private person and narrating persona, between autobiography and fiction, lost their significance. This belief, which, as we shall see, has informed much of the Japanese intellectual tradition, tells us perhaps as much as anything why "invention" played such a minor role in the *shishōsetsu* and in Japanese literature generally. Originality never became the touchstone that it has been in western literature since the rise of the novel in the eighteenth century, because the writer saw his task as the faithful transcription of a reality there for all to see rather than the creation of one in need of illumination. In fact, creation and fabrication were seen as two sides of the same coin; such attempts to "mediate" reality could only lead back to the same illusionist, representational quagmire. To say that originality has never been a dominant cultural value in Japan is not to deny the writer's artistic sensibility nor indeed even to deny creativity in a certain sense, because the informed and informing hand is always at work in any artistic project. The artistic demands made on a writer were simply of a different nature than they were in the west; that a different kind of literature would result from these expectations was only natural.

This is not to say that western fiction lacks parallels to the *shishōsetsu*. The "lyrical novel," for example, provides fruitful ground for comparison. In both, discourse prevails over story: the protagonist's actions, depicted linearly against the background of a clearly delineated "milieu," are subordinated to his perceptions, spatially juxtaposed in a series of image-laden moments. Like the *shishō-*

setsu, the lyrical novel "transcends the causal and temporal movement of narrative within the framework of fiction" and reduces the world to a point of view equivalent to that of a diarist, confessor, or first-person narrator.[12]

We should not, however, let these very real similarities blind us to some important differences. The early twentieth-century lyrical novel is a creature of romanticism and a reaction against the dominant realist and naturalist traditions. The *shishōsetsu* is the product of an altogether different literary history, which had no specifically realistic tradition against which to react; such terms as "romanticism" and "naturalism" in the Japanese context can be considered profitably only in conjunction with the indigenous categories with which they interacted. Both forms, it is true, downplay the matrix of human relationships that informs the conventional novel. But while the highly symbolic lyrical novel "shifts the reader's attention from men and events to a formal design,"[13] the adamantly concrete *shishōsetsu* reminds the reader constantly of the already-constituted events or perceptions that precede any design in such a way as to put history at war with the imagination. More important than the narrative urge to give shape to the external workings of time or the lyrical urge to give shape to the internal workings of the poet's mental landscape is the diarist's or confessor's urge to transcribe lived experience, letting the course of the life itself determine the shape of subsequent transcriptions.

The question of formal classification often perplexes outsiders exploring Japanese literature. *Shōsetsu* itself covers far more literary territory than "novel" or even "fiction," being used to describe everything from Victorian triple-deckers to meditative essays or sketches. Because the classifications we take for granted overlap only approximately those in the Japanese terminology, the *shishōsetsu* is referred to throughout this book as a form rather than as a genre or subgenre, in order first that it retain its suprageneric aspect and second that it *not* be distinguished qualitatively from *shōsetsu*, the term that shall be used rather than novel or short story for any modern Japanese prose fiction. The issue is a large one, for as we shall see in Chapter 3, deciding what to call the *shishōsetsu*

12. Ralph Freedman, *The Lyrical Novel*, 1, 8.
13. Ibid., 1.

has determined to a significant degree how critics in Japan have evaluated it.

The problem of classification, and particularly the nonfiction-fiction distinction, is apparently common to many other non-western literatures as well. If this is so, then the strict bifurcation employed so confidently in the west may be the exception rather than the rule.[14] The advent of the "new journalism" and "nonfiction novel" since the 1960s in the United States is one sign of a rebellion underway in the west against this bifurcation. But whereas these new genres use the techniques of the classical narrative to emplot actual events, *shishōsetsu* use the techniques of essay, diary, confession, and other nonfictional forms to present the fiction of a faithfully chronicled experience.

Granted that our own expectations about modern Japanese literature cannot be the same as those of the original audience, we need not deny the validity of our own special perspective. What, then, is our task as readers of *shishōsetsu*? It would seem to be threefold. First, since the form's roots tap deeply into the indigenous literary and intellectual tradition, we must examine in some detail how that tradition molded the early twentieth-century writer's thinking about fiction, realism, naturalism, and the many other western literary concepts that bore the great prestige of an "advanced" civilization. Second, because the *shishōsetsu*'s development is connected so intimately with Japanese perceptions of the evolution of their literature in the modern period, we cannot avoid tracing, again in some detail, the form's critical assessment in the decades following its inception. We must, in short, reinterpret the *shishōsetsu*'s interpreters. Third, we must examine as many examples of the *shishōsetsu* as possible in the limited space of a single study in order to prevent the process of selection from con-

14. See, for instance, the introduction in Miriam Cooke, *The Anatomy of an Egyptian Intellectual*, which points out the difficulties of assigning the stories of a major Arab writer (in this case, Yahya Haqqi) to any single category. Cooke's specific example, "The Saint's Lamp" (1945), offers a perspective on the world that "should not be obscured because of externally imposed criteria of categorization, such as genres," which ultimately define "not only the mold of thought, but the thought itself" (ibid., 2–3). Thus, the story "may be used as an autobiography . . . as a long short story; as a historical document; as *Bildungsroman*" (ibid., 3). It is interesting that it is an Egyptian critic, no doubt trained in western literary thought, who denies the story's status as fiction. See ibid., 147 n. 4.

cealing the form's remarkable variety, particularly since so few examples are otherwise available in translation.

The selection process has had one obvious result: the limitation of the discussion to a single gender. The decision is in fact not as arbitrary as it might first appear, since all but a few major writers during the time of this study were men. Higuchi Ichiyō, that meteoric, mid-Meiji talent, had died before the turn of the century, and the energies of prominent female writers working in the 1910s and the 1920s (such as Yosano Akiko and Hiratsuka Raichō) were devoted as much to feminist causes as they were to literary production. Nogami Yaeko, like her mentor Natsume Sōseki, did not write *shishōsetsu*. It was not until the 1930s, when the feminist movement allied itself with the proletarian movement, that a number of influential writers, including Miyamoto Yuriko, Hayashi Fumiko, Sata Ineko, and Hirabayashi Taiko, began to make their mark on the literary scene, using the *shishōsetsu* as their principal medium.

The argument that it is possible for an author to be better and more important than any one of his works[15] may also hold true for the *shishōsetsu:* that is, the form itself is more engrossing and far more important than any single text or oeuvre that it comprises. Several authors are treated here, therefore, in hopes of providing a broad picture and avoiding the sort of extended biographical criticism that has all too commonly obscured each writer's narrative project and the nature of *shishōsetsu* in general. The key to understanding these writers is not simply their lives or their times but also the system of narrative presentation that informs the *shishōsetsu* as a whole, which can be evaluated only by a survey of several authors' works. Our focus, then, is first and foremost on the form itself and on how the writings of a particular author illuminate its study.

15. Edward Seidensticker, *Kafū the Scribbler*, v.

1

THE "TRANSPARENT" TEXT

1

Fictions and Fabrications

> When it comes to fiction I can write nothing but lies; and
> because I so believe, I simply cannot be serious about it.
>
> Fubatatei Shimei,
> "Watakushi wa kaigi-ha da"

> I think that truly creative writing involves . . . discovering
> something in yourself, not dreaming up some formally sat-
> isfying story.
>
> Yasuoka Shōtarō, "Gendai ni okeru
> watakushi shōsetsu"

There is an unmistakable mystique about the *shishōsetsu*, begotten
by the special status it enjoys as a "truthful" account of its author,
which has traditionally discouraged anything more than a cursory
analysis of it as a literary artifact. Writing about the *shishōsetsu* is
not unlike pursuing a desert oasis only to watch it recede and finally disappear altogether as you approach it, or like peeling an
onion, skin after skin, in a vain attempt to get at the "core"; there
is something inherently elusive about the entire project. How is
one to analyze a form that critics have debated for well over half a
century but for which they have failed to come up with a workable
definition? How does one go about isolating a form that is commonly thought to differ significantly from the *shōsetsu*, yet has no
clearly identifiable linguistic marks? And finally, how is one to describe in English a form the very name of which comprises two
seemingly neutral but in fact highly problematical and quite un-
translatable elements, *shi* (*watakushi*) and *shōsetsu*? Raising such
awkward questions at the commencement of a study perhaps bodes
ill for its outcome, but it seems wisest to alert readers at the outset
to the illusory nature of this most "realistic" (as Japanese critics
would have it) of narrative modes.

The *shishōsetsu* appears all the more illusory in translation. "I-novel" is an unfortunate misnomer for a form that differs fundamentally from the novel and contains no "I" in the sense we are accustomed to thinking of the word. *Shōsetsu*, a Chinese compound with its own long etymological and cultural history, is the word chosen by the early-Meiji students of western literature to render "novel" into Japanese. From the beginning, however, its much broader meaning and scope defied the neat definition of "novel" that the students, in all good faith, originally assigned to it. In the first place, *shōsetsu* refers to a prose fiction of any length. The distinction made in English between the novel and the short story is nonexistent, although the Japanese do classify texts as "short," "medium," or "long."[1] In the second place, *shōsetsu* can refer to texts that westerners ordinarily do not think of as fiction. Essays, sketches, memoirs, and other discursive and reflective pieces, which we would normally subsume under the rubric of nonfiction, very often fall under the category of *shōsetsu* in Japanese.

Shishōsetsu is a loose approximation of the German *Ich-Roman*, after which it appears to have been named. The *Ich-Roman* is a full-length novel in which the narrator gives a first-person account of his experiences. This genre is hardly unique to German literature (which has examples from *Werther* to *The Tin Drum*) or to western literature as a whole; modern Japanese literature, too, has its examples—*Wagahai wa neko de aru* (I am a cat, 1905–6) and *Botchan* (1906), both by Natsume Sōseki, being among the earliest and best. Japanese readers would never think of calling these texts *shishōsetsu*, however, because the narrators bear little or no resemblance to their author. Sōseki is no alley cat, after all; nor is he a reckless, ne'er-do-well teacher in Shikoku like Botchan (although he did teach there once). The *shishōsetsu*, moreover, need not have a first-person narrator at all. A story narrated in the third person may still be considered a *shishōsetsu* if the hero is clearly modeled after the author.[2]

---

1. *Tanpen, chūhen,* and *chōhen,* respectively. These forms have no distinguishing structural characteristics or absolute word count. Hirano Ken, for example, calls Chikamatsu Shūkō's *Ko no ai no tame ni* a *tanpen shōsetsu* in *NKBD* 2:382 but calls the same work a *chūhen shōsetsu* in Itō Sei et al., eds., *Shinchō Nihon bungaku shōjiten,* 765.
2. For a discussion of the *Ich-Roman* and the *shishōsetsu,* see, for example, Satō

The nature of the *shi/watakushi* in *shishōsetsu*, however, invites further examination. *Watakushi* can hardly be translated other than as "I," but it most assuredly does not mean the same thing. Indeed, the single first-person pronoun nearly all languages employ is no more useful to Japanese than the word "snow" is to Eskimo; it is much too general to serve any purpose. *Watakushi* is actually one of a half dozen or so first-person pronominals that any *one* person commonly uses to refer to oneself, depending on the occasion (e.g., public or private) and on the relative social position of the listener and/or the referent. A man might use one pronominal (e.g., *ore*) to refer to himself when speaking to family members or to close friends, another (e.g., *boku*) when speaking to his peers at work, and still another (e.g., *watashi*) when speaking to his boss. (A woman is generally limited to the use of *watashi* or *watakushi* in the standard dialect.)[3] Each first-person pronominal has distinct nuances that greatly affect a writer's style. We shall see in Part 3 how Chikamatsu Shūkō, for example, uses the relatively formal *watashi* to lend an air of solemn, matter-of-fact dignity to his zany accounts of depraved love; how Shiga Naoya uses *jibun* to distance himself from his experience and at the same time draw the reader into it; and how through Kasai Zenzō's kaleidoscopic usage of first-person pronominals we "see" one man's sense of self disperse before our eyes.

This remarkable variety extends to the second- and third-person pronominals as well, which if anything are even more numerous. The incidence of so many pronominals in the language speaks eloquently for a very protean notion of self, one that depends for its existence more on the person or situation with whom or with

---

Kōichi, "Ihi-roman." For a comparison of the *shishōsetsu* with the French *roman personnel*, which is no more closely related, see Shirai Kōji, "Roman perusoneru ni tsuite."

3. *Watakushi*, the most public and formal of the first-person pronominals currently in use, is a curious choice of labels for a form that presumes to describe the author's "private" life and thoughts. The original meaning of *watakushi*, to be sure, is "private" or "personal" as opposed to "public" or "communal" (whence such words, still in use, as *watakushigoto* ["private matter"] and *watakushigokoro* ["private emotions"]), but the *watakushi* in *watakushi shōsetsu* is clearly an example of the pronominal usage, as is illustrated by the term once used alternately with *watakushi shōsetsu*: "*watakushi wa* shōsetsu." (*Wa* is the topic-indicating particle.) See the entry on *watakushi shōsetsu* in *NKBD* 4:539. As an alternative, Kasai Zenzō elected to call his *shishōsetsu jiko* ("self") *shōsetsu*, although this term, too, is problematic.

which one is associated at a given moment than on one's own uni-laterally initiated thoughts and acts. We can think of a true pro-noun as a sign of separate and autonomous presence, marking an indelible boundary between self and other. The existence of only one first-person pronoun in western languages like English makes that presence all the more inviolable. The abundance of first-, second-, and third-person pronominals in Japanese, however, each used in accordance with the speaker's social relationship with a specific hearer and referent, tends to undermine that sense of sepa-rate, autonomous presence and blur the boundary between self and other.[4] In short, self-expression in Japanese is forever a contin-gent activity, dependent on the relationship between speaker and hearer and, by extension, between writer and audience. *Shi/wata-kushi shōsetsu* becomes in this way a metonymy for what is in Japa-nese a continually variable communicative act. The narrator cannot even utter the word *watakushi* or *boku* or *ore* until he has posited a specific relationship with the narratee. The *shishōsetsu*, then, is as much "we-novel" as "I-novel."

REALITY, MEDIATION, AND THE FICTIONAL CONTRACT

Creating a viably intimate narrative relationship is, however, fraught with contradictions and forces each writer to come to terms with the nature of writing. Insofar as the *shishōsetsu* is a prose fiction, it can never be a completely personal communicative act; the narrator does not know the recipient of his discourse in the same way as, say, the writer of a letter. As Roland Barthes exuberantly claims: "Writing is the destruction of every voice, of every point of ori-gin. . . . As soon as a fact is *narrated* no longer with a view to acting directly on reality but intransitively . . . this disconnection occurs, the voice loses its origin, the author enters into his own death, writing begins."[5]

---

4. It is interesting to note in this connection that words like *onore* have been used historically as either a first-person or second-person pronominal, depending on context, while the modern reflexive pronominal *jibun*, depending on context, can signify the first, second, *or* third person.

5. "The Death of the Author," in *Image, Music, Text,* 142. (Emphasis in original.)

And yet, we find, the *shishōsetsu* is weaned most reluctantly from its author. Or, to put it another way, the *shishōsetsu* resists becoming "writing" in Barthes's sense and flaunts its "personalism" by encouraging the reader to disregard its textual boundaries and view "real" world and "fictional" world as an unbroken continuum. The question of an author's "presence" in the text has assumed great importance in Japanese letters, as it alone is believed capable of establishing the text's "authenticity" (that is, autobiographical purity or nonfictionality), the highest value attached to writing. We shall discover that in Japan the notion of what is "real" or "authentic" is traditionally limited to personal observation and experience, with the result that fiction, insofar as it deviates from what "actually" happens, connotes a "fabrication" inapplicable to reality rather than a plausible, equally valid version of it. A story written in 1920 by Uno Kōji (1891–1961), which relates one man's affair with a country geisha, plays on this notion. The narrator-hero interrupts his account and addresses his readers:

> I have mentioned that I am a writer. When *Hitogokoro*, which I had completed during my previous stay in Shimosuwa . . . was published last January, it created something of a sensation there, small town that it is, because I modeled the character "Yumiko" after Yumeko. Surely any intelligent reader has noticed a peculiar development in much recent Japanese fiction, namely the appearance of a nebulous figure known only as "I." One reads nothing about his looks, much less about his behavior or his profession. What *does* one read, you ask? Merely a string of impressionistic musings. Soon you realize that the "I" is none other than the author himself; indeed, this is almost always the case. The "I," therefore, is a writer, and the reader never seems to question this curious convention whereby the author uses first-person narrative to point to himself. Now, even though there is nothing wrong with having the narrator double as the hero and the hero pose as a writer, it is regrettable that readers have come to equate him automatically with the author and think of all the story's incidents as actually having taken place. At any rate, because *Hitogokoro* is written in the first person, people believed everything in it to be true and assumed that I had based my character "Yumiko" on Yumeko—which was all right by me, but I'm afraid it caused Yumeko no little consternation. . . . I hurriedly sent her a letter of apology.[6]

---

6. *Amaki yo no hanashi*, in *Uno Kōji zenshū* 2 : 442–43. First published in *Chūōkōron* (Sept. 1920). Translations from the Japanese are original to this study, unless otherwise indicated.

This often-quoted passage may be the first literary reference to what only later became known as the *shishōsetsu*, and it well illustrates the kind of osmotic relationship that exists between author and narrator-hero—the one seemingly flowing into the other through a very permeable text. Uno knew that his audience would immediately recognize the by-then familiar formula of author = narrator = hero. A careful reading of Uno's discursive aside, however, suggests that it is not a critique. What sounds at first like an ironic disclaimer turns out to be an apt description of this very story. Indeed, it seems calculated to collapse the distinction between real world and fictional world by enticing readers into believing that the author has recorded events from his own life rather than invented them. The narrator laments the "regrettable" equation that readers ordinarily make between author and literary persona, yet implies that he too is "none other than the author himself" by listing in rapid succession the many properties that he the narrator and Uno the author have in common: the same profession ("I have mentioned that I am a writer"), the same piece of writing (*Hitogo-koro*, which appeared in the same magazine as this story), and the same personal life ("people . . . assumed that I had based my character 'Yumiko' on Yumeko—*which was all right by me*").[7]

Much of this story's impact, then, derives from the conceit, which Uno simultaneously ridicules and exploits, that the real-life author and his literary persona are one and the same. This, we might think, is impossible. Uno the author exists independent of the literary medium; Uno the persona, because of it.[8] And in fact

---

7. Elsewhere the narrator engages in a game of name-dropping, presumably to establish himself further in the readers' minds as a historical personage rather than as an imaginary character. He chats with another guest at the inn where he is staying who claims the acquaintance of Tanizaki Jun'ichirō, the famous author. "In that case, you must know Satō Haruo, too," he retorts, for he is aware, as no doubt are his readers, that Satō and Tanizaki were close friends. The guest quickly takes the hint and tells of his drinking acquaintance with Nagata Mikihiko, another of Tanizaki's literary friends. Ibid., 427.

8. Distinctions between author, "implied" author, and narrator on the one hand and between reader, "implied" reader, and narratee on the other should be kept in mind when analyzing a highly reflexive form like the *shishōsetsu*. See Seymour Chatman, *Story and Discourse*, 147–51 and passim, for an account of the narrative process. See also Gérard Genette, *Figures of Literary Discourse*, esp. chap. 7 ("Frontiers of Narrative"), for an explication of narrative distinctions relevant to this study, as well as *Narrative Discourse*, by the same author. References in this study to *shishō-setsu* writers, insofar as they are the "heroes" of their own texts (as suggested by

what will be argued here is that author and persona even in a *shi-shōsetsu* are *not* fully interchangeable, because authorial "presence" must always be, in the final analysis, a product of representation. This is not to say that we can simply isolate persona and text from the author and his life, for they are all part of a literary and cultural field that determines in large measure how the reader regards—or indeed whether he has any interest at all in—such notions as "author," "intention," "text," and "fiction." To confuse persona with author, however, no matter how close the resemblance, is to confuse the telling with lived experience: the former is accessible to the reader in a way that the latter simply is not. Gérard Genette, in his study of narrative, reminds us, for example, that "even the references in *Tristram Shandy* to the situation of writing speak to the (fictive) act of Tristram and not the (real) one of Sterne; but in a more subtle and also more radical way, the narrator of *Père Goriot* 'is' not Balzac, even if here and there he expresses Balzac's opinions, for this author-narrator is someone who 'knows' the Vauquer boardinghouse, its landlady and its lodgers, whereas all Balzac himself does is imagine them; and in this sense, of course, the narrating situation of a fictional account is *never* reduced to its situation of writing."[9]

The common practice in the Japanese literary establishment, or *bundan*, however, has been to reduce the narrating situation to its situation of writing. We shall see in Chapter 2 that the structure of the Japanese language provides some justification for this reduction, since the language's fundamental speaker orientation is most compatible—*regardless* of narrative person—with a limited point of view that is easily identified with the author's own.[10] There is of course no dearth of examples in twentieth-century western literature that invite a similar practice (one recalls the writings of Gide, Miller, and Proust), but the emphasis on fictional autonomy has prevailed.[11] The *bundan*, meanwhile, has historically believed lived

---

William F. Sibley in his *The Shiga Hero*), will accordingly be to the literary personae as opposed to the extraliterary persons.

9. *Narrative Discourse*, 214. (Emphasis in original.)

10. Genette's strict distinction in *Narrative Discourse*, 185–89, between "point of view" (who sees?) and "voice" (who speaks?), therefore, is not entirely valid in the Japanese case. We will find that ambiguity of narrative voice is structurally built into the Japanese language. See the discussion in Chapter 2, below.

11. Proust, for example, insists in *Contre Sainte-Beuve* that a literary text not be

experience to be more "authentic" than any literary version of it, and has read the *shishōsetsu* in the confidently referential manner in which we read a biography or legal document, finding meaning in it only insofar as it sheds light on the author's private life. In this view, the *shishōsetsu* narrator is less a storyteller than a spokesman who has eschewed fictionalization in favor of direct expression. Narrative is thus wholly subordinated to discourse.

A writer's notion of fiction is of course predicated on his concept of the "real." The Japanese view of history, the individual's place in society, the native literary tradition, and the language itself have all been instrumental in forming the concept of reality through which the early twentieth-century writer regarded his world and against which notions of fiction had to compete. As used here "fiction" suggests any plausible, alternative vision of "reality," rather than simply the "fantastic" or the "nonreal." John Fowles offers a credo for the fiction writer when he says, *"We wish to create worlds as real as, but other than the world that is."* [12] The great tradition of realism that flourished in the nineteenth century attests to the essential compatibility in western culture between the "imagined" worlds one reads about in novels and the "real" world of personal experience. It is less important that an event has actually occurred than that it *could* have occurred, given the particular situation. Fictional world and phenomenal world are both based on the premise, underwritten by the post-Enlightenment secularization of culture, that "reality" is as much mediated by the human mind as it is an entity unto itself; it is a function of the very manner in which it is apprehended and then represented. [13] Fictive imagination is just as much a part of this reality as actual experience, because *both* are products of mediation and are in this sense created.

Fowles's fictional credo, however, does not square with the Japanese perception that the unmediated presentation of lived experi-

---

confounded with the life of its author and that in the text the writer creates a self distinct from his biographical one. See Stephen G. Kellman, *The Self-begetting Novel*, 17, 21.

12. *The French Lieutenant's Woman*, 81. (Emphasis in original; the quotation appears in chapter 13.)

13. We should note the important distinction between the "gentile" or historical, and the "sacred" or original, that Vico makes in his philosophy of a *human* history. See the concluding chapter of Edward W. Said's *Beginnings*, esp. 347–53, for an excellent introduction to Vico's thought and a discussion of the evolution of an intellectual environment conducive to narrative creativity.

ence *is* possible when "freed" of fictional elements. Maruyama Masao, in a highly suggestive discourse, attributes the dearth of fictional "imagination" in modern Japanese literature to a traditional social organization that can accommodate only experience that is directly perceived. Maruyama distinguishes between two kinds of reality, "mediated" and "immediate," and argues that the western intellectual tradition stresses the former while the Japanese tradition stresses the latter. Modern society is founded on "mediated" reality, that is, "fictions" of social organization that transcend direct and tangible interpersonal relationships (such as the lord-vassal contract) and see people as individuals capable of independent action. Westerners, very much at home since the Renaissance with abstractions to govern their legal, philosophical, and social lives, have applied them naturally to the literary realm as well. The term "fiction," then, can have very positive connotations in the west, for it means "to fashion" or "to invent" as well as simply "to imagine" or "to pretend." Such a view of fiction derives from a fundamental faith in "mediated" reality, a faith so great that it rates the product of intellectual activity higher than perceptual or "immediate" reality. Fiction is natural in a society that believes individual action to be a determining force in social behavior and the natural order. "It is precisely because the reality does not appear directly," says Maruyama, "but as a 'mediated reality' depending on the positive participation of the human spirit, that we can call it fiction."[14]

In Japan, however, man's intellectual and spiritual side is neither differentiated nor independent from perceptual nature. Like medieval European society, Maruyama argues, Japanese society sees interpersonal relationships as static and irrevocable. It naturally follows that the social environment, which modern society recognizes as man-made, assumes for the Japanese the same kind of reality ("immediate" rather than "mediated") as the natural world. Human intercourse is conceived of in the same dimensions as birth, death, or the passing of the seasons. "When people view their society as a *fait accompli*," Maruyama suggests, "they don't just automatically start thinking in terms of fictions."[15] The result is that the Japanese, who feel uncomfortable about fiction, try

14. "From Carnal Literature to Carnal Politics," 251.
15. Ibid., 255.

to push it in the direction of firsthand, perceptual experiences. Whereas the western view of fiction is rooted in a fundamental faith in mediated reality, unmediated "fact," in the Japanese view, becomes itself a kind of faith. Maruyama concludes that the notion of fiction as the intellectual construct of an individual mind is rooted in modernity, for it could not exist without the individual imagination freed from a predetermined social order. Fiction becomes "real," that is, a viable entity, only when one sees oneself as independent of the natural environment and views intellectual constructs not as useless abstractions but as thoroughly relevant to daily life.

Although Maruyama's analysis reveals a socioevolutionary slant that virtually equates post-Restoration Japan with pre-Enlightenment Europe, it articulates persuasively a "modern" society's need to employ fictions and a "premodern" society's absence of such a need. In a culture that views "reality" only as immediate experience of the natural world, literature not surprisingly becomes a chronicling or transcribing of that experience rather than an imaginative reconstruction of it. And in a culture that views human relations as a predetermined part of the natural order, a fictional form such as the novel, which thrives on fluidity in human relations, is clearly out of place. Traditional Japan was such a culture; so, to a considerable degree, were Meiji and Taishō Japan. And if one accepts Nakane Chie and others' arguments that the transformation in Japan from a preindustrial to an industrial society was not accompanied by the kind of radical change in social organization that occurred in the west,[16] then it comes as no surprise that the novel's emphasis on individual autonomy and on serendipitous relationships is not to be found in abundance in the early twentieth-century shōsetsu.

Yet it was precisely the rise of individual autonomy and serendipitous relationships, Ian Watt suggests, that paved the way for the development of modern fiction in the west. Like Maruyama, Watt argues that modernity is the product of an individual-centered world in which one is "responsible for his own scale of moral and social values." Not only did the rise of individualism weaken communal and traditional relationships, it fostered the

16. See Nakane Chie, *Japanese Society*, esp. 7–8.

"stress on the importance of personal relationships which is so characteristic both of modern society and of the novel—such relationships may be seen as offering the individual a more conscious and selective pattern of social life to replace the more diffuse, and as it were involuntary, social cohesions which individualism had undermined."[17]

Beginning with Montaigne and Rousseau, the self in western literature has continually been celebrated and probed. The driving force in "classical" fiction (whether autobiographical or not), from *Tom Jones* and *Emma* to *Wilhelm Meister* and *Rudin*, has been socialization through individuation, achieved by rigorous personal scrutiny and dynamic interpersonal relationships and leading to the protagonist's confrontation and integration with society. A character's sense of "self" is brought about by a strong awareness of, and interaction with, the "other." Even such antisocial acts as, say, Werther's or Madame Bovary's suicides are depicted as having been committed in despair by individuals who had been thoroughly engaged in their societies.[18] The Japanese, however, have been less convinced of (we might even say they have been uninterested in) the self's tangibility or value, even after their massive exposure to western civilization in the Meiji period. The driving force in much of Japanese fiction, therefore, has been what might be called "naturalization" rather than socialization, achieved by a studied withdrawal from society and often leading to the hero's identification with nature.

The often-discussed "search for selfhood" (*jiko tankyū*) in modern literature actually harks back to the traditional "pursuit of the

17. *The Rise of the Novel*, 177.
18. The goal of self-determination in the west may have proved increasingly elusive since the late nineteenth century, but the individual has remained, nonetheless, the point of reference. Despite volumes of criticism in Japan and the west to the contrary, however, all emphasizing the impact of western thought, modern Japanese fiction springs from a tradition that did not take the individuated self as its point of departure and against which, therefore, it could not react in expressions of fragmentation and alienation so familiar to us in modernist literature. It is true, of course, that many heroes in western fiction, beginning perhaps with *Crime and Punishment* and continuing with such works as *A Portrait of the Artist as a Young Man* and *The Stranger*, have become less and less socialized and that alienation from one's society is a theme common to both twentieth-century western and Japanese fiction. The difference, however, is that alienation in western fiction still represents a deviation from the norm, whereas in Japanese fiction (such as the works of Shiga, discussed in Part 3) it can actually approach an ideal.

Way" (gudō). Both are steeped in the Buddhist emphasis on libera-
tion from the bonds of society and on yielding to life's inexorable
cycle: the "four trials" of birth, aging, sickness, and death. The
achievement of selfhood in the Japanese context, then, means in a
very positive sense the loss of one's individuality. This is a recurrent theme in many shishōsetsu but most conspicuously in those of
Shiga Naoya, whose "Kinosaki nite" (At Kinosaki) and An'ya kōro
(A dark night's passing) are particularly powerful depictions of the
authorial persona's communion with nature and of what the early
twentieth-century philosopher Nishida Kitarō calls "emptying the
self," achieved by the perceiving subject's identification with the
object.[19]

Shishōsetsu are saturated with the author's personal experiences,
to be sure, but not with the aim of revealing a core of personality that is clearly defined in the process of socialization or self-
analysis, as we might expect in western literature. It is ironic that the
so-called "I-novel," treated by many Japanese critics as the showcase
of the "modern self" (kindai jiga), actually questions what it ostensibly champions.[20] Indeed, the shishōsetsu is less the vehicle for personal affirmation that critics frequently make it out to be than a
theater where the hero acts out his ambivalence toward the self.
The medieval scholar Nishida Masayoshi, one of the few to reex-
amine the shishōsetsu from a non-Eurocentric perspective, sees little
validity in claims for the shishōsetsu as an expression of a burgeon-
ing individuality appropriate to a "modernized" Japan; indeed, he
is skeptical about the entire enterprise of reading into the shishōsetsu the awakening of a western notion of selfhood.[21] Takahashi
Hideo, in his revisionist study, also urges that we revise our notions of the self in Japan. Rather than equate it with modern west-

19. The Problem of Japanese Culture, 869.
20. See Yasaki Dan, "Jiga no hatten ni okeru Nihonteki seikaku" (part of a longer
work entitled Kindai jiga no Nihonteki keisei [1943]), for a sample of that thriving
subgenre, the kindai jiga essay, which takes the "modern self" to be, in the words of
Kenneth Strong, "the key to the vagaries of modern Japanese literature, or at least
of modern Japanese fiction" ("Downgrading the 'Kindai Jiga,'" 407). (Emphasis in
original.)
21. "The code of the 'watakushi' in shishōsetsu," writes Nishida, "is the obliterat-
ing of self by confession. It would seem to have succeeded remarkably in enriching
the writer's spiritual quest by aspiring ultimately to the kind of 'ego-shedding' [da-
tsugasei] that approaches the emancipating experience of the 'no-self' [muga] of traditional Buddhism" (Watakushi shōsetsu saihakken, 72).

ern society's individuated self, which has been largely weaned from nature and tradition, he concludes it is more properly conceived of as a premodern "element" of man that aspires to fusion with its surroundings. The *shishōsetsu's watakushi* has brought new meaning to the "self," Takahashi argues, not by an assertion of individuality but by its reversion to sel*f*lessness, as exhibited in the protagonist's return to the comforting embrace of nature, family, and tradition—to which we might add, in the case of those politically motivated writers in the 1930s who underwent ritual "conversion" (*tenkō*), the state.[22]

In short, the diffuse, involuntary social cohesions of a strictly hierarchical society suggested by Maruyama were still very much intact in early twentieth-century Japan. The Japanese writer in the Taishō, let alone Tokugawa, period, never knew the range of selection and choice in human relations experienced by an individual in the England of Defoe, Richardson, and Fielding that Watt describes. Contact with western culture, to be sure, awakened writers to the idea of individualism. Yet while individualism in the west suggests a dynamic (as opposed to regulated or tradition-bound) relationship between the self and the other, it came in Japan, because of the traditional equation of spiritual autonomy with aloofness from society, to imply just the opposite: a withdrawal into the world of nature and private experience. This notion of individualism as a form of isolated self-contemplation may have been the only avenue to spiritual independence in a society that placed severe constraints on interpersonal relations. The typical Japanese writer, moreover, aware of the limits of his intellectual and social liberties, may have seen in his private life the only area he could exploit with confidence. In a society generally hostile to nonconformist behavior, he discovered in confession a literary form that matched his conception of self: something fulfilled by unilateral and almost instinctive expression rather than by integration in a matrix of human relationships. He saw confession, moreover, as an embodiment of his uniqueness, insofar as it could be authored only by one person, namely, himself. The *shishōsetsu* was eminently suited to this view of individualism. Its protagonist becomes an "individual," as it

---

22. *Genso to shite no "watakushi."* See the introductory and concluding essays, esp. pp. 23–24 and 288–89.

were, by virtue of his monopolized point of view and, not infrequently, by his occupation of an otherwise empty stage.

THE PLACE OF FICTION IN
JAPANESE LITERATURE

As we have seen, the starting point in much Japanese "fiction" has not been the construction of a hypothetical situation but the observation of an actual one. This modus operandi is hardly unique to the *shishōsetsu;* precedents can be found in such classical forms as the *zuihitsu* (discursive essay), *kana nikki* (poetic diary), *haibun* (haiku and prose), and *kikōbun* (travel sketches), all of which are literary descriptions of lived experience. Even the stories and settings in an innovative and "fantastic" form like *jōruri* are generally rooted in actual events or previous literary accounts. Both "contemporary" (*sewamono*) and "period" (*jidaimono*) pieces are based on a large but finite number of "worlds" (*sekai*), well-known historical events or literary depictions with fixed casts of characters.[23] The accepted practice was to work with material already familiar to audiences rather than fashion entirely imaginary characters or situations. Playwrights worked within these established frames of reference, fleshing out the action and characterization as they saw fit.[24]

The radical transformation of the old literary language into something approaching the colloquial, the experiences of modernization and urban growth, and the influx of western thought, all of

---

23. The *Sekai kōmoku* (late eighteenth century) lists some 150 "worlds" along with their historical or literary source and names of characters. See Barbara E. Thornbury, *Sukeroku's Double Identity,* 22–23.

24. James R. Brandon notes, "Precisely because a world was already significant in legend or history, or in the case of sewamono through public scandal, it was considered appropriate for the stage" (*Kabuki: Five Classic Plays,* 25). The same is largely true of other theatrical forms, including No and Bunraku. Katō Shūichi argues that there is little in Kabuki of "the universal, the paradoxical or the abstract" and that the playwrights' lines concern specific characters and situations but "say nothing about human feelings in general or about the human condition" in the manner of a Shakespeare. The reason for this, he concludes, is that Edo-period townsmen were interested in "specific subjects, not universal considerations." The somewhat negative cast of Katō's argument aside, this concern with specificity over universality would seem to apply equally well to post-Edo fiction. See *A History of Japanese Literature,* vol. 2, *The Years of Isolation,* 201.

which preceded the *shishōsetsu's* emergence, insured that the gap between classical and modern Japanese literature would be unbreachable in certain respects; yet we should not overlook the modern writers' attempts to come to terms, in various and subtle ways, with the classical forms. It was, of course, never simply a matter of incorporating the classical vocabulary or aesthetic. For more than a millennium, the language served as a repository of richly connotative images and associations shared by the literate community.[25] With the demise of old Japanese after Ozaki Kōyō (1867–1903), however, the familiar vocabulary of pivot words (*kakekotoba*), prefaces (*jo*), epithets (*makura kotoba*), association words (*engo*), and poetic place-names (*uta makura*), which for many centuries had provided a context for meaning and had made such ostensibly "personal" genres as the *zuihitsu* and *kana nikki* both highly conventional and more accessible to their audience, died out rather suddenly with no comparable system of literary conventions readily available to take its place. By the turn of this century, Japanese writers were looking to naturalism and other European literary movements for inspiration; but the western tradition, itself the culmination of many centuries of independent development, could not be readily assimilated. Writers now faced the task of formulating a new poetic vocabulary and repository of associations on which to draw. Unable to rely any longer on the "worlds" and associations of classical literature or in any coherent way on an alien literary tradition, they began exploring the possibility of using their own lives as "world." Once the writer established his persona as a legitimate subject of literary discourse, he was working, as far as he and his audience were concerned, with familiar material and could allude to it in subsequent works in the knowledge that readers would be conversant with it. This "world" gained further legitimacy as its author gained a name; and personal experience, as presented in the work, became part of the public literary domain. Just as Sei Shōnagon (fl. early eleventh century) challenged her readers in *The Pillow Book* to pit themselves along with her against the tradition of literary allusions, the early *shishōsetsu* writer chal-

---

25. The extraordinary richness of this repository is demonstrated by Mark Morris in "Sei Shōnagon's Poetic Categories," 29.

lenged his readers to gain a similar fluency in the newer and narrower "tradition" of his recorded life. He sought in this way to validate his experience as a kind of history.

The *shishōsetsu* writer was preoccupied with such a legitimizing project in the first place in part because of fiction's subordinate relationship to history in traditional Japanese letters. We have observed that any author's view of fiction is predicated on his notion of reality, which is itself a mutable entity; concepts of just what constitutes reality vary with the age, culture, and artistic temperament, as E. H. Gombrich, among others, makes clear.[26] The common understanding in the west has been that literary fictions are very much a part of "reality"; fiction, no less than history, aims at a credible representation of the world. Far from being opposed to history, it offers a competing and basically similar strategy of representation. (Henry Fielding, after all, calls his great novel about a foundling a "history.") Many novels could pass for histories, and vice versa. Hayden White goes so far as to say: "Viewed simply as verbal artifacts histories and novels are indistinguishable from one another. We cannot easily distinguish between them on formal grounds unless we approach them with specific preconceptions about the kinds of truths that each is supposed to deal in. But the aim of the writer of a novel must be the same as that of the writer of a history. Both wish to provide a verbal image of 'reality.'"[27]

The difference between the two, then, is a very subtle one indeed. It certainly does not lie in the dubious notion that the historian "finds" his stories, whereas the fiction writer "invents" his. Such a notion obscures the extent not only to which "invention" plays a part in the historian's operations but also to which "discovery" can play a part in the fiction writer's operations. It is tempting to say that history deals with what actually happened (events already constituted) and hence with "truth," and fiction with what might have happened (events not already constituted) and hence with "untruth." Already constituted events, however, are by no means the historian's exclusive domain. They are a part of any "fictional" work as well. Likewise, events that exist "inside" the writ-

---

26. See *Art and Illusion*, esp. 84–86, which discusses the triumph of an established artistic vocabulary over an unfamiliar "reality" or setting.
27. Hayden White, "Fictions of Factual Representation," 122.

er's consciousness are not the exclusive domain of the fiction writer. In his *Metahistory*, Hayden White posits the fictive nature of historical reconstructions, which are generated necessarily by various contending modes (romance/metaphor, tragedy/metonymy, comedy/synecdoche, and satire/irony) of emplotment, and argues convincingly that no mode of conveyance of historical "fact" is neutral or definitive or inherently truer than any other. "Commitment to a particular form of knowledge," White concludes, "predetermines the *kinds* of generalizations one can make about the present world."[28]

At the center of this view of historiography as an essentially poetic act lies the assumption that history, like fiction, is a form of narrative. Although White never specifically defines "narrative," it is clear that he uses the term to designate a verbal construct that is more complex than either a chronicle (a chronological, open-ended arrangement of data) or a story (a chronicle to which culminations and resolutions have been added) and utilizes a plot—that "provider of significance to mere chronicity" as Frank Kermode puts it.[29] Unlike a simple story that is content with a chronological ordering (asking the question "What happened next?"), an emplotted narrative imposes an internal, nontemporal, overriding order on events (asking, "What is the point of it all?"). The aims of both novelist and historian are realized through this synchronic ordering process.

White takes both "chronicle" and "story" to be "primitive elements" in the historical (and by inference the fictional) account;[30] but it is precisely within this "primitive" realm that much of Japanese history and fiction reside. Although narrative in the west, beginning with the Old Testament, has been informed by a dramatic poetic of emplotment that insists on a causal relationship between events,[31] the traditional Japanese "narrative" (*monogatari*) is informed by the highly conventionalized aesthetics of the native verse forms and the nondramatic historiography of Chinese chronicles.

In the absence of a highly representational mode, the influence

28. *Metahistory*, 21.
29. *The Sense of an Ending*, 56.
30. *Metahistory*, 5.
31. See, for example, Erich Auerbach's analysis of Genesis as an emplotted narrative in *Mimesis*, chap. 1.

of a more self-consciously presentational mode on Japanese fiction has been enormous. The latter mode has played no small role in western literature as well—as the continuing interest in tropes, for example, demonstrates—but it has not had the sweeping impact, especially on prose, that it has had on Japanese literature. Whereas prose in the west, whether "history" or "fiction," has been inextricably tied to the emplotted narrative, the Japanese have been more at home with literary forms that tend to undermine or circumvent the narrative flow. The presentational mode infuses not only *waka*, *haikai*, and other poetic forms but also such prose forms as the "fictional tale" (*tsukuri monogatari*), "poem tale" (*uta monogatari*), "story of the 'floating world'" (*ukiyo zōshi*), "poetic diary" (*kana nikki*), and discursive essay (*zuihitsu*), to name the most prominent examples. In all these forms, imagery, polysemy, and canonical allusions do not simply counterpoint the action but may actually interrupt or even overwhelm it.[32]

Although Japanese prose had by the early twentieth century lost not only the rhythm but the poetic vocabulary of the old literary language, it was by no means on a comfortable footing with the emplotted narrative still so prominent in western fiction. The difference, of course, is the cause of much consternation for western readers of the *shōsetsu* who even today talk of its "inaccessibility," bemoan the "lack" of an ending, and ask what is the "point" of the story they have just read. The *shōsetsu*, however, needs no overall plot signifier to enable its discourse. Getting there, for readers of the *shōsetsu*, is not just half the fun; it is *all* the fun. In fact, there is no "there" or "here"—that is to say, no privileged event indicated by the emplotting narrative mechanism; the *shōsetsu* narrative goes everywhere and nowhere.

The Chinese annalistic model for the writing of history also had a considerable influence on Japanese letters, including modern *shōsetsu*. Beginning with *Nihongi* and the other "Six National Histories" (*Rikkokushi*, 720–901) and continuing with the hybrid "fictional histories" (*rekishi monogatari*) written in the late Heian (794–

---

32. The presentational and serial nature of *Genji* and other Heian *monogatari* is brilliantly analyzed in Richard Hideki Okada, "Unbound Texts." Of particular interest is his discussion of the tenseless character of old Japanese and the ambiguity of narrative voice in *monogatari*, a feature that survives in the modern *shōsetsu*. See Chapter 2.

1192) and Kamakura (1192–1333) periods, Japanese texts take after the Chinese chronicle in their essentially descriptive rather than investigative bent and likewise make no attempt at synthesis or at establishing a hierarchy of significance. What mattered was that an event had actually occurred; having occurred, it was dutifully recorded. Even more important, the continental tradition guided Japanese thinking as to what constituted history and ultimately what constituted literature. The Chinese regarded literature as a public institution that had as its purpose the maintenance of the Confucian orthodoxy, a political and social system of bureaucratic government entrusted to a class of highly literate civil servants who owed their place in the administrative ranks to their fluency in the four major categories of literature: histories and biographies, the classics and their commentaries, philosophy, and belles lettres.[33] The last category included poetry but no prose; fiction was not included in scholarly discourse until the influx of western literary theory in the twentieth century. Traditional commentators who wrote on prose fiction at all quite naturally criticized it in terms of history, the highest form of literature and the only body of prose narrative that, because of its unquestioned respectability, could serve as a standard of comparison.[34] Even during the heyday of Chinese prose fiction in the Ming (1368–1644) and Ch'ing (1644–1911) dynasties, most authors wrote anonymously and lived out their lives in obscurity—the price to pay for indulging in such a minor art.[35]

The content of "literature," then, for all intents and purposes, was poetry and nonfiction prose. The former served as a vehicle of expression and the latter as the moral guideline for the literati class. The highest forms of literature were public and utilitarian in orientation and meant to aid in the art of government. The Japanese civil service, under the control of either the aristocratic or military classes, never became as dominant as its Chinese model, and we see both literature and history take on a less public face. *Rekishi monogatari*, for example, are more likely to describe an outing of

33. Liu Wu-chi, *An Introduction to Chinese Literature*, 5.
34. C. T. Hsia, *The Classic Chinese Novel*, 14–15. Ssu-ma Ch'ien's *Shih chi* (*Records of the Grand Historian*) was the most frequently invoked historical text against which classical Chinese prose fictions were measured.
35. Liu, *An Introduction to Chinese Literature*, 195, 228.

court ladies than a meeting of ministers. In the Edo period, however, the Tokugawa shogunate developed a deeply conservative political system that looked eagerly to the Chinese Neo-Confucian philosophy to legitimize its rule. Literature came to be regarded, officially at least, solely as a vehicle for propagating the dominant sociopolitical ethos. Indeed, literature was understood to be useful only insofar as it contributed to the Confucian worldview or "Way."[36]

Literature that inspired the populace to socially correct behavior, then, clearly served a useful function in the Confucian scheme of things. In Tokugawa Japan, the writing of histories, biographies, and moral treatises was encouraged, while other forms were merely condoned. The poet Matsuo Bashō's (1644–94) witty, self-deprecating assessment of *haikai*—"My art is like a fire in summer or a fan in winter; it serves people no purpose"[37]—expresses, however ironically, the prevailing official bias against any forms of poetry except *kanshi* (poetry written in Chinese) and *waka*. The bias against prose fiction was even stronger and also reflected Chinese literary tastes. The word for prose fiction itself (*shōsetsu* [*hsiao-shuo* in Chinese] originally meant "unofficial history" and referred to popular, loosely historical accounts written in the vernacular) is indicative of the low esteem in which it was held. *Shōsetsu* might be translated literally as "small talk"; a *shōsetsuka* was therefore someone who collected "street talk" and "roadside gossip" and committed them to writing.[38] The Chinese expended great efforts preserving and handing down histories and the other categories of "refined" literature; the "vulgar" texts of prose fiction, however, were commonly ignored, lost, and even destroyed.[39] The *Han shu* (History of the Former Han) lists in its catalogue of learning ten "sages" in descending order of importance—the Confucianist, Tao-

---

36. The Confucian scholar Hayashi Razan (1583–1657), adviser to the first Tokugawa shogun, writes: "Where there is the Way [*dō*] there are letters [*bun*]. . . . They are different manifestations of the same principle. . . . Letters branch out from the great trunk of the Way. Since the branches are few, they are healthy and firm" (quoted in Hiraoka Toshio, *Nihon kindai bungaku no shuppatsu*, 13). Razan's concept of the nature of literature echoes the words of Emperor Wen of the Wei (A.D. 186–226): "Literature: a vital force in the ordering of the state" (quoted in Burton Watson, *Early Chinese Literature*, from the epigraph opposite the title page).

37. Quoted from "Kyoroku ribetsu no kotoba," in Sugiura Sei'ichirō et al., eds., *Bashō bunshū*, 205.

38. Liu, *An Introduction to Chinese Literature*, 141.

39. Watson, *Early Chinese Literature*, 4.

ist, Legalist, diviner, logician, Moist, diplomatist, eclectic, farmer, and finally "small-talk writer"—but quickly adds that only the first nine are worth mentioning.[40]

The notion of what constituted literature in Tokugawa Japan is examined with remarkable insight by Kitamura Tōkoku (1868–94), a noted poet, essayist, and critic. Tōkoku posits two distinct strains in Tokugawa letters: "refined" nonfiction literature that commented seriously on life and "vulgar" nonliterary fiction that burlesqued life.[41] Into the former category went the histories, biographies, and other erudite texts that appealed to the ruling samurai class, in which fiction had no place; into the latter, the witty picaresques and other "popular" narratives that appealed to commoners, in which fiction figured large. Tōkoku's distinction is noteworthy, for it shows that Tokugawa literature had no lack of fiction. On the contrary, a great deal was being written in the form of *gesaku*, a generic term for such forms as the *kibyōshi* (illustrated "yellow-covered books"), *sharebon* ("sophisticated books" about the gay quarters), *kokkeibon* ("humorous books"), *ninjōbon* ("amatory books"), and *yomihon* (didactic "reading books"). Its very name (literally, "playful composition"), however, suggested its "frivolous" and therefore nonliterary character. *Gesaku* were often authored (usually anonymously) by samurai intellectuals, but their primary audience was the lower classes, mainly townspeople.

The idea that fiction and literature were entirely separate concerns—the former frivolous, the latter serious—continued into the Meiji period. It held true even for the man who made the first sustained attempt at writing in the colloquial idiom. Futabatei Shimei (1864–1909), author of *Ukigumo* (Drifting clouds, 1887–89), abandoned his effort at fiction writing for nearly two decades before trying again in 1906, only to abandon it for good a year later. Influ-

---

40. Noguchi Takehiko, *Shōsetsu no Nihongo*, 10–11. That this low view of fiction has continued even into modern times is demonstrated by an influential essay by Chou Tso-jen, written in 1919, which argues for the superiority of the classical genres of prose and poetry over fiction and drama. See Hsia, *The Classical Chinese Novel*, 3–4.
41. *Nihon bungaku shi kotsu* (also known by the subtitle of its only extant portion, *Meiji bungaku kanken*), in *Kitamura Tōkoku shū*, 124. My discussion of Tōkoku is based largely on Hiraoka, *Nihon kindai bungaku no shuppatsu*, esp. the section entitled "Futatsu no bungaku," 7–24. See also H. D. Harootunian's stimulating article on Tōkoku and Takayama Chogyū, "Between Politics and Culture."

enced as much by his samurai lineage and Tokugawa heritage as by his studies of western literature, Futabatei was very uncomfortable with the idea of a literary career, which he regarded as decidedly unprofessional. The contemporaneous success of the Ken'yūsha, a school of writers that carried on the Edo *gesaku* tradition, no doubt increased his distaste for such a "frivolous" calling. In a late essay, he insists on the impossibility of writing fiction of any worth. "No matter how good one's technique," he argues, "one cannot write the truth. One may know the truth, but it inevitably becomes distorted when one speaks or writes of it. . . . When it comes to fiction [*shōsetsu*] I can write nothing but lies; and because I so believe, I simply cannot be serious about it."[42] In the end, the only way he could be honest with himself was to quit the life of a writer and embark on a more respectable career in the bureaucracy. Futabatei continued his literary activities both as a translator of stories from the Russian (which won him his initial fame) and as a contributor of *kansōbun* (short pieces that allow a writer to reflect on virtually any subject) to various journals, but he considered this part of his life an avocation.

By the early twentieth century, the original sense of *shōsetsu* had been largely supplemented, if not superseded, by the western concept of the novel that Tsubouchi Shōyō (1859–1935), author, translator, critic, and student of English literature, first grafted onto the Chinese word when he published his famous interpretation of European literature (*Shōsetsu shinzui*; The essence of the novel, 1885–86). And yet, the west's literary impact notwithstanding, the word *shōsetsu* could not be stripped so quickly of its two-thousand-year-old connotations. As Noguchi Takehiko suggests, such connotations explain not only why Edo-period writers, with a mixture of shame and defiant pride, would use the derogatory term *haishi shōsetsu* ("trivial history and small talk") to refer to their literary productions but also why the term *sakka* ("artist"; literally, "maker of things") is looked on even today with more favor than *shōsetsuka* in identifying someone as a writer.[43]

Early twentieth-century writers, then, could not help feeling ambivalent toward their literary heritage. To wear the label of *shō-*

42. "Watakushi wa kaigi-ha da," in *Futabatei Shimei zenshū* 5:230–31.
43. *Shōsetsu no Nihongo*, 12.

setsuka was to acknowledge the vulgarity of one's calling. The Confucian tradition had disenfranchised *shōsetsu* from any of the legitimate categories of literature. Moreover, the new European model was still not so well established that it could counter the prejudice that *shōsetsu*, unlike the classics or histories, did not tell the "truth," that is to say, a referential truth that pointed to some external reality outside the text and gained its significance from that reality. A few, like Noguchi, argue that it was the destiny of the *shōsetsu* as fiction, aided by the positive western conception, to transcend the limits of referentiality imposed by the dominant culture and to present its own kind of truth, a reality that exists nowhere but in language.[44] Pressures on the *shōsetsu* and on its cultural context, however, worked both ways. To the same extent that its verbal energy as a fictive text tended to propel the modern *shōsetsu* beyond referentiality, the modern *shōsetsuka*, in hopes of gaining respect for his work, tried to contain it within the referential framework of traditionally accepted prose forms and thereby elevate it to the level of "true" ("refined" as opposed to "vulgar") literature. Thus, the legitimizing rationale for the *shōsetsu* as fiction was soon countered by a movement to free the *shōsetsu* of fiction altogether. Out of this movement came the *shishōsetsu*.

The concern about telling "lies" is still very much alive today. Witness the following sentiments, delivered to a lecture audience in 1971, by the contemporary *shishōsetsu* author Yasuoka Shōtarō (1920–):

> In a *shishōsetsu* you write, somewhat tediously, about your own life and nothing else. A *shishōsetsu* has . . . no shape, no form, no style. It has none of these—and yet in writing about that ordinary, everyday life . . . a person's unique individuality manages to surface. "Everyone has his quirks," as the saying goes . . . but it's very difficult to discover those quirks for oneself. . . . Still there are those fleeting moments when you become detached and see yourself for what you really are . . . just as clearly as if your eyeball were attached to the wall over there. I think that truly creative writing involves that kind of searching for and discovering something in yourself, not dreaming up some formally satisfying story. Anyway, that's how I got started. It took me about half a year to write my first story, a mere thirty pages long. I'm in no position to judge its worth, but writing has made me understand—how shall I put it?—the value of life. Or,

44. Ibid., 20.

to put it another way, I feel that by writing I'm continually able to affirm my existence.[45]

Yasuoka is speaking in an age of high democratic capitalism beyond the postwar era, at a time when the sociocultural constraints on "mediated" expression to which Maruyama Masao alluded might be presumed no longer operative. And yet there is no sign, if these words are any indication, that the privileging of lived experience has waned. Its appeal lies on one level in its patently narcissistic value as a kind of literary graffiti that affirms the scribbler's existence. Even more important for Yasuoka are its revelatory powers, its ability to plumb the "truth" about the writer and about life in a way that no "formally satisfying" fictional work can. A story is naturally formless if it follows life, naturally "unique" if it accurately describes its author, whose life is by definition one of a kind. For Yasuoka, then, true originality lies not in the possible but in the actual, not in imagining but in living. Any attempt to stray from lived experience is bound to result in mimicry and fabrication, which in this scheme are seen in opposition to originality. In a move that effectively challenges the western conception of the fictional enterprise, he tells of his efforts to "invent" an original, formally convincing prose fiction—the product, he claims, of a pure flight of imagination—only to discover that a virtually identical story already existed in the *rakugo* (comic monologue) repertoire.[46] For Yasuoka, the lesson is clear: no such duplication is possible if a writer draws solely from his own life. Fabrication can only lead one away from the truth of lived experience.

There is still another kind of appeal, however, which Yasuoka only hints at, namely, the voyeurism inherent in reading what one knows to be a record of experience and not invention, a record not so valuable for what it says in itself as for whom it says it of. It may be impossible for the writer to see himself, as Yasuoka argues, except during a few fleeting moments of heightened awareness; but he is always in view of the reader, who is constant witness to the author's "quirks." The *shishōsetsu* may have no shape or form, but it does have a peculiar "style," contrary to Yasuoka's assertion, which is none other than its reputed *absence* of style. The *shishōse-*

45. "Gendai ni okeru watakushi shōsetsu," 34.
46. Ibid., 33–34.

tsu's whole raison d'être rests on the powerful illusion of its textual transparency—its sincerity—which lets the reader view the author's experience "unmediated" by forms, shapes, structures, or other "trappings" of fiction. Again and again we shall encounter the belief, articulated here with such conviction by Yasuoka, that the *shishōsetsu* lets the reader view through the window of its "transparent" language the private goings-on in the author's glass house in a way simply not possible through the mediated language of fiction.

One of our central concerns, of course, is just how "transparent" the language of the *shishōsetsu* really is. We may not notice that the glass in this window on life is tinted or warped or even *there* until it is opened, rolled down, or otherwise exposed. How, if at all, does it differ from the language of fiction? And if it does not, then what makes readers and writers believe nonetheless in a difference, as if literary will took precedence over linguistic evidence? We shall grapple with these questions in the following two chapters.

2

Language and the
Illusion of Presence

The essence of writing . . . is to prevent any reply to the
question: who is speaking?

Roland Barthes, *S/Z*

In most books, the *I*, or first person, is omitted; in this it
will be retained. . . . We commonly do not remember that
it is, after all, always the first person that is speaking. I
should not talk so much about myself if there were anybody
else whom I knew as well.

Henry David Thoreau, *Walden*

Why the preponderance of first-person narration in modern Japanese *shōsetsu*? We are led by the insights gained in Chapter 1 to
conclude that it is due paradoxically to a lack of a sense of self—
and to the concomitant lack of an isolable, autonomous "other." If
this is so, however, the term "*first-person* narration" itself becomes
problematic, because, as we noted earlier, pronominals in Japanese
do not mark an indelible boundary between self and other. The
shishōsetsu turns out to be not so much a first-person as a single-
consciousness narration (whether first *or* third person), and one,
moreover, that makes no distinction between the *narrated* and the
narrating subject.

To repeat, then, in terms that do more justice to the texts we
shall analyze: why the preponderance of single-consciousness or
subject-oriented narration in modern Japanese *shōsetsu*? In Chapter
1, we attributed the phenomenon in part to a worldview, rooted in
the indigenous and continental cultures, that privileged "unmediated" over "mediated" reality and made the Japanese (as Maruyama
Masao put it) try to push fiction in the direction of firsthand (although not particularly individuated) experiences. In later chapters,
we shall examine the influence of contemporary intellectual, criti-

cal, and literary developments on early twentieth-century writers' narrative technique. In this chapter, we shall see what the Japanese language itself can tell us about the preference for subject-oriented narration.

Examples of such narration can be found in all periods of Japanese literature: *waka*, of course, and in such prose forms as the *zuihitsu* (*Makura no sōshi, Tsurezuregusa, Hōjōki*, etc.), *kana nikki* (*Tosa nikki, Kagerō nikki, Sarashina nikki, Towazugatari*, etc.), and *haibun* (*Oku no hosomichi, Shin hanatsumi, Ora ga haru*, etc.). Even in an ostensibly "third-person" form like *monogatari*, the narrator's presence is too tenuous and particularized to be considered omniscient; indeed, the storyteller seems at times to merge with the characters.

In the classical western novel, from Fielding to Fowles, the narrator's omniscient perspective is validated solely by the novel's internal consistency; the narrator need not be situated vis-à-vis the characters in any concrete relationship, since s/he commands a suprahuman authority. Note, for example, how George Eliot's narrator in *Adam Bede* (1859) establishes complete control over her fictional world:

> With a single drop of ink for a mirror, the Egyptian sorcerer undertakes to reveal to any chance comer far-reaching visions of the past. This is what I undertake to do for you, reader. With this drop of ink at the end of my pen, I will show you the roomy workshop of Mr. Jonathan Burge, carpenter and builder, in the village of Hayslope, as it appeared on the eighteenth of June, in the year of our Lord 1799.

The Japanese *monogatari*, on the other hand, features a linguistic relationship between narrator and characters that automatically situates the former *within* the world depicted. Even *The Tale of Genji*, whose narrator is perhaps the most ubiquitous presence in the classical canon, is not a truly omniscient narrative. The *Genji* text contains frequent asides about the inaccessibility of certain information concerning the characters, and an honorific language that places narrator, characters, and audience in a specific social and linguistic relationship. At the same time, the virtual absence in classical Japanese of pronouns, which would serve to identify characters plainly and distinguish them from the narrator, as well as the absence of clear diacritical and grammatical demarcations between the "framing" discourse and the "framed" story, radically closes the distance between narrator and characters. Compared to the autonomous and highly authoritative narrator in *Adam Bede*, who reigns so confidently over her novelistic kingdom, the *Genji* narrator is indeed an amorphous presence.[1]

In short, omniscient narration is not operative in classical Japanese literature. This is not to say that the language itself lacks the tools with which to create a truly omniscient narration, only that it would be very unnatural to use them to that end. A number of recent studies have drawn attention (with the intent of finding parallels in western languages) to the existence in Japanese of two distinct narrative styles: one that does and one that does not observe the speaker-hearer paradigm and epistemological restrictions of actual linguistic performance. However, none have made the strong case needed to be made for the preferred *usage* in Japanese of the former over the latter. An examination of this clear preference should shed some light on the nature of narration in the *shishōsetsu* and Japanese prose fiction in general.

REPRESENTATION VERSUS TRANSCRIPTION

In the early 1970s the linguist S.-Y. Kuroda posited two mutually exclusive narrative styles in Japanese, the "reportive" and the "nonreportive," which distinguish grammatically between the restricted knowledge of a speaker or narrator in actual linguistic performance and the more general kind of knowledge to which a fictional narrator is privy. A narrative is reportive if related by a single-consciousness narrator who addresses a specific audience as if engaged in an act of communication; it is nonreportive if related by a multi-consciousness narrator whose utterances are not a part of actual linguistic performance. The reportive style offers a single point of view (that of the narrator's own consciousness); the nonreportive style, any number of points of view. Since the former situates the narrator specifically vis-à-vis the characters and events in the story and the latter depersonalizes the narrator entirely, the two narrative styles cannot be used interchangeably.

1. For a thorough study of the mechanics of narration in Heian texts, see Richard Hideki Okada, "Unbound Texts," esp. the discussion of *Genji*, 206–12.

Kuroda's main insight is that the reportive style's single-consciousness narrator[2] can speak in a cognitively definitive sense *only* about what he "knows" experientially, which is to say, his own feelings and sensations, and must resort to a different morphology when observing or describing the feelings or sensations of any other person. In short, grammar mirrors epistemology in the reportive style.[3] "The narrator in the reportive style," Kuroda observes, "however successfully he might otherwise transcend the world the story describes, can be pointed to by a mechanism of reference in grammar which exists independently of any assumption we might make concerning the ontological status of the narrator." He can never, in other words, be completely effaced from

2. Not to be confused with the first-person narrator; for as we shall see below, the "third-person" narrator in the *shishōsetsu* is no less a single-consciousness narrator who identifies psychologically *and* grammatically with the hero.

3. "Where Epistemology, Style, and Grammar Meet." Kuroda argues the grammatical distinction by presenting two classes of sensation words, the first of which (e.g., adjectivals such as *atsui* ["hot"] or *kanashii* ["sad"]) the speaker/narrator can use to describe only himself, whom he knows experientially to be in a particular state, and the second of which (e.g., verbals such as *atsugaru* ["to act hot"] or *kana-shigaru* ["to act sad"]) he uses to describe someone other than himself, whom he must judge through observation to be in a particular state. Thus, the speaker/narrator in the reportive style can make an epistemologically unequivocal statement (that is, one based on experiential knowledge and not merely on judgment) only about himself. To make epistemologically unequivocal statements about others requires the use of the nonreportive style.

The above example is actually one of several grammatical forms in the language that make the same epistemological distinction. Suffixes such as *-rashii, -yō (na)*, and *-sō (na)* indicate the narrator's judgment (on the basis of observation or hearsay) about attributes of people or things beyond the narrator's own experiential knowledge. (Such words as *kawairashii* ["cute"] and *kawaisō [na]* ["pitiable"], in which the suffix has become fused with the root word to form an essentially new word, are excluded from this characterization.) Although it is true that a narrator in the reportive style can use *-garu* and similar "judgmental" suffixes to refer to himself, their use is limited to those instances, such as the state of drunkenness, when the narrator is unsure of his own actions and thoughts or when he wishes to objectify himself by distancing narrating and narrated consciousness, as in the sentence, "Omoshirogatte yatte mita ga, tsumaranakatta" (I gave it a try, making a show of interest, but found it a bore).

Although an impossibility in Japanese, a first-person narrator can make unequivocal statements about other characters' sensations and feelings in English. Here is an extreme example, in which Mike Hammer describes his gunning down of two opponents in Mickey Spillane's *One Lonely Night*: "They *heard* my scream and the awful roar of the gun and the slugs stuttering and whining and it was the last they *heard*. They went down as they tried to run and *felt* their legs going out from under them. I saw the general's head jerk and shudder before he slid to the floor, rolling over and over" (quoted in Umberto Eco, *The Role of the Reader*, 164; emphasis added).

the narrative. The depersonalized narrator in the nonreportive style, meanwhile, communicates "in a way which is essentially different from the paradigmatic linguistic performance. One might say that the secret of the writer's artistic creation lies partially here."[4]

The interest for our discussion lies in Kuroda's claim that his "case study from Japanese" may be universal in its application. In her study of prose fiction narrative, *Unspeakable Sentences*, Ann Banfield takes a cue from Kuroda's argument to describe a form of depersonalized narrative (variously described as *style indirect libre*, *erlebte Rede*, and in her own terminology, "represented speech and thought") that presents the character's own point of view directly rather than through any mediating voice. Banfield argues that Kuroda's distinction between the reportive and nonreportive styles does exist in the grammar of English and the other European languages, revealing itself however not in a morphological distinction between sensation adjectives and verbs but rather in the grammar of reported speech. Banfield's study bears close scrutiny, then, because of its self-professed ramifications for narratives in all languages including Japanese. It describes an "unspeakable sentence," peculiar to narrative, which reconstructs or "represents," in a fictional "here and now," the speech and thought of characters in a prose fiction.

Banfield notes that the development of represented speech and thought parallels that of the novel between the seventeenth and the nineteenth century and that the form comes into its own with the emergence of such "stream-of-consciousness" novelists as Joyce, Woolf, Lawrence, and Proust. Contrary to direct and indirect speech, which reports a speaker's utterances with varying degrees of accuracy, represented speech and thought brings to light what a character may never have actually said or even consciously thought.[5] Further, it is marked by shifted pronouns and modals that make possible the use of the past tense to describe thought and speech

4. Kuroda, "Where Epistemology, Style, and Grammar Meet," 388.
5. Thus, such direct- and indirect-speech forms as: (1) "She said, 'I am tired,'" and (2) "She said (that) she was tired," to quote from the example that begins Banfield's book, become: "She was tired, she thought," in the represented speech/thought paradigm, in which parentheticals such as "she thought" are a commonly used but optional phraseology. See *Unspeakable Sentences*, 23.

in the fictional present. This style has the advantage, Banfield argues, of being able to present the consciousness of a character directly without the intervention of a narrator. In ordinary linguistic performance, subjectivity is limited to the "I" of the speaker, whereas in narrative, and particularly in the mode of represented speech and thought, an entirely separate sense of subjectivity can be expressed. Indeed, rather than being "narrated" at all, consciousness in this style is represented without the intervention of any judging point of view. In Banfield's words, "No one speaks."[6]

Since Banfield draws her conclusion from the premise that represented speech and thought is not modeled after actual linguistic performance, she is led to a radical counterposing of narration to discourse and valorizes the former in literary texts. "It is the dominance of the communicative function in speech," she argues, "which . . . accounts for the absence of the features of narrative style in speech, and it is writing . . . which frees linguistic performance from the tyranny of the communicative function."[7] Represented speech and thought is essential to the fictional enterprise, she concludes. "The linguistic cotemporality of PAST and NOW and the conference of [the nonnarrating] SELF and the third person supply a language for representing what can only be imagined or surmised—the thought of the other. *By separating SELF from SPEAKER, this style reveals the essential fictionality of any representation of consciousness.*"[8]

Like Kuroda, Banfield argues against the hypothesis put forth by Todorov and others that every text has a narrator and hence conforms to the communication model.[9] Yet Todorov's model of literature (including, of course, the category of represented speech and thought) as an act of communication cannot be dismissed lightly. According to this model, the narrator, regardless of whether he actually "appears" on the scene, arranges the material and its se-

---

6. Ibid., 97. Although certain literary forms, such as the epistolary novel and the *skaz*, do clearly address a second person, most narrations, Banfield contends, need no first person to intervene; where one does, "a narrator narrates, but addresses the story to no one" (ibid., 171).

7. Ibid., 227.

8. Ibid., 260. (Emphasis added.)

9. See for example Tzvetan Todorov, *The Poetics of Prose*, 26–28, which asserts the complementary relationship of story and discourse, both of which, he argues, are aspects of "utterance" or communication.

quence, orders its telling and its perspective, chooses between dialogue and "objective" description, and otherwise makes his "presence" felt, however indirectly. Is it possible, we want to ask, for there to be an *unnarrated* consciousness? To whom, if not a narrator addressing an audience, do we attribute the parenthetical consciousness verbs such as "think," "reflect," "feel," and "wonder" that appear so commonly in represented speech and thought for the purpose of establishing a point of view? The narrator may not be "needed" to "report" every sentence to the reader, but we sense his presence whether he comments on, or simply makes us aware of, the reflection that takes place in a character's mind. Regardless of how "unspeakable" certain narrative sentences seem, none of them can be said to be *unlistenable*—which is why the argument for an author addressing his narrative to an audience of readers, in conformance to the speaker-hearer paradigm, remains so compelling.[10]

More than in any specific problems with Banfield's discussion, our interest here lies in its applicability to the Japanese narrative, and in particular to the *shishōsetsu*. Banfield's argument, which is not without merit in the English case, rests of course on Kuroda's analysis, which she credits for presenting evidence that Japanese also possesses a narrative sentence of represented consciousness. The evidence to support this claim, however, turns out on closer inspection to be surprisingly slim. Kuroda's entire article, cited earlier, quotes not a single passage from an actual Japanese text. (His examples appear to be reworkings of English sentences into Japanese.) A later article on narrative theory quotes only one—but how revealing an example it is! Kuroda sets out to prove that the grammar of the reflexive pronoun *jibun* differs in narration and in discourse (arguing that in the former mode it can indicate the point of view of a referent who is not the topic/subject) but demonstrates in the process the curiously reportive nature of his nonreportive style in the Japanese case.

10. Gerard Genette addresses the issue succinctly with an example from the *Odyssey*: recounting Ulysses's slaughter of Penelope's suitors is just as much an action as the slaughter itself. "Without a narrating act, therefore, there is no statement [i.e., narrative text], and sometimes even no narrative content [i.e., story]" (*Narrative Discourse*, 26). Of these three senses of the term "narrative," Genette suggests that the narrative text of "discourse" is the only one directly available to textual analysis, but he never loses sight of the other two.

Let us examine the lone textual example on which Kuroda bases his analysis of *jibun* and, by extension, the nonreportive style.[11] After admitting that such examples are not abundant in written Japanese, he then presents, in a footnote, the opening passage of *Mon* (1911), the third book in Natsume Sōseki's famous trilogy, quoted in part below:

> Sōsuke wa sakki kara engawa e zabuton o mochidashite, hiatari no yosasō na tokoro e kiraku ni agura o kaite mita ga. . . . Sono sora ga jibun no nete-iru engawa no, kyūkutsu na sunpō ni kuraberu to, hijō ni kōdai de aru. Tama no nichiyōbi ni kō shite yukkuri sora o miageru dake demo, daibu chigau na to omoinagara.

> (Sōsuke had brought a cushion on to the veranda and plopped himself on it, cross-legged, and was now basking in the midafternoon sun. . . . Viewed from the tiny veranda, [the sky] seemed extremely vast. It made quite a difference, he reflected, to be able on an occasional Sunday to gaze leisurely at the sky like this.)[12]

Here, indeed, is a typical example of the reflexive pronominal *jibun* working to establish the point of view of the referent, in this case the hero Sōsuke: the sky as seen through Sōsuke's eyes. The reflexive pronoun is absent from the English translation, but the verb "seemed" in "[the sky] seemed extremely vast" leaves no doubt who the referent is. Kuroda suggests in the same footnote that the sentence "Sono sora ga jibun no nete-iru engawa no, kyūkutsu na sunpō ni kuraberu to, hijō ni kōdai de aru" (Viewed from the tiny veranda, [the sky] seemed extremely vast) could be made more "objective" or at least more "grammatically neutral"—closer, in other words, to an omniscient narration—by replacing *jibun* with the third-person pronominal *kare* and that it as well as the entire passage could be rewritten in the first person by replacing the words *Sōsuke* and *jibun* with *watashi*. It is doubtful, however, that a Japanese writer would in fact wish to be "objective" by using *kare*

11. Kuroda offers his own rather unidiomatic example of the shifting point of view made possible by a depersonalized narrator roaming from consciousness to consciousness—an unlikely occurrence in Japanese fiction. See "Reflections on the Foundations of Narrative Theory from a Linguistic Point of View," 119. The example also appears in "Where Epistemology, Style, and Grammar Meet."
12. "Reflections on the Foundations of Narrative Theory," 122–23. Kuroda uses the English translation by Francis Mathy, p. 5.

in place of *jibun;* for to do so would seem to introduce another point of view rather than point back to Sōsuke. Neither would *jibun* be replaced by *watashi* in a first-person narration. The sentence, quite as it stands, is perfectly interchangeable with first-person narration and could be so read in another context. It is the absence of proper names and pronouns in a narrative, once a point of view has been established, that makes this possible. There is nothing in the sentence itself that marks it as third-person narration. Indeed, there is nothing in the entire opening passage that marks it as third-person narration, other than the single mention of the name Sōsuke at the very beginning. Unlike the English "he," which of course refers to any male person previously mentioned or understood, *kare* has a far more circumscribed denotation in Meiji and Taishō literature: specifically, the protagonist, through whose eyes the narrator sees and through whose mind the narrator thinks. Indeed, what appears to be a pronoun, a placeholder for any subject of discourse, is in fact more correctly thought of as a proper name, because the use of *kare* is restricted to a single character.[13] That is why a story's protagonist may be introduced from the very first as *kare* and only later, if at all, by a given name.[14]

Nor is that all. In the very next sentence we find what looks like a typical example of represented speech and thought: "It *made* quite a difference, he *reflected*, to be able on an occasional Sunday to gaze leisurely at the sky like this." But is it really typical? The use of the past tense contemporally with the fictional present and the use of the parenthetical insert ("he reflected") identify the style

13. This tendency can be observed in the contemporary colloquial language as well. Young women often identify their boyfriends exclusively as *kare* (or *kareshi*), using names or titles to identify other men. Similarly, young men often identify their girlfriends simply as *kanojo* ("she").

14. Very little has been written in Japanese on this subject. For a brief review of the use of *kare* in modern literature, see Yanabu Akira, "*An'ya kōro* ni okeru 'kare.'" Yanabu notes that *only* the hero in Tayama Katai's *Futon*, for example, is designated as *kare*. (The hero's given name is not introduced until the second chapter.) Although *kare* does not refer exclusively to the hero in a work like Shiga's *An'ya kōro*, the exceptions seem almost to prove the rule (see Chapter 8 below). This usage is observed by writers of both sexes. In Okamoto Kanoko's *Boshi jojō* [1937], for example, *kanojo* denotes only one character, the heroine, throughout the story, while various nonpronominal words are used to denote other female characters. See also Kumakura Chiyuki, "Nihongo no shukansei ni tsuite," for an important analysis of what he calls the Japanese language's "subjectivity" (i.e., speaker orientation), to which my discussion is indebted.

for us clearly enough in the English translation. A closer look at the original Japanese reveals a very different arrangement, however. "Daibu chigau na to omoinagara" (It made quite a difference, he reflected) is more literally rendered, "It makes quite a difference!—thus, as [I/someone] reflect[s/ed]." There is nothing to distinguish this expression of "represented" thought from direct utterance. (The particle *to* normally follows utterances/reflections of any kind.)[15] It is context, then, not grammar, that determines whether the sentence in *Mon* translated as "It made quite a difference . . ." is to be read as represented speech/thought rather than as direct utterance/reflection. Indeed, the general sense one gets from reading the Japanese is that there is not the essential difference between these two forms that there is in western languages. The staple features of represented speech and thought, namely, the shifts in tense and pronoun usage, are nowhere to be found. The Japanese sentence, in short, is doing precisely what the English version cannot do: "representing" a character's speech or thought by *imitating* that character's very own words/thoughts.[16] The "unspeakable" in English becomes the only way to talk—or write—in Japanese.

THE WRITTEN REPORTIVE STYLE

That such sentences are in fact grammatical is not so surprising in itself; we might expect certain expressions, rejected in one language, to be perfectly acceptable in another. What is significant for our discussion is the impact of their grammaticality on the Japanese narrative enterprise. The first effect of this rejection of the past tense for utterances in "represented speech/thought," combined

15. It is deleted only after certain forms of indirect command. See Samuel E. Martin, *A Reference Grammar of Japanese,* 998.

16. Two more examples of what are considered "unacceptable" expressions in English may help clarify what is meant here. Banfield asserts that consciousness verbs cannot introduce direct quotations and may be used only as parentheticals following an expression of represented speech and thought: thus, *"She noticed: 'He is getting fat'" and *"She remembered, 'Ah dear, it is Wednesday in Brook Street'" are unacceptable transformations, respectively, of "He was getting fat, she noticed" and "Ah dear, she remembered—it was Wednesday in Brook Street" (*Unspeakable Sentences,* 45). But the structure of "represented" speech and thought in Japanese (if one were to translate the above examples) is in fact almost identical to the unacceptable form in English, except that the communication/consciousness verb usually comes after the utterance/reflection in Japanese.

with the absence of pronouns or other semantic markers that distinguish types of narration, is the extraordinary sense of immediacy that obtains. The use of the past tense in English (even if it loses its "pastness," as Banfield argues) has the effect of creating a much sharper distinction between utterance and narration, between character consciousness and reader awareness, than exists in Japanese. Without a tense that insists on its own fictional autonomy or a pronoun usage that insists on the otherness, the externality, of the character(s) in the narrative, the Japanese narrative presents the speech and thought of a character in a way that not only posits an audience but also invites the reader's identification— indeed, assimilation—with the character's train of thought. And if this is true even for "fictional" narrations like *Mon*, it is all the more true for "autobiographical" (whether first- or third-person) narrations like the *shishōsetsu*.

Second, and a consequence of the first, the reportive and non-reportive styles in Japanese, which are quite distinct in Kuroda's theoretical argument, merge in narrative praxis into a hybrid style that rejects depersonalized, multi-consciousness narration and approximates, but does not exactly duplicate, the speaker-hearer paradigm. Because of its special language, such a style—let us call it here the written reportive style—posits an audience without precisely identifying it. Locating the audience too specifically or denying it altogether would push the style toward either the reportive or the nonreportive pole. The written reportive style, with its restricted point of view, is the overwhelming preference of authors writing in a language that favors the transcription (in as literal a way as possible in writing), over the representation, of speech and thought.

To return to Banfield's conclusion, we see that whereas "the linguistic cotemporality" in western languages "of PAST and NOW and the coreference of SELF and the third person supply a language for representing what can only be imagined or surmised—the thought of the other," the absence of those two features in Japanese makes representation (in Banfield's sense) a linguistic impossibility. The written reportive style would seem to undermine the Japanese writer's belief in the legitimacy of "invention"—that is, the right of (or simply the possibility for) individual imagination to supplant an experiential, single-consciousness "reality" with a more compelling one (abstract and remote from immediate experience though it may at first appear) told from an omniscient perspective. Rather than acknowledge "the essential fictionality of any representation of consciousness, or any approximation of word to thought," Japanese yearns for the authenticity—however illusory—of an unmediated transcription of consciousness, in the language of an ever-present speaker.

For such a transcription to be truly convincing, however, it must be of the one consciousness that the narrator knows directly—namely, his own. Japanese prose fiction is therefore quite comfortable with first-person narration, since it does not aspire to a universal brokerage of consciousness afforded by omniscient narration or the nonreportive style. Yet this particularity of narrative voice, with which a Japanese reader identifies so closely and which the written reportive style exploits so expertly, works just as well with "third-person" as with first-person narration. In a "third-person" *shishōsetsu*, the pronominal *kare* typically has only one referent: the hero himself. Since voice and point of view readily converge in the absence of grammatical and tense markings, narrator and hero easily merge: not only do they appear as one in a *shishōsetsu*, they even "speak" and "think" as one.

Perhaps it would be useful here to offer a new narrative paradigm consistent with the written reportive style: let us call it the recorder-witness paradigm, which rejects the wholly representative author-reader paradigm of the nonreportive style while approximating the communicative speaker-hearer paradigm of discourse. This paradigm is central to the *shishōsetsu*, in which narrative voice and point of view become thoroughly intertwined. The grammar of the written reportive style reflects an epistemology that asserts that knowledge founded on personal experience is the only kind worth relating. A narrator situated within the confines of this epistemology is not aiming to reveal "the essential fictionality of any representation of consciousness," as is the case with Banfield's narrator of represented speech and thought, nor is he interested in the kind of "artistic creation" that Kuroda suggests is linked with the use of the nonreportive style. He is a happily nontranscendent figure, anchored in the narrative he both acts in and produces. And whereas the omniscient narrator in a classical novel distances himself from the narrative and invites the reader (as Henry James does so explicitly and eloquently in his prefaces) to join him in witnessing his production unfold, the *shishōsetsu* narrator "reports" on experience from an epistemological perspective that sees no further than the narrated subject.

The *shishōsetsu*'s recorder-witness paradigm thus pretends to a far more direct relationship than does the author-reader paradigm and can itself become a story's central or unifying element. Although it differs from the speaker-hearer paradigm in being a product of writing and not of speech, it presents, as the latter does, an intelligence no greater—or more distant—than that of any sentient being. Yet this intimacy between recorder and witness derives ironically from the rejection of a specific reader as the narrator's intended audience. Given a language in which a precise and subtle system of honorifics operates to situate speaker, hearer, and referent in a particularized and hierarchical relationship, the recorder had to discover a mode of expression that would radiate an equal sense of authenticity to any witness regardless of the actual social relationship that obtained.[17] The recorder was in no position to maintain the fiction—and it could only be a fiction—of a universally valid relationship with his audience as superior or inferior or equal. This inherently ambivalent narrative situation stimulated the development of a style that was familiar yet circumscribed. Unable on the one hand to address a specific reader without potentially ruling out discourse with another, and on the other to address all readers as one without distancing them, the recorder essentially became his own audience, writing a "story" in the style of a sketch or memoir and inviting the witness—any reader—to examine it.

And yet although the *shishōsetsu* writer's goal was to have the recorder-witness paradigm come as close as possible to the communicative act and thus do away with the mediative quality of written language, it was doomed to failure, as each writer was to dis-

17. The great task of modern Japanese writers in general was to develop a colloquial style that would close the immense, centuries-old gap between the spoken and written languages and call less attention to itself as a rhetorical medium. Masao Miyoshi, in his already-classic treatise, argues persuasively, however, that the language of Japanese prose fiction never did develop into a truly colloquial idiom, because spoken Japanese precluded the kind of undifferentiated audience that the novel demands. See *Accomplices of Silence*, esp. xiii–xiv and 11–14.

cover in his own way. Chikamatsu Shūkō began his first important series of writings by positing a specific, epistolary audience (his wife, addressed as "you" [*omae*]) but eventually abandoned the project as unworkable. For Shiga Naoya, the only way a writer could maintain the pretense of "talking" naturally while writing was to talk to oneself; but doing so resulted in a style that was strangely aloof. Kasai Zenzō, meanwhile, discovered for himself, and revealed to us through "slips" in his colloquial narrative style, the nature of his writing as writing. He was forced to "talk" in unexpected ways and engage in a series of feints that only served to remind him of the textuality of his "discourse," the closer he approached a pure colloquial style.

All these writers worked to camouflage the fictionality of their writing, a fictionality produced not by the nonreportive style's "lie" of narrated consciousness but by the lie of authorial "presence" featured in the written reportive style. From this style has sprung the myth of "sincerity," in which the totally accessible author relates his experiences through the totally transparent text. Yet these writers would discover, in ways that will be elaborated in Part 3, the surprising opacity of their supposedly glass-clear medium. The written reportive style turned out not to be fiction-free: the very act of expressing themselves in writing, they realized, was in effect to don a mask, to supplant person with persona. Each effort to suppress the textuality of their enterprise and to valorize narrative immediacy was undermined by the very process of mediation in which they were engaged. As a result, many *shishōsetsu* that seem at first glance to be neutral descriptions of experience, dependent for their legitimacy on an extratextual, referential world, take on a decidedly metafictional tone.

Such arguments for the *shishōsetsu*'s awareness of its own textuality, however, are not intended to equate it with "postmodernist" fiction: the latter thematizes overtly—and the former only covertly—the text's linguistic self-awareness and ontological independence from the referential world.[18] Rather, they simply confirm

18. See, for example, Linda Hutcheon, *Narcissistic Narrative* (esp. chaps. 1 and 6), which treats fiction as an autonomous universe, dependent on intratextual validity rather than extratextual "truth." See also Patricia Waugh, *Metafiction*, 21–61, for a discussion of the self-conscious nature of textual production, which is to be found in the *shishōsetsu* (esp. in the writings of Kasai Zenzō) as well.

the assertion that "all great fiction, to a large extent, is a reflection on itself rather than a reflection of reality."[19] The question of the *shishōsetsu's* "greatness" aside, we shall find numerous examples in Part 3 of the form's reflection on the medium it is constrained to employ in the textual reproduction of lived experience.

While Taishō-period writers were forced by the very mechanics of their narrative art to reconsider the meaning of such concepts as sincerity and authorial presence in literature, critics were busily engaged in the mystification of these terms. That many of these critics were also writers does not undermine the argument that writers were in fact aware of the paradoxical nature of their project; it only suggests the degree to which that awareness had been suppressed to a subconscious level. Writers, as writers, reckoned with the language of the text; as critics, they drew back from the texts and embraced the mythology of sincerity and authorial presence. If we find that Japanese writers were more linguistically than critically attuned to the nature of fictionality and referentiality, it is because the *shishōsetsu* had so thoroughly established its own legitimacy as a cultural (and not simply as a literary) artifact, weighed down with a large set of conventions to determine meaning. Both the *shishōsetsu's* admirers and its detractors were slaves to these conventions, founded on a referential view of literature, and both addressed the issue of the *shishōsetsu's* beneficial or deleterious effect on Japanese letters from essentially the same position. It is a position that we must now locate and explore.

19. The assertion, by Raymond Federman, provides the epigraph to Hutcheon, *Narcissistic Narrative*.

3

Shishōsetsu Criticism
and the Myth of Sincerity

When one looks at the statue of Kannon adorning the
Dream Hall in Hōryūji Temple, the farthest thing from one's
mind is the person who carved it. This is a special case, for
the statue has taken on a completely separate existence
from its producer. If I were able to produce literary text of
equal caliber, I doubt that I would feel compelled to sign
my name to it.

> Shiga Naoya, Preface to the 1928 *Gendai*
> *bungaku zenshū* single-volume edition of
> his writings

If we forget that fictions are fictive we regress to myth.

> Frank Kermode, *The Sense of an Ending*

Thus far we have seen how a literary tradition of equating
"serious" writing with nonfiction and a language well suited to the
reportive style's epistemology have nurtured the belief in an
author's "unmediated" presence in the text, especially in a text so
clearly autobiographical as the *shishōsetsu*. This belief has in turn
prompted the *shishōsetsu*'s admirers and detractors alike to appeal
to a biographical "pre-text" in establishing the proper context for
evaluation. In the eyes of the detractors, *shishōsetsu* writers were
unimaginative gossips whose stories' very intelligibility depended
on a prior familiarity with details of their private lives. In the eyes
of admirers, they were a special breed of artists whose candid confessions inspired a confidence between author and reader that did
away with the need for fiction. These seemingly contradictory but
in fact interlocking views have informed the *shishōsetsu* from its
emergence in the critical consciousness at the end of Taishō down
to the present day.

Three major periods of critical debate concerning *shishōsetsu*—the first in the mid-1920s, the second in the mid-1930s, and the third in the 1950s—will provide the focus of our discussion here.[1] We should note that even the earliest criticism appeared when the *shishōsetsu's* popularity and influence had already reached their zenith; nearly all texts by the writers analyzed in Part 3, for example, date back to the 1910s and early 1920s. But there is no question that the values that eventually surfaced in the form of criticism were in place from the *shishōsetsu's* very beginnings. An examination of those values should tell us a great deal about a cultural product that was packaged from its inception as a "purer" and "sincerer" prose form than ordinary fiction, and by that measure somehow more uniquely Japanese.

THE FIRST PERIOD: "PURE" SHISHŌSETSU
VERSUS "TRUE" NOVELS

In 1924 Nakamura Murao (1886–1949), author, publisher, and critic, inaugurated the first period of critical debate with an essay championing what he called the "true novel" (*honkaku shōsetsu*) against the *shinkyō shōsetsu* (a variant term for *watakushi shōsetsu / shishōsetsu*). The true novel's principal concern, Nakamura writes, is the realistic depiction of characters in society. Since the author reveals his philosophy only parenthetically, by his characters' speech and actions, the reader's understanding of such a text does not depend on a familiarity with the author's private life. The *shinkyō shōsetsu's* principal concern, by contrast, is the direct communication of lived experience. Since the author has no interest in creating characters or dramatic situations and it is just as important to know *who* is writing as it is what is being written about, the reader's understanding greatly depends on his knowledge of the author. The descriptive shorthand used in the *shinkyō shōsetsu* makes the form resemble the haiku in its economy, to be sure; but economy is no virtue in fiction, Nakamura insists, and he offers *Anna Karenina* as the consummate example of what he looks for in

---

1. Some critics alter this periodization slightly. For example, Katsuyama Isao divides the same three decades into four periods: the first in the mid-1920s, the second in the mid-1930s, the third during the Pacific War, and the fourth right after the war. See "Shoki watakushi shōsetsu ron" (1953), in *Taishō, watakushi shōsetsu kenkyū*, 187 n. 1.

a novel. Japan has no hope of producing a Tolstoy, because writers have become too bogged down in their private lives and because the critics have become voyeurs whose preoccupation with autobiographical truth has undermined the incentive to create imaginative fictions. In an atmosphere where curiosity about private life reigns supreme over concern for literary excellence, any writer's attempt at authoring true fiction is derided as "vulgar" literature.[2]

Although we have used *watakushi shōsetsu / shishōsetsu* exclusively in our discussion, we should note here that the term *shinkyō* ("mental state") *shōsetsu* has also had wide currency down to the present day. The terms are often used interchangeably. Kume Masao (1891–1952), for example, argues that the *shinkyō shōsetsu* is a "purer" form of *watakushi shōsetsu* (see below), but either term would be appropriate in Nakamura's essay. Some critics have worked out elaborate schemes for distinguishing one from the other. The predominant postwar view is that the *watakushi shōsetsu* is a literature of crisis, to which writers turn in desperation and at the risk of disrupting their private lives, while the *shinkyō shōsetsu* is a literature of harmony and salvation, through which writers find peace with themselves and their surroundings. The latter is commonly conceived as an even more evocative, discursive, and nondramatic presentation of experience than the former.[3] A writer is usually regarded as the author of one form or the other, depending on his commitment either to unmitigated self-exposé or to more controlled confession. Hirano Ken (1907–78) offers the best-known exposition of this critical perspective in his opposition of the presumably "unabashed" writing of Chikamatsu Shūkō and Kasai Zenzō to the more "guarded" prose of Shiga Naoya. The rationale for distinguishing between two varieties of confession lies, not surprisingly, in the pre-text of private life. Writers like Shūkō and Kasai, their personal lives a shambles, had nothing to lose by their candor, Hirano argues, while those like Shiga, their domestic lives more or less intact, had everything to lose by letting their "confessions" get out of hand.[4] This distinction is not really useful, since

2. "Honkaku shōsetsu to shinkyō shōsetsu to."
3. Howard Hibbett reflects this critical view, which ascribes a more resonant and elevated tone to the *shinkyō shōsetsu*, when he calls it a "contemplative" (as opposed to a "confessional") novel. See "The Portrait of the Artist in Japanese Fiction," 348.
4. See *Geijutsu to jisseikatsu*, 25–45 and passim. Hirano's view is shared by Honda Shūgo, who likewise makes an explicit contrast between the "destructive"

it is impossible to determine objectively just how much an author "reveals" of himself in his work. It *is* valid, however, with regard to the author's literary persona. Thus, the Shiga hero's "confessions" predictably conform to the persona of a morally conscientious author-sage, for example, while the Kasai hero's conform to that of a forever-victimized, ne'er-do-well artist. We shall examine these personae in detail in Part 3.

But now to continue our discussion of early critics. Nakamura is representative of those who believed that the *shishōsetsu* (by which is meant either *watakushi shōsetsu* or *shinkyō shōsetsu*), although a faithful record of "real-life" events, was inevitably inferior to the true novel as art because it was not informed by an overall conception that transcended the author's personal experience. He was supported by an even severer critic of the *shishōsetsu*, Ikuta Chōkō (1882–1936), who insisted that the world's truly great authors, from Shakespeare to Saikaku, best expressed themselves through imaginative creation rather than documentary accounts of their private lives.[5]

Support for the *shishōsetsu* came first from a practitioner, Kume Masao. In perhaps the most widely quoted essay on the subject, Kume confides that as an author he has always felt more comfortable writing *shishōsetsu* than "fiction" and that as a reader he has always placed his greatest trust in other *shishōsetsu* writers. He then presents an argument that epitomizes the Japanese writer's skepticism of the fictional contract.

> I cannot believe that art in the true sense of the word is the "creation" of someone else's life. . . . I see it rather as the "recreation" of a life, of an experience, that actually took place. To be sure, a Balzac can write a voluminous narrative like *The Human Comedy* and portray his usurers and aristocratic ladies so vividly that they seem to come alive. Yet I cannot but regard such a narrative as a fabrication, nor can I place in it the trust I do in even the most off-handed remark the author might make about, say, the difficulties he encountered

---

literature of Shūkō and Kasai and the "constructive" literature of Shiga. See *"Shira-kaba" ha no bungaku*, 125. Hirano's strict opposition between these two types of literature has been questioned by later critics. See, for example, Katsuyama, "Taishōki ni okeru watakushi shōsetsu no keifu" (1966) in his *Taishō, watakushi shōsetsu kenkyū*, 248–53. Few critics, however, question their own ability to ascertain the accuracy of an author's confessions by an examination of the life.

5. "Nichijō seikatsu o henchō suru akukeikō" (1924).

writing his stories. The world has known a handful of great authors—true geniuses (Tolstoy, Dostoevsky and in particular Flaubert)—who have been able to communicate something of themselves
in their writing. The moment these authors express themselves
through other characters, however, they distance themselves from
their readers. Inevitably, embellishments and technical flourishes—
convenient fictions, all—creep in. Their novels may be superior as
entertainment, but they do not ring true to me. Once, during a lecture, I went so far as to say that Tolstoy's *War and Peace*, Dostoevsky's
Crime and Punishment, and Flaubert's *Madame Bovary* were really no
more than popular novels [*tsūzoku shōsetsu*]—first-rate examples of
their kind, to be sure, but popular novels nonetheless. In the final
analysis, they are mere fabrications—just so much entertainment.[6]

For Kume, then, the *shishōsetsu* is the purest of prose forms because it allows the author to express himself candidly without having to "fabricate" his thoughts in the guise of a novelistic character.
Wary of the essential fictionality of represented consciousness, he
yearns for a literature of "unmediated" experience told directly by
the subject as opposed to one told through the "mediation" of an
omniscient narrator. To a reader with Kume's sensibilities, Balzac's
memoirs would have greater appeal than any of his novels (which,
however brilliantly fashioned, were mere "fabrications"), because
they brought the reader closer to Balzac the man. Kume appears to
qualify his faith in unmediated experience when he later insists
that the true *shishōsetsu* is not "mere" autobiography or confession
but "first and foremost a work of art." But art, in Kume's view, is a
product of one's mental state. Only properly harmonized thoughts
can generate an unerring depiction of self. The line Kume draws
between art and nonart corresponds to the distinction he makes
between the *shinkyō shōsetsu* (a word that he claims to have coined)
and the ordinary *watakushi shōsetsu*.[7] Kume argues that the *shinkyō
shōsetsu* is not simply a random account of personal experience (as
he implies the *watakushi shōsetsu* is) but a scrupulous self-portrait
that can be drawn only when one has reached a suitably contemplative frame of mind. In Kume's view, then, art is a discipline, the

6. "'Watakushi' shōsetsu to 'shinkyō' shōsetsu" (1925), 52–53.
7. According to Kume, the word *shinkyō* was used in his haiku circle and referred to the poet's mental state during composition. (Some critics dispute his claim
to be the first to use the term in connection with prose writing.) For a discussion of
the origins of *shinkyō shōsetsu* and *watakushi shōsetsu* as critical terms, see Katsuyama
Isao, "Shoki watakushi shōsetsu ron," in *Taishō, watakushi shōsetsu kenkyū*, 174–89.

shinkyō shōsetsu a vehicle for meditation, and the writer his own audience.

Many critics, whether or not they subscribed to Kume's *watakushi shōsetsu* / *shinkyō shōsetsu* distinction, believed that the *shishōsetsu* enabled the author, in the words of Uno Kōji, to "plumb the depths of the self" in a way that the ordinary novel, fettered by its conventions of "fictionalization," could not.[8] They also saw in the classical western poetics of plot, characterization, and dramatic scene a built-in artificiality that undermined the aims of sincerity, and argued that fiction was a crutch an author relied on only when he had exhausted his own life's experience or when he could not address his readers with complete candor. It followed that the best preparation for writing—itself no more than an unpretentious presentation of one's philosophy of life—was living. In this vein, Kikuchi Kan (1888–1948) insisted that a writer had to serve a rigorous apprenticeship to life before committing himself to art, which was a kind of "report card" of the life.[9] He also insisted, in a remarkable statement linking art and morality, that individual character and literary style were inseparable:

> It has long been the case that outstanding writers are also outstanding people. . . . Writing is a reflection of the entire person, and if the person's character is defective, so will be the reflection. . . . One improves one's writing by first improving one's character. . . . A writer will be successful as long as he describes his thoughts and feelings sincerely and faithfully—never mind how naive they may be. The worst possible thing is to imitate another's style and write about what one has never seen or felt.[10]

8. "'Watakushi shōsetsu' shiken" (1925), 64. Uno singles out Kasai Zenzō as the form's most brilliant practitioner.

9. See "Shōsetsuka taran to suru seinen ni atou" (1922), in *Kikuchi Kan zenshū* 12:373–76. See also "Geijutsu to tenbun" (1920), in ibid., 29–32, and finally "Chikamatsu Shūkō-shi no kinsaku" (1924), in ibid., 312, in which Kikuchi uses the term to describe Shūkō's work *Ko no ai no tame ni*. Many critics continue to speak of the *shishōsetsu* as the author's personal "report card." See, for example, Yamada Akio, "Watakushi shōsetsu no mondai," 43. Both Kikuchi and Kume Masao eventually turned away from the *shishōsetsu:* Kikuchi, because he believed that writing as a financially viable career depended on pleasing a mass audience (see, for example, his *Han jijoden* [1929–47], in *Kikuchi Kan: tanpen sanjū-san to Han jijoden*, 490); and Kume, because he believed that one could write successfully only as an avocation, without the pressure of deadlines and editorial whims (see his "Junbungaku yogi setsu" [1935], 411–13). But their critical stance toward life and art remained unchanged.

10. "Bun wa hito nari."

The assumption made by both sides in the debate, however—and here we see their common ground—was that fictionality was operative only in the author's "absence" from the text. A narrator-hero clearly modeled on the author was a sign to the *shishōsetsu's* admirers and detractors alike that all experiences related in the text, being the author's own, belonged ipso facto outside the realm of fiction. There is no more telling evidence of their common ground than the comments of Nakamura Murao, the erstwhile *shishōsetsu* critic. Ten years after he declared his preference for the "true" novel, he now confessed his partiality for "pure literature" (*junbungaku*, which, as many have noted, has been equated with the *shishōsetsu* since the Taishō period)[11] precisely in terms of the attitude toward fictionality we have discussed.

> I regard the *shishōsetsu* as the ultimate form of pure literature. It is surely the purest and the most candid of prose forms. In a conventional, objective novel [*kyakkan shōsetsu*], fiction [*uso*] inevitably creeps in; it simply cannot be written otherwise. Tolstoy, Balzac, and Flaubert are revered as "gods" of the novel. All their work contains fiction. . . . The subjective passages, in which the author reveals himself directly, are much more real to me than the objective passages, in which fiction prevails. Anyone with a modicum of talent can write a novel. That is why a novel, no matter how deft or serious its fictionalizations, does not claim my respect or appeal to me as pure literature.[12]

The notion of "pure literature" as the honest depiction of the author's own life, which might otherwise be "sullied" by incretions of fiction, was common throughout the *bundan* and continues to the present day.[13] To claim, however, as we do here that Naka-

---

11. See Katsuyama, "Shoki watakushi shōsetsu ron," in *Taishō, watakushi shōsetsu kenkyū*, 185. See also Ōi Zetsu, "Watakushi shōsetsu ron no seiritsu o megutte," 46–47, which links the equation specifically to Kume Masao's essay, discussed above.

12. "Junbungaku to shite no watakushi shōsetsu," 5. The prejudicial view of literature not based on the author's own life as being somehow less "authentic" is noted nearly three decades later by a well-known writer of detective fiction, Matsumoto Seichō, who insists that his own literary intentions are serious despite criticisms that the "fictionality" in his work makes it less "real." See Hirano Ken and Matsumoto Seichō, "Watakushi shōsetsu to honkaku shōsetsu."

13. For example, Isogai Hideo, a contemporary critic, describes the author Makino Shin'ichi in the following manner: "Makino began his literary career writing stories in the *shishōsetsu* mode; but his was not a temperament that could bear the strain of *unvarnished* confession, and he gave his works a comic and fictional *veneer*" (*NKBD* 3:225c; emphasis added).

mura's statement is a particularly cogent articulation of the myth of sincerity is to address squarely the myth's power and to acknowledge its evolution from a cultural to a precritical, "natural" artifact. The myth of "pure literature" became the *shishōsetsu's* touchstone; perhaps even more important, it became the touchstone for critical judgment of all Japanese prose fiction, whether *shishōsetsu* or not. "Pure literature" was an original site, a virgin territory that could be recovered only if purged of "objective" passages having nothing to do with lived experience. The latter, according to Nakamura and the vast majority of critics until quite recently, could be made available only in writing like the *shishōsetsu*. Such reasoning would not have made sense to the mass audience, which had no inkling of the real-life author who produced stories for their consumption, but it held sway in the *bundan* as long as writing was seen as a vestige of the life that preceded the text.

Akutagawa Ryūnosuke (1892–1927), the famous short-story writer who was frequently criticized by the *bundan* for his forays into "nonpure" fiction, attempted to collapse the distinction between *shishōsetsu* and true novel altogether by arguing that no art form was concerned with referential truth. Yet even he agreed that the *shishōsetsu* was a "fictionless" writing.[14] Tempted though we might be when reading a *shishōsetsu*, however, to exclaim, along with Tanizaki Jun'ichirō (1886–1965), "Aha! The man is writing about himself!" we need not jump to the conclusion that we are "reading a nonfiction piece" and "immediately lose patience with it."[15] If we do, we only confuse the fictive product (however "true-to-life") with the producer whom we do not know and whose connections with the text are severed once pen leaves page.[16]

14. "'Watakushi' shōsetsu shōken" (1925), in *Akutagawa Ryūnosuke zenshū* 8:39–46. Akutagawa's statement is important nonetheless, for he suggests that a work's basis in fantasy or fact has no bearing on its artistic value. He uses an example from painting to illustrate his point. The physical "reality" of the Mount Kōya monastery's *Red Fudō*, with flames rising from the deity's back, is not at issue, he argues, but rather the painting's overall design. Likewise, the *shishōsetsu's* apparently faithful representation of life does not by itself make it superior as art. "Honest" representation may be a moral imperative, he concludes, but it is not an artistic one.

15. *Jōzetsu roku* (1927), in *Tanizaki Jun'ichirō zenshū* 20:72.

16. Tanizaki himself took advantage of just this sort of confusion and enticed naive readers to equate fictive and real-life authors. He made enough independently confirmable referential asides in his *Shunkinshō* (1933), for example, to have sent some gullible critics scurrying to an Osaka cemetery in search of the heroine's nonexistent grave.

Shishōsetsu authors may lie or they may tell the truth about them-selves. But unless we are prepared to privilege the biographical pre-text over the written text to the extent that we deprive the latter of any autonomy, we gain nothing from having distinguished "truth" from "falsehood." The act of writing, however confes-sional, actually liberates the writer, however unwillingly, from lived experience. Therefore, a text whose protagonist has a clearly recognizable model is no less autonomous than a text that has none. If any one *shishōsetsu* text does not stand up on its own, it is simply because it exists in a discursive field where it is radically contiguous to other texts (not to the life it presumes to "repre-sent"). Either way a text is condemned to independence from its author.

Thus, the anonymously produced statue of the Kannon goddess adorning the Hōryūji Dream Hall, which Shiga Naoya gazes at so fondly in the epigraph to this chapter, is not a "special case" after all. Shiga, even by signing the texts he writes, paradoxically con-firmed his biographical absence from them. The seeming overlap of author, narrator, and hero notwithstanding, the author's "pres-ence" in a *shishōsetsu* is, finally, an artistic illusion like perspective or coloring or shading: it may add a dimension of "realism" to a text (the kind that Taishō-period readers were particularly enam-ored of, to be sure), but it does not bring the text any closer to "reality." Nor should it; only by transcending life—by transform-ing experience and perception into the written word—can litera-ture be free to represent it. Even Shiga, the *shishōsetsu* author par excellence, was apparently aware of this theorem of fictionality and its corollary of the illusion of authorial presence.

THE SECOND PERIOD:
WRITER AND SOCIETY

When the debate over the *shishōsetsu* intensified a second time in the mid-1930s, attention shifted from fiction's place in literature to the citizen's place in society—a legacy of the proletarian move-ment's concern for social engagement. The *shishōsetsu* came under attack by various groups, from the modernist school known as the Shinkankaku-ha (Neo-perceptionists) to the proletarian writers, for its extreme introspection and lack of social consciousness. In his essay "Junsui shōsetsu ron" (1935), Yokomitsu Riichi (1898–1947), the Shinkankaku-ha's leading member, urges writers to offer a broader vision of society than can be had in the autobiographical *junbungaku* ("pure literature"), yet to avoid the frivolity of popular fiction (*tsūzoku shōsetsu*). He borrows a term from André Gide and champions what he calls the "pure novel" (*junsui shōsetsu*), which combines the former's moral seriousness with the latter's structural cohesion. Only the pure novel, Yokomitsu maintains, can bring together these two divergent strains, which he argues are carryovers from the "autobiographical" diary (*nikki*) and "imaginative" narrative (*monogatari*) traditions, respectively.[17]

Yokomitsu's advocacy of a new literary synthesis leads him to challenge the notion of "realism" prevailing in the *bundan*. For *junbungaku* writers, Yokomitsu claims, realism simply means the faithful chronicling of personal experience. Following in the *nikki* tradition, the author-narrator focuses exclusively on a single character—himself. Because Japanese "realism" has no place for sustained plot and character development, the typical *junbungaku* *shōsetsu* is fragmented and short-winded. *Junbungaku* writers, Yokomitsu argues further, have misjudged the serious artistic intentions of the great nineteenth-century western "realists" like Balzac or Tolstoy or Dostoevsky in whose works accident often plays a crucial role, because their narcissism has rendered them oblivious to anything outside their own immediate experience and consequently to the links between the particular and the universal. A great novelist skillfully orchestrates fortuitous occurrences in his characters' lives, he concludes, whereas the *junbungaku* writer, preoccupied with authenticity, seeks to eliminate them altogether.[18]

Yokomitsu's answer to "pure literature's" limited narrative perspective and resultant particularity is a radically different, al-

17. "Junsui shōsetsu ron," 146–47. For additional commentary on this essay and its dubious debt to Gide, see Dennis Keene, *Yokomitsu Riichi: Modernist*, 181–83.

18. "Junsui shōsetsu ron," 144–45, 149–50. (One is reminded of Akutagawa's comment that "true-to-life" fiction contains far fewer coincidences than one probably encounters in one's own experience ["Shuju no kotoba," in *Akutagawa Ryūnosuke zenshū* 7:448].) Yokomitsu would no doubt have agreed with Georg Lukács, who wrote a year later in his classic comparison of Tolstoy and Zola that without chance all narration was dead and abstract and that the secret of representation lay in its elevation of chance to the inevitable. See "Narrate or Describe?" (1936), in *Writer and Critic and Other Essays*, 112.

though vaguely defined, point of view he calls the "fourth person," capable of seeing both the inner self and the world at large; he holds up Stendhal's *Charterhouse of Parma* as a model for writers to emulate.[19] "Fourth person" suggests that Yokomitsu realized the easy tendency of "third-person" narration to merge with first-person narration in Japanese and hoped to construct a narrative in which the distance between narrator and hero did not collapse. Yet this comprehensive narrative perspective, which directly challenged the epistemology that underlies Japanese realism and the pervasive mode of expression we have provisionally called the written reportive style, was never to gain much currency in the *bundan*. One reason, perhaps, is that Yokomitsu's proposed "synthesis" of two traditional forms (*nikki* and *monogatari*) is of elements not as disparate as he makes them out to be. By contrasting the "autobiographical" *nikki* with the "imaginative" *monogatari*, Yokomitsu equates the latter with western fiction; yet we have already noted that both forms lack the teleological worldview that predominates in western narrative. Moreover, *monogatari* did not provide the precedent for omniscient-narrative overview that Yokomitsu was looking for. Japanese realism was not to be divorced so easily from the narrator-hero's perspective and voice.

Shortly after the appearance of Yokomitsu's essay, Kobayashi Hideo (1902–83) responded with "Watakushi shōsetsu ron" (1935), a kind of postmortem on the *shishōsetsu*, although he acknowledges in his famous conclusion: "The *shishōsetsu* is dead, but have people vanquished the self? The *shishōsetsu* will doubtlessly reappear in new forms, so long as Flaubert's celebrated formula, 'Madame Bovary—c'est moi,' lives on."[20] He argues that the *shishōsetsu* is rooted in Japanese naturalism and that *Futon* is its prototype, a view that has assumed the status of critical orthodoxy.[21] He discounts any similarities between the *shishōsetsu* and European personal fiction. Unlike the latter, which has its roots in the romantic movement inaugurated by Rousseau's *Confessions* and the subsequent flowering of self-awareness, the *shishōsetsu* is a product of

19. "Junsui shōsetsu ron," 150, 154.
20. "Watakushi shōsetsu ron," 201–2.
21. Ōi Zetsu, "Watakushi shōsetsu ron no seiritsu o megutte," 43. Yoshida Sei'ichi offers a representative example of this view in "Watakushi shōsetsu no mondai ni tsuite," 19.

the Japanese naturalist movement's faith in literature as nonfiction document. This faith, he notes, was crystallized in Kume Masao's 1925 essay that denounced several great nineteenth-century novels as "mere" fabrications. Kobayashi argues that Kume spoke for an entire generation of skeptics about the fictional enterprise.[22]

Kobayashi's most penetrating remarks about the *shishōsetsu* have to do with the relationship between self and society and how radically it differs in Japan and in the west. Kobayashi maintains that Japanese writers casually imported the idea of "self" from European literature without domesticating the social, intellectual, and scientific institutions on which it was based. The individual in modern European literature has always been situated in a broad social milieu. However much the romantics questioned the individual's place in society, they did not turn their backs on that society. Rousseau and his successors never sought refuge in depictions of private life for their own sakes; they confidently featured their self-portraits in sweeping canvases of society. Writers of personal fiction from Goethe to Gide were thoroughly assimilated into their communities and steeped in a tradition of individualism nurtured by what Kobayashi calls the "socialized self" (*shakaika-shita watakushi*). Japanese writers, of course, lacked this tradition. And although fascinated with naturalism as a literary technique, they were incapable of truly appreciating, let alone transplanting, the positivistic philosophy from which it derived. "No writer, however great a genius he may be, can create singlehandedly a zeitgeist or social philosophy," writes Kobayashi; ". . . he can only articulate in his works a philosophy that already lives among the people."[23] Unable to take root as a system of thought, then, the literary naturalism imported by Japanese writers yielded, inevitably, nothing more than technically brilliant depictions of the writers themselves living in studied isolation.

Kobayashi makes his point by contrasting the views of Flaubert and Shiga on the place of private life in art. Flaubert epitomizes for Kobayashi the European tradition of subordinating private life to artistic production. "The artist must conduct himself in such a way as to make later generations believe he never existed," he quotes

22. "Watakushi shōsetsu ron," 182.
23. Ibid., 185.

Flaubert as saying. And further: "The only way to escape misery is to cloister oneself in art and completely disregard all else. I have no desire for wealth or love or passion. I have divorced myself irrevocably from my private life."[24] This credo, argues Kobayashi, is antithetical to that of a *shishōsetsu* writer like Shiga, whose desire to overcome crises in private life become both the motivation *for* and the motif *in* his writing. The notion that private life was off-limits to his creative career was no doubt behind Flaubert's yearning for anonymity. For Shiga, however, private life was the main arena of his art. Shiga recognized that a truly great work of art was, in the final analysis, independent of its author, as his remarks on the Kannon statue (which Kobayashi cites) make clear. Yet this recognition, Kobayashi suggests, did not translate into action. What are we to make of the long silence that followed those remarks? Shiga was able to gaze complacently at the statue at a time when he had already achieved personal contentment and had exhausted his store of creative material. Anonymity was no longer a choice; it was his destiny.[25]

Shiga's case may have been extreme, but it was far from unique; sooner or later all *shishōsetsu* writers faced this crisis of creativity. Having exhausted his private life as a creative resource, Shimazaki Tōson (1872–1943), for example, turned to the writing of history, while Masamune Hakuchō (1879–1962) turned to criticism. Still other writers turned to popular fiction, including Kume Masao, whose bold pronouncements a decade earlier had figured large in the first *shishōsetsu* debates. Kume now argued (in "Junbungaku yogi setsu," 1935) that the *shishōsetsu* could be pursued only as an avocation, that it was not worth sacrificing one's livelihood for, and that making such a sacrifice actually defeated the purpose of writing by destroying the elevated mental state one wished to write about. Kobayashi calls Kume's essay an example of wishful thinking by a writer unable to turn his own life into a work of art.[26]

Kobayashi and Yokomitsu, then, were in general agreement over the baneful influence of *junbungaku* on Japanese letters. Both, however, were quick to pronounce the *shishōsetsu* a failed form without

24. Ibid., 186.
25. Ibid., 186–87.
26. Ibid., 187–88.

coming to grips with its continued popularity. Like most writers and critics of the time, Kobayashi and Yokomitsu were influenced by their readings of European, and especially French, literature, which enjoyed tremendous prestige. (Yokomitsu goes so far as to say that Japanese writers knew more about Europe than Asia and that their own tradition *was* French and Russian literature.)[27] A decidedly evolutionary view informed their thinking; they were confident that Japanese letters would follow in the path of, and eventually merge with, European literature, the unquestioned standard. To be sure, Yokomitsu perceptively linked *junbungaku* to the native tradition when he noted its similarities to the poetic diary; and Kobayashi described Japanese naturalism (and by extension the *shishōsetsu*) as more "feudal" (i.e., premodern) than "bourgeois" (i.e., modern and western)—an idea that shocked his contemporary audience, which had thought of it as having made a clean break with the past.[28] Yet neither they nor their contemporaries seriously questioned the belief that Japanese literature *ought* to have developed along the lines of European "antecedents" and that any deviation was in fact a "distortion." Their literary evolutionism and corollary expectations about the self's relation to society blinded them to their own shrewd insights into the nature of Japanese naturalism and the *shishōsetsu*.

Kobayashi in particular interpreted the *shishōsetsu* in terms of the western literary aesthetics he had so thoroughly assimilated. He accused Japanese writers of adopting the trappings of European literature and placing them in a barren context, and he accused Japanese society of depriving writers of the means to relate to a world larger than their own immediate surroundings. Yet although he remained discouragingly silent, except for the one parenthetical remark noted above, about their native lineage, one can nonetheless surmise what he imagined those roots to be. In an essay on the medieval poet-priest Saigyō (one of a series of essays he wrote during the Pacific War addressing various topics and figures in classical literature), we find a remark that might qualify as an answer.

---

27. "Junsui shōsetsu ron," 153.
28. "Watakushi shōsetsu ron," 191. To Honda Shūgo and his compatriots, Kobayashi's characterization came like a "bolt from the blue." See "Kaisetsu," in *Nakamura Mitsuo zenshū* 7:620.

Saigyō introduced afresh the concept of man's loneliness into the world of poetry. This theme permeates his verse. It might be said that loneliness was a treasure with which Saigyō was born. I think it no exaggeration to call his way of life as a priest and a recluse a mere expedient that served to preserve this treasure.[29]

It seems safe to say that Kobayashi saw the *shishōsetsu* writer in terms of the time-honored aesthetic recluse who engages in solitary contemplation at a distant remove from society. If we substitute "prose" for "poetry" and "writer" for "priest" in the passage above, we have a fair picture of the *shishōsetsu* writer's situation some eight centuries after Saigyō. Kobayashi suggests that the only modern writers who were in a position to reflect seriously on the nature of the self in society were Mori Ōgai (1862–1922) and Natsume Sōseki (1867–1916). Authors of unusual learning, they understood fiction's ability (and Japanese naturalism's inability) to universalize experience. Neither cast his lot with the *shishōsetsu*. The other writers, lacking fully "socialized selves," were left to seek a kind of "self-purification" achieved by recording one's mental state.[30]

Yet purification was surely more than an aesthetic exercise; it was for the *shishōsetsu* writer the staking out of a position vis-à-vis society as well. The isolated writer quite naturally wrote about the writer in isolation. He received no aesthetic or social encouragement to write of anyone else. That such a literature would appeal to readers may be surprising; yet the *shishōsetsu* did in fact command a steady although by no means vast audience, as we shall see in Chapter 6. This "distortion" of European models flourished in spite of the continual pronouncements against it. That is why critics of this period regarded the *shishōsetsu* as such a mystery; like a bumblebee, it seemed to have no business getting off the ground, yet it managed to buzz effortlessly about the *bundan* and beyond despite the efforts of the best critics to shoot it down. Many decried its lack of content. Kobayashi was particularly concerned about its preoccupation with "style." It was not enough that *junbungaku* writers had turned their private lives into open books; their obses-

---

29. "Mujō to iu koto," in *Shintei Kobayashi Hideo zenshū* 8:35.
30. "Watakushi shōsetsu ron," 187–88.

sion with writing seemed to trivialize the content of their stories even further. Japanese naturalists, who took it as an article of faith that art imitated nature, always had before them something to write about, he argued. However much they struggled with their material, they never thought to publicize that struggle. The *shishō-setsu* writers who followed in their wake, however, did just that. Circumstances forced them to produce stories whose subject matter was none other than the writing of those stories, and the presentation of reality became a more important theme than reality itself.[31]

And yet this concern with "style," which Kobayashi so abhorred, may well be the saving grace of the *shishōsetsu* writer's art. The content of daily life becomes far less "trivial" when it is problematized by its container—the "prison-house of language," to borrow Fredric Jameson's term. Efforts at sincerity of presentation are undermined time and again by the writer's own awareness of the sheer artifice of presentation, of the frame that shapes the "content" of his life. If a literary form like the *shishōsetsu* does not even pretend to talk about society and if the aesthetics of isolation are its guiding force, then it makes little sense to censure it for being a "distortion" of the western novel, with which it has only a tenuous relationship. It is one thing for a Japanese author to read widely in an alien literature, but quite another to write in a manner that actually ignores the indigenous tradition's deeply held epistemological and linguistic assumptions. It does not seem at all strange that modern Japanese prose fiction (and the *shishōsetsu* in particular), with a centuries-old history antedating all contact with the west, should have taken on an entirely different character from that of the novel. As long as confessional "content" remained the issue, however, the critics of Kobayashi's generation naturally judged the *shishōsetsu* as inferior to its purported model, the western narrative.

31. Ibid., 197–98.

THE THIRD PERIOD:
FUGITIVES AND MASQUERADERS

Nakamura Mitsuo (1911–) wrote even more disparagingly of the *shishōsetsu* than Yokomitsu and Kobayashi did. With "Watakushi shōsetsu ni tsuite" (1935) he inaugurated a career that was to culminate in such devastating critiques of modern Japanese literature as *Fūzoku shōsetsu ron* (1950) and *Shiga Naoya ron* (1954). As with Yokomitsu and Kobayashi, Nakamura's strong background in French literature deeply colored his judgments of the native literature and particularly of the author's relationship to society. After reiterating Kobayashi's assessment of the individual in the west as a "socialized self," however, Nakamura carried his analysis of *jun-bungaku* one step further. "Unlike western romantics," he writes, "*shishōsetsu* writers had no awareness of any confrontation between society and the individual. Indeed, they lacked the concept of 'society' altogether. Society for these writers was only those people who had a direct impact on their sensibilities: family, friends, lovers, etc."[32]

This is a shrewd observation. Rather than argue, as Kobayashi did, that the Japanese writer possessed no "socialized self," Nakamura redefined society on a scale commensurate with the writer's consciousness, which extended to his immediate acquaintances ("family, friends, lovers") and not to some larger, more abstract system of institutions and relationships. His comment that personal experience in early twentieth-century Japan was felt to be a perfectly adequate mediator between the writer and this micro-society, moreover, underscores Maruyama Masao's theory of traditional social organization that we reviewed in Chapter 1.

Nakamura summed up his argument fifteen years later in a sweeping critique of modern Japanese literature, *Fūzoku shōsetsu ron*. This work differs markedly from the period's other major essays on *shishōsetsu* in its relentlessly critical tone. Nakamura singles out 1906–7 as a watershed in modern Japanese literature, when a "duel" took place between Tōson's *Hakai* (1906) and Katai's *Futon* (1907). The literary "revolution" sparked by the former's broad social awareness was nipped in the bud, he argues, by a second revo-

32. *Nakamura Mitsuo zenshū* 7:134.

lution sparked by the latter's claustrophobic self-consciousness.[33] Now the naturalists and their followers were exempted from modern literature's most difficult task, which was to write about oneself and one's life in universal terms. *Futon's* success changed the course not just of the naturalist movement but of all twentieth-century Japanese letters. "Most of the Taishō period's best works . . . were written in a style imitative of *Futon*," he writes. "This is most unfortunate when we consider its innumerable defects and shortcomings."[34]

An obvious difficulty with Nakamura's analysis lies in his acknowledgment of good works, and even masterpieces, in a form he argues has no redeeming qualities. It is a paradox he never quite resolves, because his assumptions have inevitably generated a set of literary guidelines that modern Japanese letters simply do not meet. Even as he redefines the perimeters of "society" in accordance with the writer's marginalized existence, he cannot bring himself to abandon the social vision and narrative perspective offered by the classical western novel. Although he repeatedly notes the early twentieth-century Japanese writers' great attraction to western literature, it is finally Nakamura himself who succumbs most completely. By western standards, Japanese naturalism, not surprisingly, is inferior to the European model. Nakamura never questions the motives, which he doubtlessly considers reasonable, of Japanese writers who try to assimilate the western view of literature. Assimilating this particular aspect of western culture is just one more way of competing at all levels with a hegemonic power. Nakamura speaks to this idea very bluntly in an essay he wrote two years earlier.

> Foreign influence has a characteristically great impact on the literature of second- or third-rate nations. It would not, however, result in an endless succession of schools or movements in a first-rate nation—that is, one with a first-rate literature. I think that it would be profitable to compare literary circles in Japan with those in such second- or perhaps third-rate nations as Romania or Poland. The latter are susceptible to any new literary trend that develops in Paris. I am sure that this is the case. In this regard, modern Japanese literature has little to brag about. Many Japanese, I know, believe that their

33. *Fūzoku shōsetsu ron*, 29–31. See also the discussion below, 113–14.
34. *Fūzoku shōsetsu ron*, 53.

own literature is not worth studying at all and that they would be better-off reading translated literature.[35]

The political implications of this statement, written just three years after Japan's defeat at the hands of the Allied Powers, are unmistakable. A nation's literature is only as viable and as reputable as its global position, as can be seen in Nakamura's equation of a first-rate literature with a first-rate power. Nakamura is quite naturally at a loss how to assess a literature that appears to be subordinated to the hegemonic culture but is in fact anything but derivative.

Another difficulty with the analysis lies in its exaggerated assessment of *Futon* as the turning point in Japanese letters. Katai's narrative indeed helped spark the "revolution" in literary confession of which Nakamura speaks. But it provided, at most, the trigger, not the powder. When we note *Futon*'s marked similarities to Katai's previous writings and its differences from the *shishōsetsu* that followed (as we shall do in Chapter 5), we can only conclude that the work was not in fact a radical break with, but rather a stage in, the process of development in the Japanese narrative that took place over a significant period of time. If anything, *Futon* was as much a result as it was the cause of this narrative development, which we have already traced to the Edo-period literary tradition. This is not to deny the importance of Katai's particular achievement or to minimize the influence—perhaps it would be more correct to say the overwhelming presence—of a narrative form legitimized by (in the eyes of the Japanese) a superior culture. It is only to remind ourselves that these "revolutionary" developments actually grew out of the literary tradition.

Itō Sei (1905–69) thought carefully and productively about the *shishōsetsu* as a species of narrative quite disparate from the novel. His *Shōsetsu no hōhō* (1948) is probably the most comprehensive study of modern narrative written in Japan up to that time. Like Nakamura, he acknowledges the great prestige of western literature. In his preface, Itō provides readers with a list of "required readings," of which nearly half the titles are European.[36] But his recognition of the indigenous narrative tradition is apparent as well

35. "Kindai Nihon bungaku," in *Nakamura Mitsuo zenshū* 7:415–16.
36. *Shōsetsu no hōhō*, 9–10. Included, incidentally, in these "European" texts are two stories by Poe.

in his inclusion of texts from the premodern canon (from *Genji mo-nogatari* to *Kōshoku ichidai onna*) and in his discussion of the modern Japanese narrative against the background of its premodern pre-decessors. Itō argues that it makes much better sense to talk about the stories of an author like Masamune Hakuchō, for example, who writes about the literary company he keeps, in terms of *Tsu-rezuregusa* or *Hōjōki* than in terms of western narrative.[37]

Itō thus connects the *shishōsetsu* with certain premodern forms and opposes them all to the western novel, arguing that compari-son with the latter can only be counterproductive. He emphasizes, moreover, as no one did previously, the role that a small homoge-neous audience played in the *shishōsetsu's* development, spotlight-ing the peculiar literary economy known as the *bundan*. Regarded as social outcasts and usually living in poverty, *bundan* writers had little opportunity to experience the world outside their immediate surroundings. And so they wrote, inevitably, about themselves, their peers, their sordid affairs, their hand-to-mouth existence, and their struggles to meet publisher's deadlines, because this was the only life they knew. Since the audience consisted mostly of their own peers, such things as character depiction and plot were as unnecessary as introductions at a club. Poverty may have cramped the imagination, but the limited narrative scope also turned out to be a blessing, Itō argues: it eliminated the need for fictionalization and allowed writers to focus on what they considered to be the most pressing issue, which was not how to write but rather, as reclusive rebels unconcerned with social convention, how to live.

Itō's argument builds on the assumption that the self and the personal voice to which it gives rise are the primary concerns of modern literature, whether Japanese or western. The two litera-tures differ, Itō suggests, in the way the authors present their "selves." Paradoxically, it is the more modern society that places greater constraints on self-expression. European writers, unwilling to subject their private lives to public scrutiny, resort to fiction be-cause it provides the facade they need to function in society. Japa-nese writers, on the other hand, excluded by their professions from respectable society, have nothing to fear from confession be-cause they have no social position to lose in the attempt.[38]

37. Ibid., 15–16.
38. Ibid; see esp. 55–56, 106–7.

"Masqueraders" (*kamen shinshi*, literally, "gentlemen in masquerade") and "fugitives" (*tōbō dorei*, literally, "runaway slaves") are the picturesque terms Itō coined in a contemporaneous essay to describe these two groups of writers. In this essay, which summarizes many of the arguments in *Shōsetsu no hōhō*, Itō poses several important questions. What is it about fiction (*shōsetsu*) that moves Japanese readers, and how does western fiction differ from it? Is fiction's essence in its structure or its philosophical content? And what is fiction's role in the two cultures? He argues that the *shōsetsu*, as a "report" of the writer's life, moves the reader to the degree that it is able to depict that life unerringly. One cannot have one's "philosophy" and fictionalize it, too, Itō seems to be saying. *Bundan* writers may be social outcasts, but they are also part of a respected literary tradition that idolizes the writer—a Saigyō or a Kamo no Chōmei or a Bashō—who rejects society and the material world.[39]

Whereas Nakamura measures the *shōsetsu* against the standard of the European novel and argues that it comes up short, Itō argues that it is by no means inferior just because it moves away from fictional narrative and toward essay and autobiography. The *shōsetsu*, he insists, is an ideal medium for intimate expression that would suffer from too much attention to structure. The only way to write successfully in such a medium is to live, as a morally free person in an otherwise restrictive society, with a mind to documenting one's life as faithfully as one can.

Itō's assessment of the *shōsetsu* is a valid one. But his faith in the importance of content ("philosophy") over form ("structure") leads him inevitably into the trap we identified earlier as the myth of sincerity. "The Japanese have no use for masks," Itō states flatly. "Fiction is rubbish—good only for writers who would dress up in coattails for the evening. Fugitives need not stand on ceremony. They can dazzle their readers with the slightest handiwork. But they must take great care not to overdo it lest they be labeled phonies and ostracized by their peers."[40]

39. "Tōbō dorei to kamen shinshi" (1948), in *Itō Sei zenshū* 16:286–91; see esp. 287–88.

40. Ibid., 291. See also *Shōsetsu no hōhō*, 71. In *Literature and Sincerity*, Henri Peyre provides a useful corrective to Itō's argument that the western writer is necessarily less sincere because he has determined (as in Stendahl's case, to take one of Peyre's examples) that "only in fiction could he reach truth" (190). Although this

THE MIRAGE OF AUTHENTICITY

As Itō sees it, then, *bundan* writers in effect consigned fiction to the dustbin of literature and opted for a less structured, autobiographical medium. Yet we still want to know how such a move could make their writing sincere. In an essay in *Writing Degree Zero* on narrative presentation, Roland Barthes identifies the preterite and third person (to which we might add Banfield's represented speech and thought) as the signposts of fiction in the classical western narrative. Together they "are nothing but the fateful gesture with which the writer draws attention to the mask which he is wearing."[41] There is no escaping the mask, because language itself points to it. "The third person, like the preterite . . . supplies its consumers with the security born of a credible fabrication which is yet constantly held up as false."[42]

Although Itō and others argue that the *shōsetsu's* all-important philosophical "content" determines its "sincere," "structureless" form, Masao Miyoshi's commentary on the *shōsetsu* in light of Barthes's analysis seems closer to the truth:

> It is the reverse of the novel: rather than a "credible fabrication which is yet constantly held up as false," the *shōsetsu* is an incredible fabrication that is nonetheless constantly held up as truthful. Art is hidden, while honesty and sincerity are displayed. Distance is removed, while immediacy is ostensive. . . . The *shōsetsu* is thus an art that refuses to acknowledge art.[43]

In short, narrative intimacy is itself an ideologically motivated form and in no way subordinated to content. Form is naturally suppressed in a culture that privileges sincerity over design, experience over word. It has not disappeared, however, only assumed

---

felt need for fiction may confirm Itō's characterization of western writers, it does not change the fact that the concept of sincerity and the struggle to give it form in literature has occupied countless writers in the last two centuries and given birth to what Peyre calls the "personal novel." See ibid., 161–202.

41. "Writing and the Novel," 40.

42. Ibid., 35. Although he does not elaborate, Barthes implies that first-person narration is just as much of a fabrication as third-person narration, when he notes the ability of the former to confer on the narrative the "spurious naturalness of taking the reader into its confidence (such is the guileful air of some stories by Gide)" (ibid).

43. "Against the Native Grain," 233. See also Miyoshi's account of the western narrative form and the Japanese alternative, 231–33.

the guise of style. As a verbal construct, "sincerity" in the *shōsetsu*, no less than design, is part of a rhetorical rather than a referential field.

This distinction is easily demonstrated by considering the criterion used to judge sincerity. We saw in Chapter 1 the Japanese writer's struggle to transcend his calling and achieve a moral legitimacy by offering his life (however derelict) as an example to his community of readers. The stakes of appearing sincere were therefore very high, and it is no wonder that a great many writers and a vast number of readers conceived of the *shōsetsu* in Itō's terms: the choice was indeed between fiction and philosophy, between "how to write" and "how to live." It goes without saying that the writer who most successfully understood (dare one say "exploited"?) the myth of sincerity became the object of deification. Shiga Naoya's nickname, *shōsetsu no kamisama* ("the god of the *shōsetsu*"), is, then, no gratuitous label but the ultimate signifier of this mythical hierarchy. Criticism of Shiga (and by extension any less successful would-be recorder of "truth") necessarily centers on the touchstone of emotional honesty. In the words of Honda Shūgo (1908–), for example, a principal defender of the myth:

> The *shōsetsu* of Shiga Naoya contain no false notes [*uso*, literally, "lies"]. . . . There is not a single false note in the author's feelings toward his characters or toward nature. Instead of "no false notes," I could just as easily say "no idle phrases" or "no empty rhetoric." . . . To put it more positively: each and every Shiga sentence harbors profound emotion and a powerful sense of authenticity.[44]

Honda's statement is significant less as a critique of Shiga than as an implied ideal for Japanese literature, in which the authentic transcription of the author's feelings becomes the paramount aim of writing, and the correct identification of (perhaps even communion with) those feelings becomes the chief task of the reader/critic. But just what does this lack of deception really mean? Is the emotion in question felt at the time of writing or at the time of the incident about which the author writes? Honda argues in favor of the former; but to argue either way is in effect to acknowledge the mediation involved in any "authentic" transcription.

44. *"Shirakaba" ha no bungaku* (1954), 155.

This leads to an even more awkward question. How do we know that Shiga or any author is not "lying"? That is, how exactly are we to judge the authenticity of the author's feelings? Clearly, we must engage in an act of faith and believe that the author is telling the truth. The critic's only recourse in determining the author's credibility, other than relying on documentation that is never fully verifiable, is to appeal to the author's style. Thus Honda's sonorous refrain: "No false notes." In that style, Honda suggests, is a leanness and a ruthlessness necessary and appropriate for honest self-scrutiny. In short, it is a style that says, "I mean business." This surely is what Honda means when he argues that Shiga's writing contains no idle phrases or empty rhetoric. But style itself is rhetoric, the literary equivalent of acting, the concealed art without which the honesty and sincerity could not be "revealed." It turns out, then, that form is indeed the key to content. For what is sincerity in literature but the donning of a verbally well-wrought mask, the masterful *display* of honest emotion? In the words of Benjamin Crémieux: "Is not the greatest artist also the greatest *imposter*, the most capable of giving form to whatever imaginary reality, of bestowing upon it, through *expressing* it, a soul and an *appearance* of truth which others than the creator will accept?"[45] That a writer like Shiga really does sound more sincere than others, then, is a tribute not to his honesty but to his mastery of the rhetoric (the intimate voice, ellipses, allusions, etc.) of authenticity.

Honda and others argue that the test of any *shishōsetsu* lies in the recognizability of its author. In fact, the author is "recognizable" only through a style made familiar from previous texts. The role played by sibling texts as a guide to reading an author, therefore, is a crucial one, and those who overlook its significance are all but forced to scavenge the author's private life in order to supplement a given text. (This matter will be addressed more substantively in Part 3 and especially in the chapter on Kasai.) Itō Sei clearly has an inkling of the problem when he writes:

> [The *shishōsetsu*] was written with the expectation that the reader would know the hero's (that is to say, the author's) personal history without explanations of his circumstances and position. The hero in

45. Quoted in Peyre, *Literature and Sincerity*, 336. (Emphasis added.)

such a text is therefore a virtual nonentity, so superficially is he described. . . . The reader had to glean what information he could about the hero's personality and circumstances from gossip about the author current in literary circles, *or be familiar with the hero from previous texts that reported on the author's private life.*[46]

Itō, however, ignores the ramifications of his own insight: namely, that the reader need not rely on the finally inaccessible life. The oeuvre is enough. Regular readers of literary magazines, as we shall see in our discussion of the *bundan* in Chapter 6, would have no trouble piecing together the "lives" of the authors about which they read.

It is not just the writer, then, who must master the rhetoric and assume a role: the reader, too, must cast himself in a very specific relationship with the text. The *shishōsetsu*'s style demands it. We need not go as far as Walter J. Ong's claim, although it is probably a valid one, that the writer's audience is always a fiction to understand that the relationship between writer and audience is founded on rarely articulated but nonetheless concrete assumptions about the text and the world that must be accepted in order for communication to take place. Regardless of how seemingly intimate the narrative voice or how casual the allusions, the author does not, cannot, know his readers. He has to "make his readers up," as Ong puts it, "fictionalize them."[47] Narrative intimacy—or narrative distancing, for that matter—is part of the fictionalization. Although it may surprise *shishōsetsu* readers to learn that they are not the only audience intimately addressed or expected to possess background information, there is no question that Ong's observations concerning the Hemingway narrator in the opening passage of *A Farewell to Arms* are applicable to our study.

The reader—every reader—is being cast in the role of a close companion of the writer. . . . It is one reason why the writer is tight-lipped. Description as such would bore a boon companion. What description there is comes in the guise of pointing, in verbal gestures, recalling humdrum, familiar details. . . . The reader here has a well-marked role assigned him. He is a companion-in-arms, somewhat later become a confidant. It is a flattering role. . . . Hemingway's exclusion of indefinite in favor of definite articles signals the

46. *Shōsetsu no hōhō*, 66. (Emphasis added.)
47. "The Writer's Audience Is Always a Fiction," 11.

reader that he is from the first on familiar ground. He shares the author's familiarity with the subject matter. The reader must pretend he has known much of it before.[48]

This argument recalls Itō Sei's on the *bundan* readership, with one important exception: Ong's emphasizes the pretense involved in the act of writing and reading. Sincerity has a new twist here: it is the *product* of style, not its generator.

The myth of sincerity develops to its logical conclusion in Hirano Ken's *Geijutsu to jisseikatsu* (1958), an exploration of the links between the modern Japanese writer's life and art. The discussion quickly gravitates toward the *shishōsetsu*, which provides the subject matter for the work's major theoretical essay, "Watakushi shōsetsu no niritsu haihan." We noted at the beginning of this chapter Hirano's characterization of the *watakushi shōsetsu* as the literature of destruction and of the *shinkyō shōsetsu* as the literature of harmony and salvation, a characterization generally supported by Hirano's contemporaries, including Itō Sei. Hirano's aim is to cast Japanese writers in two broad types: those who accommodate, and those who turn their backs on, the obligations of private life. Hirano suggests that the *shishōsetsu* writer's art is by its very nature stimulated by crisis and stifled by tranquillity, anchored as it is to the vicissitudes of lived experience. *Shinkyō shōsetsu* writers, therefore, whose twin goals of domestic harmony and candid expression harbor an insoluble contradiction, are faced sooner or later with the choice of betraying either their families or their profession. Accommodators that they are, they usually choose the latter course.[49] No such contradiction exists for *watakushi shōsetsu* writers, on the other hand, because they have already forfeited domestic tranquillity in order to chronicle lives that are often bent on destruction. Ostracized and poverty-stricken, their raison d'être lies entirely in their utter truthfulness as artists.[50]

Hirano sees "sincerity" (and its companion ideals of "candor" and "truthfulness"), then, as the only positive, if ultimately undefinable, quality of writers who would mine their own lives for any material whatever the cost. The result of this reification is an in-

48. Ibid., 13.
49. *Geijutsu to jisseikatsu*, 29–37.
50. Ibid., 36–37.

flated and exalted signifier curiously drained of meaning, a capricious looking glass reflecting nothing but the authenticity of its own persuasion. The French poet Luc Estang's wry characterization is apt: "Sincerity is to itself its own mirror. In literature, we find only reflected sincerities."[51] But Hirano, like Honda and Itō before him, is apparently satisfied with tautology, asking no more than that sincerity be sincere.

The myth of sincerity is founded, as we have seen, on the illusion of authorial presence. Japanese critics have expended enormous efforts buttressing the myth, perhaps because they have feared to ask whether the *shishōsetsu* would still contain anything of value should the author in fact be inaccessible. To remove sincerity (and by extension authorial intention) from the text would be to deprive it, a record of otherwise "trivial" events, of its most important "content" and thus of any interest.

We have also seen that sincerity is not an ethical goal to which the artist aspires but a strategy of discourse, motivated by the desire of writers to legitimize or at least strengthen their position within the *bundan* and vis-à-vis society and governed by the *shishōsetsu* form itself. Arguing that the author is "absent" from the work, therefore, far from denying the referential world to which *shishōsetsu* writers constantly allude, actually helps us recognize a highly complex negotiation between art and life that a reified notion of sincerity fails to suggest. For, once we grasp sincerity as an ideology rather than as a vague, ultimately inaccessible emotion, we can understand how it controls the mode of literary production. Candor becomes a commodity that writers have no choice but to produce and critics no choice but to appraise.

The critical posture toward the *shishōsetsu* during the period we have reviewed, from the mid-1920s through the 1950s, has remained essentially unchanged and continues to dominate present-day thinking. Critics of all persuasions, including those most skeptical of the *shishōsetsu* writer's art (from Akutagawa Ryūnosuke to Nakamura Mitsuo), have unfailingly acknowledged the value of the *shishōsetsu* as confession of a different order from other literatures and have thus actually contributed to the form's mystique. For that reason the *shishōsetsu*, despite all attacks, has occupied a

51. *Invitation à la poésie*. Quoted in Peyre, *Literature and Sincerity*, 328.

critical sanctuary in which a variety of powerfully nostalgic and ethnocentric emotions concerning the form's "purity," "Japaneseness," and philosophical "honesty" are heavily invested.

That some writers would rebel against this ideology was perhaps inevitable. What is surprising is how early in the shishōsetsu's history the rebellion occurred; parody was common almost from the start. Yet the norm of sincerity was so pervasive that its deifiers generally failed to recognize the parody in other writers' texts. Members of the supposedly close-knit bundan would typically contrast their own productions, which they regarded as art, with the "bald" confessions of their peers. That they were able to question the absolute priority of experience over writing in their own work at least (as we shall see in Part 3), is justification enough for us to challenge the shishōsetsu's claim to uniqueness in world literature (and the corollary claim of its unintelligibility to outsiders), even as we situate the form more precisely in its specific linguistic and cultural environment—ever mindful that particularity is no synonym for sacred exclusivity.

2

THE RISE OF A FORM

4

Harbingers (I):
Tōkoku, Doppo, Hōgetsu

I have never troubled myself over stylistic matters, as form is not my object in writing. . . . Only by putting down precisely what you feel and expressing your thoughts frankly and without deception or decoration, no matter how awkward the attempt, can you create a genuine and appealing work of literature.

Kunikida Doppo, *Byōshō roku*

I cannot now construct a viable philosophy. I would do better simply to disclose my doubts and uncertainty as they are. That would be telling the truth; saying anything more promises to be sheer invention. . . . Ours is indeed an age of confession. Perhaps we shall never go beyond it.

Shimamura Hōgetsu, "Jo ni kaete"

Western writers at least since the Enlightenment, steeped in an intellectual tradition that has understood reality to be mediated by the human mind and therefore by the act of writing itself, have regarded imagination as very much a part of reality and fiction as fundamental to the production of literature. Indeed, as Hayden White notes in his discussion of narrative emplotment, imagination necessarily generates a particular reality, and the tropical forms or "modes" of romance, tragedy, comedy, and satire inevitably impose themselves fictively on the "free flow" of life. Early twentieth-century Japanese writers, however, hailed from an intellectual tradition that, as Maruyama Masao argues, denied that reality is mediated at all. They were far less willing to concede that writing necessitated a conscious patterning of experience and kept faith in the possibility of chronicling the free flow of life. Iwano Hōmei (1873–1920) speaks for many writers when he equates in all seri-

73

ousness (although with typically outrageous hyperbole) life and literature at a level that he believes precludes fiction: "Now that the shōsetsu is no longer a fabrication, our state of mind, whether we take up our pens to write or our chopsticks to eat, is one and the same."[1]

Writing is hardly the spontaneous physical act that Hōmei makes it out to be, however. It is both active and reflective, at once experience and the representation of experience. Eating has no parallel to this latter aspect of writing, and in this sense picking up one's chopsticks to eat is quite dissimilar to writing about the act. To be sure, the physical act of eating (or writing) needs no representation. But by writing about eating (or about writing, for that matter) one moves from experience to expression, which must be represented through another medium—that is, "mediated"—to be communicated. Yet Hōmei was not alone in thinking of writing as an unmediated act to which invention and fabrication were as foreign as feigning satiety was when sitting down hungrily to eat. Rather than examine fiction's role in literature, many writers denied that it played a role at all.

In order to appreciate fully the views of Hōmei and his contemporaries, we would do well to investigate more closely the literary and intellectual climate immediately preceding the rise of the shishōsetsu. We shall find not only that the traditional bias against fiction as a vehicle for serious comment on life persisted into the twentieth century, but also that the elevation of the shōsetsu into the realm of true literature, which *did* in fact occur, required its transformation from a "frivolous" form of nonliterary entertainment in the eyes of the writers themselves to a "serious" form of moral and philosophical inquiry in which fiction was deemed out of place. Although the choice of whom to single out for discussion is necessarily an arbitrary one, the careers of three writers in particular—Kitamura Tōkoku (1868–94), Kunikida Doppo (1871–1908), and Shimamura Hōgetsu (1871–1918)—were so bound to issues surrounding the purpose of literature as to reward even the brief study with which we must content ourselves here. Doppo

1. From the preface to *Tandeki* (1909), Hōmei's first collection of prose fiction, in *Hōmei zenshū* 18:81.

wrote short stories; Tōkoku and Hōgetsu, essays—although we shall see that categorizing their work according to such generic classifications is itself problematic and one reason why the clear identification of one author's writing as "fiction" and another's as "nonfiction" can be difficult if not impossible. Our discussion of these three writers will provide a backdrop for a fourth writer, Tayama Katai (1872–1930), whose work, to be discussed in the following chapter, represents the culmination of the initial stage in the Japanese writer's interior focus. We shall then consider briefly how the early twentieth-century literary world's general intellectual climate provided such an amenable environment for the *shishōsetsu* writer.

It is unquestionable that the three Meiji writers in the ensuing discussion contributed significantly to the inward turn literature took in the Taishō period. The Japanese writer's apparent focus on himself, however, should not be interpreted as the birth of "modern" consciousness or as an attempted validation of the "self," as is so commonly argued, without first delimiting the terms "modern" and "self" in such a way as to strip them of their culturally specific connotations.[2] In her synthesis of the Shōwa Japanese critical consensus that expression of the "modern self" (*kindai jiga*) is the dynamo that drives the modern Japanese "novel," Janet Walker sees Japan becoming modern and the Japanese discovering themselves as individuals through contact with the west.[3] But modernity and selfhood are more properly characterized as historical processes emerging from a particular intellectual tradition than as commodities readily available for consumption, like so much technological hardware; they are not concepts that translate easily from one culture to another. If, as Walker claims, modernity in the west is the outgrowth of a socioeconomic system based on post-Renaissance secularism, positivism, capitalism, and individualism, and the middle-class individual is its cultural hero, and if, as she also claims, it was just this "happy coexistence of private ideals of

2. Masao Miyoshi, in a recent essay, shows just how problematic the term "modern" is in the Japanese context. See "Against the Native Grain," 224–25. See also p. 232 for a discussion of the nature of "individuality" in Japan.
3. *The Japanese Novel of the Meiji Period and the Ideal of Individualism;* see esp. the introduction.

individualism with liberal economy and political systems"[4] that was absent in Meiji Japan, then where are we to observe the ideal of modern consciousness, so specifically defined, in Meiji thought?

Nowhere at all, according to Kenneth Strong, who writes in a seminal essay, "One wonders whether the emphasis on *kindai jiga* [modern self], particularly in the period that began the postwar rediscovery of Kitamura Tōkoku, has not resulted in a somewhat distorted evaluation of the modern period."[5] Strong describes Shimazaki Tōson's first novel, *Hakai* (The broken commandment, 1906), generally acclaimed the pioneering expression of the modern self, as "prophetic of the *non*-expression of the *kindai jiga* in most of modern fiction"[6] and sees in its principal character's much-described but never realized inner conflicts, in its sensitive feeling for nature, in its lack of any real dialogue between characters, and in its failure to embody its concerns as a unified, symbolic whole, the same introverted, reclusive tendencies that appear in the works of many later writers whose inability or unwillingness to achieve true fictions manifests a great deal more of "traditional Japanese ways of thinking and feeling . . . than is sometimes assumed to be the case."[7]

Walker contends, meanwhile, that the western-educated writers of Meiji Japan concerned themselves, despite the inherent difficulties, with the discovery of the individual. She treats in this context Shimazaki Tōson and three "forerunners" (Futabatei Shimei, Kitamura Tōkoku, and Tayama Katai), all of whom she argues were "sympathetic to the ideal of individualism and creatively involved with it in their works."[8] Yet she curiously dismisses Natsume Sōseki, perhaps the *only* Meiji or Taishō writer to comprehend fully the meaning of individualism in Japanese society, from her study, finding his attitude toward the self "at best ambivalent."[9] If she can make such a claim (which would seem to be a valid one) of Sōseki, how much more it holds true for Tōson, the focus of her study, or a writer like Shiga Naoya, whose most powerful works represent

4. Ibid., 28.
5. "Downgrading the 'Kindai Jiga,'" 407.
6. Ibid.
7. Ibid., 408.
8. Walker, *The Japanese Novel of the Meiji Period*, ix.
9. Ibid.

the very antithesis of individualism yet whom Walker characterizes as having been born (although scarcely a decade after Tōson) in an age that already "assumed the validity of the self"![10]

For our purpose, then, modernity in the Japanese intellectual context takes on this paradoxical meaning: it is no more—and no less—than the institutionalized process by which Japanese continue to apply traditional (and specifically non-western) modes of thinking to contemporary social, economic, and political issues; selfhood, again paradoxically, is the state of separation from society ("premodern" *or* "modern") that Japanese can attain, although not without certain material and psychological risks. Whereas modernity and selfhood in the west are conceived of as two sides of the same coin, in Japan they stand for two quite diverse traditions: public versus private—or what Tetsuo Najita has characterized as the tradition of "bureaucratism" (*kanryōshugi*), which was always considered central to the realization of political or social well-being, versus the less easily defined idealist tradition of impassioned "spiritualism" (*ningensei; kokoro*), which aspired to enlightenment and to acts of self-sacrifice.[11] The inward turn taken by the writers we shall presently examine was therefore not an expression of "self-validation" in a "modern" society but rather a move, inspired only tangentially by western models, away from political and social integration promoted by Meiji bureaucratism and toward a quietist and separatist ideal of domestic exile that makes possible a peculiarly Japanese kind of selfhood: a nonparticipatory and nonconfrontational existence by which a Japanese, normally that most social of social animals, turns his back on society and loses himself in the aesthetic life and in nature.

TŌKOKU AND THE PRIVATIZATION OF LITERATURE

The life of Kitamura Tōkoku anticipated the transition made by intellectuals as a group from publicly to privately oriented careers. Itō Sei calls Tōkoku the modern intelligentsia's charter member, in that, after a brief but heady period of cooperative involvement by

10. Ibid., 283.
11. *Japan;* see chapter 1, esp. 2–7.

earlier intellectuals in the affairs of state, he was the first to recognize the intellectual's and literature's oppositional role in society.[12] "Oppositional" is probably too strong a word. H. D. Harootunian argues persuasively that the public-private transition was emblematic of a shift in people's concern in late Meiji and Taishō from "civilization" (i.e., the development of the state) to "culture" (i.e., the development of the person) and from socially motivated "education" to privately motivated "cultivation."[13] "Rather than offer either alternatives or opposition," writes Harootunian, "[Tōkoku] defined with great detail and clarity the area of privatization (*watakushigoto*) permitted by arrangement of authority" and provided "the means for writers and intellectuals to operate safely in the officially sanctioned space relating to 'private affairs.'"[14] Tōkoku's essays offer an archetypal portrait of the litterateur acting in a nonparticipatory, nonconfrontational role vis-à-vis society, which we will find repeatedly portrayed in the early twentieth-century *shōsetsu* and especially the *shishōsetsu*.

Tōkoku started out as an activist interested in citizens' movements, until fear of harsh government suppression—and disillusionment with the violent tactics of his colleagues—led him to take up his pen during the last half decade of his two-and-a-half-decade life. Realizing that naive forays into politics would be quickly subdued by the Meiji state's enormous power, Tōkoku attempted to cordon off for himself a private realm that was beyond the reach of the state and answerable only to aesthetic and spiritual values.[15] In

12. "Nihon kindai bungaku no shutai" (1946), reprinted in *Kitamura Tōkoku shū*, 348.

13. "Introduction: A Sense of an Ending and the Problem of Taishō"; see esp. 15–18, where Harootunian contrasts the late Meiji and Taishō intellectual's "ethics of being" to the early and mid-Meiji intellectual's "morality of doing."

14. "Between Politics and Culture," 138 and 154. This valuable essay sketches the conceptual evolution of the public and private realms in post-Restoration Japan and shows that they failed to intersect. The 1889 Constitution, the Imperial Rescript on Education, and the Civil Code all demonstrated, Harootunian argues, that "politics as a mediation between private and public not only had disappeared but, more importantly, had never existed in any form other than a vague promise. What started as a celebration of the political importance of individualism ended as the argument that 'unpoliticality,' the rejection of politics, was a necessary requirement to the preservation of individualism" (ibid., 112). The very limited literary precedents in the traditional canon for the expression of sociopolitical consciousness, moreover, no doubt encouraged easy acquiescence to the statist requirements of "unpoliticality."

15. H. D. Harootunian comments, "If the relationship between private and public was in fact one of distance, if separation was the condition of the common exis-

Chapter 1 we observed Tōkoku's useful distinction in the Edo period between the "refined" literature of the samurai class, which comprised morally edifying histories and treatises and served the goals of the central government, and the "vulgar" literature of the townspeople, which offered the breezy and anti-heroic "street talk" and "roadside gossip" of plebeian life. The Confucian view that true literature was nonfictional in content, moral in persuasion, and utilitarian in function, however, continued basically intact into Meiji times. Tōkoku was impressed by the high place of belles lettres, particularly prose fiction, in nineteenth-century western literature, and he questioned, perhaps even more forcefully than Tsubouchi Shōyō did, the traditional hierarchy of literary forms that had supported the moral and political status quo for centuries. His mission, he believed, was to alter the prevailing view of literature as an institution serving public ends into a vision of literature as a purely personal concern, the value of which could not be reduced to its social utility.

And yet Tōkoku made little impact on the literary hierarchy he attacked with such vehemence. In fact, he typically voiced his sympathy for commoner-oriented, "nonliterary" fiction through the (originally) samurai-oriented medium of nonfiction "literature." Other than three stories and a few long poems, he wrote nothing but essays and short, contemplative sketches (*kansō*) in which he made direct appeals, in the traditional format, for his new and "private" literature. To be sure, he criticized the utilitarian view of writing advocated at the time by the great majority of critics and insisted that literature could be at once serious and very personal. For example, he attacked the critic Yamaji Aizan's (1864–1917) celebrated dictum that writing was a practical "enterprise" ("Bunshō, sunawachi jigyō nari"). Judging literature by such a utilitarian standard, Tōkoku argued, was to lose sight of its true value, which lay in its support of the individual's spiritual growth and not its immediate social relevance.[16] Elsewhere he expressed profound disappointment in the traditional culture, which he believed denied the individual an inner life.[17] His disappointment did not prevent him, however, from choosing a solution for engaging in the

---

tence, then it was virtually impossible for the self to reach out sympathetically to move others and to change the outer world" (ibid., 136).

16. "Jinsei ni aiwataru to wa nan no ii zo" (1893), in *Kitamura Tōkoku shū*, 115.

17. "Naibu seimei ron" (1893), in ibid., 143–44.

inner life that was actually sanctioned by tradition: namely, voluntary withdrawal from society. If the current political climate failed to recognize the individual's spiritual growth as a legitimate pursuit, then he would renounce politics altogether and embrace literature as a preserve for solitary meditation. The literature he embraced was not prose fiction, however. If his own literary output is a fair indication, the *shōsetsu* played a small role indeed in the kind of literature he envisioned as championing the quest for personal artistic achievement. For Tōkoku, literature was still as predominantly a moral enterprise as it was for his Tokugawa predecessors, although centered on the private rather than the public realm. His essays are exercises in self-exhortation.[18]

Adhering, then, to a view of literature as a fundamentally moral endeavor but finding at first little in tradition to support his pursuit of the inner life, Tōkoku turned to Christianity and its promise of an autonomous, private realm. He was not alone in looking to the alien faith for the self-fulfillment unattainable in a public career, nor is it a coincidence that so many young Meiji writers were attracted to an essentially "inward, individualist and self-conscious kind of religion."[19] For Tōkoku and others who could not identify with the Meiji government's statist goals, Christianity offered a set of positive values that justified their heretical posture toward society. They rejected the government's (and most of society's) equation of private interests with public values. Such commitment to personal priorities usually led to disassociation from the public sphere, but its reward was the freedom to explore a more autonomous, private realm.

Yet Tōkoku's withdrawal from politics and society resulted only partially from the tenets of his adopted faith. It has been aptly noted that even though western religion occupied a disproportion-

---

18. Francis Mathy, in his study of Tōkoku, notes that Tōkoku's first steps in the literary world were motivated by a resolve to influence society as a writer and by a determination to become another Victor Hugo—in short, they were motivated by the very didacticism he subsequently denounced in the Min'yūsha and other writers. This motivation was to take other forms later in his career but it never disappeared completely. See Mathy, "Kitamura Tōkoku: The Early Years," 12. See also the other two parts of Mathy's important study, listed in the Bibliography.

19. The characterization is Ian Watt's in *The Rise of the Novel*, 177. Other writers discussed in this study who were at one time drawn to the faith include Kunikida Doppo, Shimazaki Tōson, Iwano Hōmei, and Shiga Naoya.

ately prominent position among Meiji intellectuals, one must not "overestimate the influence of the particular tenets of Christianity as a faith, or even of its underlying view of man and his society, on important styles of modern Japanese consciousness—much less of the more deep-rooted creative sensibility."[20] Indeed, one finds numerous parallels in Tōkoku's career to a pattern of aesthetic life, rooted in traditional culture, that was in many ways hostile to the notion of selfhood posited by Christianity. This pattern, although difficult to discern in terms of concrete, formative events in Tōkoku's life, was, it seems fair to say, a guiding force in shaping his worldview and in situating the self in his aesthetic universe. The Japanese have of course lived and continue to live by values that have emphasized corporate or familial goals over personal ones. They have, however, tolerated a greater amount of freedom in the realm of the arts, which along with meditative activities is traditionally one area where an individual, normally integrated in a network of hierarchical relationships, can enjoy relative independence.[21] The social and even physical alienation that often attend a person's independence offer a compensatory spiritual autonomy that is attained, paradoxically, by submergence in the beauties and the inexorable changes of nature. The wanderer or hermit is a recurrent figure in the classical literature: Nōin, Saigyō, Sōgi, Bashō, and the reclusive priests of *Tsurezuregusa* and *Hōjōki*. He lives frequently by choice, occasionally by necessity, away from society and seeks in the natural world a diversion from human relations. He is typically depicted in isolation and in moments of contemplative awareness that establish his relationship to nature and to a reality that dwarfs the world of human concerns. Finally, he is often depicted as a "seeker of the Way" (*gudōsha*) after the fashion of Buddhist ascetics, and as one who sees his literary pursuits as a form of spiritual discipline.

There is no question that Tōkoku identified with such a way of life, which is primarily Buddhist in its inspiration, despite his sometimes vitriolic indictment of Buddhism's pessimistic world-

20. William Sibley, "Review Article: Tatsuo Arima, *The Failure of Freedom*," 260.
21. The discussion here is indebted to the instructive analysis of Japanese society by Robert N. Bellah. See, for example, "Values and Social Change in Japanese Society"; "Continuity and Change in Japanese Society"; and *Tokugawa Religion*, esp. chap. 2 ("An Outline of Japanese Social Structure in the Tokugawa Period").

view in "Naibu seimei ron" and other essays. (Nor is it a coincidence that, of all the forms of western thought to which he was exposed, he was attracted most strongly to Emerson's transcendentalist philosophy of a self submerged in nature and an impersonal God.) Buddhism, with its doctrine of impermanence and self-denial, would seem to disregard just those "inward, individualist and self-conscious" qualities that are so central to the Christian view of man and society. Unlike Christianity, which aims at uniting an individual with his personal God, Buddhism aims at liberating him from the illusion of an autonomous self and releasing him from all worldly bonds. At a time when *shusse*—"advancement in the world"—became the slogan of a newly competitive and mobile society, Tōkoku in effect called for a *shusse* in its original, Buddhist sense: a separation *from* the world, which opened the way, he claimed, to spiritual, if not political or social, fulfillment.[22] Tōkoku's essays are filled with allusions to Saigyō (1118–90) and Bashō (1644–94), the two most celebrated of the reclusive premodern poets, whose works are infused with a contemplative sensibility and a profoundly negative view of the self. Tōkoku sensed an attraction to self-eradication in their works, moreover, which he believed could not be found in the western tradition. Pondering the reason why Bashō wrote no verse commemorating a visit to the fabled bay of Matsushima during his journey to the far Northeast, for example, Tōkoku concludes that the poet had reached an ecstatic state of selflessness in which personal expression had no place.[23]

One wonders whether the tenets of Buddhism, which have infused Japanese literature almost from its beginnings, do not challenge the validity of fiction as well as that of selfhood, despite the religion's receptivity to various allegorical "modes" with which to impress its doctrines on believers.[24] The author's urge to "play

22. Earl Kinmouth makes this point in his *The Self-made Man in Meiji Japanese Thought*, 149.
23. "Matsushima ni oite Bashō-ō o yomu" (1892), in *Kitamura Tōkoku shū*, 75. Bashō did of course provide a lengthy prose description of Matsushima in *Oku no hosomichi*; that Tōkoku chose to disregard it is perhaps all the more revealing of the nature of his argument. Yet Bashō's description, bristling with allusions to scenic spots in China that the poet himself had never seen, is not an especially personal passage to begin with.
24. I use William LaFleur's rendering of *hōben*; see *The Karma of Words*, 84–85. In

God" in the Judeo-Christian sense and create a separate, autonomous life would not seem to occur readily in a God-less culture (from the monotheistic viewpoint) that sees life as a cycle of rebirth and the world as an illusion and encourages passive acceptance in the face of this recognition. Buddhism's cyclical view of history (with its doctrines of transmigration and of nirvana as the ultimate release from it), moreover, can be contrasted with the Judeo-Christian teleological tradition, in which history by definition has an ultimate purpose, an overall design. Given this "emplotment" of history on a macrocosmic level, it is only natural that western writers would use the same strategy in their microcosmic "histories" of men—that is, novels. Tōkoku and other Japanese writers and intellectuals who converted to Christianity were not so easily converted to this teleological worldview, which lends itself readily to the idea of emplotment, either in politics (in the form of activism) or in literature (in the form of narrative). Consciously or not, Tōkoku was sympathetic to the Buddhist perspective, in which history (on the macrocosmic level) and literature (on the microcosmic level) become the chronicling of man's illusory attachments to life, doomed to be repeated throughout time. For him transcendence did not mean the salvation of a personal soul so much as it meant the escape from the vicissitudes of life.

Clearly, Buddhism is not the sole factor in the Japanese distrust of fiction any more than the Judeo-Christian tradition is the sole root of its broad acceptance in the west; and clearly, many cultural forces other than Buddhism have been at work in Japan, especially in its more recent history, when Buddhism's influence has undergone a considerable decline. (We have already seen, for example, the impact of Confucian thought on belles lettres in Tokugawa and Meiji Japan.) Yet Buddhist tenets, which provided the governing intellectual force during an entire millennium of medieval Japanese history, have unquestionably left recent Japanese consciousness more receptive to the belief that any attempt at creating a world according to the whim of imagination is just another illusory exercise. Buddhism no doubt also encouraged, along with Confucian-

---

the "Hotaru" chapter of *The Tale of Genji*, Genji lectures Tamakazura on literature and comments on the Buddhist sanction for using "lies" to uncover the truth. "Even in the writ which the Buddha drew from his noble heart are parables, devices for pointing obliquely at the truth" (Seidensticker translation, 438).

ism, a didactic approach to literature that took authorial intention to be of primary importance in assigning meaning to a text. It therefore had little use for fictional texts that, because of their conscious "fabrications," seemed to conceal authorial intention and thereby undermine their own seriousness. The influence of both Buddhism and Confucianism may have waned in modern Japan, but the question of seriousness and sincerity of intent is one that, as we shall have ample occasion to see, remained foremost in the minds of early twentieth-century Japanese writers.[25]

Tōkoku, then, despite his brief career and small literary output, set a powerful example for those writers who, disillusioned with Meiji society's utilitarian values and the Confucian emphasis on a didactic literature, reached into the pool of tradition for other values, primarily Buddhist in inspiration, that provided a rationale for their withdrawal from society and their embrace of the aesthetic instead of the political, the contemplative instead of the active, life. Significantly, Tōkoku chose to present his case for the contemplative life by showcasing the narrating subject rather than suggesting by dramatic narrative a greater degree of character involvement with the outside world than he was prepared to acknowledge. He was no doubt comfortable with the narrative stance sanctioned by the classical tradition in both poetry (*waka, haikai,* etc.) and prose (*kana nikki, zuihitsu,* etc.). Tōkoku's narrator, like those in classical literature and those that followed, defines with his own presence the scope and limits of the essay he narrates, since he is at once the meditating subject *and* the object of meditation. Tōkoku's piece on Bashō cited above, for example, is no expository disquisition on the *haikai* poet but a highly self-conscious discourse in which the narrator himself emerges as the essay's central figure. Each allusion to Bashō's poetic journey to Matsushima is overlaid with an account of the narrator's own experience at the islet-studded bay. In "Issekikan" (1893), to take another example, Tōkoku turns what might have been a speculative, metaphysical tract on nature and self into a concrete, experiential account. This last of his important essays is worth quoting at length.

25. A number of scholars, most recently William LaFleur, make a forceful case for the persistence of the "medieval" *episteme* in "modern" Japan (see his *The Karma of Words,* esp. chap. 1)—all the more reason, surely, to measure carefully the weight of the "traditional" outlook on modern writers.

One evening I lie before my window at a seaside village. The autumn is deep, the weather fine; but all things, all forms oppress me, as if to laugh at my insincerity, mock my cringing ways, scorn the poverty of my words and wits and will. Why does nature pierce me thus to the quick? Who am I but a mere clod of earth that cannot hope to comprehend her?

The moon, late to rise, is still below the horizon. When I look up at the deep blue sky I see a canopy dotted with countless stars above my head. When I contemplate my own diminutive form and then my inner self, I am dismayed by the vast distance that separates me from nature. Immortality, imperishability: these are hers. Decline, decrepitude, disease, death: these are mine. I rise and leave the cottage. . . . Anguish is still knotted in my breast. I walk a short way and throw myself down finally in a deep thicket of autumn grasses. The shrill chirping of insects suddenly strikes my ears. A change comes over me. As I listen on, my heart grows lighter. What I thought to be anguish is not that at all. Look: those insects that seem to mourn the autumn—what is there for them to lament? If I take them to be mourning nature, then I too am sad; if I take them to be singing, then I too am bursting with song. Yet in another frame of mind, I see that there is no nature, no self—only myriad lanterns suspended in the vast firmament.

I stroll down to the water's edge. White-capped waves carry the echo of distant ages. Blue waters reflect the hue of eternity. I gaze with folded arms at the azure sky. I forget myself; time seems to slip from me like so many old rags.[26]

What are we to make of this memoir-essay, this lyric sketch, this modern-day *zuihitsu*, which strains any single generic label to the limit? It treats the abstractions of time and space yet situates the subject in a specific setting. It tells the "story" of a character who yearns to melt into the embrace of all-pervading nature. Its first-person narrator is the text's focus and yet remains himself out of focus, a permanent blur seemingly no amount of textual analysis can resolve. In its tone and mood, its perspective and specificity, this piece that is neither story nor essay nor hybrid contains the seed of what two decades later would develop into the *shinkyō shōsetsu*, the sketch (one can scarcely even say chronicle) of the narrator's mental state that, as a variant of the *shishōsetsu* form, was to take the Taishō literary world by storm. But to look forward in Japanese letters is commonly to look back as well. The strategy of depersonalizing one's emotions ("What I thought to be anguish is not

---

26. *Kitamura Tōkoku shū*, 222. About half the text is translated here. Francis Mathy includes a complete translation in "Kitamura Tōkoku: Final Essays," 54–55.

that at all") recalls nothing so much as the pose struck by Bashō in such famous verses as these:

Tsuka mo ugoke	Move, thou tomb!
Waga naku koe wa	My wailing voice—
Aki no kaze	Autumn wind.
Uki ware o	O mountain thrush:
sabishigarase yo	Turn the sadness I feel
Kankodori	Into Loneliness.

Perhaps most important, Tōkoku's essay transmits a seriousness of intent that makes, however, little attempt at universalization; its urgent and even didactic tone, moreover, would resurface in the stories of later *shōsetsu* writers. Here was a form that could be at once serious and personal. Posing as a self-conscious narrator-protagonist, furthermore, Tōkoku the "critic" would encourage future "novelists" to adopt a similar pose and blur further the line between story and essay.

Once this form was thus denarrativized and defictionalized, the *shōsetsu* practically merged with it to take its place in the family of "refined" literature. Tōkoku's essay-sketch-memoir—in which there was room for little more than the narrator's own voice—was published a decade before naturalism appeared on the Japanese literary scene. The generation of writers following Tōkoku (especially the "romantic" poets, including Tayama Katai and Shimazaki Tōson, who later as "naturalists" turned to prose for their depictions of personal experience) discovered in it a form far better suited to the expression of the contemplative life they led than a more dramatic narrative form could possibly be. Inspired by the many poetic personae in the classical literature to meditative isolation and liberated from the priorities of public interest mandated by the Meiji Confucian ethic, their voice emerged after Tōkoku to become a major literary presence, and the *shishōsetsu's* raison d'être.

DOPPO AND THE PERSONALIZATION OF NARRATIVE

Kitamura Tōkoku's call for a serious literature was overshadowed by that of Tsubouchi Shōyō, whose *Shōsetsu shinzui* (The essence of the novel, 1885–86) ostensibly rejects the didactic hermeneutics of

Edo-period letters in favor of nineteenth-century western "realism" (*shajitsu*). But Shōyō's criticism was no more successful than Tōkoku's in bringing fiction—insofar as it was equated with omniscient, emplotted narrative—into the realm of serious literature. Not only was he himself unable to create a literary work that successfully illustrated his theories; his most brilliant student, Futabatei Shimei, soon gave up his occupation as a full-time writer because of deep reservations about literature as a career and about fiction as a legitimate literary medium.

Shōyō insisted that a work's merit was based on psychological verisimilitude rather than on didactic intent and chastised the Edo-period writers who would defy all bounds of credibility to make a moralistic point; yet he considered fictional imagination an essential part of the novel's art, without which a work lacked coherence and direction. A novel, he argued, differed from a historical account or travelogue by virtue of its tightly controlled plot, which gave significance to all the characters and events it depicted. A novel that refused to articulate the relationship between events was not a novel at all but a queer piece of writing in which events were simply recorded as they occurred, one after another.[27]

Such queer pieces of writing, of course, flooded Japanese letters after the turn of the century. The naturalist critics in the early 1900s found Shōyō's attack against the overly contrived plotting in the Edo *gesaku* equally applicable to such mid-Meiji forms as the *seiji shōsetsu* ("political fiction") and the *katei shōsetsu* ("domestic fiction"), and in particular to the writings of the Ken'yūsha school led by Ozaki Kōyō. The Ken'yūsha's hegemonic position in the literary world in the 1890s effectively squelched the kind of writing that Shōyō tried but failed to achieve and that Futabatei Shimei achieved but chose not to pursue. The naturalist movement grew up largely in reaction to what it saw as the Ken'yūsha's maintenance of the "nonliterary," fictional strain of Edo-period literature, and it took Shōyō's call for "realism" to mean a rejection of the author's license to invent.

Flourishing during the years between the Russo-Japanese War (1904–5) and the end of Meiji, the naturalists—a diverse group of writers with far more varied styles and sensibilities than their label

27. Shōyō's remarks on fiction and plot can be found in the opening passage of the "Shikumi no hōsoku" section of *Shōsetsu shinzui*, 43.

suggests[28]—developed a relatively unadorned and colloquial style and gave Japanese letters a body of landmark texts that exerted a profound influence on successive generations of writers. In their generally pessimistic portrayal of men and women who succumbed to the larger forces of heredity and environment, they clearly revealed their debt to writers like Zola and Maupassant. They were, moreover, fascinated by (although they never wholly identified with) the writer's role as dispassionate anatomist, dissecting the human animal and exposing it for all to see. The word "nature" had been practically a synonym for beauty during the previous millennium in Japanese literature, as the canon of classical poetry demonstrates, but in 1902 Kosugi Tengai (1865–1952) could write:

> Nature is simply nature. It is neither good nor evil, beautiful nor ugly. The people of a certain time and place, grasping only a single aspect, merely label it as such. . . . The poet has no concern with the reader's emotional response. His only imperative is faithful depiction. A portrait painter, noting that his model's nose is too big, cannot, after all, plane the model's face. Likewise, the writer must not breathe a hint of subjectivity into his imagery.[29]

Despite this and other bold manifestos about "objective" description, "naturalism" in Japan was in fact domesticated by "subjectifying" experience, that is, presenting in the form of a plotless narrative (precisely that "queer" sort of writing against which Shōyō so vociferously inveighed) what the author himself knew from personal experience, usually from the viewpoint of his fictional alter ego. Naturalism's first great impact, predictably, was on writers who had begun their careers as romantic poets in the 1890s: Kunikida Doppo, Tayama Katai, Shimazaki Tōson, and Iwano Hōmei, all of whom turned to prose when they found that they could adopt the same subjectified voice that had served them well in their verse. Not that they themselves saw their writing in these terms: on the contrary, they regarded it to the man as a revolutionary break with the past, through which they could comment critically on society. But the whole force of the movement, from its inception, was in the direction of collapsing the distance between

---

28. Just how diverse is illustrated by William F. Sibley's essay "Naturalism in Japanese Literature," esp. 166–68.

29. From the preface to *Hayari uta*, in *KBHT* 2:418.

the author and his protagonist and increasing it between the protagonist and the rest of society.

Kunikida Doppo was perhaps the first writer, naturalist or otherwise,[30] whose stories lent themselves to a positing of a close author-narrator or author-protagonist relationship. Like Tōkoku, Doppo became interested in writing only after he had grown disillusioned with politics and discovered that the privatized realm of literature was one of the few that offered, within the limitations outlined above, a modicum of expressive freedom. He looked on his Ken'yūsha rivals with distaste while reading enthusiastically the works of Wordsworth and Turgenev. What attracted Doppo to western literature was its personalized narrative voice in poetry and prose; this, he found wanting in the literature of his contemporaries. The Ken'yūsha writers' greatest sin, he believed, was their lack of emotional involvement with their characters—the inevitable result of their concern for mass appeal at the cost of silencing their own thoughts and yearnings. Doppo regarded the Ken'yūsha as a group of latter-day *gesaku* writers, mere "entertainers," and saw himself as an artist with rather more serious pretensions, writing to please only himself. Serious literature was not a showcase of stylistic brilliance, nor was it necessarily a "good read"; it was a medium through which the writer expressed matters closest to his heart. In a memoir recounting his literary career, he offers a keynote for the succeeding generation that would complete the task of privatization: "My stories are honest depictions of my own deepest feelings. . . . I want never to lose touch with those anguished moments when I first wrestled with life's questions and merely become immersed in art for art's sake. I shall always be prepared to submit a 'report on my study of life.'"[31]

Here again, as in the case of Tōkoku, we are presented with a theory of writing that lays claim to its importance by de-

---

30. Doppo claimed on many occasions that he did not belong to the naturalist "school." He identified closely with the movement and with writers like Tōson and Katai, however, and conceded, in his posthumous *Byōshō roku* (1908), that he might profitably be called a naturalist. See *Kunikida Doppo zenshū* 9:65.

31. "Ware wa ika ni shite shōsetsuka to narishi ka" (1907), in ibid. 1:498. Doppo did not believe that the author's feelings alone made a story or that a story had to be literally true to life to contain a kernel of artistic or philosophical truth. His narrators' strongly personal voices and close identification with their protagonists, however, give his writing an unmistakably intimate tone not found in works of the Ken'yūsha school.

emphasizing the role of artifice. One becomes "immersed in art for art's sake," according to Doppo, only at the risk of losing touch with personal experience and the moral lessons to be derived therein. In one such "report" on his life, Doppo celebrates the mysteries of existence in a way that suggests that personal awareness is more important than wisdom gleaned from any external source. "I do not wish to penetrate the mysteries of the universe," his pensive hero remarks, "but simply to be moved by them. . . . I would become a great philosopher, but if my wish to be moved by these mysteries were not granted, then I could only look upon myself as a hypocrite and brand myself a liar."[32] Doppo's view of literature as a form of spiritual discipline given unmediated expression, then, unmistakably reveals the same sensibility that motivated Tōkoku; and his rejection of a literature of entertainment is informed by an eminently moral vision worthy of the Confucian "Way" that has simply been turned inward.

Doppo's literary rise and the prominence of the naturalists in general in the years following the Russo-Japanese War was due largely to these writers' success in elevating prose fiction to a level of seriousness on a par with the traditionally respected genres of nonfiction prose and poetry. Doppo achieved this on the one hand by rejecting ornate style and on the other by injecting personalism into his works. For Doppo, these two aspects of writing were intimately related, as can be seen in his comments collected in *Byōshō roku:*

> I have never troubled myself over stylistic matters, as form is not my object in writing. I am simply concerned with how to express the thoughts that fill my breast. And so I have written some of my stories . . . in an epistolary style, others . . . in a quasi-lecture style, and still others . . . in diary form or . . . a hybrid of fiction and essay. I am not interested in the merits or demerits of a particular style. I seek only to convey my own true voice. . . . To take up your pen out of a desire to produce fine writing is to ignore your own true feelings and make it impossible to move others. Only by putting down precisely what you feel and expressing your thoughts frankly and without deception or decoration, no matter how awkward the attempt, can you create a genuine and appealing work of literature. . . . The task is simple: give vent to your emotions. If you do, then one work in ten at least is sure to be true literature.[33]

32. "Gyūniku to jagaimo" (1901), in ibid. 2:384, 383.
33. Ibid. 9:75–77. I am indebted to Jay Rubin's unpublished Ph.D. dissertation, "Kunikida Doppo," 4–5, for alerting me to these passages.

Paradoxically, Doppo's personalism did not undermine the didactic strain that had nurtured "serious" literature in the earlier tradition, but built on it. Doppo constructed the role of the poet-philosopher who was attuned to the "voice" of humanity. This moral teacher was in an ideal position to communicate his message to the rest of the world. The message was personal rather than political, but the existence of such a vehicle of expression helps explain why the political ambitions of Doppo, and Tōkoku before him and most writers after him, were so easily displaced by literary ones, once the latter were reinstated as morally legitimate. In his study of Doppo, Jay Rubin notes that Doppo's stories, even when ineptly composed, always had a point. "He wrote only when he wanted to say something, never just to write. He read books for what they could teach him as an individual, never for what they could teach him about writing. He quotes Turgenev and Wordsworth at length in some of his stories because he wished to pass on what he has learned from them: not so much ways of writing as ways of seeing. Perhaps it was this, more than anything else, which Doppo gave to Japanese literature: a new kind of didacticism, a belief that literature could teach men about the world they live in."[34] To write such a literature, one needs no master but only to learn from one's own heart. In one of his attacks on the Ken'yūsha, Doppo proclaims: "Literary art has no need for a master-disciple relationship. A writer's only master is the body of work that strikes a responsive chord in his breast. Do not seek a single master; seek many. . . . Literature is not an art that can be taught or learned; it must be developed using one's own strength."[35]

Doppo's diminutive stories attracted few readers and received little critical notice at first. In 1905, however, three years before Doppo's death, Masamune Hakuchō, himself one of the three or four most important naturalist writers, published an essay on Doppo's second short-story collection that may surpass in significance the stories he reviewed. It deserves quoting at length.

> If one defines prose fiction [*shōsetsu*] as the objective and dispassionate depiction of character and milieu, then most of the stories in his collection are not fiction. One might better describe them as sketches

34. Rubin, "Kunikida Doppo," 91–92; see also the discussion, 36–37.
35. *Kunikida Doppo zenshū* 9:76.

or impressions, and the characters in them mere likenesses of the author himself. . . . The author lacks the kind of aesthetic distance needed for realistic description that even the mediocre artist has at his command when mechanically painting a landscape or portrait. He has a burning, poetic passion, and he seems compelled to unburden himself at all costs of his brooding thoughts on love, marriage, and life. Those who share his passion will read these stories with great interest; those who do not will think them rather tedious. He can hardly be expected to enjoy the popularity of a domestic-fiction writer.

The author has a clumsy narrative style—downright crude, in fact, if one judges "good writing" by the presence of embellishments and pretentiousness, by the way an author carries on about the sky or moon or about who laughed or cried, when such things actually do not matter to him in the slightest, or by the way he hides his true feelings and writes down only transparent fabrications. It is gratifying to encounter a writer who communicates his personal view of life with such great economy.[36]

Hakuchō's remarks set a major critical precedent, because they posit an identity, never before so clearly articulated, between the author and his protagonist and with it the possibility of an "unmediated" literature. It is perhaps the first piece of evidence we have of the defictionalized *shōsetsu* being created in large measure by its mode of reading. The implications of such a reading, which evaluates a text more on the basis of its fidelity to the author's personal experience than on its internal coherence, are profound.[37] For Hakuchō, Doppo's endearing subjectivity and clumsy style have the ring of truth. Sympathetic readers respond to the author's emotional integrity with a depth of feeling that the pulp writer, who hides his "true feelings" and puts down only "transparent fabrications," simply can not evoke. Literature's proper function, Hakuchō insists, is to communicate the author's own private world rather than create an imaginary one. Because "fabrication" is by definition incompatible with the author's own experience, it does

---

36. "*Doppo shū o yomu*" (1905), in *Masamune Hakuchō zenshū* 6:24–25.

37. Doppo frequently based his stories closely on "real life," but rarely without conscious alterations. In "Yo ga sakuhin to jijitsu" (1907), he groups his stories in four categories: one in which both characters and plot are completely "imaginary," one in which the author uses some idea from an incident or character in real life, one in which incident and character from real life form the story's core, and one in which the author "faithfully" transcribes an incident from real life exactly as it had occurred (*Kunikida Doppo zenshū* 1:519–24)—and thus the significance of Hakuchō's preoccupation with Doppo's stories as personal statements rather than as fictional texts.

not deserve an emotional investment on the reader's part. Writing thus shorn of aesthetic distance can of course be expected to attract few readers. This small audience, however, is precisely the elite segment that, seeing beyond the *shōsetsu*'s function as entertainment, will transform the traditionally "nonliterary" form into a bona fide literature of edification. The *shōsetsu*'s perceived importance is thus directly proportional to its nonfictionality. This is the lesson that Tayama Katai and others learned from Doppo. Shortly after Doppo's death, Katai wrote that without his colleague's influence, he would never have turned to literary confession.[38] We shall examine in detail the fruits of this influence in the following chapter.

HŌGETSU AND THE TRIUMPH OF INTROSPECTION

While Doppo and other writers were experimenting with a more privatized style, Shimamura Hōgetsu, a highly respected naturalist critic, provided a comprehensive intellectual rationale for their new approach to literature. As a student of aesthetics and the theater, Hōgetsu spent three years at Oxford and Berlin before returning to a professor's chair at Waseda University in 1905 and assuming the editorship of the university's prestigious literary journal, *Waseda bungaku,* which became one of the naturalist movement's principal voices. At first, Hōgetsu was wary of the movement's penchant for "truthful" description. He regarded naturalism in Japan as just a passing phase—necessary ground to be traversed on the way to the more rewarding field of symbolist literature—as had been the case in the European literary circles he had observed firsthand.[39] Art's ultimate goal was beauty, he argued, not truth (by which he meant the accurate observation of life); the latter had value only insofar as it led to the apprehension of the former.[40] Beauty was

---

38. "Kunikida Doppo ron" (1908), in *Kunikida Doppo zenshū* 10:410.
39. In one essay he writes, "I think naturalism is good thing. . . . It may have arrived here twenty years late, but . . . if Japanese literature, which has so much ground to cover, can move even one step forward (and by that I mean to experience something new), then that is progress. In this sense, at least, novelty has its value" ("*Futon* gappyō" [1907], 430).
40. "Shizenshugi no kachi" (1908), 209–10.

central to Hōgetsu's conception of literature, because it inspired the writer to transcendence; art was not far from religion.

Hōgetsu, however, eventually became caught up in the intellectual malaise that afflicted writers after the Russo-Japanese War, and he waxed less and less metaphysical in his later essays. His desire to see Japanese literature evolve after the European model gave way to a resigned acceptance of the strict taboos on sociopolitical statement in the Meiji state. Unlike painters, musicians, and other artists who received, on occasion, official government recognition and support,[41] writers were the frequent targets of censorship and other harassment. But even though this treatment further isolated them from the rest of society, it also nurtured among them a sense of solidarity and fierce pride. This camaraderie among writers, which united them (albeit entirely passively) against the politico-economic establishment, had become quite strong by late Meiji, when skepticism about the regime's political objectives was reaching new heights. The statist goal of early Meiji Japan—building a "rich, militarily powerful nation" (*fukoku kyōhei*) that could repel any external threat—had been achieved in large measure by the turn of the century and finally with demonstrable success in its hostilities with Russia. Thus, after 1905 the sense of imminent national crisis—the cornerstone on which the government had founded its program of rapid modernization—had dissipated considerably, and nation building was no longer the top priority it had been since the Restoration. The majority of the people had united in support of government efforts to strengthen the military and the economy, at least until the Russo-Japanese War. The Meiji period's final years, however, were characterized by the more open pursuit of private interests in the face of waning national priorities. Such concepts as independence and autonomy, which had heretofore been interpreted only in a national context, now took on new meaning on a personal level, although they remained somewhat ill defined. The critic Tokutomi Sohō (1863–1957), an early advocate of civil liberties who later championed nationalism and expansionism, lamented shortly after war that the early Meiji values that

41. In a panel discussion, Hirano Ken and Takami Jun note ways in which the Meiji government supported the fine arts, including the sponsorship of exhibits for painters and the establishment of a public university for musicians. See Hirano Ken, Takeuchi Yoshimi, and Takami Jun, "Bundan," 141.

placed public interests over private had been overturned; people now valued personal prosperity over national strength.[42]

This awakening of private consciousness occurred at a time when opportunities for individual advancement in public life had been severely curtailed. The relative political and social mobility of the post-Restoration decades had lost momentum as the leadership in government and the bureaucracy consolidated its authority. By the end of the Russo-Japanese War, political opportunities had grown so limited that many young intellectuals were forced to abandon hopes for public careers.[43] The fast-rising careers in the academy and in government awaiting the small elite who graduated from a university in Tsubouchi Shōyō's day were no longer available to those reaching adulthood after the turn of the century, when sheer numbers, combined with fewer openings, sent the market value of educated youth tumbling.[44]

The forces that frustrated the political aspirations of many young intellectuals also curbed the outlets of creative thought. Having introduced a series of "peace preservation" laws in the late nineteenth and early twentieth centuries, which effectively controlled participation in the political process, the government kept a tight rein on literary activities to insure that the writer's political consciousness (in the few cases when it was expressed) did not stray from the national interest. Censorship was swift, severe, and sparing of no writer who offended, in the eyes of the bureaucrats, the sacrosanct sensibilities of public morality. Even a writer like Mori Ōgai, whose "establishment" credentials were impeccable (he was an army doctor who rose to the rank of surgeon general), did not escape the censor's scrutiny. His *Vita sexualis* was banned within a

42. "Fukuzatsu naru shakai" (1906), cited in Oka Yoshitake, "Nichiro sensō-go ni okeru atarashii sedai no seichō," 2. Confronted with this diminishing nationalistic fervor and with a younger generation that seemed inclined more toward vague and romantic spiritual pursuits than toward its obligations to the state, Sohō exhorted his readers to "love the nation, if you must love at all" ("Chihō no seinen ni kotauru sho" [1906], in ibid., 12).

43. See Kenneth B. Pyle, *The New Generation in Meiji Japan*, 199–200.

44. See Kinmouth, *The Self-made Man in Meiji Japanese Thought*, esp. 220–21. Kinmouth contends (ibid., 228) that this explanation for the much-discussed "anguish" (*hanmon*) of the age undermines Oka ("Nichiro sensō-go ni okeru atarashii sedai no seichō") and others' argument that waning national priorities prompted the privatization of interests. The two theses, however, appear to be not antithetical but complementary explanations for what was both a political *and* an economic phenomenon.

month of its publication in July 1909, and he was warned soon after by a high government official not to sign his articles in the newspapers.[45] Finally, the trial in 1910 and subsequent execution of Kōtoku Shūsui and other radicals who had allegedly plotted the emperor's assassination demonstrated to intellectuals across the political spectrum the extent to which the government was willing to exercise its power in the interests of political and cultural domination.

In 1911, hoping to fend off any concerted reaction by writers, the government reestablished its national committee (Bungei Iinkai, originally organized in 1909) for the purpose of "fostering" literary activities, which meant of course discouraging any potentially subversive writing. H. D. Harootunian sees in this bureaucratization of literary taste not only the government's desire to inhibit writers from treating subjects of a social and political nature but also its continuing strategy of separating politics and culture and insuring that individualism as a concept would remain entirely nonpolitical in its ramifications.[46] By all indications, the strategy worked. Writers had long viewed individualism as something achieved not because of one's relationship with society and the state but only because of one's independence from them, and they were not about to alter this formula now. "I believe firmly that we should live in the world," writes the influential critic Takayama Chogyū (1871–1902) at the turn of the century, "but it should be remembered that the individual does not exist within state and society. State and society exist within the individual. We have to conduct our spiritual lives under these conditions."[47] Chogyū is proposing the tacit agreement that would be in force throughout the

---

45. Richard John Bowring, *Mori Ōgai and the Modernization of Japanese Culture*, 139.
46. "Introduction: A Sense of an Ending and the Problem of Taishō," 26. Jay Rubin, in his informative study, contends that at the end of the reestablished committee's brief tenure, the struggle between writers and the bureaucracy ended in a draw (see *Injurious to Public Morals*, esp. 9, 205–19). But if this is so, it is because the writers had already learned well the value of self-censorship, as we can see from the opinions of six major writers and critics on the uses of censorship collected in the January 1909 issue of *Taiyō*. Of the six, only one, Shimamura Hōgetsu, comes out unequivocally against censorship in any form, although he limits his defense to what he calls "true literature," which he does not define. The response of Kosugi Tengai is more typical: writers should avoid getting involved in quarrels with government. See *KBHT* 3:397–406, esp. 404–5.
47. Quoted in H. D. Harootunian, "Between Politics and Culture," 154.

first half of this century: if the state allows the artist the freedom in his private realm to lead an irregular life and hold unorthodox views concerning literature and philosophy, the artist will in turn abstain from criticism of the state and involvement in politics.[48] Chogyū's celebration of the privatized aesthetic life, in which "nothing was more important than the 'gratification of instinctive desires,'"[49] would provide the rationale for many *shishōsetsu* writers in the second and third decades of this century and most especially for Shiga Naoya, who made a career of depicting, probably unconsciously, the private, instinctual man living in a political vacuum.

For all their caution, Chogyū's comments were among the less guarded political statements to be uttered by early twentieth-century intellectuals. The attitude of Nagai Kafū (1879–1959), when he heard about the Kōtoku trial and its verdict in 1911, was far more typical:

> Of all the public incidents I had witnessed or heard of, none had filled me with such loathing. I could not, as a man of letters, remain silent in this matter of principle. Had not the novelist Zola, pleading the truth in the Dreyfus case, had to flee his country? But I, along with the other writers of my land, said nothing. . . . I felt intensely ashamed of myself as a writer. I concluded that I could do no better than drag myself down to the level of the Tokugawa writer of frivolous and amatory fiction.[50]

Silence, however shameful, was preferable to jail or worse. To be sure, Kafū was one of the modern culture's most strident critics. Yet his was the voice of a man incensed by sheer bureaucratic ineptitude and by the loss of an irrecoverable tradition, not that of a guilt-ridden progressive lamenting his missed chance to serve humanity. As Edward Seidensticker notes, "It is one thing to complain about the dirt and clutter of Meiji Japan, but quite another to fight for social justice."[51] The latter option was in actual fact practically nonexistent. The way to the writer's development as an "individual," no matter how critical and discerning, lay in the renunciation of political involvement.

48. Ibid., 152.
49. Ibid., 149.
50. "Hanabi" (1919), quoted in Edward Seidensticker, *Kafū the Scribbler*, 46.
51. Ibid.

"Renunciation" is perhaps too strong to describe what was essentially a passive, apolitical stance. The writings of the naturalists show that they were intensely interested in society, but "society" as a much more circumscribed institution than that depicted by their French counterparts, as the titles of many works suggest: Tayama Katai's *Sei* (Life) and *Tsuma* (Wife), Mayama Seika's *Minami Koizumi Mura* (South Koizumi Village), Tokuda Shūsei's *Arajotai* (New household), Masamune Hakuchō's *Ni kazoku* (Two families), to name a few. For Japanese writers, the *ie*, or extended family, *was* society; what lay beyond it was quite literally out of their world. It was inevitable that one of those works would bear the title of *Ie*. Tōson's ponderous work describes with great power the strictures that the *ie*, even when transplanted from the country to the more fluid urban scene, placed on the individual. An autocratic national government could hardly do more to restrict one's freedom of action and movement. The incestuous turn that personal relations took for the hero Sankichi and his niece seems an almost logical conclusion to a life so involuted, and to human relations so constricted, that the daily constitutional provides the only chance for solitude and freedom.

The fact remains, however, that the government did not rely on intellectual ennui and malaise or the traditional preoccupation with the *ie* for political acquiescence but sought aggressively to silence writers before they spoke. Given this intellectual climate, it is hardly remarkable that writers were less than enthusiastic about expressing their political views—if, indeed, they had any—or that their writings tend on the whole to focus on man in his isolation from, rather than his relationship to, society. The government's demonstration of force during the Kōtoku trial provided just one more incentive for writers to steer clear of any incident that smacked of subversion—and "subversion" in the late Meiji and Taishō context meant virtually any written expression of political or social concern.[52] It was not worth risking one's artistic freedom,

52. In the words of H. D. Harootunian: "Here, in this *fin de siècle* world of late Meiji and early Taishō, men discovered that what a European like [Thomas] Mann was to defend as a free choice . . . —to act or not to act politically—was in Japan no choice at all. The situation was reversed, and to refuse to act politically was the precondition to freedom, individualism, art and culture, and the surest guarantee of their continuation. . . . This is perhaps one reason why such concepts as indi-

however circumscribed, to display too keen an interest in, let alone righteous indignation over, public affairs. (It was difficult enough for writers to combat the censors' charges, laughable nowadays, of prurience in many of their works.) These pressures compelled writers to treat subjects that from the government's perspective harbored no obvious "threat" to society. The least offensive literature was one in which, not surprisingly, broad social issues did not figure at all and the largest perimeter of human affairs was the writer's family circle or his literary coterie. Naturalism became a rallying point for the privatization of literature, and writers applied their powers of observation to the last realm in which they enjoyed even a limited autonomy: their personal lives.

Hōgetsu, too, became attracted in time to this introspective enterprise. In a skeptical age like the present one, he argued, art no longer transcended life; it had become mired in life. And when the writer's sights were limited to personal experience, the result, inevitably, was a record of disillusionment. At first, Hōgetsu insisted on an inviolate demarcation between life and art. In an essay assessing the "value" of naturalism, he argues that a writer's authorial stance and his personal behavior are of two entirely different dimensions.[53] He later exhorts his readers: "We desire to contemplate life through art. We do not wish, however, to act out our lives through it. If our aim is action, we do not turn to fiction or poetry; we turn to our hands and feet."[54] When the goal of art shifted in his eyes from transcendental "beauty" to experiential "truth," however, the demarcation seemed less defensible, and literature appeared destined to become an exercise in personal confession.

Hōgetsu was quick to recognize Japanese naturalism's potential as a vehicle for confession in his critique of *Futon* (1907), which he called a "stark, utterly candid revelation of a man stripped naked."[55] In what is perhaps his most famous essay, which prefaces a collection of his writings on naturalism, he explores his own need

---

vidualism, freedom and liberty could never lead to concrete political action. . . . To have turned outward in search of one's individuality would have risked conflict with public expectations and the state" ("Between Politics and Culture," 114–15, 123–24).

53. "Shizenshugi no kachi" (1908), 213.
54. "Kanshō soku jinsei no tame nari" (1909), 247.
55. "*Futon* gappyō," 431.

for a more direct expression of personal sentiments and concludes that confession is the only appropriate literary form in the present age. In this essay he paints a bleak picture of the intellectual life, devoid of spiritual and moral underpinnings. He longs for something to believe in and curses an intellect that has produced only doubt. "I can hardly believe in my own philosophy of life, let alone someone else's," he laments. "My first impulse is to criticize. I can believe nothing, admire nothing. The true believer must certainly have peace of mind; but restless is the heart of a critic."[56] Hōgetsu's next words, which reveal the anguish of a man who has lost his intellectual bearings, are hauntingly prophetic, for they, like none before, articulate the need of writers to make their private lives the focus of their literary attentions:

> I cannot now construct a viable philosophy. I would do better simply to disclose my doubts and uncertainty as they are. That would be telling the truth; saying anything more promises to be sheer invention. When I look around me in this frame of mind, moreover, I cannot help believing that other seekers after life's meaning are in similar straits. Should that be the case, then we may be entering into an age of confession. Very well. Let us do away with falsehood. Let us dispense with decoration. Let us scrutinize ourselves and acknowledge frankly what we are. Is that not the most suitable credo for our times? In this sense, ours is indeed an age of confession. Perhaps we shall never go beyond it.[57]

In a sequel to the essay quoted above, Hōgetsu argues that literature is better equipped than either philosophy or religion to reflect on life, the meaning of which lies in its very uncertainty. Because literature (and here he clearly means "naturalist" literature) faces squarely the skepticism of the age and refuses to rely on "invention," it provides, he concludes, the most persuasive description of reality. In it one can express one's doubts in a straightforward manner that rings truer than any metaphysics. Philosophy and religion are fated to explain the inexplicable, while literature—the depiction of the unfathomable reality that one sees all around and within oneself—acknowledges the inexplicable as life itself.[58]

56. "Jo ni kaete jinseikanjō no shizenshugi o ronzu" (1909), 256–57. The collection *Kindai bungei no kenkyū* (1909) includes all the Hōgetsu essays cited above.
57. Ibid., 257.
58. "Kaigi to kokuhaku" (1909), 274–82.

Hōgetsu thus found meaning in the very skepticism that was undermining his beliefs. Rather than ignore the feelings of doubt that plagued him, he celebrated them. Masamune Hakuchō saw in Hōgetsu's matter-of-fact expressions of intellectual bewilderment the most representative statement of Japanese naturalism.[59] Yamazaki Masakazu, writing nearly thirty years later, reached a similar conclusion. The Russo-Japanese War brought to an end both the Meiji Restoration and the urgent sense of purpose that had mobilized the population for nearly four decades, he writes. Hōgetsu's naturalism articulated the disorientation felt by intellectuals. It was not a positive approach or a method in itself but an expression of skepticism directed at all methods.[60]

Hōgetsu's position was at the same time an eloquent defense of the traditional epistemology, which favored "immediate" over "mediated" reality. Since reality as perceived by others was no longer credible ("I can hardly believe in my own philosophy of life, let alone someone else's"), one was compelled to fall back on one's own perceptions, however limited, as the point of literary departure. The writer had no alternative but to rely on personal experience, the sum total of his introspective world. In an age of confession, Hōgetsu seems to be saying, the "mediated" reality of creative imagination has no purpose. As long as literature is limited to the expression of an "unmediated" personal reality ("I would do better simply to disclose my doubts and uncertainty quite as they are. That would be telling the truth; saying anything more promises to be sheer invention"), there is no room for fictional constructs that posit worlds as real as, but other than, the world that is.

Hōgetsu's reversion to what seemed an epistemologically secure realm of immediate, perceptual reality not only typifies the late-Meiji writer's stance,[61] it reveals a great intellectual debt to his native tradition. In asking literature to fill the shoes of philosophy

---

59. *Shizenshugi seisui ki* (1948), in *Masamune Hakuchō zenshū* 12:316. In a similar vein, Tayama Katai remarks that Hōgetsu expressed more forcefully than anyone the spirit of the age. See *Kindai no shōsetsu* (1923), in *Tayama Katai zenshū* 17:338.

60. *Fukigen no jidai* (1976), 117–18.

61. Other naturalists shared Hōgetsu's views. In an age of disillusionment, argues Hasegawa Tenkei (1876–1940), when religion and metaphysical speculation have been debunked, tales spun from the author's imagination are as out of place as belief in a heaven and a hell. See "Genmetsu jidai no geijutsu" (1906).

and religion and in disassociating it from mediation and fabrication, Hōgetsu shows remarkable consistency with premodern thinking about its nature and purpose. The old notion of two separate literary traditions—the nonfiction that is "literature" and the fiction that is not—was still very much alive in the minds of Hōgetsu and the naturalists, as was the conviction that the *shōsetsu* as serious literature must free itself of fabrication and become the unmediated voice of its author.

5

Harbingers (II):
Katai, Hōmei

> What struck me most [about these works] was the futility
> of imagination.
>
> Tayama Katai, "Sōshun"

> The author does not understand others as he understands
> himself. . . . It is impossible for a writer to be purely objec-
> tive, . . . and by trying to be so he irresponsibly takes a
> position only God can take.
>
> Iwano Hōmei, "Gendai shōrai no
> shōsetsuteki hassō o isshin suru boku no
> byōsha ron"

Although the writings of Shimazaki Tōson, Iwano Hōmei, Tokuda
Shūsei (1871–1943), and Tayama Katai among others can all be examined with regard to the "unmediated," experiential worldview
articulated by Hōgetsu's naturalist creed, it is primarily on Katai
that we shall focus here; for whether or not he deserves his reputation as the *shishōsetsu's* progenitor, his *Futon* (The quilt, 1907),
more than any other single text, inspired a reading of the *shōsetsu*
that challenged its fictional autonomy and thereby set modern
Japanese letters on a course that continues (as demonstrated by
Yasuoka Shōtarō's comments quoted in Chapter 1) to the present
day. To be sure, this singular mode of reading did not develop
spontaneously with the appearance of Katai's story. Indeed, it
would have been impossible without the trend toward privatization
of consciousness we noted in such writers as Tōkoku, Doppo, and
later, Hōgetsu. Only after *Futon*, however, did it gain ascendancy.

It would be wrong of course to place responsibility (and with it,
depending on one's critical camp, the praise or blame that accrues)
for the *shishōsetsu's* genesis on the shoulders of a single author, for
to do so would be to underestimate both its significance and the

inevitability of its development. Other authors were pushing the *shōsetsu* in the same direction as Katai was, and it is safe to say that the *shishōsetsu* would have emerged with or without the appearance of *Futon*. (Later we shall review arguments that *Futon* was not the first "true" *shishōsetsu*.) But the fact remains that no previous text was so thoroughly critiqued with regard to its fictionality—or lack thereof. As we shall discover, two major critical "schools"— one culminating in Nakamura Mitsuo's *Fūzoku shōsetsu ron* (On the novel of manners, 1950), which argues that the unabashed confession in *Futon* began the *shishōsetsu* tradition, and the other culminating in Hirano Ken's *Geijutsu to jisseikatsu* (Art and private life, 1958), which argues that *Futon* is a mixture of fact and fiction— both make fictionality the modern *shōsetsu*'s central issue and referentiality the touchstone of the critical act.

KATAI AS "NATURALIST"

Futon is the story of Takenaka Tokio, a writer nearing middle age and married to a woman who is indifferent to his artistic strivings. He falls in love with Yoshiko, a young admirer whom he has taken into his home as a student, only to discover that she already has a boyfriend, Tanaka, who has abandoned his theological studies in Kyoto to be with her in Tokyo and become a writer. Shocked at the young couple's openness about their relationship and hurt that he himself is not the object of Yoshiko's affections, Tokio informs the girl's father of the affair, forcing Yoshiko to return to her home in the provinces. The story concludes with the frustrated Tokio alone upstairs in Yoshiko's now-deserted room, his face pressed against her bedding.

Nothing in its plot greatly distinguishes *Futon* from any number of Katai's earlier, equally lachrymose and melodramatic writings that describe the hero's infatuation with a "new breed" of young, educated woman, which shall be discussed presently. Indeed, Katai, who wrote poetry and fanciful, sentimental stories for years before the publication of *Futon*, seemed an unlikely candidate as standard-bearer for a new movement. Of his encounter with European naturalism shortly after the turn of the century, through the writings of Maupassant, he wrote: "I felt as if I had been clubbed on the head. My beliefs were completely overturned. . . .

I had formerly gazed only at the heavens, I wrote then in a brief essay. Of the earth I knew absolutely nothing. What a superficial idealist I was! From then on I wanted to be a child of the earth."[1] The naturalist penchant for sordid themes and settings reveals itself as early as 1902 in a work entitled *Jūemon no saigo* (The end of Jūemon), the story of a physically deformed man whose string of arsons leads fellow villagers to lynch him; but it was not until 1904, the year after Ozaki Kōyō died, and with him the authority of the Ken'yūsha, that Katai issued his famous manifesto, "Rokotsu naru byōsha," which combined Kosugi Tengai's critique of a gilded literature with a call for a new, unadorned style that described ordinary life.

> Any intelligent person will agree that writing whose style does not match its content is less than worthless. And yet present-day stylists persist in using pretty phrases unsuitable to the ideas they express, stringing together one blatant lie after the next and calling it all "fine" and "elegant" writing. It hardly needs mentioning that the purpose of writing is communication. It is enough that the writer convey his meaning. . . . He should not have to agonize over how to arrange his phrases or color his words. . . . It is this bold, straightforward description—precisely the kind of writing stylists condemn as crude and incoherent—that I believe will become our literary world's lifeblood and moving force. . . . A commonplace style suits commonplace material; a blunt style suits blunt ideas. This is only natural.[2]

Naturalism in Japan collectively depicts, with considerable depth and breadth, a world closer to the experience of the average Japanese than can be found in most previous Meiji literature; but the individual writer felt most comfortable with a style of presentation that allowed personal observation of one's immediate surroundings to speak only for itself, unanalyzed, rather than for society at large. Here is where Katai and his literary colleagues differed plainly from their French precursors, because the latter would not hesitate to generalize about the whole range of human experience. For a writer like Zola, universal truth always lay waiting to be grasped from specific circumstances and naturally propelled writing beyond the realm of personal experience. The spirit of inquiry was

---

1. "Maruzen no nikai," in *Tayama Katai zenshū*, vol. 15, *Tōkyō no sanjū nen*, 565–66.
    2. *KBHT* 2:360–62.

turned outward, and observations of individual behavior were linked logically and necessarily to entire groups or classes of people: to wit, the coal miners in *Germinal*, the slum dwellers in *L'assommoir*, or the peasants in *La terre*, with whom the author was not even casually associated.

In one of his essays on naturalism, it is true, Zola speaks of the novelist's role as a stenographer who "forbids himself to judge or draw conclusions." Imagination no longer has a function in the novel, he claims; "Nature is all we need . . . we say everything: we no longer select, we do not idealize."[3] Yet even this self-styled champion of "scientific" journalism keenly understood the role of a synthesizing narrative intelligence that readily gave the settings and characters in his best work a symbolic significance. The mines of Le Tartaret and the Paris slums fairly strain from the page, in a tropically dense language, to transcend their own time and place. "The truth," as Zola himself argues, "ascends in winged flight to the symbol."[4] In his naturalist manifesto, "The Experimental Novel" (1880), Zola is supremely aware of fiction's mediating force in representing (with a view to universalizing) the limited data of personal observation. Indeed, the "experiment" in his experimental novel sounds very much like the leaven of fiction giving prose its shape and direction. In answer to the "stupid reproach made against us naturalist writers . . . that we wish to be merely photographers," Zola declares: "The idea of experiment carries with it the idea of modification. We begin certainly with true facts which are our indestructible base; but to show the mechanism of the facts, we have to produce and direct the phenomena; that is our part of invention and genius in the work."[5] Maupassant is no more satisfied with the label of photographer. Only by transcending reality, he argues, can the writer describe it truthfully in fiction:

> The realist, if he is an artist, will endeavor not to show us a commonplace photograph of life, but to give us a presentment of it which shall be more complete, more striking, more cogent than reality itself. To tell everything is out of the question. . . . A choice

3. "Naturalism in the Theater" (1880), in George J. Becker, ed., *Documents of Modern Literary Realism*, 207–9.
4. Quoted in Harry Levin, *The Gates of Horn*, 327.
5. Becker, *Documents of Modern Literary Realism*, 168.

must be made—and this is the first blow to the theory of "the whole truth." . . .

"Truth" in such work consists in producing a complete illusion by following the common logic of facts and not by transcribing them pell-mell, as they succeed each other.

Whence I conclude that the higher order of Realists should rather call themselves Illusionists.[6]

The notion that the writer's task was to transcend everyday life by a process of "modification" (as Zola put it) or "illusion" producing (as Maupassant put it) was precisely what Katai resisted most, conditioned as he was by a nonteleological narrative tradition, by an intellectual climate conducive to private musings, by a movement to rid the *shōsetsu* of fabrication in order that it might take its place among the more prestigious literary forms, and perhaps by the language itself, which as we have observed so clearly privileges the narrator's consciousness in the written reportive style, whether first- or third-person. Like so many of his colleagues, Katai equated truth with the recording of events personally documented. In the wake of his success with *Futon* and the trilogy (*Sei* [Life], 1908; *Tsuma* [The wife], 1908–9; *En* [The bond], 1910) that followed, Katai carried his views to their logical extreme. He took Ozaki Kōyō posthumously to task for instructing his disciples to "write nothing that seems unnatural, even if it really happened, and write only about things that seem natural, even if they never really took place," and he turned the exhortation around: "Write about what really happened, even if it seems unnatural—precisely because it *did* happen. Write nothing that did not actually take place, however natural it may seem."[7] Gone were the days, he was to write later, when one "read a novel as a novel"; the author who wrote only the "truth"—that is, what had actually happened to him or to those he knew—had no use for "fictionalization." Even the names of people one wrote about were better left unchanged.[8] The author's preoccupation with demonstrable "fact" could naturally scandalize his models. But art had no ethics, Katai insisted. It was simply the "duplication of phenomena" (*genshō no saigen*), and the artist was

6. From the preface to *Pierre et Jean* (1888), trans. Clara Dell. Quoted in Philip Stevick, *The Theory of the Novel*, 397–98.

7. *Katai bunwa* (1911), in *Tayama Katai zenshū* 15:180.

8. *Kindai no shōsetsu* (1923), in ibid. 17:309–10.

not to blame for revealing embarrassing truths, whether about himself or those he knew. A writer had but one task: to record his own experience faithfully.[9] At issue was authenticity, not morality. The only artistic sin was fabrication. Reviewing a crop of contemporary stories, Katai wrote:

> What struck me most was the futility of imagination. None of the stories spun from fantasy have any authority or any power to move the reader. Whenever I came across a fine passage in one of them, I had no difficulty surmising that here the author was not writing from imagination at all. . . . The ability to write the truth untainted by fabrication, no matter how slight—or should I say, to achieve a state of mind in which it becomes possible to write in such a way— this is the source from which a new literary spring shall well.[10]

Katai did not and probably could not elaborate on what he meant by a "fine passage" or on how he could detect truth untainted by fabrication, but his clear preference for (perhaps it was a blind faith in) unmediated presentation over mediated representation reflected the prevailing view of his time.

Thus, as is the case with so many "influences," naturalism taught Katai only what he wanted to hear. It advocated the recording of "truth": what could be truer than the events and feelings one had witnessed and experienced oneself? It rejected narrative contrivance: what could be more "natural" than one's own life, plainly described? If "nature" was synonymous with personal experience (as he argued in an early essay),[11] it followed that the writer's task was to observe himself. Writing, then, was an experiment in self-portraiture, and the author became his own hero.

Perhaps the most important fact concerning Katai's articulation of the relationship between life and art is the sheer number of writers who agreed with him. Katai, it turns out, spoke for a good many who professed to be his critics; despite the opposition to naturalism by other writers, the movement away from universalizing fictions to particularized reflections was a trait common to all: naturalist and antinaturalist, aesthetic and decadent, proletarian and neo-perceptionist. Satomi Ton (1888–1983), a major writer in

9. *Katai bunwa*, in ibid. 15:184–85.
10. "Takujōgo" (c. 1911), in ibid. 15:335–36.
11. "Sakusha no shukan" (1901). See Wada Kingo, "Kaisetsu," in Wada Kingo and Sōma Tsuneo, eds., *Tayama Katai shū*, 29.

the Shirakaba school, which is commonly said to have arisen in reaction to the naturalist movement, notes just how little the various coterie labels have to do with styles of writing.

> If one mentions the word "Shirakaba" people soon start on about its "confrontation" with naturalism, and one can't say that there wasn't one, but our differences with the naturalists arose mostly from questions of upbringing. We were aristocrats, whereas "naturalism" meant to us that crowd cooped up in lodgings around Waseda University; and being young, there didn't seem much chance of our getting along with them. But as far as literature was concerned I don't actually recall any real criticism as such being made.[12]

Satomi rightly stresses that the distinction made between these groups of writers, naturalist and otherwise, is one of pedigree rather than literary predilection. Although critics could point with some justification to the naturalists' preoccupation with life's darker, seamier side, the naturalist label was more a value judgment than a literary one and came to stand for boorish provincialism in the eyes of the urbane natives of Tokyo.

FUTON AS AUTOBIOGRAPHY

Futon is by no means modern Japanese literature's first roman à clef. Mori Ōgai's "Maihime" (1889), a story told in the first person about a Japanese student who loves and then leaves a German girl in Berlin, is based on the author's experience in Germany, although it differs somewhat from actual events.[13] It was common knowledge that the protagonists in the Meiji period's two most popular books, *Konjiki yasha* (1897–1902) and *Hototogisu* (1898–99), had real-life models. But as Kimura Ki notes in his memoirs, no scandals resulted because no harm was done.[14]

All that changed with the rise of naturalism. What distinguishes this body of writing from previous writings is not simply the high autobiographical content but also the portrayal of characters in a distinctly unfavorable light. Shimazaki Tōson in particular found

12. Nakano Yoshio, ed., *Gendai no sakka* 58–59. Quoted with slight modification from Dennis Keene's translation in *Yokomitsu Riichi*, 18.
13. For a discussion of "Maihime," see Richard John Bowring, *Mori Ōgai and the Modernization of Japanese Culture*, 47–55.
14. *Watakushi no bungaku kaiko roku*, 101–2.

himself the target of criticism. The publication of one of his early stories was stopped by Yamaji Aizan, who notified the Ministry of Home Affairs that it treated the widow of Aizan's mentor, one Kimura Kumaji, with disrespect.[15] "Namiki" (1907) caused a furor because of the uncomplimentary portraits of Tōson's colleagues Baba Kochō and Togawa Shūkotsu. *Suisai gaka* (1904), the story of an artist who discovers that his wife harbors a lingering affection for the man she loved before she married, was based on the author's own life. Tōson used as his model, however, another couple, a painter and his wife, who promptly brought suit against him. This same story reappeared as an episode in a later text, *Ie* (1910–11), which describes Tōson's early married life.[16]

Shinsei (The new life), which chronicles Tōson's affair with his niece Komako, caused the greatest scandal of all when it appeared in the pages of the *Asahi* newspaper from 1918 to 1919. Although a somewhat later work, it deserves mention here, for it shows the direction that the confessional element in Japanese naturalism was inevitably to take. Tōson began writing long before he knew the outcome of the affair, in hope of ending it once and for all and severing relations (and their incumbent financial obligations) with his brother (Komako's father). The hero, who has recently lost his wife, becomes intimate with a niece who assists in the care of his children. He then abandons the pregnant niece and exiles himself to France, intending to abort the affair before it becomes public knowledge, only to continue it on his return to Japan two years later.

This much Tōson himself knew when he first picked up his pen. He could not have known however what his story held in store for the rest of his life. He (and consequently his hero) finally decided to reveal the affair in the form of a newspaper serial, which resulted in his (and his hero's) being disowned by his brother and in his niece's hasty removal to Taiwan, then a Japanese colony, in disgrace. The ramifications of this scenario are unsettling, to say the least. *Shinsei* records not simply the affair itself but also its trans-

---

15. Ibid.
16. Tōson did have his supporters. Kunikida Doppo argued that models from real life took on an existence of their own when they appeared in a work of art and that a painter, of all people, should have realized that fact. Recalled in Tayama Katai, *Kindai no shōsetsu*, in *Tayama Katai zenshū* 17:313.

ferral from the private to public domain. In other words, the text's very appearance generated a new crisis in Tōson's life, which Tō-son proceeded to record in *Shinsei* and which generated further crises, and so on, ad infinitum. Referentiality was turned on its head: even as "real-life" events changed the *shōsetsu*'s course, the *shōsetsu* just as easily altered the course of "real life." It was one thing to write about a past affair; it was quite another to write about an affair in progress and in such a way that the progress report itself played a role in the outcome as great as, or greater than, the feelings of the participants. (This point will be brought home in our examination of a cycle of stories by Shiga Naoya in Chapter 8.)

Needless to say, *Shinsei* caused a sensation and gave Tōson's sag-ging career a tremendous boost. Akutagawa Ryūnosuke wrote, not without justification, that he had never before encountered so crafty a hypocrite as the hero of *Shinsei*.[17] Komako, recalling much later the scandal that her uncle's writing had caused, said essen-tially the same thing, although in understandably more deferential terms.

> I am afraid that I read [*Shinsei*] merely as an apology by a man trying lamely to philosophize. . . . It tells the truth so far as it goes, yet leaves out episodes that could have incriminated its author. . . . *Shinsei* is a landmark in the author's growth as a thinker and as an artist, but for me it was only an ordeal, an unbearable photograph that, when exposed to public view, made it impossible for me to live the life of an ordinary woman.[18]

As confession, *Futon* may have been surpassed by later ex-amples, but in no previous writing is there such a clear correspon-dence in every detail between the text and the life. Like Tokio, Katai was a writer who had to make ends meet with a dull editorial job. Like Tokio, Katai had an uneducated wife and three children. Like Tokio, Katai took in a young female admirer who, after living for a month at his home, moved to his sister-in-law's house and enrolled at a nearby woman's school in Kōjimachi Ward—and so on. The psychological parallels between hero and author are, of course,

17. "Aru ahō no isshō," in *Akutagawa Ryūnosuke zenshū* 9:334.
18. Hasegawa Komako, "Higeki no jiden," part 1, p. 285. For a more sanguine and artistic appraisal of *Shinsei*, see Janet A. Walker, *The Japanese Novel of the Meiji Period and the Ideal of Individualism*, esp. 239–43 and 269–82.

more problematic. The author himself suggests that they are indeed close in his memoir, *Tōkyō no sanjū nen* (My thirty years in Tokyo), published in 1917, ten years after *Futon*. In the chapter entitled "My Anna Mahr," [19] Katai claims that he wrote *Futon* knowing that it would destroy any potentially intimate rapport with his student yet hoping that it would establish his reputation as a major writer. "My Anna Mahr was at her parents' home in the provinces," he reminisces. "I had visited her there while traveling during the previous autumn, and her memory now was even more sharply etched in my mind. Should I write about her and abandon all hope for love? Or should I refrain from writing and await the chance for it to blossom?" [20]

From the outset, critics dwelt on the text's lack of authorial distance,[21] but in doing so lent it an air of notoriety that insured its popular success. Even ridicule was good publicity, and Katai soon capitalized on it, writing in quick succession a trilogy (*Sei, Tsuma,* and *En*) based entirely on his domestic life. Other writers soon followed with accounts of their lives: Shimazaki Tōson with *Haru* (Spring, 1908), Iwano Hōmei with *Tandeki* (Decadence, 1909), Chikamatsu Shūkō with *Wakaretaru tsuma ni okuru tegami* (A letter to my estranged wife, 1910), and Tokuda Shūsei with *Kabi* (Mildew, 1911). Masamune Hakuchō argues that Katai's success in exploiting his private life was interpreted by other writers as a green light for self-exposé, a course that would not have occurred to them had *Futon* not met with such critical acclaim and notoriety.[22]

This observation is no doubt true as far as it goes, but it is useful here to note the comments of Chikamatsu Shūkō, who questioned,

19. "Watakushi no Anna Māru." The title alludes to the principal female character in Gerhart Hauptmann's drama *Einsame Menschen* (Lonely lives, 1891), which is mentioned several times in *Futon*. See below.
20. *Tayama Katai zenshū* 15:602. Katai recalls the response to *Futon* (owing to its apparently confessional nature, which he never denies) in a later essay entitled "*Futon o kaita koro*" (1925), in which he writes: "Critics made a terrific fuss when *Futon* first appeared. People sitting next to me at work shot furtive glances in my direction. One person sent me a letter announcing that he was breaking all ties with me" (quoted in Iwanaga Yutaka, *Shizenshugi bungaku ni okeru kyokō no kanōsei*, 116).
21. The view of Katagami Tengen (1884–1928), a naturalist critic, is typical: "The author seems unable to write except in a way that suggests a personal involvement in his material. He lacks objectivity and is incapable of universalizing his predicament. He attempts to observe himself, but with his face flush against the mirror" (*KBHT* 3:423). Tengen's review is one of several included in a survey of contemporary opinion under the title of "*Futon* gappyō," originally appearing in *Waseda bungaku*, Oct. 1907, the month following the publication of *Futon*. See *KBHT* 3:417–32.
22. "Tayama Katai ron" (1932), in *Masamune Hakuchō zenshū* 6:295.

at a time when critical consciousness of the *shishōsetsu* was just emerging, what most believed to be the overriding influence of *Futon* in that form's development. Shūkō tells us that it was not Katai's text but Futabatei Shimei's *Heibon* (Mediocrity, 1907), a brilliantly humorous meditation on mundane existence first serialized scarcely a month after *Futon* appeared, which inspired his own notoriously confessional *Wakaretaru tsuma ni okuru tegami*. He argues that *Heibon*'s peerless colloquial style and first-person narration had an enormous influence on him and other writers and that Futabatei, not Katai, should be credited with originating Japanese naturalism and by extension the *shishōsetsu*. Shūkō had been a great admirer of writers like Ozaki Kōyō and Higuchi Ichiyō (1872–96) and their mastery of the classical idiom, but *Heibon* awoke him to the vernacular's power as a literary instrument, and he determined to exploit Futabatei's style in his own fiction.[23] This essay is of interest not simply because it challenges the established view of *Futon* as the *shishōsetsu*'s true precursor but because it downplays the role of confession. Autobiography is really not at issue, Shūkō suggests. *Futon*'s confessional content no doubt inspired writers like Shūkō, despite his disclaimer; but *Heibon* provided them with the modus operandi to convey that content with the greatest impact.

But to return to *Futon*. Despite the many obvious parallels between the text and the life, it is by no means certain that the text transcribes the life with complete fidelity. What is significant for Japanese literature, however, is that both Katai's critics, who see no attempt at fictionalization, and his defenders, who do, have justified their positions with referential readings of the text that rely more or less completely on extratextual evidence. We shall benefit from an examination of both positions, since taken together they set the tenor of critical perceptions concerning not just *Futon* and the *shishōsetsu* but modern Japanese literature as a whole.

Nakamura Mitsuo's views are representative of the former position. Nakamura sees in *Futon* the first clear breakdown in modern Japanese literature of the fictional contract, which resulted in a form rooted in imaginative bankruptcy. He lays the "blame" for the *shishōsetsu*'s inception squarely on Katai in a number of strident essays, most notably *Fūzoku shōsetsu ron*, and argues that the form

23. "*Wakareta tsuma o kaita jidai no bungakuteki haikei*," 15–18.

has never created life but only plagiarized it. "To reveal the secrets of one's personal life must indeed have required a certain courage," he remarks wryly of Katai and his imitators. "But they had the audacity to believe that simply by describing their personal experience they could automatically move their readers. They wrote of their private miseries without thinking to analyze or objectify them. . . . I do not doubt that literature is the art of portraying the writer's feelings to the reader. But only the *shishōsetsu* is founded on the naive belief that so vulgar a portrayal would have any reader appeal."[24] Nakamura subscribes to a kind of devil theory of literature in which the appearance of Katai's text single-handedly changed the course of Japanese naturalism at its headwater, transforming it from a promising stream of realistic fiction modeled after the classical European novel (as exemplified by Tōson's *Hakai*) into a wayward torrent of confessional autobiography. "A duel of sorts was fought between *Hakai* and *Futon*," Nakamura concludes, "and in terms of influence wrought on literary contemporaries, *Futon* emerged the overwhelming victor. . . . Today it has reached the point where *Hakai* is itself judged in terms of literary standards established by *Futon*."[25]

Hirano Ken's views are representative of the latter position. According to Hirano, *Futon* is clearly a fictional text. But because it had aroused such a clamorous response, he argues, Katai later began thinking of it in purely autobiographical terms and thereby deceived even himself (into contemplating, for example, how his writing would affect the relationship with his "Anna Mahr" in *Tōkyō no sanjū nen*), not to mention his readers, about its true character. Hirano examines Katai's relationship with the people on whom he modeled his characters—his wife, Okada Michiyo (the model for Yoshiko), Michiyo's parents, and Nagayo Shizuo (the model for Tanaka)—and argues on the basis of numerous documents that Katai consciously distorted the psychology of his teacher-pupil relationship with Okada Michiyo (while faithfully recording all its superficial aspects) and that the parties directly involved (namely, Katai's wife, Okada, and her parents) condoned

---

24. "Watakushi shōsetsu ni tsuite" (1935), in *Nakamura Mitsuo zenshū* 7:121–22.
25. *Fūzoku shōsetsu ron*, 29. Nakamura goes on to cite Satomi Ton, whose critique of *Hakai* written in 1948 parallels Katai's own, written twenty-five years earlier.

his creative license. He stresses that the association between Katai and Okada as teacher and pupil continued unbroken and with the blessings of Katai's wife and Okada's parents even after the story's publication. The only rational conclusion to be drawn, he reasons, is that the amorous innuendos in *Futon* have no grounding in reality. He goes on to cite an article published by Okada in 1915 stating that although the innuendos in *Futon* disturbed her, Katai's own morals were impeccable and that his portrayal of a jealous teacher lusting furtively after his pupil was a complete fabrication. Hirano concludes that the models in question could never have misconstrued *Futon* as a confession of adultery, even though many readers have.[26]

In effect, both critics argue their positions using the same referential touchstone. The former condemns Katai for "copying" life, while the latter defends him for "fictionalizing" it. Nakamura and Hirano are not alone in making referential readings, however; the principals themselves do the same. We have noted Katai's allusion in *Tōkyō no sanjū nen* to his quandary over whether to conceal the "truth" about his feelings for his pupil or to unburden himself of it. Okada Michiyo, meanwhile, chides Katai for writing a fairy tale at her expense and doubts that she is in fact the model for Yoshiko. She accuses him of exercising "poetic license" in a manner calculated to scandalize all his models, when it was his task as a self-proclaimed naturalist to record experience as accurately as possible. She argues that Katai's motive for this distortion was to slander Nagayo and charges that Katai's defamatory characterization ruined Nagayo's fledgling literary career. Katai depicted Nagayo as a weasel while painting her in the most flattering manner imaginable; his reputation as a naturalist was so firmly established that readers (including, we are perhaps to assume, Nagayo's prospective contacts in the publishing world) were deceived by his gross misconstrual.[27] These accusations are of special interest because they reveal the treachery of a literature that claims to deal only in "facts" and appeals to critics on a purely referential level.

26. *Geijutsu to jisseikatsu*, 88–89. The article Hirano cites is entitled "*Futon, En, oyobi watakushi*" and originally appeared in the Sept. 1915 issue of *Shinchō* under the name Nagayo Michiyo, since Okada had become the wife of Nagayo Shizuo ("Tanaka" in *Futon*).
27. "*Futon, En, oyobi watakushi*," 266.

Okada is saying in effect that Katai, after having primed a gullible reading public over the years with platitudes about naturalism's mission to document personal experience, duped it into believing that he was writing the sordid truth, resulting in brisk sales for the author and embarrassment for his acquaintances.

Okada's interpretation lends support to Hirano's position that *Futon* is indeed a fictional account and not merely, as Nakamura would have it, a "plagiarism" of life. But it brings us no closer to an understanding of the work. By establishing her own experience as the criterion for judgment, Okada merely traded one literalist point of reference for another and quite naturally overlooked any artistic intent behind Katai's "distortions" of experience. Her interpretation does not take into account, for example, why Katai himself, in his incarnation as Tokio, emerges as the most pathetic of all the characters. *Futon* has two comic scenes in which Tokio, drowning his frustrations in drink, collapses first by his toilet and later in the muddy precincts of a Shinto shrine while on his way to visit Yoshiko. The irony is driven home when we see Tokio, who is busily comparing himself to numerous heroes in western literature, viewed through the eyes of other characters (his wife at the toilet, a passerby at the shrine): this would-be hero of his own romance, this master of the house and godlike (to Yoshiko) mentor, has fallen as low as he can fall. Okada's interpretation also fails to explain why Katai did not see fit to include, as an episode in *Futon*, his departure for the front as a correspondent covering the Russo-Japanese War, which had just broken out—why he makes it look as if domestic jealousies, rather than professional necessity, were the sole reason for Yoshiko/Okada's removal from Tokio/Katai's home after just one month.[28] (This discrepancy of course does not disprove that domestic jealousies were in fact the "real" reason for Yoshiko's/Okada's removal but merely suggests that even a referential interpretation cannot accommodate all the "facts" surrounding such an incident.) It fails, moreover, to explain why Katai consistently depicted Tokio as a jealous spoiler destined to lose his happy if platonic relationship with Yoshiko by tattling on her to her parents and forcing her return to the country; for we know on the

---

28. Katai left for China in March 1904, the same month that Okada left his home for his sister-in-law's residence, which was nearer Okada's school.

strength of more than a dozen letters written by Katai to Okada's parents that he was actually the young couple's most ardent supporter.[29] Finally, it fails to explain why Katai so idealizes his heroine—a gesture that troubles even Okada herself.

Why indeed did Katai offer these "distorted" portraits, presenting his heroine in such a complimentary light and himself in such an uncomplimentary one? Clearly, the author's biography cannot provide the whole answer. Katai was doubtlessly guided by personal experience in writing *Futon*. But the question we must always ask is why he (or any author) wrote about one particular experience rather than another, and it is here that our knowledge of the author's life proves surprisingly unhelpful. We must turn instead to other texts and take note of the sensibility that pervades Katai's entire oeuvre. One of the trademarks of a Katai story is the presence of a blatantly sentimental hero of the narcissistic, brooding sort that one would expect to find in writings of a more romantic than naturalist cast. *Futon*, which along with Shimazaki Tōson's *Hakai* is said to have ushered Japanese letters into the naturalist era, is no exception. Katai's shift of emphasis to what was "natural" (i.e., the realm of private life) as the only legitimate subject matter did not alter his predominantly romantic sensibility. What is significant is not that *Futon* is based so heavily on personal experience but that it conforms so closely to the same motif of forbidden love that informs his earlier, pre-"autobiographical" and pre-"naturalist" writings. Most critics, preoccupied with *Futon* as confession and unconcerned with how it fits into the context of Katai's oeuvre, have virtually overlooked that motif. In numerous Katai stories, a man beset with middle-age angst and disillusioned with domestic life yearns for a romantic attachment. Yoshiko is yet another incarnation of Katai's feminine ideal: a woman who is at once intellectually stimulating, emotionally supportive, and sexually attractive.

Katai himself hints at his heroine's ideal qualities when he refers to Yoshiko/Okada Michiyo as "my Anna Mahr" in his memoir

29. "Katai *Futon* no moderu o meguru tegami," in Yoshida Seiichi, ed. *Tōson, Katai*, 317–35. The letters were originally published in *Chūōkōron*, June 1939, nine years after Katai's death. In them, Katai praises Okada for her conscientiousness and Nagayo for his intelligence and urges Okada's parents even after her return home that her marriage with Nagayo would be the happiest and most expedient solution.

Tōkyō no sanjū nen. Anna Mahr is the principal female character in Gerhart Hauptmann's drama *Lonely Lives,* to which *Futon* frequently alludes. Katai's text finds some of its inspiration in this drama of an intellectually and spiritually troubled man who gains no solace in family life or religion and who seeks understanding and companionship, in the face of his wife's and parents' obvious distress, from a young woman who rooms in his home. Here, too, is a story of forbidden love doomed to an unhappy end. Katai was not interested in all aspects of Hauptmann's play, however. *Lonely Lives* concerns the conflict between science and religion, and the struggle for values by a hero who rebels against the old morality yet is unable to construct a viable new code of personal ethics. *Futon* has no such intellectual pretensions, nor does it concern itself with the theme of existential loneliness that so pervasively informs *Lonely Lives;* it focuses solely on the hero's infatuation with his student and on his efforts to save face when his love is not reciprocated. But even though Katai's emphasis may differ from Hauptmann's, his allusions to *Lonely Lives* themselves clearly bespeak a broader engagement than simply with personal experience and belie his own suggestion, cited above in *Tōkyō no sanjū nen* ("Should I write about her and abandon all hope for love?"), that he merely intended to document an incident in his life. Despite his theoretical insistence on the privileged status of lived experience, then, Katai's allusions to other literary texts can only be described as a conscious attempt to mediate that experience.

The Katai scholar Tosa Tōru notes that Zola's *Thérèse Raquin* may well have been the inspiration for the notorious conclusion in *Futon,* in which the hero buries his face in his beloved's quilt. In chapter 9, Thérèse has just left Laurent: "He lay sprawling on his bed, sweating, flat on his stomach with his greasy face buried in the pillow where Thérèse's hair had been. He took the linen between his parched lips and inhaled its faint perfume, and there he remained, breathless and gasping."[30] This passage bears more than a passing resemblance to the final scene in *Futon:* "Tokio drew [the bedding] out. The familiar smell of a woman's oil and sweat excited him beyònd words. The velvet edging of the quilt was noticeably dirty, and Tokio pressed his face to it . . . He spread out the mat-

---

30. *Thérèse Raquin,* trans. L. W. Tancock, 82.

tress, lay the quilt out on it, and wept as he buried his face against the cold, stained, velvet edging."[31] Tosa argues convincingly that the direct and copious tribute that Katai pays in *Futon* to such authors as Hauptmann, Turgenev, and Sudermann is mere window dressing and that Katai is curiously silent about his work's most critical literary source. He goes on to suggest that this calculated suppression led readers to believe that any of the hero's thoughts or actions not "footnoted" in other literary texts were to be interpreted as the author's own experience.[32]

More important than any of these literary antecedents, however, are those in Katai's own oeuvre, most notably *Onna kyōshi* (The woman schoolteacher, 1903), published more than four years before *Futon* and more than a year before Katai had made the acquaintance of Okada Michiyo. An episode in *Futon* alludes to the earlier work and foreshadows the hero's abortive relationship with Yoshiko. Tokio, disillusioned with the wife he once loved and yearning for a more satisfactory mate, carries on a fantasy tryst with a beautiful young schoolteacher whom he sees occasionally on the way to his office.[33] *Onna kyōshi* is an elaborate treatment of that fantasy. It is the story of a writer whose pastoral life and connubial bliss are shattered by the passion he develops for a young schoolteacher named Kuniko, who is not only beautiful and personable but also intellectually supportive in a way that his wife cannot be.

In general outline, *Futon* and *Onna kyōshi* are quite similar. In both, the hero is a married man nearing middle age who fears the prospect of an intellectually and emotionally bankrupt life[34] and seeks rejuvenation by contact with a young educated woman, an avid admirer who has requested his tutorial guidance. But the simi-

31. *The Quilt and Other Stories by Tayama Katai*, trans. Kenneth G. Henshall, 96.
32. "Futon no nioi," see esp. 119.
33. *Tayama Katai zenshū* 1:525–26.
34. Katai actually uses the English phrase "lonely life" in *Onna kyōshi*, in what appears to be a reference to Hauptmann's play. Katai very likely had made his acquaintance with the play by this time through the English translation, which was first published in 1898. (The first Japanese translation was not made until 1922.) Shimazaki Tōson wrote a letter to Katai in 1901 thanking him for lending his copy of "Kodoku shōgai"—Tōson's rendition, apparently, of the English title *Lonely Lives* (*Tōson zenshū* 17:60). See the discussion in Ogata Akiko, "Futon zen'ya," 46. Katai wrote a critical essay on one of Hauptmann's plays (*Die versunkene Glocke*) as early as 1903. See *NKBD* 4:362c.

larity does not stop there. The heroines have the same outgoing personalities and physical attributes; they are both described as fair-skinned with expressive features and as keepers of tidy rooms lined with books. Certain scenes and descriptive passages in the two works, moreover, are nearly identical. In both works the hero visits the heroine on a moonlit spring evening, notes the beauty of her makeup, and leaves her very late at night having barely controlled his emotions, she accompanying him partway home. In both the hero is about to dash off to see his beloved only to be detained by his wife, who suspects mischief. In both the hero imagines to himself that his pregnant wife dies in childbirth and leaves him free to pursue his forbidden love. (In *Onna kyōshi*, the wife actually does die, but too late for the hero to consummate his relationship with Kuniko.) In both, the hero lectures the young woman on literature, love, and feminism. And in both he presides over her departure at the end to distant lands (Yoshiko to her parents' home in western Japan, Kuniko to Taiwan), resigning their parting of ways to "fate." In short, not just in theme and overall tone but in the construction of scenes as well, the two works resemble each other strikingly.

These observations are hard to reconcile with Katai's own pronouncement on the composing of *Futon*: "I merely attempted to write down faithfully what I saw and heard and thought."[35] If *Futon* is indeed completely true to life, as it is widely presumed to be, with every character based on a recognizable model, while *Onna kyōshi* is purely imaginative, then it is certainly curious that the heroine in *Futon* should so closely resemble—in appearance, personality, speech, and gesture—the "fabricated" heroine in *Onna kyōshi*. We are witnesses either to a remarkable coincidence between "fact" and "fantasy" or, far more likely, to rather impressive evidence that Katai modeled Yoshiko as much on his own personal feminine ideal as on the young female student he took into his home one spring day in 1904. Private life, it turns out, does not have the only say in Katai's text. Rather, the vectors of experience and imagination intersect on the author's thematic graph of forbidden love.[36]

35. "Shōsetsu sahō," quoted in Hashimoto Yoshi, "*Futon* ni kansuru memo," 66. The discussion of the similarities between *Onna kyōshi* and *Futon* is indebted to this article.
36. See Ogata Akiko, "Futon zen'ya," for yet other examples of texts featuring

It is of course hardly unusual for an author to treat the same
theme more than once—or even with a repetitive obsession (as we
shall witness especially in the works of Chikamatsu Shūkō, in Part
3). Katai does vary his approach the second time around, however.
Having already developed the theme of forbidden love as fully as
he was able in *Onna kyōshi,* he burlesques it in his remake from
"real life." That Katai is capable of poking fun at his hero, and himself, is evident in the short story "Shōjo byō" (1907), which both
recalls *Onna kyōshi* and anticipates *Futon.* "Shōjo byō" is the story
of a man approaching middle age whose continual gawking at
schoolgirls riding on the train he takes to and from work causes
him one day to fall absentmindedly right off the train to his death.
In appearance (he is a very large, "animallike" man), circumstances
(he works for a publishing firm), and family life (he lives with his
wife and small children in Tokyo's Yoyogi district), the hero closely
resembles the author. Like Katai, the hero is the literary world's
laughingstock as the writer of saccharine love stories that are popular only with young female readers. Like Katai, he languishes at a
boring editorial job.

    In "Shōjo byō," Katai carries self-parody to its comic extreme:
the hero's literary pursuit of the ideal woman brings him only re-
proaches from his peers; and his pursuit in real life, a preposterous
death. The parody in *Futon* is more tentative than in "Shōjo byō," [37]
but its melodramatic scenes retain a comic tone. The narrator in-
dulges his hero mightily, to be sure, but manages an occasional
wink at him as well—as in the toilet and shrine scenes. Whereas
the hero in *Onna kyōshi* appeals to lofty sentiments in justifying his
love for the young schoolteacher, Tokio is preoccupied with his
lust. Whereas the hero in *Onna kyōshi* loses ultimately to propriety,
in the form of the schoolteacher's saintly concern for his wife, Tokio
loses to the prurient desires of the former theology student, Tanaka. The latter work's frenzied tone, moreover, recalls nothing so
much as an Edo-period *jōruri.* Indeed, *Futon* smacks of a Chika-

---

Katai's feminine ideal written in the years before *Futon.* In tracing the "transformation" of Katai's sentimental romanticism to naturalistic realism, Ogata notes the
unchanging pattern of supportive, intellectually stimulating, "modern" female
characters in Katai's writings.

    37. It is not so tentative, however, as to warrant the opinion of Nakamura Mi-
tsuo, who writes, in an unfavorable comparison with Goethe's *Werther* and Constant's *Adolphe,* that *Futon* distinguishes itself only by its complete lack of authorial
distance (*Fūzoku shōsetsu ron,* 44).

matsu domestic play, with its thematic linchpin of *giri-ninjō*, in which the protagonist agonizes interminably over whether to follow the dictates of social and/or familial obligation or of personal sentiment—except that Katai's farce is an inversion. Here the hero ends up following the dictates of social obligation (as Yoshiko's protector and mentor, in deference to Yoshiko's parents) instead of sentiment (as her potential lover) as is the case in a Chikamatsu play. To the last, Tokio struggles gallantly but awkwardly to save appearances. After turning Yoshiko over to her parents, he can only fling himself on his beloved's old quilt in a spasm of secret self-pity.

Thus, despite arguments to the contrary, *Futon* does not distinguish itself by its portrayal of individualistic consciousness. An indulgent narrator charts a course for his hero that leads paradoxically to the repression, rather than the affirmation, of self. The elusive *kindai jiga* is nowhere to be found. Having squelched personal desire, Tokio ends up supporting the social order (by opting for his role as guardian over the one as lover) and thus insures his estrangement from Yoshiko. The scenes in which Tokio asserts himself even tentatively end significantly in parody, as if to nip that assertion in the bud. Tokio's most aggressive form of behavior is drunkenness, a socially safe form of self-expression that predictably leads him no closer to his secret love than the toilet or the muddy shrine grounds. He asserts himself only through repressive acts. In this sense, at least, his vain, furtive shedding of tears into Yoshiko's quilt after the final separation is a fitting conclusion to a tale of sublimation.

The aesthetic or ideological failings of *Futon* by no means heralded an inauspicious beginning for the *shishōsetsu*, because literary excellence was not the primary criterion for judgment. The story brought to itself an unprecedented degree of critical attention (it was the subject in just the first month after publication of no fewer than thirteen reviews in two major literary magazines), most of which catalogued, with various degrees of outrage, the correspondences between literature and private life. Far greater than its importance as a literary text, then, was *Futon*'s role as catalyst; and it is here that its influence far exceeded that of *Heibon*, which Chikamatsu Shūkō shrewdly and perhaps correctly labeled the *shishōsetsu*'s true precursor. In an age preoccupied with cultural privatization and with a literature that privileged "philosophy" over style, *Futon* helped spawn a critical method that evaluated a text by how "faithfully" it depicted its author's life. In this sense, *Futon* is indeed the prototypical *shishōsetsu* and the *shishōsetsu* a distinct form, not because of any truly distinguishing characteristics but because readers attuned to the new literature, insisting on the referentiality of literary art, made the accurate description of the author's personal experience the supreme standard in their evaluations.

KATAI AND HŌMEI: "SURFACE" VERSUS "SINGLE-DIMENSIONAL" DESCRIPTION

Futon differs in one important respect from *shishōsetsu* to follow: Katai's narrator accommodates several points of view. Although focusing primarily on Tokio, the narrator presents freely if briefly the thoughts of Yoshiko, Yoshiko's father, Tokio's wife, and even a curious neighbor. Katai never felt compelled to restrict narrative perspective to that of the protagonist. Rather than strive for a unified point of view in his later works, he moved in the other direction, with the stated goal of adopting no point of view at all. This was the substance of his famous "surface description" (*heimen byōsha*); and *Futon*, although by far his best-known work, might profitably be characterized as no more than a dry run for works like *Sei* and *Inaka kyōshi* (The country teacher, 1909), which more successfully exemplified his technique. In "*Sei* ni okeru kokoromi" (1908), Katai claims to follow in the footsteps of the Goncourt brothers by championing a style that allows the narrator to treat all events and characters with the same degree of studied aloofness. Katai argues that his purpose in writing *Sei* was to describe accurately and dispassionately what he saw and heard and to avoid all interpretation of events and characters. "By refraining from petty, subjective interpretation and from analyses of phenomena about which I had no direct understanding, and by presenting my material in unaltered [*ari no mama*] form," he concludes, "I believed that my descriptions would actually come closer to the truth and would of themselves suggest the inner significance of things."[38]

---

38. *KBHT* 3:450. Katai's alleged debt to the Goncourt brothers should be viewed

In his effort to legitimize this narrative technique, Katai had important company. Shimazaki Tōson's first autobiographical text, *Haru* (1908), was being serialized in another newspaper at the same time as *Sei*. Tōson, whom Edwin McClellan argues was "as responsible as any single writer could be for the prevalence of the idea in Japan that the novel need not or should not be a creation of the dramatic imagination,"[39] also utilized in this and later writings an aloof narrator who makes little effort to probe his characters' minds. Katai was quick to recognize the similarity of their efforts and took note of Tōson's achievement in "*Sei* ni okeru kokoromi." The same dispassionate style, carried if anything to an even greater extreme in the writings of Tokuda Shūsei, prompted Natsume Sōseki, for one, to describe it disparagingly as an endless stream of words with no direction, no informing idea, no life.[40]

Katai, too, had his critics, most notably Iwano Hōmei, who argued that Katai's failure to invest his works with a specific point of view deprived them of meaning and interest.[41] Hōmei championed what he called "single-dimensional description" (*ichigen byōsha*), arguing that it avoided the epistemological pitfalls of Katai's technique. "There is no life outside the self," he asserts in one of his first major critical statements, "and literature is the product of the

---

as skeptically as that to Zola. Katai was no doubt familiar with the Goncourts' various pronouncements on the novelist's role as historian, including the following: "We passed through history to arrive at the novel. . . . On what basis does one write history? On the basis of documents. And the documents of the novel are life" (quoted in Richard B. Grant, *The Goncourt Brothers*, 30–31). But Katai apparently took no note of the Goncourts' concern with style and their awareness of the mediative powers of their form, which they argued could miraculously attract the reader's interest in "a human story that we know never took place" (ibid., 114). These self-styled clinicians of truth frequently acknowledged their aesthetic motivations: "Art for Art's sake, art which proves nothing, the music of ideas, the harmony of a sentence, that is our faith and our conscience" (ibid., 16). The Goncourts, then, never aspired to the "unaltered" transcription of life any more than Zola did.

39. "Tōson and the Autobiographical Novel," 348.
40. "Bundan no kono goro," in *Sōseki zenshū* 16:723–25.
41. Hōmei is an anomaly in Japanese letters. Although usually grouped with the naturalists, he was something of an outsider who relished his role as gadfly to the *bundan*. Like Mishima Yukio, he took as much, or more, pride in being a man of action as he did in being a man of letters. Confronted with failure at every turn in private life, from his business ventures to his relations with women, he celebrated his defeats in his writing, creating a hero who presided bellicosely over his own demise. After establishing his reputation as a fiction writer with *Tandeki*, which describes his liaison with a syphilitic geisha, he went on to produce a monumental, five-part account of his pursuit of wealth and love in Tokyo, Sakhalin, and Hokkaido (usually referred to as *Hōmei gobusaku*, 1910–18).

author's subjective tone or attitude. . . . A writer cannot hope to portray life conscientiously if he cuts himself off from his own subjectivity."[42] It is clear from the ironic dedication to Katai of his first anthology that Hōmei was conscious from the beginning of his polar position vis-à-vis the author of *Futon,* despite (by Hōmei's own admission) the latter's influence.[43] Nor was Hōmei alone in sensing this polarity. Major naturalist critics like Shimamura Hōgetsu and Hasegawa Tenkei saw Hōmei and Katai as embodying two divergent trends in the naturalist movement. Tenkei, for example, contrasted Hōmei's passionate, "self-revelatory" (*jiko kokuhaku*) style with Katai's aloof, "self-contemplative" (*jiko seikan*) style and argued that Hōmei's was a throwback to the romantic period while Katai's represented naturalism's true path.[44]

While his critics were dwelling on degrees of emotional distance between author and hero, Hōmei was concerning himself with the mechanics of representation. In an essay entitled, with typical immodesty, "Gendai shōrai no shōsetsuteki hassō o isshin subeki boku no byōsha ron" (My theory of writing, which will revolutionize thinking on the *shōsetsu,* present and future, 1918), he articulates his position on narrative.

> This is not a world in which we know everything about everyone else. All people and all things are actually reflections of our own minds. We reign as sovereigns over our private worlds and we allow no rights to others. . . . This said, let us consider what it means to be a writer. The author does not understand others as he understands himself. . . . It is impossible for him to be purely objective . . . and by trying to be so he irresponsibly takes a position only God can take. . . . I will use my subjectivity, not narrow-mindedly but to its fullest potential, to enter into the feelings of a single character, whether A or B or C. Just as we cannot know what another person thinks in real life, the author cannot know what B or C thinks if he has identified with the feelings of A. There is almost no one here or abroad who realizes this fact, except for myself and those who have fully digested my theory on this subject.[45]

42. "Gendai shōsetsu no byōsha hō" (1911), in *KBHT* 3:366.

43. See the preface to Hōmei's *Tandeki* (the anthology), in *Hōmei zenshū* 18:78–81.

44. "Jiko bunretsu to seikan" (1910), 207–9.

45. *KBHT* 5:88–90. For discussions of this essay and its place in Hōmei's critical project, see Yoshida Seiichi, *Shizenshugi no kenkyū* 2:449–60; Wada Kingo, *Byōsha no jidai,* esp. the chapters on Katai's "surface" and Hōmei's "single-dimensional" description, 103–72; and Noguchi Takehiko, *Shōsetsu no Nihongo,* 197–210.

In this and other writings, Hōmei never insists that the author re-strict his point of view to a character modeled after himself, only that he be consistent. It was the Taishō literary establishment that would go on to interpret Hōmei's definition of "single-dimensional description" in an even stricter sense than Hōmei himself had ever advocated: namely, that the author could do no better than to nar-rate lived experience from his own point of view.[46]

Yet Hōmei presents here something rather close to what would emerge as the mainstream *junbungaku* worldview (even though he portrays himself as the lone voice of reason in a critical wilder-ness—encouraged, to be sure, by a literary establishment that took him only half-seriously).[47] That is surely why he aroused the ire of *junbungaku* opponents. Ikuta Chōkō, for example, whose critique of the *shishōsetsu* we noted in Chapter 3, argued that however much Hōmei's thesis held true for works of a confessional nature (diaries, travel essays, autobiographies, etc.), in which a single point of view was most convincing, it had no bearing on fictional works, which appropriately might have several protagonists and several points of view. The "best" method of representation, Ikuta concluded, was simply the one that best suited a particular writer.[48] The philoso-pher and critic Tsuchida Kyōson (1891–1934), continuing the at-tack, insisted that Hōmei was on extremely shaky epistemological ground when he argued that the author's perceptual world over-lapped the protagonist's. Tsuchida's Kantian system divided the world into two categories of perception—the things, people, and other "objects" (*taishō*) in nature that exist independent of each in-

46. Hōmei stressed in many of his essays that the point of view need not be the author's own. Among his own writings, the group of stories published near the end of his life focusing on a character named Ōsei are examples of this. (See, for in-stance, *Ōsei no shippai* [1920], which chronicles the heroine's loss of her boarding-house to a wily carpenter on whom she has naively relied to make improvements. [*Iwano Hōmei zenshū* 8:387–488]) Hōmei also insists in the face of repeated attacks that the hero, even when modeled after the author, should not be equated with the author himself. See Wada, *Byōsha no jidai*, 132 and 136, for extracts of his protesta-tions, of which Wada himself seems skeptical. Noguchi Takehiko, meanwhile, ar-gues that Hōmei was more successful than Katai or Tōson at transforming his per-sonae into autonomous characters. See *Shōsetsu no Nihongo*, 204–9.

47. Ino Kenji, in his study of Meiji writers, notes that Chikamatsu Shūkō aligned himself solidly with Hōmei against the likes of Hōgetsu and Katai on the issue of narrative perspective and suggests that it was Shūkō and not Katai who, as heir to Hōmei's narrative theory, fixed the *shishōsetsu*'s course. See *Meiji no sakka*, 401.

48. "Iwano Hōmei shi no byōsha ron" (1918), in *KBHT* 5:97–100.

dividual's apprehension of them as images, and "subjects" (*naiyō*) in need of an "I" to see them—and he claimed that Hōmei made no distinction between the two.[49] Both reached the same conclusion: to argue as Hōmei did that "this is not a world in which we know everything about everyone else" and that "all people and all things are actually reflections of our own minds" was, in a literary context at least, the height of naïveté.[50]

Hōmei's "naïveté," however, was characteristic of a great many Taishō writers who, while making no pronouncements of their own, adhered to the tenets Hōmei set forth. Ikuta and Tsuchida's condemnations notwithstanding, Hōmei had an unerring sense for the mode of narrative presentation that would triumph in the Taishō era. In essence, he was championing what we identified in Chapter 2 as the written reportive style. Hōmei's critics correctly pointed out its constraints, but they underestimated the enormous power it held over the Taishō literary community. Hōmei's theory helped legitimize the *shishōsetsu*'s mode of presentation to the extent that it came to be regarded as "natural," and finally transparent.

A few years after Hōmei's death, Katai conceded in his memoir *Kindai no shōsetsu* (*Shōsetsu* in the modern era) that Hōmei's "single-dimensional description" was, in principle, the ideal to which literature should aspire and that the truly great writers utilized just such a technique.[51] Such a concession on Katai's part was probably less a shift in his own position than an acknowledgment of the *shishōsetsu*'s dominance in the early 1920s. Given the popularity by this time of first-person narration and the critical insistence on the equation of author and hero, the Jamesian-style narrative that focused on a single character distinct from both author and narrator never became the dominant mode in Taishō letters. Even though Hōmei had some success (as did Tokuda Shūsei and of course Natsume Sōseki) in building a narrative around a character not modeled after himself, the Taishō literary establishment took far less interest in works to which the author-hero formula could not be applied.

49. "Iwayuru ichigenteki byōsha o ronzu" (1918), in ibid., 101–6.
50. Ibid., 100, 101.
51. In *Tayama Katai zenshū* 17:357.

6

The *Bundan:*
Readers, Writers, Critics

I really get the feeling that your reading . . . is based on a
knowledge of, and a sympathy for, the author's private life.
Chiba Kameo, in a roundtable discussion

I simply could not force myself to become more intimate
with society merely in order to write stories that any young
girl would then be able to understand.
Tayama Katai, in a roundtable discussion

The *shishōsetsu* so dominated the Taishō literary world that the
phrase "Taishō literature" (*Taishō bungaku*) now connotes its heyday. This phenomenon was due in no small measure to the rise of
the *bundan*. The existence of a literary subculture in which writers
came to associate with one another more as social acquaintances
than as artists and which encouraged gossip about one's peers, by
word of mouth and ultimately in print, contributed immensely to
the critical consciousness of the *shishōsetsu* as being uniquely true
to life and therefore the only *shōsetsu* form of any importance in
Taishō letters. Although it would be wrong to isolate the *bundan* as
the *shishōsetsu's* sole formative element when we have already
linked several significant literary, linguistic, and intellectual factors
to its inception, there is no doubt that it played a crucial role in
legitimizing critical focus on the writer's life as much as on his
writings. In such a climate, the writer freely assumed readers'
familiarity with—and curiosity about—the details of his personal
life, and publishers actively solicited stories that exploited this
curiosity.

Although the *bundan* in its broadest sense includes any person
or coterie active in the literary world, it is used here in its more
restricted sense to include only those writers, critics, and publishers associated with what is commonly called *junbungaku*, or "pure"

(i.e., confessional or autobiographical) literature, as opposed to *taishū bungaku*, or "popular" literature. The distinction between "pure" and "popular" is almost certainly a carryover from the Edo-period dichotomy, noted in Chapter 1, between the nonfictional literature of edification and the fictional "nonliterature" of entertainment, bolstered by the naturalist school's stress on lived experience as the only legitimate source on which the author could draw. It was also intimately related, surely, to the values of a select as opposed to a mass audience.

The *bundan*, in the narrow usage considered here, was a product of three crucial trends that came together during the Taishō period: the literary journal's emergence as the "pure literature" writer's single most important medium, the popularity of shorter works, and a camaraderie among writers nurtured by physical proximity, social alienation, and contemporary journalistic demands. These trends were so pervasive and intimately related that they became self-perpetuating and often transcended their status as mere professional realities, with which an author had to cope in the process of writing a story, to become a central theme *in* a story. (We shall see this theme explored to its fullest extent in our discussion of Kasai Zenzō.) And since literary purity was measured in terms of how closely the author adhered to the details of his personal life, a writer had a good deal of motivation to model his characters after his acquaintances, for example, or to cite his previous stories (as Uno does in *Amaki yo no hanashi*, quoted in Chapter 1), or even to refer self-consciously to the very manuscript which he was then writing. These factors in turn provided the *bundan* audience, composed largely of writers and would-be writers, with a powerful incentive to read and criticize stories entirely on a referential level.

At the heart of the *bundan*'s raison d'être is the *junbungaku* writer's elitist consciousness, born of common education (most writers went to universities, typically Tokyo or Waseda or Gakushūin, before launching their literary careers), geography (Tokyo, the hub of cultural activity, was the home or adopted home of virtually every *junbungaku* writer), and aloofness from a society that generally took a dim view of the writer's profession. Traditional social prejudice against the writer of "nonliterary" fiction (*gesaku*) worked, as we have seen, against the early twentieth-century *shōsetsu* writer as well. The authors of "pure literature" believed that their writing was not "fiction" in the sense that popular literature was, since they, too, were imbued with this prejudice. But society as a whole (i.e., non-*bundan* society) was less inclined to distinguish one kind of writer from another. In an achievement-oriented world that paid special reverence to university graduates, who were expected to pursue socially useful careers, writers, with few exceptions, were second-class citizens. Mori Ōgai earned respect as a man of letters largely because he had already distinguished himself in the medical profession. And Masamune Hakuchō suggests that Natsume Sō-seki's reputation as a scholar helped sell his novels. (Sōseki had been a lecturer at Tokyo Imperial University before joining the staff of the Tokyo newspaper *Asahi* in 1907 as editor of the newspaper's literary page.)[1] Hakuchō and his naturalist colleagues, meanwhile, met with little commercial success, in part because their many stories set in the provinces did not appeal to an urban audience but also because of the traditional view of the "fiction" writer as an outsider or outcast.

Just what constitutes an "outsider" is of course in itself problematic, but it depends at the very least on the existence of an "insider." Kawakami Tetsutarō defines insiders as those established intellectuals who maintain the orthodox system of thought; he suggests that modern Japan has had no orthodox, traditional system (such as Neo-Confucianism in Tokugawa Japan) to which an intellectual could ally himself, and thus no true insiders. The most likely candidate for an "orthodox" system of thought in post-Restoration Japan, Kawakami argues, was the utilitarian philosophy, with its emphasis on success and service to the state. By this standard, at least, the man of letters—whose very act of writing, when not clearly utilitarian in intent, was considered antisocial in Meiji and Taishō Japan—was very much an "outsider."[2] This common view of the writer manifested itself even at the level of daily life. One writer reported to his friends in astonishment that he was willingly let a house even after he had defiantly announced his calling to the landlord—rare treatment then for one of his kind because of his low social and economic status.[3]

1. *Shizenshugi seisui ki,* in *Masamune Hakuchō zenshū* 11:308–9.
2. *Nihon no autosaidā,* 11–12 and 206–7.
3. The writer was Hirotsu Kazuo. See Ōkubo Fusao, "Bundan ni tsuite," in *Bun-*

The *junbungaku* writer's career revolved, at least at the beginning, around his coterie and its publication, known as a *dōjin* (or
dōnin) *zasshi,* which catered to a small and homogeneous audience.
Unlike contemporary coterie magazines, which often have a na-
tionwide membership, the Taishō magazines were very exclusive
and their memberships defined by mutual acquaintance and common purpose, a fact that resulted both in fast friendships and bitter
infighting.[4] Kasai Zenzō, for example, published his earlier stories
in one such coterie magazine, *Kiseki,* which he and his Waseda
University colleagues put out monthly from September 1912 to
May 1913. *Kiseki* was but one of several dozen *dōjin zasshi* appearing at the time. Although most were quite short-lived, they made
up the Taishō *bundan's* lifeblood. Shiga Naoya established his career
by his many contributions to a *dōjin zasshi* called *Shirakaba,* which
was one of the most successful. The coterie magazines, edited and
distributed by the contributors themselves, provided an ideal vehicle for the aspiring young author who lacked a name but possessed the boundless energy needed to publish a magazine on a
shoestring budget. Coterie members were plagued by a lack of
funds, and the attrition rate was high; a typical magazine lasted
perhaps a dozen issues. *Kiseki* (1912–13), for example, had 9 issues; the first four and by far the most significant series of *Shinshi-
chō* (1907–17) had anywhere from 6 to 11; *Ningen* (1919–22) had 24.
There were exceptions to this law of evanescence, the most notable
being *Shirakaba.* A total of 160 issues appeared from April 1910
to August 1923. Its longevity was due in large measure to its
strong financial backing and to the contributing members' relative
affluence.[5]

Printings of most *dōjin zasshi* were in the very few hundreds, or
less. Only a smattering of copies were sold at bookstores on consignment; the majority were distributed gratis to important literary
figures in hopes of catching their attention.[6] The *Kiseki* group

shi to bundan, 243. In the same book, Ōkubo notes the literati's growing social prestige and affluence since the war ("Bundan no sengo," 163–234).
    4. See Yamamoto Kenkichi, "Dōjin zasshi hyō," 177–78, for a general
description.
    5. Chikamatsu Shūkō was the only writer discussed in Part 3 who never be-
longed to a coterie. He began his career as a critic, writing in newspapers like the
Yomiuri, before starting to write fiction.
    6. Ibuse Masuji, in a conversation held on 1 March 1985, recalled that the strat-

printed two hundred copies of their first issue and placed one hundred of these in bookstores like Kinokuniya on consignment sale. The twenty-eight copies that actually sold, however, are said to have been bought in twos and threes by the *dōjin zasshi* members themselves in an effort to save appearances.[7] Again, the exception is *Shirakaba*, whose monthly circulation numbered in the thousands and peaked at well over ten thousand around 1920. Its broad appeal as a magazine of the arts helped insure the popularity of its major contributors: Arishima Takeo (1878–1923), Mushanokōji Saneatsu (1885–1976), and Shiga Naoya.[8]

By the time a coterie magazine had folded, however, some of its contributors would have made enough of a name for themselves to be invited to write for the more prestigious literary and commercial magazines, which included *Shinshōsetsu* (1889–1950, with interruptions), *Chūōkōron* (1899–present), *Shinchō* (1904–present), *Kaihō* (1919–33), and *Kaizō* (1919–55). Fully half of Kasai's fiction (roughly forty stories), for example, appeared in these five magazines; the rest is scattered in some thirty other periodicals. Perhaps a third of Shūkō's nearly two hundred stories appeared in these same magazines, and a good many more in *Bunshō sekai* (1906–20), one of the naturalist movement's strongholds; *Waseda bungaku* (1891–present, with interruptions), one of the great university-supported magazines along with Keiō University's *Mita bungaku* (1910–present, with interruptions); and *Bungei shunjū* (1925–present), a well-known general-interest magazine, which began as a literary magazine. Shiga emerged as a major literary figure with the publication of *Ōtsu Junkichi* in *Chūōkōron* in 1912, and he serialized his crowning achievement, *An'ya kōro* (1921–37), in the pages of *Kaizō*.

Most readers of *dōjin zasshi* and of all but the largest literary magazines were writers and would-be writers themselves, nearly all of whom lived in or near Tokyo. Precise figures are hard to come

---

egy used to catch the influential critic's eye in his early *dōjin-zasshi* days (late Taishō–early Shōwa) was to send the magazines by registered mail. See also Ibuse, "Dōjin zasshi no koro," 222–24.

7. Kōno Toshirō, "*Kiseki* kaisetsu," 13.

8. See the entries in *NKBD*, vol. 5, on the various magazines in question. The information on *Shirakaba* circulations is gleaned from a personal correspondence (12 Feb. 1985) from Miyazaka Eiichi, the magazine's last editor.

by, but the circulation of a purely literary magazine like *Shinchō* in early to mid-Taishō is thought to have ranged from three to five thousand. Magazines like *Kaizō* and *Kaihō,* which also catered to literary audiences, had circulations of around thirty to forty thousand in 1920. Only *Chūōkōron,* far and away the largest general-interest magazine, could boast a circulation of over a hundred thousand at this time.[9]

This high concentration of writers in Tokyo bred familiarity on a social as well as a professional level. The major literary magazines, moreover, served as clearing houses of information and gossip about writers. They also served as forums: published interviews with writers and roundtable discussions between writers and critics provided an inexhaustible supply of literary grist. Writers, therefore, sharing not merely the pages of the same magazines but also frequently participating in the same roundtable discussions, were in constant contact with one another and held few secrets. Rare was the *bundan* critic, therefore, who failed to note the correspondences between a story and what he knew of its author. In the following panel-discussion excerpt, we see how the discussion of a short story ("Isan," 1924) quickly gravitates toward its author, Kasai Zenzō.

CHIBA KAMEO: Why must one criticize the author's life as well as his writing? . . . Can't one simply criticize the writing itself?

NAKAMURA MURAO: I didn't say I know anything about Kasai's private life. But after reading the story, I can see how he has woven the complex emotions of his life into every phrase.

CHIBA: I really get the feeling that your reading of Kasai is based on a knowledge of, and a sympathy for, the author's private life.

SATOMI TON: I think Nakamura's reading is merely based on what you yourself referred to as "common knowledge" that circulates around the *bundan.*

9. The figures are based on the following sources: Hirano Ken and Matsumoto Seichō, "Watakushi shōsetsu to honkaku shōsetsu," 133; Dōmeki Kyōsaburō, *Shinchōsha hachijū nen shōshi,* 14; Yokoyama Haruichi, *Kaizō mokuji sōran sōmokuji,* 11; and Maeda Ai, *Kindai dokusha no seiritsu,* 173. See also Yokozeki Aizō, *Watakushi no zakki chō,* esp. 5–9, for further information on circulations and on the *bundan* in general.

NAKAMURA: I read this story as an autonomous piece but
           got through it a sense of the author's character
           and way of life. . . .

CHIBA: Doesn't Nakamura get that sense because of
           what he already knows about Kasai through
           gossip or hearsay?

KUME MASAO: That's the question, isn't it![10]

Nakamura Murao's claim that he read "Isan" as an autonomous text of fiction in effect goes unsubstantiated. Like nearly every critic of the age, he reads a text in such a way that knowledge of the author's private life becomes essential to its understanding. It follows, then, that Nakamura would say of Kasai, in another discussion: "What makes [Kasai's] stories interesting is the writer himself. They may not be so interesting to readers who don't know him, though." [11] Here again, private life is seen as the Ur-text of pure literature.

Although literary magazines reached their zenith in the mid-Taishō period, daily newspapers like the *Tokyo Asahi* and the *Yomiuri* were also an important medium for prose writers through the end of Meiji and early Taishō. One of their greatest contributions was serial publication. Many of the naturalist writers' longer works first appeared in the major dailies: Tayama Katai's *Sei* (*Yomiuri*, 1908), *Tsuma* (*Nihon*, 1908–9), and *En* (*Mainichi shinpō*, 1910); Shimazaki Tōson's *Haru* (Tokyo *Asahi*, 1908), *Ie*, part 1 (*Yomiuri*, 1910), and *Shinsei* (*Asahi*, 1918–19); Tokuda Shūsei's *Kabi* (*Asahi*, 1911) and *Arakure* (*Yomiuri*, 1915). (The *Asahi* also published all of Natsume Sōseki's fiction from mid-1907 until his death in 1916.)

It is difficult to understand why newspapers would have an interest in publishing some of these authors (who, however important to literary history, had only a small following) unless we realize that the newspapers themselves did not enjoy anything close to the mass audience that they do today. Although all the major dailies now boast circulations in the many millions, they served a far more elite clientele until mid-Taishō or later, as Table 1 shows.

Papers like the *Asahi*, *Tōkyo nichi nichi*, *Jiji shinpō*, and the *Yomiuri* appealed to a highly literate audience and devoted far greater space to literary matters than any of the major papers do today. Let us

10. *Kasai Zenzō zenshū bekkan*, 410. Originally published in *Shinchō*, Mar. 1924.
11. Ibid., 408.

Table 1.   Circulations of Major Tokyo Dailies

Newspaper	1905	1910	1915	1920	1925
Yomiuri (1874–)	40,000	30,000	70,000	100,000	90,000
Tōkyō nichi nichi (1872–1943)	30,000	70,000	230,000	350,000	600,000
Jiji shinpō (1882–1936)	60,000	40,000	70,000	100,000	350,000
Asahi (1888–)	100,000	110,000	130,000	250,000	420,000
Kokumin (1890–1942)	70,000	130,000	190,000	200,000	230,000
Yorozu chōhō (1892–1940)	160,000	150,000	100,000	120,000	90,000

Sources: Yamamoto Fumio, *Nihon Shinbun hattatsu shi*, 199–200, 290–92, and passim; Sōma Motoi, *Tōnichi nanajū nen shi*, 360; Yamamoto Taketoshi, *Kindai Nihon no shinbun dokusha sō*, 410–12; Mori Masamichi, ed., *Shinbun hanbai gaishi*, 115; Shashi Hensan Iinkai, ed., *Mainichi shinbun nanajū nen*, passim; and Yomiuri Shinbun Hyaku Nen Shi Henshū Iinkai, ed., *Yomiuri shinbun hyaku nen shi bessatsu*, front foldout. See also the entries on the various papers in *NKBD*, vol. 5, and on *shinbun shōsetsu* in *NKBD* 4:242–44. Some of the figures are rough estimates. Numbers are rounded off to the nearest 10,000.

examine the one that devoted the most space to literature: the *Yomiuri*.[12] In early Taishō it, like most other papers, was only eight pages long. Page 1 of our randomly chosen 4 May 1914 issue is dominated by two serials, plus the daily editorial. Political and international news is relegated to page 2; local and cultural news, to page 7. Page 3 includes a travel essay and an installment of translated literature. Two critical essays appear on page 4 and two more on page 5, along with a long poem in the "new style." An installment of still another *shōsetsu* appears on page 6, and of a historical tale told in the old *kōdan* style on page 8. All this—plus the usual assortment of haiku, tanka, senryu, and reviews. In addition to publishing fiction and criticism by professional authors, the *Yomiuri* held competitions in various categories for aspiring writers. The paper advertised its first short-story competition during May 1914, and the prize-winning story appeared in the 8 June issue, complete

12. See Ikegami Kenji, "*Yomiuri shinbun* to Tayama Katai," for an analysis of the importance of the *Yomiuri* as a literary organ in mid- to late Meiji.

with the judges' critiques in a format anticipating the Akutagawa and Naoki prizes begun by *Bungei shunjū* in 1935.

"*Yomiuri* bundan" (page 4), a regular feature, always contained one or two essays, reviews, or travel pieces by well-known authors. Newspaper photos are still rare in this period (averaging only about one per page), yet one often finds a commemorative photograph of a gathering of writers at some restaurant or publishing house. But the most remarkable item on this page is a daily column called "*Yomiuri* shō" (*Yomiuri* notes), which kept readers up to date on recent and future publications as well as the activities of the nation's major writers. On 3 May 1914, for instance, we learn that a volume of essays by Shimamura Hōgetsu has gone through the final proofs and now awaits publication by Shinchōsha. On the sixth, we learn that a two-hundred-page manuscript by Iwano Hōmei will appear at long last in the June issue of *Chūōkōron*. On the nineteenth, we learn that *Shinchō*'s May issue has been taken off the market by authorities, the victim of official censorship. On the twentieth, we learn that Hōgetsu's above-mentioned volume of essays was published the previous day. Throughout the last week of May the column lists articles and stories (including Hōmei's) that have appeared in the major literary magazines' latest issues.[13]

The activities of Chikamatsu Shūkō, already an established writer by this time, are faithfully reported. We learn that he will publish a short story entitled "Haru no yukue" in the June issue of *Bunshō sekai* (5 May). He leaves Nara, his first stop on a provincial tour, on the fourth for Dōgo Spa in Shikoku (8 May) and later returns to his home in Bizen (Okayama) for a brief visit (18 May). On the nineteenth he moves to Kyoto and lodges at a boarding house (22 May). The column dutifully notes his address. Finally, on 5 June, Shūkō boards the 9:00 A.M. express for Tokyo (7 June). Shūkō himself reports on his travels in a number of articles appearing on the same literary page. In "Ryojin" (Dusty road, 18 May), he describes his journey from Tokyo to Nara, and in "Bunraku-za yori"

13. Thanks to Professor Sasaki Yasuaki of Ibaragi University for introducing this fascinating column. A similar but less detailed column appears in *Jiji shinpō* ("Bungei shōsoku") and also in the major literary magazines like *Shinshōsetsu, Shinchō, Waseda bungaku,* and *Bunshō sekai,* although the latter could not compete with the dailies for timeliness and comprehensiveness.

(From the Bunraku Theater, 8 June), he writes further about his sojourn in the Kansai area. Read together, *"Yomiuri* shō" and the articles provide thorough coverage of Shūkō's movements. The latter, in the popular travelogue style, rewards the curiosity that the former has piqued.[14]

Since coverage of Shūkō represents only a fraction of the total, it is easy to imagine from this sampling the tremendous reader interest in even the most peripheral literary matters. The writer lived the life of a celebrity, although on a much smaller and more intimate scale than the word implies today, and virtually any activity was considered "news." That his "personal" life (e.g., travels, boardinghouse addresses) was just as newsworthy as his "professional" life (e.g., writing, publication plans) reminds us once again of the general disinclination to distinguish between the two. In his readers' eyes (and no doubt in his own), the writer comported himself necessarily as writer in everything he did. Being an author was by definition a twenty-four-hour-a-day occupation—not simply a livelihood, but a way of life.

Ironically, it was when the newspapers began commanding truly sizable audiences (circulations of most major dailies had reached the hundreds of thousands by the end of Taishō) that their literary significance declined. As circulations increased, literary editors looked for authors with broader appeal, forcing *junbungaku* writers to turn to the literary magazine as their principal medium. "Forcing" may be the wrong word, given the *bundan* writer's elitist consciousness. There are stories of *bundan* literati who in some cases did not wish to appear even in the same magazine with a writer who was thought to have made concessions to "popular" tastes. Akutagawa Ryūnosuke, for example, himself a victim throughout his career of critical attacks against his tendency to "invent" stories rather than tell the "truth" about his own life, once refused to have a story published in the same issue of *Chūōkōron* with Muramatsu

14. A passage in Shūkō's *Giwaku zokuhen* (1913) gives us an idea of the monitoring function of this and similar columns. The story's narrator-hero is surprised to learn from a maid at the Nikkō inn where he is lodging that his former wife, whom he has not seen in years, knew that he was in Nikkō and had inquired about him when she arrived. "How did she know that I was here?" he muses. "She must have read about me in the newspapers. She obviously checks up on me every chance she gets" (*CSS*, 59).

Shōfū (1889–1961), a very popular (and very lowbrow, in Akuta-gawa's opinion) writer of historical fiction.[15]

One of the victims of this popularization of newspaper *shōsetsu* was Tayama Katai. A pioneer along with Shimazaki Tōson of a rad-ically new kind of serialized fiction that seemed devoid of any concession to reader interest, Katai saw his own popularity decline as the literary audience of the expanding dailies grew more diffuse. His rationalization of his position is worthy of any *bundan* writer in its disdain for the nonliterati:

> I had believed that if I only knew more about society as a whole, I could write stories with greater popular appeal. I tried, and I failed . . . and I ultimately abandoned the attempt. I simply could not force myself to become more intimate with society merely in order to write stories that any young girl would then be able to un-derstand. I feared that I would end up sacrificing my art in the at-tempt. And that frightened me.[16]

Beginning in late Taishō, Katai published an increasing num-ber of his serialized *shōsetsu* in the less high-powered provincial dailies.

Thus, the literary magazine became the Taishō *junbungaku* writ-er's mainstay. Fees were low, however, and even frequent publica-tion in the more influential magazines did not provide a sufficient income, although it did enhance a writer's reputation. (Nakamura Murao writes in 1925 that a literary magazine like *Shinchō*, with a circulation of barely ten thousand, could afford to pay a writer only seven or eight yen per page, while women's and entertainment magazines, with circulations in the hundreds of thousands, paid writers twenty to thirty yen per page.)[17] *Kaizō* editor Yokozeki Aizō recalls that "Kura no naka" (1919), for example, earned its author Uno Kōji instant recognition and numerous solicitations from lit-erary magazines but no appreciable change in living arrangements. Uno shared his quarters with another writer and usually had only enough money to buy a one- or two-day supply of rice at a time.[18] No early Taishō-period writer—not even the likes of Sōseki or

15. *NKBD* 4:476d.
16. Tayama Katai et al., "Shinchō gappyōkai," 59.
17. "Bungei zasshi no koto," in *Bundan zuihitsu*, 112.
18. *Watakushi no zakki chō*, 8–9.

Tōson—could afford his own home, aside from certain independently wealthy "Mita School" and "Shirakaba School" writers, who inherited theirs. (Tayama Katai, a rare exception, managed to build a small house in the suburbs in late Meiji.) Writing, even full-time writing, was not a money-making proposition. Since most writers had little to live on, they commonly took advances, and it was the policy of most literary magazines to offer them freely in order to encourage—or prod—writers into producing manuscripts.[19]

Nor could most writers count on book royalties to supplement their income by any substantial amount. A first printing often numbered in the mere hundreds of copies, and a famous author did well to sell at the very most one or two thousand copies in this period. Even Sōseki's books sold only a few thousand copies in their initial years of printing.[20]

The best way to grasp the scale of the bookselling business in late-Meiji and Taishō Japan is to review the admittedly scanty data on sales of that period's most popular works. *Hakai* (1906), which catapulted Shimazaki Tōson (then known only as a poet) into the ranks of leading fiction writers, met with extraordinary success. The first private printing of fifteen hundred copies sold out almost immediately, and within a year ten thousand copies had been sold. This not-enormous figure was virtually unprecedented for its time. We have already noted the sensation that Tayama Katai's *Futon* created. When it first appeared in book form (in a collection of Katai's stories entitled *Katai shū*, 1908), it went through seven printings in six months, which seems remarkable until one realizes that each printing after the first most likely numbered only in the hundreds.[21]

The data on Natsume Sōseki's books are of considerable interest, because they bring home to us the limits of success that one could expect as a writer in the early to mid-Taishō period. Sōseki was far

19. Ibid. See also Nakamura Murao, *Meiji Taishō no bungakusha*, 47–48 and passim, for useful information on the *bundan*.

20. Nakamura Mitsuo, "Taishō bungaku no seikaku," in *Nakamura Mitsuo zenshū* 7:503.

21. The figures on printings are gleaned from Senuma Shigeki, *Hon no hyaku nen shi*, 123–28. *Hototogisu* (1898–99), the most widely read book of the Meiji period, sold just nine thousand copies in its first year but eventually sold a half-million copies over a twenty-five-year period. *Konjiki yasha* (1897–1903) also sold extremely well, but Senuma offers no concrete figures. See ibid., 77–84.

and away the most popular writer of his time; yet his books hardly made him a wealthy man. Matsuoka Yuzuru (1891–1969), Sōseki's son-in-law and an author in his own right, compiled figures on most of Sōseki's books and surmises that sales of all books during Sōseki's own lifetime (from the publication of *Wagahai wa neko de aru* in 1905 to his death in 1916) totaled perhaps one hundred thousand copies, or roughly ten thousand a year, and that sales of his four most popular works—*Neko, Botchan* (1906), *Kusamakura* (1906), and *Gubijinsō* (1908)—accounted for fully half the total.[22] The first printings of books for which reliable figures are available generally numbered only two to three thousand, and later printings only a few hundred. Sales did not pick up substantially until the appearance of popular editions late in the author's life; then they rose dramatically with his death.

Sōseki could command higher royalties than most: 15 percent for the first printing (after the first 130 copies), 20 percent for the second through fifth printings and 30 percent thereafter. These terms, gleaned from a contract drawn up by Shun'yōdō, Sōseki's principal publisher, apply specifically to *Uzurakago* (1906), Sōseki's second through fifth printings, and 30 percent thereafter. These terms, gleaned from a contract drawn up by Shun'yōdō, Sōseki's apparently good enough to arouse the jealousy of other writers. Nagata Mikihiko (1887–1964) recalls that Chikamatsu Shūkō became infuriated when he learned that Sōseki's share reached 31 percent. "I don't care how famous he is," he complained to Nagata, "that's highway robbery!"[24]

And yet, although the royalties attest to Sōseki's popularity, they did not bring him great wealth. His annual salary from the *Asahi* was three thousand yen, but his contract with the newspaper forbade him publication in other periodicals. Royalties of perhaps another two thousand yen on book sales brought his income to a total of around five thousand yen.[25] This was by no means a large sum, compared to what could be made in other professions.

---

22. *Sōseki no inzei chō,* 11. See the tables on pp. 6–17.
23. Ibid., 24–25. Matsuoka reports that Shun'yōdō eased the terms in later years, reducing the number of first-printing copies and thereby increasing the chances for further printings and higher royalty shares.
24. *Bungō no sugao,* 148–49.
25. Matsuoka, *Sōseki no inzei chō,* 26.

It was not until the beginning of Shōwa and the advent of the inexpensive *enpon* ("one-yen book") that *junbungaku* writers gained some degree of affluence. The appearance of these cheap anthologies, each featuring one or more writers and costing as much as a taxi ride (*entaku*), greatly increased sales, readership, and writers' revenues. Kaizōsha (the publisher of *Kaizō*) launched the *enpon* phenomenon with *Gendai Nihon bungaku zenshū* (1926–29), a thirty-eight-volume collection of modern Japanese literature that sold 380,000 copies, an astronomical figure for the times. Twenty-five more volumes were soon added to the set. Shun'yōdō, a rival publishing house, immediately followed suit with the fifty-volume *Meiji Taishō bungaku zenshū* (1927–32), which sold 100,000 copies. Shinchōsha extended the *enpon* frontier to world literature, and its thirty-eight-volume *Sekai bungaku zenshū* (1927–30) sold a half-million copies. In all, some two hundred collections were published in the early years of Shōwa alone. *Enpon*-based revenues may have been the single most important factor in dissipating the elitist, guild consciousness of the *bundan* writer and in integrating him into commercial society. Having become a much more broadly based and businesslike institution, *bundan* no longer had quite the same connotations in Shōwa Japan.[26]

Despite the growing number of books, the *shishōsetsu* author wrote few full-length stories, and his books were usually collections of previously published short stories. Although writers in the west have generally made their reputation on book-length fiction, the serious writer's career in Japan, especially in Taishō Japan, depended absolutely on publication of short fiction in the major literary magazines.[27] The typical *junbungaku* writer was a short-story writer: Kasai, of course, and Shūkō (although the latter's stories were frequently of novella length), as well as more famous contemporaries like Shiga and Akutagawa Ryūnosuke. Even a long-winded writer like Tokuda Shūsei had earned a solid reputation as a short-story writer by mid-Taishō. "In our age," one critic laments

26. Suzuki Haruo, "Enpon to bungaku zenshū." The sales figures are derived from Senuma, *Hon no hyaku nen shi*, 171–79; and Yokozeki, *Watakushi no zakki chō*, 6.
27. See Nakamura Mitsuo, "Bungaku zasshi to zasshi bungaku," in *Nakamura Mitsuo zenshū* 7:366–67. Masamune Hakuchō states flatly that he could not have written fiction had the magazine format not been available to him. "Watakushi shōsetsu no miryoku," in *Masamune Hakuchō zenshū* 7:378.

in a roundtable discussion (*Shinchō*, March 1925), "most *bundan*-oriented criticism, since it appears in the monthly literary magazines, passes over full-length stories in complete silence."[28] Kasai Zenzō's condescending description in *Funōsha* (1919) of long fiction well illustrates the *bundan's* belief that extended prose was by definition flaccid, unwieldy, and inartistic:

> I'm going to do my darnedest to be more productive. And I'm going to try my hand at long fiction, too. There is nothing wrong with this homely, horse-faced creature. It is no freak. Its features are all in the right place; they simply aren't arranged in the most becoming manner. And if people let you get away with writing it, I don't see why I too shouldn't give it a try.[29]

Long stories or short, the editors of the major literary magazines did not sit idly and wait for manuscripts to trickle in. They actively solicited material from writers, with the result that they devoted more of their energies to enforcing deadlines than to providing stylistic guidelines.[30] In addition to offering advances on fees, editors often sent writers to a hot spring or mountain retreat in the hope that an out-of-the-way setting would be more conducive to creativity than the bustling city. This strategy frequently backfired, however, especially when tried on the likes of Kasai Zenzō. In an absorbing account of numerous Taishō-period authors, Yokozeki Aizō tells how he sent Kasai to a spa in the mountains of Shinshū in May 1919 to write a story (*Funōsha*) for his magazine. Kasai, however, proceeded to spend not only his advance but also his entire manuscript fee and more on drink and geisha, forcing the inn to hold him hostage until Kume Masao arrived with additional funds in the form of a second advance from another publishing house. Both writers then proceeded to spend the "ransom" money

28. The critic is Kanō Sakujirō (1885–1941), and the discussion can be found in *KZZ, bekkan:* 432.

29. *KZZ*, 1:331.

30. Yokozeki Aizō, *Kaizō's* first editor, recalls that the magazine could never get enough from certain writers and was constantly pressing them for manuscripts of any sort to satisfy a devoted readership. The most sought-after *junbungaku* writers in the magazine's early days (which is to say the early 1920s) were Akutagawa Ryūnosuke, Mushanokōji Saneatsu, and two of the writers under study here, Shiga Naoya and Kasai Zenzō. (This information was gleaned from a conversation held on 20 February 1985 with the Kasai scholar Ōmori Sumio, who interviewed Yokozeki before his death.)

on more drink and geisha and had to be bailed out by yet another messenger. Kasai did not return to Tokyo until September. The example may be extreme, but it was apparently not unusual.[31] One of Kasai's stories ("Furō," 1921) describes a similar situation in which the writer travels to a seaside resort on borrowed money only to spend the entire sum and more before his creative juices begin to flow.

When an author had become fairly well established, it mattered little what he wrote; and thanks to the short-fiction format, he could satisfy a schedule-conscious editor with an open-ended story or a string of impressionistic musings, the full implications of which might be accessible only to those readers who, like members of a secret society, were already quite familiar with the author's previous work. Sōma Taizō (1885–1952), for example, a member of the *Kiseki* group along with Kasai Zenzō, Hirotsu Kazuo (1891–1968), and Tanizaki Seiji (1890–1971), could write an "open letter" to a penniless, feckless friend who (he claimed) constantly grubbed money from him, knowing that his readers would recognize Kasai as the story's model, although the content is not so specific as to be obvious to the uninitiated.[32] Pressed by editors and the ever-present deadline, the Taishō-period *junbungaku* writer turned regularly to his own life for material, as it seemed the most readily accessible, with the knowledge that such material would pique his readers' interest—and elicit even more solicitations (and deadlines) from his editors. This journalistic pressure frequently induced him to make "confessions" he might not otherwise have penned and sometimes to commit bizarre acts that might not otherwise have occurred to him, in his desperate search for new material.

Once an author had fashioned a particular persona, however, he could alter it only at the risk of appearing to act out of character and perhaps offending or even losing his audience. In order to make his writing "true to life," then, he had to continue acting out the role dictated by this literary self-image. Tail began wagging

---

31. *Omoide no sakkatachi*, 83–87.

32. Ōmori Sumio, "Kazai Zenzō," 156. The story is "Rinjin" (1919), first published in *Bunshō kurabu*. It *is* rather easy to tell that the model is Kasai in such stories as "Ashizumo" (1929) and "Shichigatsu nijū-ni nichi no yoru" (1932) by Kamura Isota (1897–1933), although the character is identified only by initials.

dog: persona now on occasion shaped the person in real life. Some writers succumbed to the illusion that they could solve their personal difficulties on the pages of their *shishōsetsu*, and not a few came to rely on the form for its practical function as an open forum. But here always lay the seeds of destruction. *Shishōsetsu* writers often discovered to their dismay that the solutions they had worked out on paper came back to haunt them in real life.

Few writers could bear such self-abuse; most turned to other projects, which gave them more narrative freedom or at the very least did not jeopardize their spiritual and even physical well-being. Some diversified in order to survive: Uno Kōji, Kikuchi Kan, and Kume Masao, for example, ventured early and successfully into the realm of popular fiction. Yet there were others, Shimazaki Tōson and Dazai Osamu (1909–48) among the most prominent, whose failures to keep their lives even one step ahead of their writing resulted in domestic tragedy and in death. These writers succumbed to the temptation inherent in a form bound intimately with private life: that of closing the temporal gap between experience and writing.

None of the three writers under study here went to quite such extremes, but neither were they particularly successful at diversifying their writing. Chikamatsu Shūkō dwelt incessantly on a very few episodes in his life and found only late in his career a diversion in historical fiction. Shiga Naoya, who did not depend on the income from his writing for a living, simply stopped writing altogether for several long stretches in his career. And Kasai Zenzō, who was by far the most dependent, both financially and psychologically, on the form, perhaps luckily had his career cut short by consumption. All three nevertheless succeeded in coming to grips with the singular treachery of writing about oneself and at their best made their lives speak with extraordinary power.

The following chapters examine how these three writers coped with the contemporary journalistic realities we have discussed, in their struggle to transform experience into art. That struggle was rendered all the more complex by a growing awareness of their medium's treacherous nature. Their success depended largely on how adeptly they extricated themselves from the quicksand of referentiality, how shrewdly they exploited the myth of sincerity, and finally how well they learned the lesson of textuality: that the production of literary art (including *shishōsetsu*), its grounding in "real life" notwithstanding, entails a mediative process that challenges the one bastion of "truth" that seems inviolable—lived experience. Such realizations rarely came easily and often came under duress. We shall look for flickers—sometimes flashes—of awareness in the seams, the folds, the fissures in their texts.

3

THREE APPROACHES TO EXPERIENCE

7

Chikamatsu Shūkō:
The Hero as Fool

Why should I have to earn a living by exposing my private
life to the public eye? I have not yet sunk so low that I must
prostitute myself in order to pay for my next meal.
Chikamatsu Shūkō, "Yuki no hi"

To what depths has literary fashion sunk now that Chikamatsu Shūkō's cheap, sordid tales are being printed five and
ten times over? I pale at the very thought.
Akagi Kōhei, "Yūtō bungaku no
bokumetsu"

Of the three writers singled out here for extended examination,
only Shiga Naoya is widely read today. Shiga's works were anthologized several times during his career and finally in the definitive
Iwanami edition shortly after his death. Chikamatsu Shūkō and
Kasai Zenzō are rather less well-known. Two definitive Kasai collections came out only recently, and Shūkō's complete works have
yet to appear. There is a mountain of Shiga criticism and a substantial if much smaller amount on Kasai. Shūkō, however, was little
studied until the last decade. Before then, even article-length essays on him were a rarity, and longer studies, with the exception
of Masamune Hakuchō's biographical memoir (*Chikamatsu Shūkō*,
1950), nonexistent. Nagata Mikihiko's 1953 collection of essays
(*Bungō no sugao*) is perhaps more significant for its inclusion of a
chapter on Shūkō alongside such literary giants as Shimazaki
Tōson, Arishima Takeo, Mori Ōgai, Izumi Kyōka, Tokuda Shūsei,
and Tanizaki Jun'ichiro than for the information it contains.

The decision in this book to focus on two relative unknowns
along with Shiga instead of on more familiar writers like Tōson
or Shūsei is based on the pervasive critical perception of all
three—Shūkō, Shiga, and Kasai—as particularly instrumental fig-

ures in the *shishōsetsu*'s development. No matter that actual practice may have differed significantly from the general critical perception: their image as the "purest" of the *shishōsetsu* writers persists.

It is partly a matter of historical chance that their names inevitably appear in discussions of the form: their debuts as writers all coincided with the *shishōsetsu*'s rise in late Meiji–early Taishō. More important, it is a matter of how they present themselves as characters in their writings. If these three highly diverse authors can be said to have anything in common, it is in how they let their heroes' sensibilities totally dominate a story. "Naturalist" authors like Tōson, Shūsei, and Tayama Katai wrote stories that are every bit as autobiographical as those of the writers examined here, but their writings are generally populated with a varied cast of characters whose mere presence on the same stage helps counterbalance that of the author-hero. In Katai's *Sei*, for example, or Tōson's *Ie* or Shūsei's *Kabi*, there is an attempt to present what we would call a "milieu" (whether family or, less distinctly, "society" at large) that provides an external backdrop against which the hero's thoughts and actions are set. In the writings of Shūkō, Shiga, and Kasai, however, we encounter a far more restricted world. In place of a "milieu" (*shakai*) is a map of the hero's "mental state" (*shinkyō*), fully legible only to those who read it as no more—and no less—than a record of the author's own perceptions. These records represent a culmination of the naturalists' desire to transcribe lived experience and the language's genius for grammatically assigning "truth" to experience related in the written reportive style, whether in the first *or* third person. Confession as perception was not primarily a means of exposing self or society but an end in itself, the raison d'être of the work. For these writers to have placed their experiences in some broader social context or other "novelistic" framework would have actually detracted from their authenticity.

EXPERIENCE, SPONTANEITY, AND
ARTISTIC CREATION

We begin our examination of individual authors with Chikamatsu Shūkō, in deference to the critical consensus that he was the first of the *shishōsetsu* writers par excellence. The critic Hirano Ken, for example, calls *Giwaku* (Suspicion, 1913) modern Japanese literature's first "true" *shishōsetsu*.[1] Hirano might have picked an earlier text, but what matters here is his recognition of the Shūkō hero's myopic preoccupation with private life. *Giwaku*, like Shūkō's other *shishōsetsu*, has no political or social or even familial backdrop; indeed, we hardly get a sense of the hero's own day-to-day existence other than his misguided passions. It is this narrative claustrophobia, however, this absence of any link to any palpable, external reality, that gives this text and so much of Shūkō's writing its distinctive flavor. His love life is a shambles, the Shūkō hero freely admits, but a shambles, at any rate, of his own making. He revels in his self-engendered doubts. Masamune Hakuchō suggests that *Giwaku* represents in fictive form the skepticism—and self-conceit—of post-Russo-Japanese-War society first articulated in the criticism of Shimamura Hōgetsu.[2] The opening scene in which the hero spins out endless fantasies in the refuge of his bed has also been read as a metaphor for the alienation that characterized this period.[3]

Although narrowly focused, Shūkō's *shishōsetsu* contain many brilliant tours de force that amply reward close study and bring certain features of the form into bold relief. The first feature is the author's depiction of what might be called an isolated (as opposed to an individuated) consciousness. The narrator-hero in Shūkō's works is typically engrossed in narcissistic absorption, as we have noted; yet he is to the last an amorphous figure. Acting in a social vacuum, he does not change or develop in the way that a protagonist, however self-absorbed, does in fiction populated with several clearly drawn characters. It is as if he has scrupulously avoided, or simply never considered, the issue of personality. The major texts

1. *Geijutsu to jisseikatsu*, 17. *Giwaku* is the masterpiece in Shūkō's first major group of stories, known as the "Wakareta tsuma" (Estranged wife) cycle, in which the narrator-hero describes his attempts to locate his wife, who has vanished without a trace. In his second major group of stories, known as the "Kurokami" (Dark hair) cycle, the narrator tells a similar story, except that here a prostitute has replaced his wife. Both cycles are discussed below.
2. *Shizenshugi seisui ki*, in *Masamune Hakuchō zenshū* 12:316. (Hakuchō alludes of course to Hōgetsu's famous essay, "Kaigi to kokuhaku," discussed in Chapter 4.) See also Hakuchō's discussion of Shūkō in ibid., 310–12 and 335–37.
3. Takemori Ten'yū, "*Giwaku* no sekai," 18. See the discussion of *Giwaku* below. Not that Shūkō himself was an escapist. By all accounts he was extremely well versed in the politics of his time and tried his hand at writing stories that treated the social issues of his day. See Nakajima Kunihiko, "Kyakkan shōsetsu e no yume."

seem ultimately to be less about human relationships than about a unilateral emotion: jealousy, in most cases, as experienced and expressed by the frenzied Shūkō hero.[4]

A second feature, also common to the *shishōsetsu* in general, is the author's penchant for dwelling repeatedly on certain periods in his life while glossing over others that would seem to lend themselves just as readily to fictional retelling. A kind of artistic vision appears to govern the organizing—and perhaps the very perception—of experience. Shūkō was not at all interested in presenting the whole of life. Indeed, what surprises one is not that he drew exclusively from his own life but that he drew so discriminately from it. His "confessions," one soon notices, are curiously selective and repetitive: in story after story, the hero chases blindly after an elusive love. Shūkō's talent as a writer, however, lies in his ability to create the illusion that nothing else really matters. His self-revelations, far from being the scandalously haphazard record of debauchery that Akagi Kōhei (1891–1949) and other moralists claimed, are in fact the product of a surprisingly contained and consistent vision of personal experience.

Such consistency, however, by no means yields a monolithic view of life, and this brings us to a third feature: Shūkō's insistence on viewing his past through the ever-changing present. To be sure, we find in the Shūkō oeuvre a number of unrelated personal episodes that have assumed an identical artistic reality: namely the hero as fool, abandoned in disgust by his beloved. Yet at the same time—and this is what makes Shūkō the provocative, bewildering writer that he is—the reality of a single episode in his life sometimes proves to be more elusive and protean than life's continuum of unrelated experiences. Shūkō approached his life as a critic approaches a text (although with varying degrees of rigorousness), finding new shades of meaning in an experience with each separate reading of it. He viewed his past as a book always in the writing, subject to constant scrutiny but yielding no definitive interpretation.

A native of Okayama Prefecture, Shūkō first came to Tokyo in

4. This is one reason why a Shūkō story differs fundamentally from the typical western autobiographical novel or first-person narrative. In a text like Hermann Hesse's *Steppenwolf*, for example, which is nearly as claustrophobic as any Shūkō *shishōsetsu*, Harry Haller does interact significantly with other characters and emerges as a meticulously drawn figure with a highly complex emotional makeup.

his early twenties to attend classes at what was to become Waseda University with his lifelong friend and rival, Masamune Hakuchō.[5] Shūkō's taste for amatory literature led him to the fiction of Ozaki Kōyō, Izumi Kyōka, and Higuchi Ichiyō as well as the dramas of Chikamatsu Monzaemon (1653–1724). Shūkō repeatedly claims that he had every intention in his youth of becoming a political commentator, not a creative writer, and that he was an avid reader of *Kokumin no tomo*, the journal of cultural criticism, long before he opened the pages of *Waseda bungaku*, the principal organ of literary naturalism.[6] He began his career writing columns and essays for newspapers and magazines, thanks to the good offices of Shimamura Hōgetsu. He met Ōnuki Masu in 1902 and began living with her the following year for a total of six years. They never wed. He continued writing critical essays (the most well-known being a collection entitled *Bundan mudabanashi*, begun in 1908) and penned an occasional piece of fiction, but he was temperamentally incapable of holding down a stable job. In the summer of 1907 he opened a notions shop and had Masu run it. The shop closed in early 1909, and in August of the same year, Masu disappeared. No one knows exactly why she left Shūkō; the "Estranged Wife" cycle suggests that his shiftlessness and infidelities taxed her patience to the breaking point.

Most of the dozen or so short stories that preceded Shūkō's "Estranged Wife" cycle are either adaptations of stories he had read in English from European literature ("Sono hitori" [1908] is a virtual translation of a section from Tolstoy's *Childhood, Boyhood, Youth*) or sketches of his home and family in Okayama and of his life with Masu.[7] Autobiographical though these latter stories are, they differ notably from the cycles that would earn him his fame. In them, the Shūkō persona usually adopts the pose of a bystander and is not

5. The following biographical information is gleaned from the chronologies in *NKBT* 22:499–505, and *MBZ* 70:429–36. It is extremely difficult to judge how far to trust the chronologies beyond the publication dates of Shūkō's texts, as compilers tend to rely heavily on the texts themselves for information—there being often no other sources available. According to Wada Kingo, all chronologies are based on one that Shūkō himself compiled and appended to his anthology *Koi kara ai e*, but the latter offers almost no details about the author's life beyond his early twenties. *Byōsha no jidai*, 226 n. 9. Hakuchō's *Chikamatsu Shūkō* is too anecdotal to be of much use as a research guide.

6. "Hakken ka sōsaku ka" (1).

7. See Endo Hideo, "Chikamatsu Shūkō shoki sakuhin kenkyū"; and Kuribayashi Hideo, "Chikamatsu Shūkō nōto."

the central figure swept up in a vortex of passion that he is in later texts. This pose suggests a distaste for self-exposé that becomes apparent when we consider what episodes in his life that Shūkō clearly chose to suppress. We learn of course of Masu's disappearance in the "Estranged Wife" cycle, but virtually nothing in these earlier texts of what brought the two together, why the two were never formally married, or what led to their separation. Shūkō often reflects on these years in memoirs published over the following decades,[8] yet curiously he offers no more than a glimpse of a period that surely formed the basic pattern of his adult emotional life.

Shūkō has nonetheless acquired a reputation as the most blatantly confessional of the *shishōsetsu* writers, a reputation founded on the apparent truth of even the most outlandish revelations, as confirmed by the author himself on numerous occasions. "There is no more definitive document with which to relate the truth of human existence," Shūkō writes in the preface to his anthology *Koi kara ai e*, "than the record of one's own experience." It is founded also in Shūkō's skepticism concerning the emplotted narrative, which was shared by *shishōsetsu* writers who followed him:

> My writings—at least those collected in this volume—contain no plot or staging. Critics frequently declare this lack to be the great defect of my work. But plot has its drawbacks: it forces the author to embellish the facts of his own life. True, an author cannot but be satisfied when his imaginative technique has succeeded in pleasing his audience, but I am of the school that frowns on letting plot or fabrication needlessly violate the truth of lived experience. . . . I have swallowed my shame and presented before the public eye frivolous incidents in my life out of a respect for historical truth.[9]

This preference for the shapelessness of lived experience over some transcendent, unifying structure has led, predictably, to charges that Shūkō (and any writer with the same preference) had a poorly endowed imagination. If this means that his best work is based

8. See, for example, "Koishikawa no ie" (1920) and "Kuseyama jōshu (1928), in *Shinsen Chikamatsu Shūkō shū*, 64–74 and 75–83. In the former piece, Shūkō dramatizes the parting scene with his wife but informs the reader he will not go into the reasons for the separation. In the latter piece, he admits only to feeling the greatest nostalgia for those periods in his life when he suffered so many disappointments. Shūkō writes in "Koi o enagara no shitsuren" (1908) that he is bothered by the knowledge that Masu had lived with another man before him, but he does not probe the matter at all in the "Estranged Wife" cycle.

9. Quoted from a commentary by the author appended to *Chikamatsu Shūkō, Uno Kōji*, 641.

wholly on personal experience and that his numerous attempts at transcending the *shishōsetsu* generally ended in failure, then these charges are quite correct. But such a view overlooks the most captivating quality of Shūkō's writing, which the Shūkō scholar Nakajima Kunihiko describes as a feeling of spontaneous and intense "interest" (*kankyō*)[10] and which is responsible perhaps more than anything else for the extraordinary emotional claustrophobia that pervades Shūkō's best work. "His heart was possessed by the woman he loved," writes Shūkō of his hero in "Otoko kiyohime," a story in a third group of stories known as the "Ōsaka no yūjo" (Osaka courtesan) cycle. "That he despised her at times and adored her at others made no difference; the obsession was itself more than enough reason for living. Nothing else in this world mattered to him. Nothing at all."[11]

Here is perhaps the most important reason for Shūkō's reputation as the last word in confession: the spontaneous interest that inspired the author to pen his self-exposés leads to his rejection of the technique of narrative distancing. Beginning with the "Estranged Wife" cycle, the narrator-hero indeed recounts like a man possessed the fiascos in his emotional life. No longer a casual bystander, he is caught up in a storm of passion and incapable of an ironic or critical perspective. No matter that Shūkō typically wrote of an event months or years after the fact. He manages to close the gap between narrative present and story time in a way that suggests a man still at the height of frenzy.

All Shūkō's best *shishōsetsu* have this incomparable feel of spontaneity about them that is lacking in his attempts at more "orthodox" fiction. Once we believe, along with the hero of "Otoko kiyohime," that nothing matters other than his amorous obsessions, then we have succumbed to the illusion of a uniquely unmediated brand of self-exposé. For Nakajima Kunihiko, the Shūkō *shishōsetsu* as epitomized in "Otoko kiyohime" is a world of intense emotion presented to the reader in the raw, without the trappings of hindsight or verbal artifice, and both Shūkō's greatness and his limitations as an artist spring from it.[12] We must not forget, however, that this passion is expressed entirely through the medium of the

10. "Kyakkan shōsetsu e no yume," 48.
11. *Shinsen Chikamatsu Shūkō shū*, 241.
12. "Kyakkan shōsetsu e no yume," 48.

written word, in which the author's thoughts can only be, after Aldous Huxley, "second thoughts."[13] There is no way, in short, to determine conclusively that Shūkō's emotions as revealed in his stories are ontologically somehow rawer and more spontaneous than those of other writers. But what is certain is that Shūkō brings to a medium whose keynote is "unmediated" expression a vibrant if less-than-perfect style, which, by its very imperfection, actually bolsters the illusion of a direct conversion of emotion into language. We shall pay close attention to this process of conversion during the course of our study.

THE "ESTRANGED WIFE" CYCLE:
PRIVATE LIFE AS LITERARY ACT

Shūkō's first major work, the four-part "Estranged Wife" cycle (1910–15: *Wakaretaru tsuma ni okuru tegami* [A letter to my estranged wife]; *Shūjaku* [Tenacious love]; *Giwaku* [Suspicion]; and *Giwaku zokuhen* [Suspicion, part 2]), revolves around the narrator-hero Yukioka's vain pursuit of his wife Osuma, who has abandoned him for another man.[14] The cycle's story time runs from August 1909 to May 1911. Shūkō relates events occurring anywhere from several months to several years prior to the telling, but the cycle reads as if those events have only just taken place. Two techniques help achieve a sense of immediacy. First, the epistolary style is used in all but the last story. The hero reports to his estranged wife in a manner suggesting that the events in question are still in progress. In real life, the outcome of Shūkō's vain pursuits was no longer in doubt, but the Shūkō hero remains in the dark. Letter after letter flows from the pen of a man who clings to the hope of

13. In Kay Dick, *Writers at Work*, 157.
14. *Giwaku zokuhen* was first published as *Aichaku no nagori* (Lingering attachment). Names of characters in the cycle vary with the story and with the edition. The narrator's wife in *Wakaretaru tsuma ni okuru tegami* is called Osuma or Oyuki. Osuma's lover Shinoda also goes by the name Kojima and Yoshida. See the table in *NKBT* 22:448; and Takemori, "*Giwaku* no sekai," 15–16 and 31 n. 3. Names tend to be variations and inversions of each other. Thus, the names *Yukioka* and *Oyuki* in the "Wakareta tsuma" cycle. Osuma is the inverse of Masu, the name of Shūkō's wife after whom the character is modeled. In a later cycle, Kasahara of *Kyūren* is called Ta*hara* in *Kyūren zokuhen*, and so on—all of them manifestations of Shūkō's obsession with repetition on a verbal as well as experiential level.

reunion with his wife. Second, narrative time moves backward, erasing the perspective that a telling distanced from the tale potentially generates. Shūkō has no interest in coolly assessing events that have receded into a psychologically distant past. Instead, he locates the narrative present at the height of the hero's emotional experience. His concern is clearly with process, not result.

Wakaretaru tsuma ni okuru tegami (April–July 1910; hereafter abbreviated as *Wakareta tsuma*) covers the period from Osuma's disappearance in August 1909 to the end of November. The narrator-hero Yukioka reflects on his past life with Osuma and hopes for her quick return, despite rumors that she now lives with another man. He devotes most of the letter, however, to an account of his rivalry with one Osada (modeled after Masamune Hakuchō) over a prostitute with whom he had become intimate in an attempt to overcome his loneliness. *Shūjaku* (April 1913) continues the action from July 1910 to April 1911, describing it as if the hero were writing sometime in 1911 rather than in the year of publication.[15] Yukioka learns that Osuma may be living with a university student who once shared the same tenement house with them. He then hears that she has become the mistress of a retired businessman. He also learns that Osuma vacationed in Nikkō in the summer of 1910 with her beau, whoever he might be, and he determines to track them down. In *Giwaku* (October 1913), Yukioka travels to Nikkō in May 1911, searches through several inn registers in hopes of unearthing a clue to Osuma's whereabouts, and finally locates the inn where she and her beau stayed. He discovers that the latter is indeed the young student, not the elderly patron as he has been led to believe, and regrets that he was so sanguine about Osuma's behavior when the student was living next door to them. Again he relates events as if he were writing soon after the fact. In *Giwaku*

15. There is evidence that at least certain portions of the cycle's later stories were written much earlier than their actual publication, which would of course add to the sense of immediacy to the events related. For example, Endō Hideo cites an essay Shūkō wrote apparently in reference to a sequel to *Giwaku* and suggests that Shūkō must have written *Giwaku zokuhen*, or at least some version of it, before *Giwaku*, published two years earlier. See "*Giwaku* ron," 82. Nakajima Kunihiko argues that Shūkō wrote a significant portion of *Utsuriga* (1915), a work related to the cycle, in the fall of 1910. See "Chikamatsu Shūkō ni okeru sakuhin keiretsu no mondai," 14–15. Shūkō's use of a "roving" narrative present, however, demonstrates his interest in immediacy as a *technique* above and beyond any commitment to emotional authenticity.

zokuhen (November 1915), the hero, writing a first-person narration this time and not a letter, traces Osuma and the student to Oka-yama and finds them after a search through the prefectural regis-ter. The story begins with an account of two chance meetings that Yukioka had on the same day with his former wife sometime in 1915. The narrative present gradually shifts back in time, how-ever, to a period immediately following the visit to Okayama in May 1911.

Two other stories are closely related to the cycle: "Yuki no hi" (A snowy day, March 1910) and *Utsuriga* (Lingering fragrance, June–July 1915; originally titled *Keien* [Bitter memories]). In "Yuki no hi," which reads as a prologue to the "Estranged wife" cycle, Yukioka and Osuma sit comfortably around the warm *kotatsu* (a physical manifestation of the hero's smoldering passion) and gaze out their room at the newly fallen snow.

> Since it was so warm on retiring to bed, I thought we would be getting rain the next day, but I awoke the next morning to a world blanketed by silver. Flakes like goose down fell silently to the ground.
> I feel very relaxed on such days. It is times like these that I feel fortunate to be without work. We closed the front gate and spent the day by ourselves, sitting face to face across the *kotatsu*. This was our conversation.[16]

This passage provides us with our first glimpse of the Shūkō hero's hermetically sealed emotional world. Content in his idleness and protected by a blanket of insulating snow, Yukioka literally closes the gate on the outside world and revels in his confinement.[17]

Yukioka prods Osuma into talking about her past and derives a certain masochistic pleasure as she becomes carried away by memories. He hopes thereby to rekindle his waning interest in her,

16. *CSS,* 7. All citations of Shūkō's works are taken from this edition, except where otherwise noted; they are henceforth inserted in the main body of the text. This edition is used more out of convenience (it is the most comprehensive Shūkō anthology now in print) than preference, as it is not always a reliable text. Shūkō made considerable revisions of his work whenever it was published. (For an ex-ample of how extensive the textual variants of *Wakareta tsuma* alone are, see *NKBT* 22:441–43 n. 1.) The *MBZ* edition of Shūkō's works is the more authoritative text, but it unfortunately contains only six stories (the "Estranged Wife" cycle plus "Yuki no hi" and *Utsuriga*).

17. The mood of confinement in "Yuki no hi" is explored in depth by Iwagiri Keiichi. See "'Yuki no hi' no teiryū ni aru mono," esp. 81–83, 93.

since for him, jealousy is synonymous with passion. Yet he also fears the pain that it will bring. The conversation Yukioka has with his wife is akin to testy verbal fencing, and the couple's dialogue intersects only tangentially.[18] Each time Yukioka seeks reassurance about his wife's fidelity, Osuma responds with yet another amorous episode from her past. In the end, Yukioka discovers that no amount of probing into Osuma's past will ignite the spark of jealous passion, and the "conversation" that was not a dialogue comes to a halt.

> My heart no longer fluttered with emotion as it used to. Why? Has my love for her cooled? Or have formerly crude, wild passions simply mellowed into a genuine affection? I don't know the answer.
> It was still snowing gently outside, and drifts were piling up. "We've had quite a talk, haven't we?" I said with a wide yawn. "How about some eel today?"
> "I'd love some."
> "I'll go order it," I said, and left the house.
>
> (*CSS*, 15)

Thus the story ends, with innuendos of emotions as cool as the snow that envelops them. Although the reference to eel, a common erotic symbol in the popular culture, suggests that passion, like the coals under the *kotatsu*, still smolders unconsciously beneath the surface, the narrator, by leaving the house, breaks his confinement and with it the magical spell that has prevailed throughout.

"Yuki no hi" is typical of stories to follow in that the narrative present is completely at odds with the chronological "facts" of Shūkō's life. The hero recounts his conversation with Osuma as if it has just taken place, although Masu has long since left Shūkō. Even the author of some of the most demeaning "confessions" in modern Japanese literature feels it necessary to separate life from art. Thus, "Yuki no hi" adumbrates the couple's tumultuous past but is silent about the "sadness, misery, and . . . jealousy" that the wife has apparently stirred in the husband. "And what of these things?" Yukioka asks rhetorically. "That is a story I shall not reveal here. In fact, I may *never* reveal it. It is something better left unsaid. Indeed, I ought never, never to talk about it!" Yukioka then offers a credo for all *shishōsetsu* writers: "Why should I have to earn a living by

18. See Nakajima Kunihiko, "Yuki no hi no gensō," 40.

exposing my private life to the public eye? I have not yet sunk so low as to prostitute myself in order to pay for my next meal" (ibid., 10). To be sure, the *shishōsetsu* writer does expose himself to a greater or lesser extent and earns his living thereby. But Shūkō's maintenance of a temporal buffer between his life and work suggests a way for the writer to contain his confessions even as he professes to tell all.

Utsuriga, like *Shūjaku*, is a sequel to *Wakareta tsuma*. Before we look at it, let us first examine the cycle's inaugural work, which was written in the precedent-setting epistolary style. Yukioka, the narrator-hero, begins as if he were indeed corresponding with his wife, with no thoughts of a wider audience:

> My dear,
>
> I suppose that I have no right to use so intimate a term as "my dear" [*omae*], now that we have separated. And if what I hear is true—that you have long since remarried and are therefore impossible to win back—then perhaps I should not be writing you at all. Yet I feel that I must, and I cannot help addressing you as I always have. Please let me do so in this letter, at least. I'm afraid there will be trouble if people find out that I have written you—I wouldn't mind, but it might cause you some embarrassment. I needn't tell you, then, to burn or otherwise dispose of this letter after you've finished reading it. I understand that we are practically neighbors, that you live right here in Koishikawa Ward, although I don't know exactly where you're located or what you're doing. I'd like to bring you up to date on my life since your departure. Do hear me out. Much has happened in the seven months since I last saw you.
>
> (*CSS*, 16)

The opening is nothing less than a manifesto. The hero announces to his ex-wife that he will use the intimate *omae* in the letter even though he no longer can face to face. He thereby creates the fiction of a relationship that has in fact already been nullified. Shūkō begins his story only after firmly setting this fiction in place.[19]

But the manifesto, and the fiction it embraces, is directed not simply at the writer's ex-wife. Insofar as the "letter" has been published in a magazine, *omae* loses its status as a private, single-person audience. The fiction of an intimate relationship, then, extends to the broader reading audience as well. We shall see that the

---

19. This point is made by Shimada Akio in "Chikamatsu Shūkō shiron," 16–17.

"Wakareta tsuma" cycle is in part the result of Shūkō's struggle to produce an audience that can correctly read his work: who could be more qualified to interpret his writing than his companion of six years—or anyone who can imaginatively take her place?

Yet although Yukioka addresses his wife directly in *Wakareta tsuma*, the story as a whole maintains only the barest pretense of a letter. The second-person pronoun appears less and less frequently as the letter progresses, and in one section about two-thirds of the way through, the narrator actually refers to Osuma in the third person (*CSS*, 57–58). Here, in a bizarre narrative oversight (or is it a sleight of hand?), the letter's "discourse" melts into the fictional "story" right before our eyes—yet another indication of Shūkō's awareness, however unconscious, of his larger audience. By the end, all trappings of an epistle have been dropped; there is not even the obligatory closing to complement the perfunctory greeting.

Insofar as the events in *Wakareta tsuma* are based on personal experience, Shūkō could not have been oblivious to how his former wife might react to publications. And yet the "letter" cannot be, as is often claimed, so much literary bait to lure his wife back to him. It has been argued that the story has less artistic than utilitarian intent—that is, Shūkō wrote it hoping that Masu would read it, take pity, and eventually return to him.[20] The argument is based, however, on the story's sequels, which of course get us no closer to the "truth." *Shūjaku* opens with the hero's explanation of why he wrote his first "letter": "I write you once again. Three years have passed since that first long letter. . . . I didn't write half of what I had intended, however. . . . I figured that, being the sensitive person you are, you'd take pity on me if I informed you of my plight" (*CSS*, 75–76). In the opening section of *Giwaku*, omitted from modern editions, Yukioka takes courage in his ex-wife's past promise to keep an eye on notices in newspaper literary columns and read his works even if they should separate. Yet the expectation of being read by a specific audience does not in itself necessitate writing in

20. Wada Kingo, *Byōsha no jidai*, 213–15. In an early (1913) essay on Shūkō, cited by Wada, Ibukata Toshirō speculates that Shūkō chose the title *Wakaretaru tsuma ni okuru tegami* in hopes that its appearance in *Waseda bungaku* or in advertisements for the magazine would catch his estranged wife's eye. See "Bundan no suhinkusu," 151–52.

the epistle form.[21] Far more likely, Shūkō's aim in employing this form was the impact it would have on his *primary* reading audience—the *bundan*—which was all too familiar with Shūkō's scandalous private life. Shūkō was ultimately less concerned with having his ex-wife see the "letter" than in having his *bundan* audience believe that the story's narrator so wished. If such was the *bundan's* interpretation, then the "letter" was indeed a success.[22] Had Shūkō truly wished to be reunited with his wife, he would of course have written directly to her in care of her relatives. And even if he were confident that she would see the "letter" in *Waseda bungaku*, he could not have expected to woo her back with stories of his philandering!

That Shūkō published, rather than mailed, his "letter," then, presupposed a wider audience, whose interest transcended the circumstances that generated the writing. As if to emphasize this point, the narrator in *Shūjaku* refers to a letter he published three years earlier, in July 1910, which just happens to correspond to the final installment of *Wakareta tsuma* (*CSS*, 76). And to insure that his literary intentions are not lost on his readers, he concludes his letter on the following note: "I plan to write a *shōsetsu* about us soon. I want to leave a permanent record of the bitter-sweet experiences of the past seven years" (*CSS*, 99). But clearly, Shūkō has already done in the "letters" what the narrator hints he will do in some future story: restructure the past into fictional form. The most striking evidence for this is the gap he inserts between narrative and chronological present. Shūkō's strategy throughout the cycle is to push the narrative present back in time toward the events in question in order to rob the hero of his hindsight. Reflection is anathema to passion, we quickly learn in Shūkō's fiction.

The narrator of *Wakareta tsuma*, who begins his first installment in the April 1910 issue of *Waseda bungaku*, writes of events only as recent as November 1909 and in a manner, moreover, that suggests he has no knowledge of events beyond that time. The half-year blank between the fall of 1909 and the spring of 1910 is never filled in. (This period is covered by *Utsuriga*, which however was not

21. This is the argument of Iwagiri Keiichi. See "*Wakaretaru tsuma ni okuru tegami* ron," 11.

22. The discussion here is indebted to Takahashi Hiromitsu, in his "'Wakareta tsuma' mono o megutte," 103.

published until 1915.) The blank is even longer in *Shūjaku*, which, although published in April 1913, treats events only as recent as April 1911. Yukioka mentions at the story's beginning that three years have elapsed since he wrote his first letter; yet other internal evidence suggests that he is actually writing from the perspective of 1911 (for example, the narrator refers to 1910 as "last year" throughout). In the final paragraph, which is a self-conscious reference to the act of writing this "letter," the narrative present appears to return to 1913; yet we get from it no sense of perspective or knowledge that the passage of two years might be expected to bring. Significantly, Shūkō dropped this paragraph when the story first appeared in book form.

The suppression of writing time in favor of a "roving" narrative present serves an important purpose: the hero comes across as a frenzied lover still blinded by his emotions rather than as a dispassionate observer. For Yukioka, Osuma's disappearance is a painfully fresh memory, not a historical event that has receded into the hazy past. In this and many other Shūkō stories, the borderline between memory and present reality is blurred to the point of erasure. Remembering becomes an aggressive act of recreation that weaves past into present. When the hero in *Shūjaku*, writing in 1913, learns in the spring of 1911 that Osuma ran off with another man a year earlier, this is his response:

> I feel no bitterness toward the man. I would just like to find the house where you two are living. There you would be, gayly dressed and happily absorbed in your house work. . . . And once I had found you, I would gun you down with a single bullet. And that would be that. Day and night, I lie in bed, the covers pulled over my head, and conjure up the scene. There is a loud bang. Through the cloud of gunsmoke I see your body, collapsed in a frightful posture. I can actually smell the smoke beneath these covers.
>
> (*CSS*, 99)

What appears to be spontaneous "confession" is in fact a highly complex portrayal of past events as if they were only just unfolding. Almost without our realizing it, the narrative present, which was clearly set in 1913 at the story's beginning, has shifted back two years. To the end, the narrator is in the dark about his former wife's whereabouts and her lover's identity, although the author was of course aware of both. In 1911, the narrative present for most of the story, the hero discovers that his ex-wife may have been to Nikkō with her lover and contemplates a visit there to search for clues. In 1913, the time of writing, Shūkō had already been there himself and knew what curious developments ensued. But he was not about to let the reader in on them yet.

Shūjaku is not by any stretch of the imagination one of Shūkō's best stories, but it contains features more typical of Shūkō's writing than the cycle's first text. For one, the remarkable roving narrative present is used here to great effect, as we have seen. The narrative flow appears to duplicate the hero's convoluted thoughts. Second, the motif of frenzied pursuit, which lies dormant in *Wakareta tsuma*, comes to the fore here.[23] Third, the story serves as the cycle's main point of reference. Both *Giwaku* and *Giwaku zokuhen* contain so many allusions to *Shūjaku* that they are in many ways incomprehensible without a prior reading of the earlier text. The "Estranged Wife" cycle is indeed just that: not a linear series but an entangled cycle of stories that reflect—and more often refract—each other several times over. True, Shūkō attempted through revisions and editing (especially in *Giwaku*) to give each of the last three texts in the cycle a measure of autonomy.[24] Yet the stories are so intertwined, the events related in one story so central in importance to the next, that the impact of any single story is lessened considerably when not read together with the rest. The "Estranged Wife" cycle, although it lacks the polish of Durrell's *Alexandria Quartet*, is also in its own way a palimpsest: the hero's memories of events and people, which appear fleetingly and are then erased in one text, reappear dazzlingly etched in the next.

An example of this erasure and reetching is Shūkō's presentation of Osuma's lover in *Shūjaku* and *Giwaku*, which simultaneously reveals and conceals his identity. The hero in *Shūjaku* reports, in the narrative "present" of 1913, that Osuma has run off with one Shinoda, a university student who lived with them in their rented house before Osuma's disappearance and whom Osuma befriended. Indeed, the narrator's very purpose in taking up his pen

23. Takahashi Hiromitsu notes that in *Wakareta tsuma* the abandonment-and-pursuit motif is introduced in the relationship between the prostitute and a former lover. The motif shifts to the main characters in *Shūjaku* and later stories. See "'Wakareta tsuma' mono o megutte," 116–17.

24. Shūkō revised both the beginning and ending of *Giwaku* no less than three times following its initial appearance. He also made several cuts when the stories first appeared in book form. See Takemori, "*Giwaku* no sekai," 10–16.

would seem to be none other than to vent his rage against the student. "Had I known then that you were hiding out with that Shinoda, I swear I'd have died" (*CSS*, 76), he exclaims. And yet, barely a quarter of the way into the story, we hear no more of her lover. After venting his rage, the narrator seems to lose all interest in his rival, becoming lost in memories that propel the narrative present backward. Action and narrative present intersect in May 1911, at which time the narrator is convinced that Osuma lives with an elderly patron, not a student. At the story's end, Yukioka appears no longer in possession of the knowledge that provoked him to write in the first place. In *Giwaku*, which picks up the action in May 1911, Yukioka searches through inn registers in Nikkō for the name of Osuma, who vacationed there during the summer of 1910, and learns to his astonishment that her companion was indeed the student and not the mysterious elderly patron he had imagined. The hero's astonishment is fully conveyed, however, only by a reading of *Shūjaku*, which sets the reader up for this curious twist.

Erasure of another sort occurs in *Utsuriga*, which describes Yukioka's affair with the prostitute with such single-mindedness that it is easy to forget the narrator's ostensible motive for penning this "letter" to his ex-wife: to win her back. We have noted that *Utsuriga* and *Shūjaku* are sequels to *Wakareta tsuma*; but whereas *Shūjaku* is quite conscious of its status ("I write you once again. Three years have passed since that first long letter"), *Utsuriga* reads as a direct continuation of *Wakareta tsuma*, although it was published five years later. Indeed, its opening lines seem to flow right out of the earlier text:

> And then I felt a lump growing in my throat, so large that I could choke. But I controlled my emotions and continued in as cheerful manner as possible to explain how I had come into possession of her sash. I acted out the story in front of them [Osada and another acquaintance], using falsetto and a woman's mannerisms.
> I left Osada's room soon after that.
> Once outside, the feeling of shame I had suppressed in my effort to feign unconcern surged through my chest, wrenching every rib on the way up.
> Whereupon, tears of vexation and chagrin streamed down my face. They felt hot against my sunken cheeks, which were chafed by a chilly evening wind.

It is hard to believe that the last three paragraphs quoted above are in fact the beginning of a new story published five years after the first paragraph.[25] To say that *Wakareta tsuma* is "unfinished" or that *Utsuriga* commences practically in midsentence, however, while true as far as it goes, does not begin to describe Shūkō's technique. Comparing the openings of *Utsuriga* and *Shūjaku*, we see that Shūkō viewed *Wakareta tsuma* as a textual fork in the road from which he could move in two different directions. When read in conjunction with *Shūjaku*, *Giwaku*, and *Giwaku zokuhen*, *Wakareta tsuma* is the tale of a man suffering the loneliness of abandonment. The amicable questioning that Yukioka directs at acquaintances about his ex-wife turns in later stories into frenzied pursuit. When read in conjunction with *Utsuriga*, however, this same work becomes the prologue to a tale of fierce rivalry between two men for the affections of a prostitute. Each theme is introduced in *Wakareta tsuma* and then is suppressed in one or the other of the sequels. What is the cycle's first story *about*, then? Whatever the particular sequel in question chooses to bring up, we must conclude. We see this sort of erasing and doubling back taking place in Shūkō's later stories as well. The "Dark Hair" cycle, for example, serves as another textual fork in the road that generates two sequels only tangentially related to each other. Perhaps we should not even call such works "sequels." Shūkō is less interested in continuing a tale than amending it. Indeed, for Shūkō, the tale is in the amending.

The Shūkō hero's foolish pursuit of his ex-wife reaches the height of frenzy in *Giwaku* (1913), which Masamune Hakuchō numbers among the classics of Meiji and Taishō literature.[26] Unlike *Wakareta tsuma* and *Shūjaku*, the epistle form is virtually abandoned except for the occasional use of the second person (*omae*). The interjectory final particles (*yo, ka, kai, da mono*, etc.) that punctuate the narrative in the cycle's first two texts and posit a specific audience disappear entirely in *Giwaku*.[27] This fact, combined with Shūkō's decision in later editions to drop the introductory section that directly addresses *omae*, suggests a concerted effort to reconstitute his audience.

---

25. The part of the citation that follows the end of *Wakareta tsuma* (*CSS*, 74) is taken from the original text of *Utsuriga*, first published as *Keien* in *Shinshōsetsu* 20 (June 1915): 157. Later editions of *Utsuriga* begin with the final paragraph in the above citation ("Whereupon tears of vexation . . .").

26. "Sono kessaku, *Giwaku*," in *Masamune Hakuchō zenshū* 6:64.

27. See Tazawa Motohisa, "Hōhō no mosaku," 30.

We have already noted certain narrative ploys that underscore Shūkō's consciousness of a dual readership, suggesting that Shūkō sought an ideal audience that could correctly—perhaps the word is empathetically—interpret his work. The second-person singular *omae*, who by definition is intimate with the narrator, is of course the perfect choice of interpreters. Thus, we frequently encounter in both *Wakareta tsuma* and *Shūjaku* phrases like "As you know . . ." and "I don't have to tell you . . ." as well as other narrative asides by which Shūkō maintains the pretense of intimacy while introducing new information necessary to the telling of his story. Shūkō must have realized, however, that appealing too strongly to a specific audience, even as a fictional ploy, ran the risk of alienating his wider audience. To note constantly that *omae* already knows this or that implies his general readership's ignorance; yet to limit the narration to what *omae* does not already know risks incomprehension.

Shūkō's answer to this dilemma, perfected in *Giwaku*, is a unique method of presentation that offers a means of relating to his wider audience as insiders. Shūkō rejects the idea of talking *to* his reader, even his intimate reader (*omae*); he instead talks to himself—with a mind, perhaps, to being overheard. He refuses, moreover, to assume the pose of a narrator who has learned from his experience and then condescends to enlighten his readers. Rather, he treats even his own memories as events in the making. He is no more aware of their significance than we are.

Shūkō's refusal to place reader and writer into two separate camps and his strategy of linking them to the same locus of consciousness helps explain why *Giwaku* begins where it does: at the end of the story, chronologically speaking, namely, the narrator's visit to Nikkō in May 1911. Along with the narrator, we learn to our surprise that Shinoda is Osuma's lover. Along with the narrator we search "our" memory (specifically, our earlier reading of *Shūjaku*) for past evidence of deceit. Yukioka has before him "proof" of adultery in a Nikkō inn register. Now he must resort to imagination to make sense out of it. True, his imagination has led him astray before. But in the absence of the culprits themselves, it is his only ally. Shinoda and Osuma appear frequently in Yukioka's recollections, but never once in the narrative present.

In short, all the action in *Giwaku*, except the initial Nikkō episode, takes place in the narrator's mind. The narrator opens it up to his reader but makes no further concessions. As insiders, we are led to, but never guided through, Yukioka's composite realm of memory and illusion. The function of the opening paragraph takes on crucial significance, then, not as a delineator of time or place—for it is neither—but as a gateway to a world of pure imagination, an abstract world that, in the eyes of one critic,[28] approaches legend and myth:

> It was a depressing, disturbing spring. I conjured up vision after vision of your death at my hands. During the daytime, when it was too light and noisy to concentrate properly, I would burrow under my quilt and imagine your murder and my imprisonment, rewriting the scenario over and over again in my head. No matter where you had gone or whose wife you had become, I was determined to find you out. Day after day was taken up with these stifling thoughts. I did not know how else to spend my time.
>
> (*CSS*, 100)

Initially, the hero muses from the vantage point of his cavelike quilt about the events of 1911 as if he were recalling experience in a discrete past. But he soon resorts to his familiar strategy of temporal regression. Rejecting the perspective afforded by a writing time two years after the events in question, he pushes the narrative present back to a time conterminous with that "depressing, disturbing spring" in 1911.[29] A quarter of the way into the text, the two-year gap between initial writing time and story time has been erased. This is perhaps the work's greatest fiction. Shūkō creates a world in which there is *no* fixed present: past, present, and future merge into a fluid continuum of emotion that, in the hero's mind, is real for all time.

Yukioka is elated when he discovers Osuma and Shinoda's names in the inn register, because they are the first "hard evidence" of an indiscretion. We might want to ask, what can he *do* with it, two years after the fact? Such questions, however, are made irrelevant by a technique that undermines the priority of recent

28. Takemori, "*Giwaku no sekai*," 21.

29. The time configuration in this and other texts in the cycle is easily established, since specific dates appear throughout. In the first page of *Giwaku*, for example, a police officer responds to the narrator's request to search for his missing wife thus: "Why are you asking us only now, in April 1911, to look for your wife, when she's been missing since the fall of 1909?" (*CSS*, 100).

perspective on past events. Returning to the Nikkō episode in the story's last lines, Yukioka resolves on the train back to Tokyo to head for Okayama, hundreds of miles to the west, where he believes Shinoda and Osuma now to be living. The chase goes on. And as long as it does, the hero's passion continues unabated.

Yukioka's idealized passion is abruptly cooled when he actually finds Osuma. In *Shūjaku* and *Giwaku*, Yukioka chases after figments with such zeal that emotions for a woman he no longer really loves overwhelm his present indifference toward her. When he finally locates his estranged wife in *Giwaku zokuhen*, the result can only be anticlimactic. He insists that he does not want to win Osuma back, but merely have his say in front of her and Shinoda.

> When she saw me slide open the door and step before her, she went pale and let out a cry. . . .
> "Well, come on in," she said, composing herself at last. . . . "How on earth did you find this place? That Sakata [a middleman who urges Yukioka to part company with Osuma] must have told you. He's a rogue. I thought he'd let the cat out of the bag sooner or later. Please sit over here." She offered me a cushion.
> "Sakata's no rogue," I said. "The person who used him is rogue. When you've done wrong, it gets out sooner or later."
> Shinoda showed up early that morning. His house was on the very next block.
> Even though they had been caught virtually red-handed, the two carried on as if nothing were out of the ordinary. They simply would not admit defeat. But I thought any further queries unnecessary.
> (*CSS*, 179–80).

Osuma's spell on the hero is broken, now that he has seen her in the flesh. Her elusive image as the embodiment of Yukioka's passion is completely overshadowed by her mundane presence. Yukioka has no use for this reality: the two go their separate ways.

The love object in the "Wakareta tsuma" cycle, then, is ultimately a construct of the hero's frenzied imagination. Yukioka lives in a confined world of daydreams and illusion that can only be shattered, as they finally are, by an actual meeting. He revels in wild-goose chases. "Damnit! Where on earth did you run off to, anyway?" the narrator grumbles during the vain search for his wife in *Shūjaku*. "Don't think for a moment I'll give up so easily. The longer you hide, the more I'll look. I've a mind to do nothing else!" (*CSS*, 91). Indeed, the narrator lives by his promise to "do nothing else" for the duration of the cycle. And since successful searches and direct confrontations can yield only disillusionment, he actually feels more secure clutching at straws. Who but the Shūkō hero would scorn a more direct method of locating his former wife in favor of searching the Nikkō inn registers on the chance he might find a clue to her whereabouts two years before!

Even when the hero finds a clue, it only leads to another chase. Yet just as this tale is in the telling, not in the resolving, the hero's life is fulfilled in the searching, not in the finding. Far more important than Yukioka's eventual meeting with Osuma is his dream of seeing her again. And for the Shūkō hero, sweet are the dreams that never come true.

THEMES AND VARIATIONS:
THE "OSAKA COURTESAN" CYCLE

In the early years of Taishō, when he was still penning his "Estranged Wife" cycle, Shūkō made an extended stay in the Kansai region, where he frequently engaged an Osaka prostitute. Several rendezvous in Osaka and at a nearby mountain spa, the woman's sudden disappearance and relocation in Taiwan as a businessman's mistress, and visits to the woman's sister in search of news, solace, and eventually affection, are recorded somewhat haphazardly in Shūkō's next series of stories known as the "Ōsaka no yūjo" (Osaka courtesan) cycle. After first appearing in five different magazines over a period of sixteen months (from December 1913 to April 1915), the cycle's seven stories were anthologized in book form roughly in the order of events: "Kurokami" (Dark hair), "Tsunokuni-ya" (Tsunokuni-ya [the name of the courtesan's house of assignation]), "Aokusa" (Green grass), "Nagare" (Drifting current), "Ada nasake" (Fleeting love), "Utsuroi" (A fading affair), and "Otoko kiyohime."

That this arrangement does not coincide with the original order of publication seems a minor point until one actually peruses the cycle from beginning to end. Even when read as a series, this odd collection of stories stubbornly refuses to congeal into an orderly narrative. Shūkō made some revisions before publishing the anthologized version, but apparently not with the intent of unifying it as he did, quite conscientiously, in the case of the "Estranged Wife" cycle. There is a considerable difference in the amount of narrative ground covered from story to story. Some, like "Kuro-kami" and "Ada nasake," present overviews of the affair; others, like "Aokusa" and "Nagare," only the briefest of episodes. Sections of several stories overlap, moreover, while the names of characters and places vary, contributing to a general feeling of untidiness.[30] Narrative voice, too, appears to vary in several works. In "Utsuroi" the first-person narrator-hero tells his own story. In "Kurokami" and "Ada nasake" an anonymous narrator introduces the hero's first-person narration; the rest are third-person narrations.

Or are they? The question of narrative person is not the simple, straightforward one it appears to be in English. We noted in Chapter 1 that the sheer variety and number of pronominals in Japanese, the use of each dependent on the speaker's relationship with hearer and referent, make their function vastly different from the autonomous placeholders in western languages. In the latter, an "I" is an "I," a "he" a "he," in all utterances, spoken and narrated; not so, however, in the Japanese. The use of *jibun* as a subjective as well as a reflexive pronoun, moreover, as we noted in our discussion of Sōseki's *Mon* and its English translation in Chapter 2, makes possible—indeed, inevitable—a blurring of boundaries between first and third person that is literally unthinkable in English.

Thus, what we might take ostensibly for third-person narration can on closer examination be identical to first-person narration. Only the presence of the hero's name or *kare* marks a passage positively as a "third-person" narration; yet these positive identifiers are often few and far between, since Japanese functions quite adequately without such English-language necessities as grammatical person and verb conjugation. Stories in the "Osaka Courtesan" cycle narrated in the "third person" often go for paragraphs without a single such identifier. The absence of such identifiers—combined with the language's natural inclination to the speaker/narrator's point of view—makes the stories read as if the narrating "I" and the acting "he" are one and the same.

So it is, for example, with "Otoko kiyohime" and the passage cited earlier about the Shūkō hero's foolish passion. Here it is translated, as it must be, into straightforward third-person narration, with the appropriate place-marking pronouns and agreeing verbs:

30. Nakajima Kunihiko examines the cycle's "untidiness" in "Tōsui to ninshiki."

His heart was possessed by the woman he loved. That he despised her at times and adored her at others made no difference; the obsession was itself more than enough reason for living. Nothing else in this world mattered to him. Nothing at all.

But let us take a closer look at the passage itself.

Tatoi uramu ni mo seyo, shitau ni mo seyo, *jibun* wa ima suki na onna no koto o omoitsumete-iru. Omoitsumete-ireba koso, soko ni *jibun* ga ikite-iru shōko de aru. Sore o nozoite sekai no nanimono o motte kite mo issai *jibun* to wa mukankei de aru.[31]

What we have translated as "he" is *jibun*, used here as a subjective case indicator. Read by itself, the passage is identical to a first-person narration. Indeed, given the language's aforementioned speaker/narrator orientation, it could be taken *only* as a first-person narration, and so it would seem at first glance in this very story. The most proximate references to a "third person" are those made to the hero, mentioned by name as "Kamo" one paragraph earlier, and to "he" (*kare*) two paragraphs later. These markers are of course reminders enough that the *narrated* subject is being presented in the "third person"—but not enough to distinguish it conclusively from the *narrating* subject. Narrator and hero thus merge as easily in third-person as in first-person narration in the written reportive style, which is used throughout.

This point is brought home (if we may digress for a moment) in a story called *Watakushi wa ikite kita* (I have lived, 1923). Shūkō's recounting of his first years in Tokyo is a "third-person" narration throughout. The hero (and *only* the hero) is identified as *kare*; the *watakushi* in the title is nowhere to be found in the text. And yet there is no mistaking the link between the "he" and the "I"; for as we have noted, "third person" and "first person" are not the autonomous entities that they are in English and the other western languages. Indeed, as we learned in Chapter 2, the "pronoun" *kare*'s extremely narrow range of usage results in a mode of narration in which third person and first person are for all intents and purposes intertwined. Regardless of the narrative "person," the hero's voice is, in the final analysis, the narrator's own. Whether a writer chooses *kare* or *watakushi* as his hero, he has committed him-

---

31. *Shinsen Chikamatsu Shūkō shū*, 241. (Emphasis added.)

self to the epistemology of that one character to the exclusion of all others. Not to do so is to jeopardize the credibility (or "authenticity," if you will) that is underwritten by the written reportive style.

But to return to the "Osaka Courtesan" cycle. Although it lacks the unique temporal regression that so distinguishes *Giwaku* and the rest of the "Estranged Wife" cycle, several stories contain marvelous depictions of the Shūkō world. Perhaps the best is "Nagare." Onatsu arrives late at a spa west of Osaka, where Mashima, a writer, is vacationing, to find that Mashima has finished supper and taken to his bed, having despaired of her ever coming at all. In a scene laced with sexual innuendo, Mashima peels a banana and feeds it to Onatsu as he scolds her for her tardiness. Proper names are dropped: Mashima becomes Man (*otoko*), the prostitute, Woman (*onna*), throughout this and much of the extended bath scene that follows. The next morning, in a reversal of roles, the woman feeds her man roasted chestnuts. Such suggestive passages make an actual love scene redundant, and there is in fact none to be found in "Nagare." The story ends with the hero chanting passages from *jōruri*—a fitting conclusion to a work that recalls a scene from an Edo-period "domestic" play. The hero blissfully inhabits (in a manner that recalls "Yuki no hi") a world sealed off from the realities of ransoms and rivalries with the woman's other clients.

The "Osaka Courtesan" cycle is unique in that it is the one major text that focuses on the Shūkō hero's relationship with a woman at its height. Shūkō wrote numerous stories following his "Estranged Wife" and prior to his "Dark Hair" cycles that depict, respectively, happier days with his wife and with the Kyoto courtesan,[32] but they pale before the anguished tales of abandonment and blind pursuit that make up the twin monuments of his oeuvre.

THE "KYOTO COURTESAN" CYCLE: WRITING AND REWRITING LIVED EXPERIENCE

As with the "Estranged Wife" cycle, the narrator's pursuit of an illusory relationship that nonetheless gives his life purpose is the

---

32. "Kuseyama jōshu" (1928) is an example of the former; *Katsuragi-dayū* (1916), of the latter.

theme of Shūkō's next extended series of stories, known as the "Kyōto no yūjo" (Kyoto courtesan) cycle. The most important of these is a group of stories referred to here as the "Kurokami" or "Dark Hair" cycle: *Kurokami* (Dark hair, 1922), *Kyōran* (Frenzy, 1922), and *Shimo kouru yoi* (Frosty evening, 1922), published together in book form in 1924. This group, which forms the second peak in the Shūkō oeuvre after the "Estranged Wife" cycle, is actually the fourth of six groups of stories treating the author's relationship with a prostitute from Kyoto's Gion quarter. It, along with *Futari no hitori mono* (Two loners, 1923) and a two-work subcycle entitled *Kyūren* (Undying love, 1923) and *Kyūren zokuhen* (Undying love, part 2, 1924; originally entitled *Kutsujoku* [Humiliation]), form a loose trilogy that treats the relationship's decline.

Like the "Estranged Wife" cycle, the "Dark Hair" cycle presents chronologically distant events in the author's life as if they had only just unfolded. The narrator-hero, nameless throughout the cycle, tells the story of his obsessive and demeaning infatuation with Osono, who deftly eludes his advances while extracting every penny from his pocketbook. The hero has returned to Kyoto after a summer sojourn in the mountains to find that his beloved has vanished without a trace. He reminisces about three previous liaisons with her over a four-year period, and in particular the month he spent with her and her mother before his sojourn in the mountains. In a long recollective sequence (extending into *Kyōran*), the time during which he lives in the woman's home becomes the narrative present. Once again the original present is suppressed in a move to collapse the distance between the hero as narrator and the hero as actor—and this is what makes Shūkō's technique of temporal regression differ so markedly from the more or less clearly delineated reflections-as-reflections we call flashbacks.

Kyōran continues the narrator's reverie where *Kurokami* leaves off, practically in midparagraph, with the hero blissfully ensconced in Osono's secluded flat. His jealousy and suspicion are provoked, however, when he discovers that there are other men in Osono's life and that Osono has squandered all the money he sent her from Tokyo. The story suddenly returning to the original narrative present set at the beginning of *Kurokami*, the hero then locates the mother but finds her suddenly hostile. Her lawyer later accuses him of having badgered Osono into illness and finally into running away, and sends him off on a wild-goose chase after his beloved to

Yamashiro, south of Kyoto. In *Shimo kouru yoi*, the hero finally discovers Osono living in a Kyoto back alley near her old flat; she has
never left the city.

As with the "Estranged Wife" cycle, one is above all impressed,
indeed flabbergasted, by what can only be described as an extremely myopic point of view. And yet this cycle's brilliance lies
precisely in the fact that it chronicles the hero's deception through
his own gullible eyes without the benefit of a perspective generated
by time. We have no way of interpreting the intentions of Osono
or her mother other than by what can be deduced from their actions and from the hero's own interpretations, which we come to
suspect are all too sanguine. The narrator is completely silent about
how he has occupied himself when not with Osono during the
years he has known her—which is most of the time, since he visits
Kyoto from Tokyo only occasionally. He is just as silent about the
inception—and outcome—of the affair. One somehow feels that
Osono has *always* been the narrator's sole preoccupation and always will be. Even the demands of his profession are beneath mention—we know only that he is a writer—and he attends to them
with the nearly involuntary movements more commonly associated with brushing one's teeth.

Also beneath mention is the nature of Osono's profession. The
narrator states several times in *Kurokami* and *Kyōran* that he has
denied himself the pleasure of a casual meeting with Osono in the
gay quarter itself. His attitude toward her suggests that of a man
toward his spouse, not a prostitute, and he is destined to be disillusioned. The ambiguity of his attitude is reflected in the dialogue.
His use of three different terms of address (*omae, kimi,* and *an'ta*)
in one short conversation near the beginning of *Kurokami*, for example, graphically illustrates the relationship's instability (*CSS,*
194).

The hero's vain attempt to become a member of Osono's "family"
finds a parallel in his efforts to assimilate himself into an exotic
environment. Indeed, the powerful depiction of this nameless,
rootless man's attempt to invade sacred territory is what makes the
"Kurokami" cycle such a striking text.[33] As an outsider, the hero
is acutely conscious of the city's physical setting (the text is rich in

---

33. The following discussion is indebted to Kōno Kensuke, "*Kurokami* ron josetsu," esp. 286–96.

descriptive passages), its cuisine, its language (the prostitute's Kyoto lilt contrasts markedly with his crisp Tokyo speech), and finally, his beloved, the likes of whom he claims could exist nowhere but in Kyoto. That Osono is an extension of Kyoto itself is driven home in the scene in which she first appears, as she seemingly materializes from the hills surrounding the city.

> We were to rendezvous near the Kōdaiji Temple grounds, a short walk from the inn. . . . The hills behind the houses were covered with dark green pines and straight, light green bamboo. I walked toward the hills up a quiet, narrow lane to a teahouse in Makuzu-gahara where we were to meet, and waited for a while. Situated high above the Kamo River basin, the area afforded a fine view of the city. The pleasant winter sun cast its golden light on Mount Atago, which rose to the west through the deep blue afternoon mist. I walked on a bit but took care not to stray too far. Glancing back at the spot where I had previously stood, I could make out among the crowd of passersby a familiar figure gliding up the slope. It was she.
>
> (*CSS*, 187)

At the city's center is the sacred space occupied by Osono and her mother: a tiny, secluded flat to which the hero gains brief access before his trip to the mountains. Thwarted at every turn in an attempt to have even so much as a chat with Osono, the hero is suddenly led late one misty, moonlit night by her mother through a labyrinth of back alleys to their home. Only after passing through a series of barriers—a gate, a low door, a narrow interior garden, yet another low door, a succession of dark rooms—does he at last reach his beloved's cozy apartment, which radiates light and warmth.

Returning from the mountains after the summer, however, the Shūkō hero finds that he has been expelled from this sacred space and that indeed the space itself has been obliterated: Osono and her mother have moved out. From this point on (*Kyōran*, chapter 3), the hero devotes his energies to an attempt to penetrate what is now a completely closed-off world. Unable to find any trace of Osono in Kyoto, he relies on a dubious lead from the lawyer and searches for her in the hills south of the city. Osono is said to have been born at the foot of a holy mountain near Yamashiro and still to have relatives there. The hero redirects his sights toward this new sacred space, but lacking a guide, he has no hope for success.

Lost in the countryside and with snow starting to fall, he reconsiders his request to beg a ride further into the hills.

> "Please get on," the driver said.
> My heart was warmed by the driver's kindness, but I could not bring myself to board the cart. One mountain range rose above another before me under the leaden sky. Why was it so difficult for me to forget about her, I wondered.
> "Thanks, but I think I'll forego the ride after all."
> With that, I abandoned my search and retraced my steps. When I reached the long wooden bridge across the Kizu River, a cold, snowy wind swirled up from the water and knifed across my face.
>
> (*CSS*, 246)

The hero is in the end utterly unsuccessful in his attempts to possess Osono. His ideal is by no means tarnished by such failure, however; if anything, it glistens all the more brilliantly when just out of reach. And if it is the chase (obviously futile to more discerning eyes), not the conquest, that inspires the hero's passion, so is it the desire to relate, rather than resolve, his affair that prompts the narrator to take up his pen. As actor, the hero lives only for love; as writer, the narrator revels in telling a story, shorn of perspective, of blind pursuit.

And telling it again. Shortly after publishing his "Dark Hair" cycle, Shūkō wrote *Kyūren* and *Kyūren zokuhen*, a two-story sequel that advances the "Dark Hair" narrative a few months. The "Kyūren" cycle is no ordinary sequel, however, in that it primarily amends and recasts rather than supplements the previous cycle. In the case of *Kyūren*, which interlaces *Kyōran*, a woof woven into the warp, the overlap is virtually complete. At times it comes dangerously close to being a rehash as well, but it merits our attention nonetheless for the insights it offers into Shūkō's narrative technique. Indeed, in dealing with this cycle, there is much to be said for the kind of approach that Gérard Genette calls a "paradigmatic reading," in which thematic rather than narrative consistency prevails in an author's corpus and in which "the text begins with the duplication of the text."[34]

---

34. *Figures of Literary Discourse*, 168. Genette applies this reading to Stendahl, author of an oeuvre that, compared with the self-contained narratives of Balzac, is "fragmented, elliptical, repetitive, yet infinite, or at least indefinite" (p. 165).

The "Kyūren" cycle presents a familiar story in a radically different format. The keynote in *Kyūren* is the hero's gradual, painful enlightenment, in contrast with his unchanging gullibility in *Kyōran*. It is not simply that a third-person narrator replaces the first-person narrator-hero; the temporal regression common to both the "Estranged Wife" and "Dark Hair" cycles completely disappears. Writing with a clear awareness of his hero's follies, moreover, the "Kyūren" narrator sees the hero less as a victim of his passion for Oryū (Osono in the "Dark Hair" cycle) than as the deliberate target of her associates' con game.

There is also a significant overlap between two other texts, *Futari no hitori mono* and *Shimo kouru yoi*. We immediately recognize the Shūkō hero in Tahara, a writer hopelessly in love with a Gion prostitute. After summarizing certain events detailed in the "Dark Hair" cycle, *Futari no hitori mono* describes Tahara's eventual discovery of Oryū and his bitter arguments with her now-inhospitable mother. The actual outcome of Tahara's maneuverings seems even of less concern than in earlier stories, however, because of the presence of a second protagonist: Tahara's friend Tsuruoka, a journalist with socialist leanings who is constantly tailed by the police. After Tahara finally gains a foothold into Oryū's house, the narrative inexplicably drops the subject and tells us no more.

Perhaps Shūkō's awareness that the "same" lived experience could generate different tellings (as we have noted specifically in the "sequels" to the "Dark Hair" cycle)[35] arose from his previous discovery that "different" experiences could in turn generate essentially the same tale. The most memorable texts in the Shūkō oeuvre are nearly all informed by the now-familiar motif of the hapless lover awaiting or chasing vainly after his beloved. Even though the "Estranged Wife" and "Dark Hair" cycles are based on experiences separated by nearly a decade, their similarities are particularly striking. Both Osuma and Osono are idealized figures who remain tantalizingly out of the hero's reach. Both disappear without warning. Both have protectors (Osuma's sister and

---

35. Narrative "amendation" of a sort occurs in texts published around the time of the "Estranged Wife" cycle as well. See, for example, "Sono ato," which overlaps *Giwaku zokuhen* almost completely and can be regarded as a draft of the latter, except that it lacks the intensity derived in the "Estranged Wife" cycle from the compression of temporally discrete events into virtually the same psychological continuum.

brother-in-law, and Osono's mother) who frustrate the hero's every effort to regain contact. The Shūkō hero travels far and wide in search of clues to his beloved's whereabouts: to Nikkō and Oka-yama in the "Estranged Wife" cycle and to Yamashiro in the "Dark Hair" cycle. In both, the hero vies with a shadowy figure for his beloved's affections: a student in the former, and a businessman in the latter. The "Osaka Courtesan" cycle also follows essentially the same pattern, sometimes so closely that one experiences a sense of déjà vu. A scene in "Nagare," for example, in which the hero mo-rosely takes to bed after an interminable wait for his beloved, an-ticipates a similar scene in *Kurokami* and at the same time recalls scenes in *Shūjaku* and *Giwaku*, in which the hero entertains mur-derous thoughts of his former wife while burrowed under his quilt.

It is tempting to attribute such parallels to coincidence: as a *shishōsetsu* writer, the author drew from his own life and thus from a limited pool of experience. Yet even a single life is vastly complex, and similar experiences can always be presented in vastly different ways. In an essay on his "Dark Hair" cycle, Shūkō expresses amazement that the same fate (of being abandoned by his beloved) would visit him twice in a lifetime. At the same time, he makes it clear that he has not left to chance the *technique* that describes that fate. "In *Giwaku* I establish as the fictional present the hero's search through the inns of Nikkō and then go back in time, writing about the past as if events had only just taken place. I do the same in *Kurokami* and *Kyōran*."[36]

The sheer number of thematic parallels in Shūkō's major texts, accentuated by the similarity of narrative presentation, suggests as strongly as anything that art has followed art as much as it has followed life, that the author has detected a pattern in his experi-ence and amplified it to a level of significance far beyond that in his actual day-to-day affairs. It is this pattern, more than each episode's autobiographical veracity, that gives meaning to these parallels; its presence, moreover, belies the simple author-hero equation that *shishōsetsu* readers tend to make, because it calls for a perspective on the part of the author that is not available to the narrator-hero in texts like *Giwaku* and *Kyōran*. It should not surprise us, there-fore, to learn that Shūkō did not pen his most satisfactory accounts

36. "*Kyōran* gakuyabanashi," in *Yomiuri shinbun*, 4 Apr. 1922, p. 7.

of his life until the events on which they were based had long since taken on the patina of history. Only when events had passed from the realm of action to that of reflection was he free to plumb his experience with all the frenzy he could muster. In real life, Shūkō was usually one relationship ahead of his fiction. At the time he was writing in *Giwaku* about his frantic search through the inns of Nikkō, for example, Shūkō was already involved with the woman in his "Osaka Courtesan" cycle; when writing in *Kyōran* about his wild-goose chase through the snowy countryside of Yamashiro, he was contemplating marriage to a Tokyo masseuse.[37] The broader perspective afforded the author by elapsed time allowed him to choose all the more rigorously those details that conformed to his masochistic vision of a fool's love.

SHŪKŌ AS "NOVELIST"

We have thus far considered the major cycles in a generally positive light, stressing Shūkō's ability to "see" the diversity of lived experience within a consistently idealized vision. This vision is maintained in his next series of stories as well, the "Ko no ai" (Doting parent) cycle, beginning with *Ko no ai no tame ni* (For the love of his child, 1924), in which the object of the hero's demeaning adoration merely shifts from an elusive beloved to two sickly daughters, whom he fathered in his late forties.

We must not, however, overlook the fact that Shūkō's experiments in narrative replay, specifically in *Futari no hitori mono* and the "Kyūren" cycle, harbored contradictions that ultimately called the very medium in which he worked into question. In the first place, while a "rereading" of episodes in the author's life could provide new insights through a changed perspective, it could just

---

37. See Hirano Ken, "Sakuhin to sakka," 424–25. Nakajima Kunihiko has since challenged Hirano's link between Shūkō's establishment of a new relationship and his writing about a past one. He argues convincingly that Shūkō did not need time for emotional recovery so much as time for artistic inspiration and that he found it, in the case of his "Estranged Wife" cycle, in the works of Arthur Schnitzler (through Mori Ōgai's translations). He concludes that even in Shūkō's case art imitates art more than life. See "Kyakkan shōsetsu e no yume," 47–48; and "*Shūjaku, Giwaku* o sasaeru mono," 106–7. Yet the fact remains that Shūkō *consistently* wrote his best work months and even years after the incidents in question had taken place—by which time Shūkō was indeed involved with another woman.

as easily result in an excessive milking of material. *Futari no hitori mono, Kyūren,* and *Kyūren zokuhen* are clearly derivative texts. In the second—and far more important—place, the later texts suffer from a loss of what might be called a narrative identity. Shūkō attempted not simply to reinterpret experience when he wrote his sequels to the "Kurokami" cycle but clearly also to grasp it in terms that transcended the *shishōsetsu*'s epistemological limitations. In short, he attempted to recast the Japanese narrative form into one that would have greater narrative autonomy and would accommodate, in the manner of a western-language novel, several points of view. In *Kyūren,* for example, the partially omniscient narrator frees us from the *Kyōran* hero's myopic perspective and, by anticipating events before they develop, generates ironies not to be found in the earlier story. Yet these seemingly requisite conditions for a successful narrative in fact produce an inferior story. Presented by a narrator who ventures tentatively into omniscience, *Kyūren* loses the gripping authenticity of *Kyōran.* In *Futari no hitori mono* the trend is even more pronounced. The tunnel-visioned, first-person narration of the "Dark Hair" cycle gives way to a self-consciously omniscient narrative that adopts the point of view of each of the two main characters. Yet the reader's sympathies are never fully engaged in either of them.

In *Futari no hitori mono* especially, Shūkō seems to be battling with the Japanese language itself. Alert as we have become and as any *bundan* reader would be to the *shishōsetsu* narrator's use of the written reportive style to present himself as a personal authenticator of experience, we want to ask: how does the omniscient narrator know what he knows, and by what authority? The linguistic and epistemological distance that such a narrator places between himself and his principal characters inevitably drives a wedge between narrator and reader as well; for we as readers, observing the grammatical signs (discussed in Chapter 2) that link narrating and acting consciousness, sense that the narrative has shifted from a "sincere" (because epistemologically immanent) recounting to an "insincere" (because epistemologically transcendent) fabrication. By revealing information about the hero's situation that the hero himself does not know, the narrator, in this reading, trivializes the latter's perceptions and discredits the narrative itself as an authentic account.

Thus it is that Shūkō's most myopic presentations (texts like *Giwaku* and *Kyōran*)—because they so successfully replicate a personally authenticated telling—make the most powerful impressions on the reader. Shūkō was doubtlessly aware of his achievement. Yet he spent a great deal of creative energy attempting to overturn the *shishōsetsu*'s restrictive epistemology. Throughout his career, he repeatedly announced his intention to transcend personal experience and write "true novels" (*honkaku shōsetsu*) that dealt objectively with the lives of others.[38] Nakajima Kunihiko, commenting on that intention, suggests that Shūkō was not equipped with the narrative skills needed to produce truly well-crafted and autonomous verbal artifacts.[39] Yet no less a writer than Akutagawa Ryūnosuke thought highly of Shūkō's *honkaku shōsetsu*. He singles out Shūkō's "Rin o nonde shinda hito" (Suicide by phosphorous poisoning, 1926) for special mention. It is the story of a man who, unhappily married to a member of the pariah *burakumin*, bungles his affair with a mistress he has installed in his home to tutor his children. Despairing of his situation, he finally kills himself. The work cannot in fact be counted among Shūkō's best, but it is easy to see what attracted Akutagawa's attention. The story's omniscient narrator reveals the consciousness of the three main characters in turn: the man, his mistress, and his wife. Because the narrator engages the reader's sympathies in all three characters (more successfully, it might be added, than in *Futari no hitori mono*) by relating events from diverse points of view, one is not sure until the end who will actually commit suicide; all have their pressing reasons. Indeed, Shūkō very likely entitled his work " . . . shinda hito" ("person who died") rather than " . . . shinda otoko" ("man who died") precisely in order to keep the reader in the dark.

In defense of "Rin o nonde shinda hito," Akutagawa cautions against judging *honkaku shōsetsu* by the standard of the *shishōsetsu*. Nothing can compare with the latter as a vehicle for confession, he allows, but its superiority in just this one respect should not lead

38. In the preface to a single-volume anthology entitled *Keien* (1915), Shūkō writes, "I have no intention of spending my entire career detailing the follies of my love life. . . . I wish to write about the broad social scene after the manner of Zola." Shūkō expresses a similar wish in "Honrai no negai" (1926).
39. "Kyakkan shōsetsu e no yume," 58.

critics to reject the *honkaku shōsetsu* out of hand.[40] "Should not,"
Akutagawa writes; but reject it (or at least view it suspiciously) the
bundan did. Although critics of the time did not spell it out in so
many words, what bothered them, as we can deduce from our examination in Chapter 3 of the mode of reading literature in the
Taishō period, was the question we asked shortly before: how does
the narrator in a text like "Rin o nonde shinda hito" know what
he knows, and by what authority? And if that knowledge does not
derive from lived experience, how can he convey it with the same
degree of authenticity as one whose knowledge does? The answer
is that he cannot. The mechanics of the Japanese language, reinforced by a long cultural tradition that has associated a transcendent epistemology with fabrication and ultimately with "nonliterature," simply will not let him. That is why Shūkō's *shishōsetsu*,
above and beyond any actual defects in his other fiction, have had
the greater appeal, his several pronouncements about *honkaku shōsetsu* notwithstanding. Autobiographical "fact" is not at issue here;
the crucial equation is between the narrator, not the author, and
his hero. Shūkō succeeded in utilizing the genius of the language
to project the narrator-hero's consciousness *as if* it were the author's
very own, knowing that the reader would interpret it in no
other way.

Shūkō learned well his lesson from Futabatei's *Heibon:* that the
hero who speaks in Japanese directly to his audience speaks most
persuasively. In his *Bundan sanjū nen* (My thirty years in the *bundan*, 1931), Shūkō recalls a conversation he had with Futabatei
about literature and truth. Art, according to Futabatei, is mere fabrication, and life too important to be transformed capriciously into
a pack of lies. But if you must write at all, Futabatei then admon-
ished, then at least write *as if* you are telling a truth that you have
personally lived—which is to say from your own limited perspective and not from the privileged perspective of an omniscient
observer.[41]

40. "Chikamatsu-san no honkaku shōsetsu" (1926), in *Akutagawa Ryūnosuke zenshū* 8:165–67.
41. P. 197. Sawa Toyohiko is perhaps the only Japanese scholar to note Futabatei's influence on Shūkō. See "*Wakaretaru tsuma* to sono hen'yō," 42–43. Futabatei's
words of course represent a major change from the narrative philosophy that guided
him in the writing of *Ukigumo*. Indeed, we can see in *Ukigumo, Sono omokage*, and

184 Three Approaches to Experience

Futabatei published *Heibon* soon after this interview; we have already noted its impact on Shūkō in Chapter 5. Elsewhere, Shūkō elaborates on how he himself wrestled with the problem of narrative presentation in the "Dark Hair" cycle:

> Once I had decided to write a self-exposé, I confronted the question of whether to narrate it in the third person or first person. During a discussion with Tokuda Shūsei and Kume Masao about the problem, Shūsei recommended the former and Kume the latter. I myself felt that using a third-person narration for such brazen confessions would only blunt the overall effect. I told Kume later . . . that I would employ a first-person narration, as I believed it the more convincing conveyor of my true feelings. . . . I have often expressed to younger colleagues my desire in recent years to distance myself and write coolly objective stories in third-person narration, and my utter distaste for recording the painful experiences of private life. Yet I ended up doing just that, once again, in *Kurokami* and *Kyōran*.[42]

We can see that Shūkō's narrative strategy here is essentially identical to the one that informs his "Estranged Wife" cycle. In both cases, he opts for the nontranscendent consciousness available with first-person narration. "I may choose of course to write what I observe or imagine someone else to be doing," Shūkō writes early in his career, "but art is by its very nature concrete and therefore tied irrevocably to one's own perceptions. . . . The more closely a story is linked to those perceptions, the greater its power."[43]

Yet even more important, this strategy informs such "third-person" narratives as the stories in the "Osaka Courtesan" cycle, where the acting "he" merges with the narrating "I." In stories like "Otoko kiyohime" (and most strikingly in *Watashi wa ikite kita*), the third-person narrator is in every sense an extension of the hero, never straying from the latter's epistemological realm. Of course, Shūkō's narrative method is hardly unique. Shiga Naoya also makes effective use of a nonautonomous third-person narrator in *An'ya kōro* (A dark night's passing), as we shall observe in the following chapter. Shūkō's stories simply demonstrate that the hero in an "I-novel" is neither an autonomous "I" nor "he" but rather a

---

Heibon a transition from a narrative form approaching (although never equivalent to) that of the western novel to the epistemologically immanent mode that would only later be termed *shishōsetsu*.

42. "*Kyōran* gakuyabanashi," in *Yomiuri shinbun*, 2 and 4 Apr. 1922, pp. 7 and 7, respectively.

43. "Omotta mama."

discerning, personless (in the grammatical sense) *eye* that perceives the world through the narrator's senses.

Although Shūkō wrote prolifically in several other forms, including *honkaku shōsetsu*, criticism, historical fiction, and travel essays, we have focused primarily on his *shishōsetsu* because his success in that form, combined with the difficulties he had creating a viable narrative voice for his other fiction, have provided us with insights into his overall technique and its import for modern Japanese literature. This technique, which matched perfectly the traditional epistemology, provided a modus operandi for scores of writers to follow. Among them were writers like Shiga Naoya, with a finer, more carefully crafted style, and like Kasai Zenzō, with a greater commitment to the *shishōsetsu* form, but none with a clearer awareness of the stakes involved in choosing one narrative form—and its supporting epistemology—over another.

Not that Shūkō was a deep thinker. Yet neither can he simply be dismissed as the raving degenerate that Akagi Kōhei and others would make him out to be. Although Shūkō very likely pursued in real life every foolish escapade he describes in his work, too facile an equation between life and art can only blind us to Shūkō's purpose as a writer. Masamune Hakuchō writes that Shūkō wanted to create love stories after Ozaki Kōyō or Chikamatsu Monzaemon; that he was a frustrated Chūbei or Jihei searching for his Umekawa or Koharu but finally unable to find her.[44] Perhaps. But his failure in real life was not necessarily detrimental to his literary project. On the contrary, it provided a vision radically different from the fulfilled if tragic loves of Umekawa and Chūbei or Koharu and Jihei in Chikamatsu's dramas. "Looking back on my life," Shūkō writes in a "retrospective" essay in 1910, near the beginning of his career as a fiction writer, "I see that I have achieved no memorable successes. Indeed, the more I reflect, the more painful experiences I can recall. And yet for one like me who does not entertain any ambitions for the future either, there is no other pleasure in life than recollecting past failures and savoring the excruciating ecstasy of suffering."[45] Already Shūkō has discovered the keynote of his literature, fashioned from emotions recalled in barely contained

44. *Chikamatsu Shūkō*, in *Masamune Hakuchō zenshū* 4:521.
45. "Bungei hyaku hōmen."

hysteria and centering on a lost and never-to-be regained ideal. "Even though he [this 'he' that is synonymous with 'I'] was starved for feminine affections," the Shūkō narrator writes three years later of his hero in "Otoko kiyohime," "he/I had no interest in seeking out a flesh-and-blood woman and becoming intimate with her. He/I had grown weary of real women; he/I preferred the women of his/my dreams. Recalling past associations and giving him/myself over to the exciting memories was far more pleasant, he/I found, than burdening him/myself with an actual relationship." [46]

The women in his life understandably wearied of his irresponsible ways and abandoned him; but Shūkō fashioned out of them a coy siren destined to elude for all time his heroes' grasp. We have seen how he rewrote the events in his own life in a way that conformed to his ideal vision. However eccentric in real life, he remained faithful to his literary aesthetic. And if we end up admiring the work more than the real-life man, are we not in fact paying Shūkō the ultimate tribute as an artist?

46. *Shinsen Chikamatsu Shūkō shū*, 232–33.

8

Shiga Naoya:
The Hero as Sage

Shiga Naoya's work is above all that of an author who has
lived a most noble life. Noble? To live nobly is in the first
place to live like a god. Perhaps Shiga's life is not to be likened to that of some incarnate deity. But the man has . . .
plainly led a pure, unblemished existence.

> Akutagawa Ryūnosuke, *Bungeiteki na,*
> *amari ni bungeiteki na*

I read a certain story by the "grand old man" of letters.
Once again it presented that stern countenance calculated
to please his patronizing crowd. It was mighty insincere
stuff. But this foolish, fawning crowd calls it "noble" and
"fastidious," and the silliest among them reverently label it
"aristocratic." . . . We must be wary of those writers who
are hailed as proudly aloof or principled or fastidious, for
they are the crafty ones. To be "fastidious," after all, is to
be selfish, stubborn, shrewd. "Fastidiousness" is utter vain-
glory; it is the desire to win at all costs. It is, if you will, a
fascist mentality, which longs to enslave others.

> Dazai Osamu, "Nyoze gamon"

What was there about Shiga Naoya's presence, his literary mystique, his sheer magnitude, that may have actually helped speed
at least two other writers to their deaths? In 1927, when Shiga had
reached the pinnacle of his career, Akutagawa Ryūnosuke, at the
end of his, wrote of Shiga in two posthumous essays in a tone
suggesting that fierce envy lay at the root of his praise.[1] Two

---

1. In *Haguruma*, Akutagawa writes: "Stretched out on my bed, I began reading
An'ya kōro. Every phase of the hero's spiritual struggle moved me. What a fool I was
compared to him, I thought, the tears streaming from my eyes" (*Akutagawa Ryūnosuke zenshū* 9 : 144–45). In *Bungeiteki na, amari ni bungeteki na*, chapter 5, he notes in
addition to the remarks contained in the epigraph above that Shiga is a realist who
never relies on the imagination for his descriptions, that he infuses his realism with

decades later, Shiga's still-considerable influence spurred Dazai Osamu to write of him, also in a posthumous essay, with an unmitigated bile that nevertheless failed to conceal his envy for an author turned into institution.[2] Both Akutagawa and Dazai of course had other reasons for killing themselves, but one cannot help wondering if frustration at their inability to compete with this towering institution did not provide additional motivation for their suicides.

In our survey (in Chapter 3) of *shishōsetsu* criticism since the 1920s, we traced the development of a literary standard that valorized the kind of writing Shiga in particular had mastered. We noted the concern with a writer's "sincerity" and "integrity" as manifested in the text's "realism." We also noted that the relationship between realism's "content" (i.e., the author's depiction of lived experience) and its "form" (i.e., his profession of sincerity) was a symbiotic and inseparable one. To say that confession in this context begat sincerity or that sincerity begat confession is to say no more than that content and form were mutually reinforcing, and mutually constraining, entities. Both confession as "content" and sincerity as "form" made special demands on writers who sought to exploit the *shishōsetsu*. We have already seen that realism in the early twentieth-century Japanese context did not mean the depiction of a broad social canvas or even the amassing of a plethora of naturalistic detail but rather the meticulous recording of the author's own experience. The so-called "fidelity" of depiction that generates realism, we also observed, is ultimately a function of the writer's style—that is, of his facility with the *mode* of sincerity—and not of the referential or psychological truthfulness of the account, which the reader can never fully determine.

No writer better appreciated this fact than Shiga, who fully understood both the potential and the limitations of a literature of sincerity. Shiga's case is particularly impressive in that the technical brilliance on which his reputation for integrity was based was evident from the very beginning. It is no accident that modern Japanese literature's most highly lauded stylist (*bunshō no kamisama*) was also its most highly lauded "realist" (*shōsetsu no kamisama*). Shiga's

---

a poetic spirit grounded in the eastern aesthetic tradition, and that he, Akutagawa, has found this last quality beyond his own powers as a writer. *Akutagawa Ryūnosuke zenshū* 9:12.

2. See "Nyoze gamon" (1948), in *Dazai Osamu zenshū* 10:296–326.

purpose as a *shishōsetsu* writer was never the complete, unerring depiction of lived experience, but rather the authoritative demonstration of his moral integrity. The natural and inevitable result of this conscious decision to market his sincerity, however, was that the Shiga oeuvre would be limited in scope and the private man largely inaccessible to public scrutiny.

It is thus with Shiga's writings that we realize the immense difference between a personal and a semi-private literature and discover how voluble the former (to wit, the writings of Dazai) and how reticent the latter can be. Whereas the avowedly autobiographical work of many writers, particularly in the west, demonstrate that even a highly personal literature (in which an articulate narrator-hero eagerly expresses his feelings and dramatizes the significant events of his life) can easily communicate itself to a wide audience, Shiga's work sooner or later provokes the question: how private can an author make his fiction and still appeal to his readers? Indeed, how private can writing be and still even be called fiction? The availability of the *shishōsetsu's* author-hero equation does not alone explain Shiga's interest in a private literature. We are puzzled not by the fact that Shiga dwells on personal experience (which is, after all, the domain of any *shishōsetsu* or autobiographical writer), but by the fact that he says so little about himself in the process. In the Taishō *bundan's* heyday, when *shōsetsu* and *shishōsetsu* were practically synonymous among *junbungaku* writers, Shiga was the reigning deity of prose "fiction," a reputation he earned by writing stories that are for the most part so purely autobiographical that critics rely on them heavily when chronicling his biography. Yet as a character in his stories, the author is a surprisingly elusive figure. Shiga is genuinely inclined to record personal experience, yet loath to reveal it in any detail.

Shiga, then, is at once reticent about his own experience and unwilling to stray far from it; and one wonders, with Nakamura Mitsuo, whether Shiga did not choose the wrong career: "If Shiga cannot imagine his life to have been anything other than what it actually was, then here alone is his greatest single failing as a writer."[3] Shiga's overriding preoccupation with his own literary persona, moreover, directs his attention away from other charac-

---

3. *Shiga Naoya ron*, 14.

ters, and one can appreciate Nakamura's criticism, again with reference to Shiga, that a novelist without interest in other people is no novelist at all.[4] Yet Nakamura readily admits (and here he concurs with the critical consensus) that Shiga is a crucial figure—perhaps *the* crucial figure—in modern Japanese letters. "Of all writers active in the Taishō period, none has made such a profound and vital impact on contemporary literature as Shiga. Not even the likes of [Mori] Ōgai or [Natsume] Sōseki compare with him in influence."[5] Takeda Rintarō puts it even more succinctly: "Shiga Naoya is Japanese literature's heartland."[6]

The precise nature of this influence, it should be added, is of as much interest as its scope. Even more than to matters of style and theme, Shiga's great contribution has been to defining the author's relationship to his writing. This ambivalent relationship, which reveals a contradictory urge to self-expression and anonymity (as the epigraph to Chapter 3 makes clear), must be clarified if we are to understand how Shiga's literature can be so candid and yet so taciturn.

WRITING AS A MORAL IMPERATIVE

This seeming contradiction can be addressed by pausing to reconsider just what it meant to be a writer in early twentieth-century Japan. In Chapter 1 we noted the Confucian prejudice against fiction and the preference for such respected nonfictional forms as biography, history, and memoirs, and we traced the residual effect of this prejudice into the modern era. One reason why the *bundan* congealed into a relatively like-minded group is that its members were viewed by society as outcasts and worse: mere entertainers on a level with vaudeville performers.

Shiga and most early twentieth-century authors were shaped by this view of fiction. One of the reasons for Shiga's celebrated breach

---

4. Ibid., 13. Nakamura echoes (in a very negative way) the view of Kobayashi Hideo, who claims that the only fully drawn character in Shiga's entire oeuvre is Tokitō Kensaku, the hero of *An'ya kōro*, but that this fact does not in itself detract from Shiga's greatness as a writer. See "Shiga Naoya ron" (1938), in *Shintei Kobayashi Hideo zenshū* 4:112–14.

5. *Shiga Naoya ron*, 5.

6. Cited in ibid.

with his father was his decision to pursue a writing career. Shiga's father voiced a quite common sentiment: outrage that any son (but particularly the eldest, as Shiga was) born to a socially distinguished family would degrade himself by indulging in such a frivolous occupation. There is a memorable scene in *Aru otoko, sono ane no shi* (A certain man and the death of his sister, 1920) in which the father interrogates his son, the hero, about his plan to become a fiction writer (*shōsetsuka*). The hero replies in his defense that Takizawa Bakin 1767–1848), the Edo-period writer of *yomihon* whom the father admires, also wrote fiction and that he, who thinks little of Bakin, intends to become a fiction writer truly worthy of the name ("motto hontō no shōsetsuka ni naru no desu").[7] The hero implies that his writing will not contain the implausible incidents and other "lies" that mar Bakin's works. Of course, Shiga was hardly alone in his predicament. Contemporaries like Arishima Takeo, a member along with Shiga of the "Shirakaba" group, Nagai Kafū, and Ozaki Kazuo (1899–1983), a Shiga protégé, met with similarly strong resistance from their families, and especially their fathers, when they revealed their desire to become writers.[8]

Since Shiga and others were nonetheless very serious about their work, it was incumbent on them to convince their readers (and perhaps even themselves in their moments of doubt) that they should not be dismissed as so many vaudeville raconteurs. The task was clear: to redefine the *shōsetsu* writer's image in terms that commanded society's respect. Masao Miyoshi has argued that the Japanese typically measure personal worth by how closely one approximates the ideal of one's professional type: one strives to become *the* teacher, *the* craftsman, *the* fisherman.[9] In Tokugawa Japan, the ideal writer was the scholar-sage—a man like Ogyū Sorai (1666–1728) or Arai Hakuseki (1657–1725), who pondered the problems of correct living and correct government through the study of history. Their treatises are unabashedly didactic. Society looked to them for moral pronouncements just as naturally as it

7. *SNZ* 2:439–40. Citations from this *zenshū* henceforth appear, where appropriate, in the body of the text.
8. Ozaki recalls in his memoir *Ano hi kono hi* (1:14) that his father thought of only *waka* and Chinese poetry as worthy of the name *literature* and regarded the *shōsetsu* in particular as beneath contempt.
9. *Accomplices of Silence*, 78–79.

looked to craftsmen or fishermen for the specialized services they rendered.[10] The obvious choice for the early twentieth-century *shō-setsu* writer, then, living in a society still influenced by the Confucian ethic, was to adopt the role of *the* writer, which had until then been assumed by authors of histories, biographies, essays, and other prose forms esteemed by tradition. By linking himself to this tradition, the *shōsetsu* writer appropriated for himself the moral legitimacy he otherwise lacked. To be sure, this modern-day "sage," in his incarnation as *shōsetsu* writer, entertained a different goal from his predecessors': he dedicated himself to his own inner growth rather than to the state. (In this sense his outlook was probably closer to the Buddhist worldview and its concern with the isolated—as opposed to the socially integrated—man, as we noted in Chapter 4.) But he mined his personal experiences in much the same spirit of edification as his Confucianist predecessors did. In his role as moralizer and philosophizer, the *shōsetsu* writer was less concerned with appealing to a wide audience than with earning society's respect. Indeed, vast popularity might have generated suspicions about his credentials as a member of the morally conscious literati. Writers with any pretensions to "seriousness" stood to gain only by projecting an image of themselves as ideals of their type.

Shiga was without a doubt the most successful of all twentieth-century writers at playing the author-sage. A great measure of his success lay in his ability to strip from his persona any qualities inappropriate to that role. It is important to understand that the role's principal requirement was seen as ethical, not artistic, in nature. It was not enough to be a facile stylist; the writer had to be, above all, a moral human being. Shiga himself articulated this credo in an unpublished manuscript, written early in his career, that downgrades the art of fiction and affirms the primacy of moral growth. "I was not born to write fiction [*shōsetsu*]. Fiction is a means and not an end. . . . I want to write about everyday life and by doing so to improve it. I shall develop into a better person, and my creative writing shall be a by-product of that development" (*SNZ* 9:528). That Shiga was aware of his mission as a new breed

---

10. Joyce Ackroyd suggests that Arai Hakuseki viewed himself as a "latter-day sage" dedicated to the service of his rulers. See *Told Round a Brushwood Fire*, 26.

of *shōsetsu* writer is further apparent in the choice of titles for his first important composition: "Hishōsetsu, sobo" (Grandmother: a non-*shōsetsu*, 1908), later published as "Aru asa" (One morning, 1918).[11]

Shiga's writing, then, as a "by-product" of what was essentially a moral endeavor, naturally focuses on subjects befitting the image of a would-be sage who offers the text of his life as an example to the reader; for the question that has most occupied the early twentieth-century *shōsetsu* writer as recorder of lived experience was simply, how to live. The reader, in turn, looked to a writer like Shiga for moral guidance that could be gleaned from the text. The *shishōsetsu* was, of course, the ideal form for nurturing such a "recorder-witness" relationship. The ever-present narrator-hero becomes the sole unifying and ordering textual element in a story stripped of plot, character, and dramatic scene. A narrating persona who did not resemble the author would in fact be a contradiction in terms.

The author-sage's underlying rationale is epitomized by the phrase "Bun wa hito nari" (writing is the person), which is to say that the writer's character determines the quality of his literary output. Numerous critics, tempted to equate literary virtuosity with the high moral ground, have singled out Shiga in particular and marveled at the apparent propinquity of life and art, behavior and words. One critic, arguing with Shiga clearly in mind, puts it this way: "A healthy and vigorously moral voice pervades every text worthy of being deemed a classic."[12]

We should not forget, however, that Shiga's "vigorously moral voice" is in the final analysis the product of a style of which Shiga was the undisputed master. That is why the above citation would seem to have the argument exactly backward: is not the writer's "morality" as textual expression more the *product* of the writing than its formative element? As consumers of that verbal product, readers become acquainted with the writer's character perforce en-

11. Ikeuchi Teruo notes in a comparison of several early manuscripts that this story about the Shiga hero's quarrel with his grandmother marks a decisive turn away from earlier attempts at more conventionally fictional subjects having no direct relation to the author's private life. See "Naoya no riarizumu," 52.

12. Yamamuro Shizuka, "*An'ya kōro o chūshin ni,*" 344. Takada Mizuho offers a similar view: "The beauty of Shiga's life gave birth to the beauty of his writings; in this fact lies Shiga's success as an author" (*Shiga Naoya*, 37).

tirely through the printed page. That they accept Shiga's prose style with so little resistance is the most persuasive proof of all of Shiga's sensitivity to his medium. Here is how Shiga analyzes his own awareness, in a miscellany entitled "Seishūchō" (1937):

> Grammar is not a set of rules (aside from those governing the use of case-indicating particles). It is something more fundamental. To say that a sentence is ungrammatical does not mean that the writer has disregarded the rules but rather that he has disregarded his own pattern of thought. That is not right. I do not know the first thing about grammar, but I do try in my writing to be faithful to the way I think.
>
> (*SNZ* 7:37)

In his *shishōsetsu*, Shiga is indeed faithful to the way he—and any Japanese—"thinks," namely by presenting a recorder (as we have labeled him) who speaks grammatically and epistemologically only for himself (whether in first or third person) and who thus by his very utterance privileges his "presence" over the narrated events. It is this unrelenting sense of presence that provides the basis for Shiga's celebrated moral authority. Shiga's approach is hardly unique; it is, in fact, the *shishōsetsu's* foundation (as we have already seen in the case of Chikamatsu Shūkō). But few have made such effective use of the narrator as recorder of his thoughts and actions and as unblinking observer of his surroundings.

In offering his own life as an example for others, however, Shiga continually felt the need to excise those experiences that would tarnish the image of author-sage, or at the very least to present them in such a way as to lessen their impact—even at the expense of a good story. Rather than contradict his scrupulously conceived literary image, Shiga would generally lay down his pen—hence the impression one gets of an impenetrable core of privacy in much of his writing. Any *shishōsetsu* writer, of course, has something to lose as a private citizen when he becomes overly zealous in penning his "confessions," but Shiga figured to lose his raison d'être as an author. The great attraction of Shiga's stories is the narrator-hero's display of candor and decorum. But this candor is a facade, a studied technique, as it perhaps must be in such an unspontaneous form of expression as writing. The author-sage is forced to steer his confessions between the Scylla of face-saving deceit, which if discovered might undermine the reader's trust, and the Charybdis of a downgraded image resulting from some true but embarrassing revelation. Consequently, Shiga, far from presenting a comprehensive picture of "real life," edited lived experience so thoroughly that his work inevitably took on a shape utterly distinct from it. Indeed, because his concern with writing's impact on private life was stronger than his urge to write, it led at times to awkwardly told stories or even to complete silence. When faced with the choice of disrupting private life or interrupting his literary career, Shiga—reputedly the supreme chronicler of personal experience, the *shishōsetsu* writer par excellence—almost invariably chose the latter.

THE AUTHOR-SAGE AS FICTIVE PERSONA

Shiga wrote little of what we would unhesitatingly call "fiction." Despite some memorable successes,[13] he is sometimes visibly uncomfortable making the attempt. That he would feel constrained by actual events when writing stories based on his own life is perhaps inevitable, but the concern with his image as author-sage is evident in his "imaginative" stories as well. The popular story "Kozō no kamisama" (The shop boy's patron saint, 1920) is one such example. In it, A, a young aristocrat and member of the House of Peers, treats the apprentice Senkichi to a meal of sushi and then disappears from the boy's life just as mysteriously as he appeared in it. The story revolves around a series of coincidences. A, who happens to see Senkichi fingering a piece of sushi he cannot afford to pay for at a stall, later chances to buy a set of scales at the very shop in which Senkichi is apprenticed. A takes the boy to a restaurant that is, again quite by chance, the same one Senkichi earlier overheard his superiors raving about. The impressionable boy begins to think of A as some kind of god.

In the story's final paragraph, the narrator, who has related events alternately from A's and Senkichi's points of view, confesses that he planned to conclude the story with yet another coincidence.

---

13. "Kamisori" (The razor, 1910), "Seibei to hyōtan" (Seibei and his gourds, 1913), and "Han no hanzai" (Han's crime, 1913) are the best-known examples and the most frequently translated of Shiga's stories into English—the result, at least in part, of western resistence to the *shishōsetsu*.

We have already learned that A signed a fictitious name and address in the shop register out of a certain diffidence about his intent to treat the boy. The narrator now thinks of having the address match that of a small shrine.

> This writer will lay down his pen. He had intended to conclude his story in the following way. The apprentice, hoping to learn his client's identity, finds out the man's name and address from the chief clerk. He decides to pay the man a visit. But he finds no house at the address, only a tiny shrine dedicated to the fox deity. The apprentice is stunned. Such was this writer's intent; but he thought that such an ending would be too cruel a trick to play on the apprentice and has decided to end the story here instead.
>
> (*SNZ* 3:75)

Akutagawa Ryūnosuke applauds Shiga for providing what is both a gloss on and an integral part of the story, and he compares the work's "perfect incompleteness" to a Rodin statue in which a figure emerges, only half chiseled, from the marble.[14] Akutagawa's own penchant for surprise endings, however, seems to have blinded him to the coda's self-consciousness, which exhibits Shiga's deep ambivalence about the author's creative function. One senses the narrator's desire to deceive neither his characters nor his readers. But such a desire is ultimately self-defeating, for it requires the narrator to assume contradictory roles. What has been an aloof, near-omniscient narrator until the story's last paragraph suddenly demystifies himself, becoming all too human and all too visible by admitting in effect that he, like A, can no longer go on performing in a godlike role and rig the story at will. After painstakingly fashioning the first two coincidences, he calls them both into question by wondering aloud about the need for a third. A narrator divided within himself cannot speak, and the story self-destructs.[15]

The proposed ending, had the narrator gone ahead with it, would have in fact provided a witty finale, for it is a logical out-

---

14. "Taishō kyū nen do bundan jōhan-ki kessan" (1920), in *Akutagawa Ryūnosuke zenshū* 4:175.

15. Shiga's narrator differs radically from those of, say, Thackeray or Fielding (e.g., in *Tom Jones*), who also expound on how they plan to dispose of their heroes. Even though the latter appear to treat their characters like marionettes, reflection on the chance-ridden fates, future or past, of their characters never prevents them from carrying on with their stories. On the contrary, it brings home to them the dramatic potential of their own creative imaginations, a thought that never occurs to the narrator in "Kozō no kamisama."

growth of the story's developments. The narrator has prepared the reader for this last coincidence by a prior exploration of Senkichi's thoughts. In an earlier passage, the apprentice, having met with serendipitous good fortune, imagines his benefactor to possess superhuman powers:

> Senkichi suspected that the client was someone very special. The man found out about that humiliating episode at the sushi stall, he had known what the clerks had been saying about the restaurant, and above all he had seen into Senkichi's heart and treated the boy to all the sushi he could eat. These were not the deeds of an ordinary mortal. Perhaps the man was a god. Or one of those Taoist Immortals. Or maybe even the fox deity incarnate. So Senkichi thought.
>
> (*SNZ* 3:73)

The coincidence of a randomly jotted address turning out to be that of a shrine dedicated to the fox deity, then, would hardly have come as a total surprise to readers, and it would have provided Senkichi with the final "proof" that his patron was indeed a supernatural being. Yet the narrator abandons this idea as a "cruel trick" that he will not play on his character. He is finally more anxious about his own moral integrity than about his story's working as fiction.[16]

Another drawback of the final authorial aside is that it fails to recognize the irony inherent in A's situation. This wealthy and privileged member of society, perceived by Senkichi as a demigod, actually suffers from low self-esteem, as we learn in several pas-

---

16. Rather than question Shiga's ambivalence about the narrative form, however, critics have typically concerned themselves with the story's "humanism" and "realism." Endō Tasuku suggests that the narrator's paternalistic attitude toward Senkichi is evidence of Shiga's humanitarian character: the author's decision to remain silent prevents the young shop boy from receiving a potential "shock" (i.e., the discovery that A is indeed a god). He further argues that the decision to end the story where it does is a credit to Shiga's healthy sense of verisimilitude, for the introduction of a third "coincidence" would only dilute the story's "reality" (in Shindō Junkō and Endō Tasuku, eds., *Shiga Naoya shū*, 591 n. 251). Yet the awkwardness of Endō's position is evident as soon as one stops to consider what an optimal number of coincidences might actually be—an impossibility without also considering their function in a particular text. In "Kozō no kamisama," the first two coincidences surely take on their full import only with the third, which Shiga proposes and then dismisses. The awkwardness becomes even more apparent when, after commending Shiga for his narrative restraint, Endō then suggests that Shiga ought to have excised the concluding apology altogether (ibid). Endō admits, if only tacitly, that calling the story's realism needlessly into question here only serves to undermine it.

sages. He sympathizes with the apprentice when he first spies him walking away hungry from the sushi stall, but he lacks the élan to take him aside and treat him to dinner on the spot. Later, instead of feeling pleased with himself for taking the boy to a restaurant following their chance meeting, he questions his self-complacency and succumbs to a fit of melancholy, quite as if he had just committed a crime. Finally, he rebukes himself for being so rash as to treat the boy at all. To have this character, so lacking in self-confidence, enshrined as a deity is a marvelous irony and also symbolic of the utterly different worlds that the apprentice and the nobleman inhabit. The story's most crucial fault, then, lies not in its somehow "damaging" fictions but in its inability to capitalize on them. Even A's painfully realized self-knowledge can only partially redeem a story that the narrator has acknowledged to be a sham. By raising doubts about the story's conclusion, the narrator casts doubt on the narrative project itself in such a way that leaves him alone as the only authentic vestige.[17]

Clearly, the image-conscious narrator is more at home in stories where he figures centrally from the start and competes with no other characters. Freed from the potentially awkward contrivances of plot, he records any personal experience that reveals himself in an appealing light. Shiga's celebrated honesty, then, is no ordinary candor. Spontaneity is sacrificed to "confessions" well calculated to service the myth of sincerity and at the same time limit the field of writing to a cautious form of autotherapy or catharsis that if successful leads, ironically, to silence. For Shiga, the writer's ideal state is one of emotional equilibrium in which writing itself finally becomes unnecessary. Writing is simply the means, like a dose of medicine, to bring about this state. One writes, therefore, only what is nec-

---

17. This is not to suggest that all such doubts are destined to undermine fictional narrative. John Fowles's *The French Lieutenant's Woman*, to take an example from recent English literature, is a noteworthy success in which the narrator concludes his tale with a multiple ending. Unlike Shiga's diffident narrator, who is an authorial second thought appearing from out of nowhere, Fowles's narrator, in the tradition of Fielding, is a well-developed personality with whom the reader has grown intimate from the novel's beginning. He is imperious, self-assertive, and never daunted into silence, even by apocalyptic musings about endings. He comments freely about his material throughout the text, and his equivocal ending is entirely in keeping with the novel as a whole. He is both omniscient and personal, a rare if not impossible combination in Japanese, given the tendency to link a "personal" narrator with a nontranscendent, non-"fabricated" narrating presence.

essary to achieve this equilibrium, and no more. Like an overdose, too much writing can adversely affect one's well-being.

The attraction of such an approach to writing, of course, is that its very reticence appears to be a sign of its integrity. Because the narrator makes so few concessions to his audience, it is easy for the reader to feel that he is witness to the author's private musings. Like the Tokugawa scholar-sage Arai Hakuseki, however, who "re-calls the past not critically but emotionally,"[18] Shiga relives past experience less to analyze than to justify his emotional state in that experience. Many of his stories, therefore, read like apologies, in which explanation gives way to rationalization. This method serves him well enough in stories like "Kinosaki nite" (At Kinosaki, 1917) and "Horibata no sumai" (Dwelling by the moat, 1925), which are the products of considerable temporal perspective. Difficulties arise, however, when the perspective collapses and the image of the author-sage is undermined by events that the author cannot fully digest.

Such is the case with the "Yamashina" cycle. In "Kozō no kami-sama" we noted the authorial persona's attempt to establish his credibility at the expense of his fictional characters. In the "Ya-mashina" cycle, the narrator-hero does likewise, only this time at the expense of a character drawn from real life. The cycle, which records the author's affair and eventual breakup with a Kyoto gei-sha (Shiga made his home in the Kansai region for fifteen years be-ginning in 1923), was written and published in the following order: "Saji" (A trivial matter, 1925), "Yamashina no kioku" (Memories of Yamashina, 1926), "Chijō" (Blind passion, 1926), and "Banshū" (Late autumn, 1926). In terms of the cycle's chronology, however, "Saji" comes third, not first, and thus it appears when the cycle first came out in hardcover in 1927. This seemingly minor discrep-ancy is in fact crucial, as the rest of "Yamashina" might never even have been written had "Saji" not been published.

"Yamashina no kioku" describes an awkward scene in January 1925 between the hero and his wife upon his return from a liaison with the geisha. Having found out about the affair, his wife de-mands an immediate end to it, but he insists that his feelings for

18. The characterization is Hani Gorō's. Quoted in Ackroyd, *Told Round a Brush-wood Fire*, 29.

the geisha will not diminish his affection for her. "Chijō" opens later in January with the hero still infatuated and unable to part with the geisha, but knowing full well that she is not really in love with him and actually feeling securer in that knowledge. Under pressure from his wife, he finally breaks off the affair and pays the geisha a solatium, although he does not feel in his heart that the affair is over. In "Saji," we learn that the hero is once again seeing the geisha. It is April. After telling his wife that he has an errand at the bank, he travels from his home in Nara to Kyoto only to learn that the geisha is in Nara herself with another client.

"Banshū" sums up the affair; in it we learn the circumstances under which "Saji" was written. It is now September, and the hero, entertaining his father visiting from Tokyo, cannot finish a manuscript in time to meet a deadline. His father is concerned that his visit has become an imposition, but the hero assures him that he has another manuscript that he can use in a pinch. In fact, the hero is troubled by the repercussions that this manuscript, if published, will be likely to cause, since it reveals that the affair he has supposedly sworn off (as we are told in "Chijō") is actually still in progress. Yielding to the pressure of the deadline, however, and not wanting to make his father feel any guiltier, he finally hands the manuscript over to his publisher. When he informs his wife that the story's contents are "unpleasant," she, no doubt recalling the episodes recorded later in "Yamashina no kioku" and "Chijō," makes a lighthearted reply about water under the bridge. But "Saji" is about the present, and not the past as he has led his wife to believe. He has been seeing the geisha again since February. The hero must finally end the liaison for good when the wife hears about "Saji" two months later (in November) from a former live-in maid, who reads the story and sends her a letter inquiring about the affair!

All four stories are narrated in the "third person," with the hero identified throughout as "he" (*kare*). The "he" is easily interchangeable with "I," however; the restricted use of *kare*, discussed in the previous chapter, applies here as well. The preface to the cycle's hardcover edition not surprisingly encourages a reading that links author and hero: "This is a record of events that already belong to the past. It is only proper that I refer to myself here as 'he'" (*SNZ* 3:613–14). But at the same time it attempts lamely to impose, by a

Table 2.   Shiga Naoya's "Yamashina" Cycle

Title	Story Time	Time of Writing	Publication Date
"Yamashina no kioku"	January 1925	December 1925	January 1926 (*Kaizō*)
"Chijō"	January 1925	March 1926	April 1926 (*Kaizō*)
"Saji"	April 1925	May 1925	September 1925 (*Kaizō*)
"Banshū"	Autumn 1925	July 1926	September 1926 (*Bungei shunjū*)

Sources: Nakamura Mitsuo, *Shiga Naoya ron*, 167–73; Kōno Tōshirō, "Kōki," in *Shiga Naoya zenshū*, 3:612–13; and Kunimatsu Akira, "'Yamashina' mono ni tsuite," 114.

mere change of pronouns, a certain distance between the author and the hero as well. One might suppose that the third-person narration would allow the author to analyze more objectively the motives for his behavior; yet he is in fact so reticent that one wonders why he has chosen to reveal the incident in the first place. Shiga later writes (in a commentary on his works titled "Zoku sōsaku yodan" [1938]): "The subject of these stories is for me a most unusual one. I had no desire to deal with it straightforwardly and took an interest in it rather for the impact it had on my family life" (*SNZ* 8:22). As it turns out, however, we learn nothing about the "impact" on the author's family life other than the wife's entirely predictable reaction to the affair: anger and jealous frustration couched in the most general terms.

A more convincing reason for the nature of the author's revelation is to be found in the circumstances of the cycle's publication. As we can see from Table 2 (which sets forth the three time periods pertinent to our discussion of the cycle), Shiga wrote "Saji" in May 1925, very soon after the described event, but did not publish it until September. There is no such gap between the writing and publication of the other three stories, however, because the affair had apparently ended by this time. Once "Saji" had gone into print and his wife had found out about it two months later (November 1925), there was nothing left to hide. Shiga wrote "Yamashina no kioku" the following month.

The question of art's fidelity to life in the "Yamashina" cycle need not concern us here; our observations will not be affected by the presence of any "distortions" or "embellishments." Our concern is rather with how art doubles back on life—that is, how the author persuades the reader, by a variety of self-references, to associate the literary persona with the real-life man. In a text like the "Yamashina" cycle, moreover, where chronological time encroaches on story time, art actually dictates the course of private life rather than the other way around. This would not have been possible, of course, regardless of the cycle's "fidelity" to life, had not *all* parties involved—the author, his wife, and the former maid—acted on the assumption that the hero was indeed the author himself. Thus, the publication and subsequent discovery of "Saji" by the hero's wife caused the affair to end more quickly than it otherwise would have. Had the hero remained silent, he could have conceivably carried on his secret trysts until the affair broke off of its own accord. But having exploited his private life for the sake of his literary career, he was compelled to mend his ways. The literary ball bounced back into private life, forcing the hero to break off completely with the geisha.

Despite its excess of self-referentiality, the "Yamashina" cycle remains curiously opaque. Rather than shed light on the affair itself, it merely reveals the author's reason for writing about the affair in the first place. "Banshū" in particular is an all-out attempt at damage control, rationalizing the hero's indiscretion by ingeniously supplying a new context for interpreting it. He never intended to brag about a humdrum affair with a geisha, the hero explains, but merely to defer to his father, whom he did not wish to make uncomfortable by his inability to meet a deadline. If he has sacrificed his wife's feelings in the process, too, then that is the price to be paid for saving his father's face. Thus, by extricating himself from one moral responsibility (to his wife) by appealing to a higher one (to his father), he reasserts his role as moral arbiter even when he is guilty of philandering.

The "Yamashina" cycle is one of the few examples in Shiga's oeuvre where writing dictated the course of experience. Unlike Shūkō, Kasai, and many other *shishōsetsu* writers whose domestic lives were in constant turmoil, Shiga, who enjoyed a relatively stable existence, generally refrained from incriminating self-exposés in the interest of domestic tranquility. Yet that very refusal to sacrifice his private life to the exigencies of his writing career had the effect of stilling his pen. Shiga realized all too well that writing uninhibitedly about one's personal life meant to endanger its well-being. He rarely took that risk; hence the several periods of silence during his career. Further, because he does not take his readers fully into his confidence, Shiga presents us with a hero who, for all his seeming candor, assumes only a superficially private role. As long as that role is not contradicted, the reader easily succumbs to the illusion that he is indeed witnessing the author's most private self. Those rare occasions when (as in the "Yamashina" cycle) it *is* contradicted, however, serve to remind us of the gap between author and persona and of how one-dimensional the persona really is.

In Shiga's *shishōsetsu*, then, the formal, public nuance of *watakushi* prevails. And because it does, conflict is depicted, even in the "Yamashina" cycle, in muted terms calculated to assuage the feelings of his characters' real-life counterparts (except, of course, those of his wife). That Shiga valued propriety above all and had little taste for portraying characters in an embarrassing or unfavorable light is made clear in an open letter ("Moderu no fufuku," published in *Shirakaba* in July 1913) protesting the way in which Satomi Ton, a friend and fellow Shirakaba member, used him as a model in *Kimi to watakushi to* (1913). In the letter, which he signs "Sakamoto," the name of the character modeled after himself, Shiga acknowledges the "truth" of what Satomi has written, but he questions his friend's right to bring up incidents that, in his mind at least, have no place in the public arena.

> What Sakamoto says and does in *Kimi to watakushi to* is by and large what I in fact said and did. I am not attacking you for any factual errors. I am simply puzzled by your desire to carry on over such trifles. . . . I just cannot understand what value there is in . . . making people look bad on paper.
>
> (*SNZ* 7:133)

Satomi rebutted Shiga's argument (in "Moderu no fufuku ni tsuite," unpublished) with no little energy, but the installments of *Kimi to watakushi to* stopped appearing.[19] Perhaps that is why Shiga never published his response ("'Moderu no fufuku ni tsuite' ni

---

19. We know from Shiga's diary (*SNZ* 10:681, 9 July 1913) that Satomi did write the essay manuscript and show it to Shiga. Satomi elaborates on his views in a letter to Shiga postmarked 8 July 1913 (*Shiga Naoya zenshū bekkan*, 116–18) and declares that, having gotten the matter off his chest, he will not publish "Moderu no fufuku ni tsuite."

tsuite") to Satomi's rebuttal, which however gives us a clear picture of how he believed a *shōsetsu* would be read.

> You say that I have no right to complain about my role as model unless that complaint takes the form of a purely literary critique of *Kimi to watakushi to* as art. Well, I have news for you. The text will be read above all, I believe, for the facts it contains. If you ask me, its author has a bad habit of extracting from the truth only those facts that appeal to people's basest interests.
>
> (*SNZ* 7:689)

Shiga did have a point. Most of the Shirakaba readership, which numbered at this time only a few thousand, had a very good idea of who *kimi* and *watakushi* were. Yet he is not interested in having Satomi alter the "facts" in order to make the characters anonymous or otherwise universalize them. The solution he urges is far more radical: stop writing. The message in these two pieces is clear. *Shishōsetsu* characters have real-life models, and it is therefore better to remain silent than write ill of someone. That Shiga practiced what he preached is apparent from a reading of *Wakai*, to which we now turn.

WAKAI

Both the power and the limitations of Shiga's confessional rhetoric are revealed perhaps most plainly in the "*Wakai* trilogy" (*Wakai sanbusaku*): *Ōtsu Junkichi* (Ōtsu Junkichi, 1912), *Wakai* (Reconciliation, 1917), and *Aru otoko, sono ane no shi* (A certain man and the death of his sister, 1920). It is united loosely by the theme of the hero's troubled relationship with his father. In *Ōtsu Junkichi*, the first-person narrator (a would-be writer) chronicles his ambivalent feelings toward his friend's sister, his special relationship with his grandmother, who raised him since he was an infant, and finally his unsuccessful attempt to marry a housemaid in the face of family opposition. The father remains in the background, although his presence is continually felt—most keenly when the narrator discovers that he was behind the maid's removal from the house. In *Wakai* the father again is very much in the background until the end. The first-person narrator merely informs the reader of a long estrangement without dwelling on the causes; his concern is rather with his own efforts to write about the estrangement. The reconciliation, initiated by the narrator's ritualistic apology, comes so abruptly that reader is not wholly convinced by the claim that it will last. It is only with *Aru otoko*, narrated by the Shiga hero's younger brother, that the reader gains some insight into the nature of the conflict, although he is encouraged by its fictional veneer (obvious to anyone even casually acquainted with the oeuvre) to disregard the content as autobiographical truth. This attempt by an author to guide the reading of a text as fiction is a crucial issue to which we shall return below.

A few comments about the trilogy's other two narratives are in order before we begin our discussion of *Wakai*. *Ōtsu Junkichi* was the first Shiga story to be published in a large-circulation, general-interest magazine (as well as the first for which he, at age twenty-nine, received payment); nearly all Shiga's previous stories had appeared in the coterie magazine *Shirakaba*. Not only was it a daring story for its time, thematizing a young man's rebellion (albeit a largely fruitless one) against family oppression, it was instrumental in making available the Shiga style to a wide audience. Ozaki Kazuo, one of Shiga's first disciples, discovered the story in 1916 and later had this to say about it:

> If I had not read *Ōtsu Junkichi*, I might never have become a writer. . . . It taught me that a *shōsetsu*, which I had thought of only as an entertaining mixture of fact and fiction, need not be that at all, and that if one had a grievance against one's father, then one should be bold enough to air it. . . . The language also took me by surprise. I had never encountered its like before. It was as though nothing came between the reader and the events described. . . . Reading this and other of Shiga's stories, I found that language actually disappears when it performs its function flawlessly.[20]

Ozaki articulates here what has been suggested throughout this study: the *shōsetsu*'s mission is to tell the "truth" about lived experience. Ozaki further argues that Shiga's language is particularly qualified to tell the truth, because it can convey the author's message, unadulterated, through a supposedly transparent medium. The cult of sincerity has already firmly taken hold. Honda Shūgo, comparing *Ōtsu Junkichi* with Sōseki's *Sore kara* (*And then*, 1909), which also

---

20. *Ano hi kono hi* 1:54. For an earlier, fuller version, see Ozaki, "Shiga Naoya no koto," 298–307.

treats a generational clash between father and son, concedes the novelistic superiority of the latter but claims that Shiga succeeds, especially in the story's second half, in removing the fictional "barriers" that separate reader and hero in Sōseki's text. "*Sore kara* enlightens the reader with its culture and insight," Honda concludes, "but *Ōtsu Junkichi* is the story that moves him."[21]

The suggestion here of course is that Shiga's transparent, "fictionless" language of the heart comes through to the reader in a way that Sōseki's rational, "fictional" language cannot. Honda never tells us just how he distinguishes between the two languages, but it is clear that the styles of the two texts differ in fundamental ways. There is an ill-defined relationship between the hero as actor and as observer in *Ōtsu Junkichi* that undercuts any analytical or ironic perspective. The letter to a friend that ends the story (dated 30 August 1907), while providing an outlet for the hero's pent-up rage against his father, offers no background whatsoever to the generational conflict. The hero gives us no assessment, moreover, of the intervening five years between the story time and the narrative present, which would appear to coincide with the year of publication (1912).[22] The lack of clues about the hero's present attitude leads us to believe that the hero has some reason to suppress it, although such an argument of course makes little sense in the context of a "fictionalized" narrative.

Ōtsu Junkichi, then, the story that immortalized Shiga's "rebellion" against his father, contains in fact little more than a few angry words about an apparition that readers never come to know. Most of the hero's rebellious behavior is aimed at his grandmother, whom he "loves and yet cannot help despising" (*SNZ* 2:299) for being such a dominant force in his life. The text is important, however, if only because it introduces us to the conflicting emotions with which the Shiga hero struggles so mightily in *Wakai*.

A word also on *Aru otoko*, which is easily the most penetrating statement in the trilogy on what Shiga calls "the riddle that the

---

21. "Jigazō sakka e no michi," 257.
22. The only suggestion we get of any perspective being applied to past events is the use of the nonpast tense *omou* ("I think/believe") to conclude certain reflective passages (one sentence in part 1, section 1; the final paragraph in part 2, section 12; and a sentence near the beginning of the last section), but even these examples cannot be conclusively attributed to a clearly discernible narrative "present."

existence of a father poses to his son" (*SNZ* 2:446). Yet it has never been as highly regarded as the other two stories. Criticism of it invariably takes the form that one scholar voices when he acknowledges the narrator's disinterested appraisal of both the Shiga hero and his father but concludes that this very aloofness deprives the story of the poignancy and stark sense of reality so manifest in *Wakai*.[23] Another scholar puts it even more succinctly: unlike *Ōtsu Junkichi* and *Wakai*, *Aru otoko* is "made up" (*tsukurareta shōsetsu*).[24]

It is one thing for a literary scholar to conclude that a story is "made up," but Shiga has a way of letting even a casual reader know he has crossed the autobiographical line into the realm of "fabrication." He cues the reader, by fictionalization of the more obvious sort, to expect a retelling of the father-son conflict that, however incisive, cannot incriminate the real-life models.[25] Once he has done so, he is then free to make his penetrating and sometimes devastating analysis of the conflict.

Shiga takes great pains to insure that the distance he imposes between subject and real-life model is plain for all to see. First, conscious perhaps that a mere switch from first- to third-person narrator will not sufficiently distance the hero, given the easy identification of *kare* with *watakushi*, he employs a separate first-person narrator (the hero Yoshiyuki's younger brother) to relate the story of his fictional alter ego. Second, he presents the hero in ways that often contradict previous portrayals. For example, Yoshiyuki in *Aru otoko* has an elder sister (and a brother-in-law who causes a scandal in his father's business), while the narrator-hero in *Ōtsu Junkichi* and *Wakai* has none. Yoshiyuki's mother dies when he is eight, while the narrator's mother in "Haha no shi to atarashii haha" (The death of my mother and my new mother, 1912) dies when the narrator is twelve. Yoshiyuki injures himself seriously when he falls out of a tree during an excursion to the country and recovers in Yugawara, a spa on the Pacific coast, while the narrator of "Kinosaki nite" (At Kinosaki, 1917) is injured when he is hit by

23. Kuribayashi Hideo, in Fukuda Kiyoto and Kuribayashi Hideo, *Shiga Naoya*, 154. Most critics would no doubt agree with Sudō Matsuo's description of *Wakai*'s characteristic feature: its "incomparable freshness." *Shiga Naoya no bungaku*, 165.

24. Kōno Toshirō, in notes to Shiga, *Shiga Naoya*, 480.

25. Shiga says as much (in "Sōsaku yodan," 1928) when he describes *Aru otoko* as a "mixture of fact [*jijitsu*] and fiction [*tsukurigoto*]," as opposed to *Wakai*, which he describes as "unembellished fact" (*SNZ* 8:14).

a train in Tokyo and recovers in Kinosaki, a spa on the Japan Sea coast. Yoshiyuki and his father never achieve a reconciliation, while the hero in *Wakai* does. The list goes on.

It is the author's hope, one suspects, that the reader, recognizing that many incidents in *Aru otoko* do not agree with what he knows about the Shiga hero from earlier, more "authentic" accounts, will not equate the relationship between father and son, as it is somewhat harshly depicted in this text, with the actual one between the real-life models. In particular, by composing a tragic conclusion that obviously contradicts the "facts" as they are recorded in *Wakai*, Shiga hints that the bitter confrontations leading up to the hero's permanent departure from home are also mere figments of the author. Whether or not they are in fact is beside the point. The hidden message of *Aru otoko* is that they are, and the reader is less inclined to ascribe even those segments that are not blatantly "false" (insofar as they do not contradict previous narratives) to specific events or circumstances in the author's life. "Fabrication" and the distance it imposes, it would seem, is indispensible for truly cogent character analysis in Shiga's autobiographical fiction. And yet, as *Wakai's* success makes abundantly clear, such analysis is not nearly as highly prized as the sense of authorial presence generated by the latter text.

Aru otoko is not without its limitations as a fictional text. A long parenthetical commentary that the narrator makes on one of his brother's letters is headed by a curious remark: "The author comments:" (*sakusha iu* [SNZ 2:500]). It is surely significant that the "speaker" here identifies himself not as the younger brother (*otōto iu*) or as "this writer" (*hissha iu*) but as "the author" and that he does so, moreover, in the plain, uninflected verb form, the only such use in the entire story. It is hard to believe that this self-conscious expression is a mere slip of the pen. Shiga had opportunities to make corrections when he anthologized the story, first serialized in a newspaper, in later editions of his writings. More likely, it is an example of Shiga's unwillingness to suppress completely his consciousness of the composition process in the interest of establishing an autonomous fictional time. Foregrounding the narrator's consciousness of writing rather than letting the drama unfold is of course a trademark of Shiga's and many other *shishō-*

setsu writers' prose. It is indeed one of the conventions that gives the *shishōsetsu* its aura of authenticity. More than any event depicted in the fictive time frame, the simple refrain, "I now write," is the single most important statement that Shiga as author can make. This same attitude surely informs the ending of "Kozō no kamisama." At certain crucial points in Shiga's writing, then, narrative representation takes second place to the recorder's self-conscious presentation of himself in the process of writing. This consciousness is most fully realized in *Wakai*.

Although *Wakai* is considered a sequel to *Ōtsu Junkichi*, a ten-year hiatus separates the events described in the two works. The narrator in *Wakai*, moreover, writes of a reconciliation that has just taken place (and of certain events preceding it), whereas the narrator in *Ōtsu Junkichi* writes of an estrangement as it stood in the (apparently) distant past. We have noted the unexplained gap between the narrator as actor and the narrator as recorder in *Ōtsu Junkichi*; in *Wakai* the two roles intertwine. We can only assume that the *Ōtsu Junkichi* narrator has actually become the writer he says he aspired to be; the *Wakai* narrator's professional status, meanwhile, is clear from the beginning. Indeed it soon becomes evident that the *Wakai* narrator has staked his writing career on the outcome of the events he describes. He is so obsessed with recording his relationship with his father that we cannot help viewing the reconciliation, which ends a decade-long rift, as a professional as much as a moral necessity.

Wakai chronicles four visits that the narrator-hero (also named Junkichi) makes from his home in Abiko, outside Tokyo, to his father's home in the city in 1917, from 31 July (the anniversary of his first daughter's death) to 30 August (the anniversary of his mother's death and the day of reconciliation). It concludes with his completion of a manuscript, inspired by recent events, in mid-September. This six- or seven-week period makes up the story's narrative time frame and it literally frames the story, occupying the first two and last six chapters. The intervening eight chapters, which bisect the four visits, chronicle incidents in previous years related to the hero's conflict with his father and his futile efforts to write about them, as well as the death of one infant daughter and birth of another. A third time frame, mentioned perfunctorily at the very end, sets the manuscript's composition time during the first half of September; it thus overlaps the final two weeks of the story's first narrative frame.

We are obliged to dwell at first on certain shortcomings and inconsistencies in *Wakai*, but we must ultimately acknowledge the spell that it undeniably casts over its readers. In order to understand more fully Shiga's verbal sorcery, we shall look beyond the story's thematic content (which Masamune Hakuchō describes with some justification as a sentimental tearjerker the likes of which might appear in any popular magazine[26]) to its singular mode of presentation. Nakamura Mitsuo has written that readers of Shiga can be divided into two groups: believers and nonbelievers.[27] This is an apt description, however ironic in intent, of the hold Shiga's prose has over its admirers. Nakamura goes on to suggest that the "believers" engage in a simple act of faith when they recognize Shiga "the man" behind his writing, but we must emphasize that this faith springs from a clearly (although perhaps not readily) identifiable technique of presentation that we have referred to as his "invisible" style, without which no myth of authorial presence would arise.

Although Shiga's brand of realism is founded on this distinctive "presence" and on a narrative that seemingly parallels the ebb and flow of life, we find in *Wakai* a number of curiously improbable events that might well have no place in a story that strictly conformed to the laws of verisimilitude: the hero's "conversation" with his dead grandfather during a visit to the family cemetery, the imagined reconciliation with his father described as part of an unfinished composition, and the hallucinatory sighting of his father hurrying away from the Tokyo house to avoid meeting him (just as he had once contemplated leaving his Kyoto house before his father made an unwelcome visit two years earlier). The impact of these unusual, even eerie, scenes would be greatly lessened were

26. "Shiga Naoya to Kasai Zenzō" (1928), in *Masamune Hakuchō zenshū* 6:181. Few critics are of Hakuchō's persuasion, however. More would seem to share the judgment of Eguchi Kan: "If anyone calls [*Wakai*] a sentimental work, he should be pitied, for he fails to understand the beauty of human sincerity." Quoted in Fukuda and Kuribayashi, *Shiga Naoya*, 154.
27. *Shiga Naoya ron*, 21.

they not grounded in the utter reality of the narrator's seemingly corporeal "presence" in the text.[28]

Of the conflict itself, *Wakai* offers extensive yet guarded treatment. We get neither the hero's case against the father nor the father's against the hero, in contrast to, say, Kafka's *Letter to His Father*, in which we get both. The hero depicts the rift to the last as a clash of roles rather than personalities. Juxtaposed with two other episodes in which human will plays but a small role—the death of one daughter and the birth of the other—the rift becomes a kind of fait accompli, much like a natural catastrophe or an act of God, or simply part of the landscape. Shiga met with criticism early on for his failure to probe in any depth the breach between father and son.[29] But he casts his work in a way that militates against an in-depth analysis of the breach. The hero is the Shiga persona, bound by the author's self-imposed rules of propriety and by the image delineated in previous texts. The author clearly feels a responsibility to that image and not to the full disclosure of his private life. The details of the discordant father-son relationship remain part of the impenetrable core behind the hero's facade of candor.

Yet a contradictory urge to tell all, which the hero continually suppresses, pervades *Wakai*. Again and again he counters this urge by deferring to a moral code, calculated to exhibit the author-sage's integrity and with it the rightness of the story itself, which effectively sabotages outright confession. We learn in the second chapter, for example, that the hero must turn in a manuscript to a certain magazine by 19 August for publication the following month. Although determined to write about his father, he finds the task far more difficult than he ever imagined.

> I was on very bad terms with Father. This was a product in part, no doubt, of the complex tangle of emotions that divides any father and son, but I believed that my enmity arose from a fundamental discord

---

28. Shiga's brilliance as a depicter of dreams, fantasies, and various psychological and physiological obsessions is well documented in William F. Sibley, *The Shiga Hero*. It has recently gained recognition among Japanese critics as well. See, for example, the chapter on Shiga ("'Shizen' to 'yume': Shiga Naoya ron") in Aeba Takao, *Hihyō to hyōgen*, 75–112; and Takahashi Hideo, *Shiga Naoya*.

29. Nakamura Mitsuo, for instance, argues that the reader of Shiga's works actually learns very little about Shiga. *Shiga Naoya ron*, 15.

> between us. I did not hesitate to speak ill of him to others. I could not bring myself, however, to show my hostility on paper. I did not wish to give public vent to my private grudge. Not only would I then feel sorry for him, I feared that doing so would tarnish my writing.
>
> (*SNZ* 2:327)

With less than a week left, the hero finally abandons his project and dashes off an "imaginary" story he planned to have published a month later in another magazine.

"I did not wish to give public vent to my private grudge." The narrator's message, repeated like a refrain a number of times in the story, is clear: writing from the "imagination" is easy; telling the "truth" is difficult. Shiga is betting, one feels, that the refrain requires no explanation, that the reader will be satisfied merely with the hero's "candid" admission of his inability to be completely candid about his personal affairs. To display sincerity while suppressing the story: Shiga observes this formula to the end.

In the next chapter, the hero recalls with chagrin the words of his father in reference to himself: "Never again will I shed a tear for that rogue, no matter what happens to him" (*SNZ* 2:334). He further recalls that "a certain attitude" he had adopted toward his father precipitated this grim remark and that he cannot blame his father for feeling the way he did. The hero gives the reader no further details; yet is it not this very reticence that underwrites Shiga's acclaimed "realism"? By implying that any further revelation will be extremely awkward, the narrator-hero makes the best possible case for his own honesty and for the story's authenticity. If his tale were indeed a mere invention, the reader might well reason, the hero could just as easily flaunt as hide such painful incidents, since, as fictions, they would lose their capacity to incriminate. In a literary culture that defined realism specifically in terms of authorial "presence" rather than in terms of verisimilitude, Shiga actually gained more credibility by making a show of reticence than he ever would have by making a "full" confession, which would in any event always run the risk of criticism for being incomplete.

Having used his "imagination" as a stopgap, the hero once again confronts the task of completing his previously abandoned manuscript in time for the next deadline, only a month later than the first. Once again he rejects the temptation to tell all and merely comments on the dangers of making revelations not thoroughly pondered beforehand.

> When writing about actual events, I was often sorely tempted to put down everything I could think of. All sorts of incidents would come to mind, and I would want to record every last one of them. All were in fact connected in some way with my subject. Yet . . . I would inevitably encounter difficulties when trying to link them together and end up . . . having to cut out most of what I had wished to write about. This was especially true when it came to writing about Father. I could not begin to chronicle all the bitter arguments we had had.
> (*SNZ* 2:334)

This one brief passage would seem to overturn the thesis, argued by so many commentators, that Shiga's writings exemplify the unity of art and life. Indeed, as we shall later see, the unity of life and art for Shiga actually means the death of art. For what is the narrator saying here if not that the gap between them is in fact unbridgeable? The author-sage is nothing if not a disciplined editor who is alert to the dangers of his profession. Thus, he recognizes the futility of recording all that he has experienced and the necessity of arranging what is left after "cutting out" the rest. Shiga's sincerity under these circumstances can never mean "candor"; at most it implies a recognition of his own vagueness and is necessarily one step removed from the spontaneity we normally associate with the word. The author presents it to us as a locked vessel that contains however no secrets, only the enigma of itself.

At the middle of *Wakai* comes a well-known section in which the narrator considers his past attempts to write about his father. Its central position is no accident, one feels, for it marks a turning point in the hero's consciousness. It deserves quoting at length.

> I don't know how many times in the last half dozen years I planned a story about the breach with Father, but the plans ended in failure every time. . . . I would always lose heart when I thought of the tragedy in real life that its publication would inevitably cause. I became especially distraught when I imagined the dark shadow it would cast on relations with Grandmother. When I was in Matsue three years ago, I composed a long narrative in hopes of keeping just such a tragedy from befalling me. . . . My object in writing down every unpleasant incident that could possibly occur between me and Father was to prevent them from actually happening. . . . In the cli-

mactic scene . . . I imagined father and son coming to blows at last, and I pondered the matter of who would kill whom. But then, at the height of these imagined hostilities, an entirely different scene suddenly appeared before my eyes in which the two of them embraced each other and burst into tears. . . .

I elected not to use this conclusion, however. It was not something to be decided on in advance. There was no telling how things would end until my writing had actually progressed that far. How wonderful it would be, though, I thought, if things would really turn out that way by so writing.

. . . I commenced writing, but made little headway. . . . Still I could not help feeling that the denouement I had conjured up, almost unconsciously, would someday actually unfold between Father and myself. I thought it entirely possible for such a scene to occur at a time when relations between us had reached their lowest ebb. I could not be sure, of course. Yet even if there was no telling how things would end until I had reached that point myself, I believed that there dwelt in both Father and me something that could effect just such a complete turnabout. I said as much to my wife and to a friend.

(SNZ 2:366–68)

This incantatory passage foreshadows, of course, the final reconciliation. It also voices the narrator's extremely complex position on the relationship between life and art, which, as posited here, harbors an insoluble dilemma. The hero wishes to prevent unpleasant incidents from happening between him and his father by writing them down beforehand, as if to cast a salutary spell on their relations. This formula proves unworkable, however. When he actually puts pen to paper, he finds that he makes little headway. He rationalizes his decision not to resolve the conflict in advance by arguing that "there was no telling how things would end until my writing had actually progressed that far." But in fact he cannot complete the story that he claims only needs writing down to turn out as planned. Clearly, imagination is not enough. The hero must be guided by experience. He can only hope that the scene he conjured up three years earlier will one day take place; perhaps *then* he can write about it. Thus the subtle but unmistakable change of focus in the last paragraph. What he at first says about his story—that "there was no telling how things would end *until my writing had actually progressed that far*"—in fact holds true for his own life: "there was no telling how things would end *until I had reached that point myself*." He can neither write nor act, and he is left with telling others close to him about the imagined denouement, as if to prevent it from dissipating completely. Having failed to turn art into life, he must wait for life to progress to the stage where it can someday serve his art.

Thwarted in his efforts to address the conflict in a fictional retelling, the hero later attempts to address it more directly in a letter to his father. The attempt is, however, doomed from the start, because his feelings are still too unstable to be pinned down by words. The failure to set down his all too volatile emotions on paper proves to be a blessing in disguise, however, since it prompts him to meet with his father face to face and to let emotions take him where they may. He is no longer bent on appealing to reason, as there are, he discovers, no "reasons," no natural explanation, for the rift.

The hero has already attempted to reason with his father some eighteen months or so earlier. Although this attempt presages in some ways the later, successful reconciliation (it features the same preliminaries, such as nervous instructions from his stepmother on how to behave, and the same somber exchange between the two principals), it ends in complete failure. Rationally speaking, he is not at fault and therefore has no reason to feel contrite, and he says so to his father, only to be promptly dismissed from the house. During his 30 August visit, he wisely airs his grievances to his stepmother in a kind of dress rehearsal before confronting his father. She asks him to put reason aside, to forget just this once who is to blame for the past and simply say that he is sorry. The hero resists at first, but then decides, as he did in the case of his aborted manuscript, that it is impossible to plan the outcome in advance. "Emotions have a momentum of their own," he tells his stepmother. "Who knows, I might find myself less hostile than I had anticipated" (*SNZ* 2:401).

Life has now indeed progressed to the stage where it can serve art: the hero having given up his attachment to reason, the long-awaited reconciliation can take place in all its formality and ceremony. And once it has transpired, his urge to finish the story begun in Matsue withers away. Now he must find something else to write about in time for the mid-September deadline. That "something else" turns out to be this very story, which he begins soon after.

We have noted the criticism Shiga received for avoiding any frank discussion of the breach. Shiga was by no means unaware of the criticism and rebutted it on several occasions on the same moral grounds he used earlier against Satomi Ton. Defending *Wakai* in an essay entitled "Kuchibiru ga samui" (1922), he emphasizes that his purpose was to describe the joy of the reconciliation, rather than to dwell on unharmonious familial relations.

> *Wakai* does not focus on a "theme"; it is the product of a more direct, immediate inspiration. That is its strength, and that is what appeals to readers. . . . *The best thing about it is that simply recording the facts, without alteration or embellishment, has made it a work of art.* . . . I noted more than once right in the story that I could not begin to chronicle the cause of the discord. . . . Do the critics simply not understand how I felt? They ask why I failed to explain the causes. I ask the critics: how was I able to depict the reconciliation so well without even mentioning them?
>
> (*SNZ* 8:109–10; emphasis added)

Effective the story may be—but not because the author has somehow succeeded in "recording the facts, without alteration or embellishment." Shiga's essay overlooks entirely the narrator's function as editor, self-charged, as is pointed out in the story itself, with the responsibility of "cutting out" the many potentially embarrassing incidents he might have recorded indiscriminately.

In an unpublished manuscript, Shiga further denounces critics who regard his reticence as a defect:

> How odd, I thought. They refuse to understand my silence about the causes of the estrangement even though they know that author and hero are one and the same person.
>
> I realized only too well that, in chronicling the reconciliation, I would first have to suffer the pain of recording the estrangement. That was only logical. And yet I could not bring myself to write about its causes. I simply couldn't. So I wrote instead about the violence of the breach. And I think that the story succeeded on those terms.
>
> (*SNZ* 9:538–39)

Even here, in a manuscript that never saw the light of print, Shiga is curiously reticent about his reticence. He regards the right to silence as natural and conceives of the writer and the reader of a *shishōsetsu* as bound by a special contract. Shiga implies that the reader, recognizing the author-hero equation and dutifully respecting the feelings of those close to the author, should not ask the latter to probe too deeply into personal matters that would only cause embarrassment to himself and his family.

The author who tells his readers to limit their expectations, however, is guilty of a double standard. He invites the reader into his world while leaving the door only half open, insisting that the reader identify with him uncritically. Of course, this is easier to do when, as is the case in *Wakai*, he elects not to question the moral position of either side in a dispute. It is no coincidence that the estrangement between father and son, presented without explanation in *Wakai*, is more akin to a motiveless act, resembling a natural calamity over which the hero has no control and for which he cannot be censured. Any concern about the characters' motivations is misguided, the author seems to reason, since those motivations were never subjected to any moral scrutiny in the first place. The author is interested only in the hero's reaction to events, and he employs the variety of strategies we have noted to lead the reader's interest in the same direction as his own.

Those who do not accept the recorder-witness contract as Shiga defines it will no doubt feel deprived of the human interaction that forms the core of fictional narrative in the west. And yet, even though it lacks any truly dramatic confrontation, *Wakai* has the power to move its readers, as many critics attest, when it describes an event that can indeed be thought of as a natural calamity: namely, the sudden and fatal illness of the hero's infant daughter, described in the work's fifth and sixth chapters. Masamune Hakuchō notes that even Shiga, whose writing, he claims, normally exudes a certain dilettantism, manages to convey extreme tension when he stands at the crossroads of destiny and confronts so grave an event as the death of his child.[30] We are reminded once again of the importance to literature of the Buddhist articulation of man's subordination to the forces of nature: the four "trials" of birth, aging, sickness, and death (*shō-rō-byō-shi*). The question of character or personality or will would seem irrelevant to experience in which

---

30. "Shiga Naoya to Kasai Zenzō," 182. Ōe Kenzaburō notes the tendency to treat such impersonal crises in the postwar *shishōsetsu* as well. The unfailing formula for moving an audience, he argues, is to present a featureless, nonindividualized narrator who confronts, in the context of his nondescript daily life, an unusual event (like death) that is nevertheless easily identified with by any reader. "Watakushi shōsetsu ni tsuite," 196.

personal volition is of no account. This "digression," which one critic likens to the large, tumorlike growth commonly seen on cherry- or pine-tree trunks,[31] makes a greater impact on the reader than the final reconciliation scene does. Here, because of their utter futility, personalized emotions are out of place, and in their stead is the more generalized pathos of the human condition. The same holds true for the tenth chapter, added when *Wakai* first appeared in book form, which describes the birth of the hero's second daughter. These segments succeed precisely because they treat events on which the conflict of character has no bearing, as it finally must on a confrontation between father and son. They succeed so well, in fact, that one is tempted to conclude that *Wakai* treats birth and death more significantly than it does the hero's celebrated rift.[32]

The segments take on an unexpected importance, moreover, because the author has succumbed to the influence of traditional narrative. What might have been edited out in the interest of emplotment is here left to gather its own momentum, as if in defiance of an overall unity. The narrator chronicles the baby's illness with no hint of the outcome, with the result that the narrative "present" regresses to a period conterminous with the events themselves. The reader is inexorably drawn in. In chapter 6, the narrator informs readers that the child died before he actually describes her death, but the announcement, again in defiance of plot, seems intended expressly to defuse the tension that has built up during the course of the previous and by far the story's longest chapter.

Because the narrative denies readers a panoramic perspective and draws them into the time frame of "recollected" events in the eight middle chapters, one feels as if far more than a week has elapsed between the story time in chapter 2 (16 August) and that in chapter 11 (23 August). There is no particular sense of pastness about events in the presumably "retrospective" chapters or of presentness about the more recent events narrated in chronological order in chapters 1–2 and 11–16. The reader experiences crises as they are remembered, sharing the hero's emotional highs and lows

31. Honda Shūgo, "*Wakai* ron," 223.

32. Shiga himself seems to have realized the death episode's special nature. It appears as a separate story (constituting chapters 5 and 6 and the first paragraph of chapter 7 of *Wakai*) entitled "Satoko no shi" (The death of Satoko) in a collection of stories and essays by Shirakaba writers, *Shirakaba no sono*.

with little anticipation of a final denouement. Although the reconciliation remains the high point in *Wakai*, it is finally but one of several climactic moments that punctuate the text. One event does not
have priority over another in the way one might expect in a conventionally emplotted narrative. As one scholar suggests, the structure
of *Wakai* recalls an *uta monogatari*, with its alternating prose passages providing a background for poems that vary the emotional
intensity without necessarily leading the narrative anywhere.[33]

We noted earlier in our discussion that Shiga purposefully casts
Wakai in such a way as to defy an in-depth analysis of the breach.
From the very beginning, the hero is at pains to demonstrate that
no appeal to reason will resolve it, since it is itself rooted in wildly
contradictory emotions that the hero is at a loss to grasp or describe—thus, the difficulties he encounters composing his long
story and later writing to his father.

Once we understand this, queries about the father-son conflict
as depicted in *Wakai* lose their relevance. It is precisely because the
rift has no clearly definable causes that no premeditated action can
bring about a reconciliation. Narrative fiction's inexorable logic of
cause and effect is replaced in *Wakai* by juxtapositions of the rage
and sympathy that the hero feels toward his father, the one seemingly inciting the other, throughout the text. That rift and reconciliation are rooted in the same tumultuous cluster of emotions, re-
quiring no change of heart and therefore no atonement, is apparent
from the hero's awareness of his own conciliatory feelings in the
midst of his deepest anger. In the text's opening pages, before his
first furtive visit to the Tokyo house on 31 July, the hero visits his
daughter's grave in the family plot in nearby Aoyama. There, in the
story's most intimate and startling scene, he "converses" with the
spirit of his deceased grandfather, asking him whether he should
visit the house to see his ailing grandmother. The encouraging answer that wells up in his heart surprises the hero both for its spontaneity and for its complete lack of reproach toward a man for
whom the hero thought he felt only hatred. The confusion of emotions is also apparent from the altogether gruff manner in which
the hero "apologizes" to his father in chapter 13. In his excitement
he speaks as if out of anger, despite the promise to his stepmother

33. Sudō Matsuo, *Shiga Naoya no bungaku*, esp. 166–67.

to behave civilly. Yet the tone is entirely natural, he insists. "Looking back on it, I believe that it was the only appropriate tone possible, given our relationship" (*SNZ* 2:403).

Shiga's seeming unwillingness to probe the conflict in depth paradoxically forced him to write what was surely a very different story than he had planned when first taking up his pen in early September, for it in fact focuses far more on the breach than on the reconciliation. In doing so, he has produced a form of writing similar to what we know in the west as a "self-begetting novel,"[34] in which the writer's preoccupation with creating a story becomes itself the "story" one reads. Whether or not we wish to think of *Wakai* as a novel, there is no question of its affinity with a species of twentieth-century western fiction that treats its own production. The word "affinity" is used advisedly here, for the dissimilarities are perhaps more readily apparent than the similarities. (One has only to think of the divergent notions of self, time, space, and metaphysics in *Wakai* and, say, *Nausea*, to realize the vastly different fictive worlds that Junkichi and Roquentin inhabit.) Yet the bond unmistakably exists and is worthy of attention, as it will enable us to assign new meaning to the word "unique," which is so often attached to *shishōsetsu*. The author struggling to write and thematizing his very struggle: a rather commonplace subject in recent decades. In 1917, however, it was not, in Japan or the west. Shiga experimented gingerly with the subject; it would be left to Kasai Zenzō to bring it to fruition.

Let us reconsider *Wakai*, then, with this "affinity" in mind. We recall that the work comprises three time frames. It is the third time frame, mentioned ever so casually a few lines from the end, that gives us pause. Why must the hero inform his readers that he decided to record the reconciliation and include the writing of it as part of the narrative? It is because, as he suggests in the long reflective passage in chapter 7 quoted above, his relationship with his father is inseparable from the writing about it.[35] We have seen

34. I borrow this felicitous label from Stephen G. Kellman's book of the same name, which traces the form from Proust to Beckett.
35. My argument here is indebted to a suggestive commentary by Hiraoka Tokuyoshi. See his *Meiro no shōsetsu ron*, esp. 146–53. Hiraoka compares the circular structure of *Wakai* to that of works by Proust, Sartre, and Butor—and to *Shi no shima* (1966–71), by Fukunaga Takehiko. Two other critics briefly note the thematic im-

that he cannot write at all about the rift without having achieved a reconciliation, yet he cannot achieve that reconciliation without having attempted to write about the rift. This dilemma of using art to solve the difficulties of life while at the same time waiting for life's experience to motivate his art can only be resolved by another paradox. The hero discovers, on the eve of reconciliation, that he can will neither the discord nor its resolution. He can only prepare himself mentally to accommodate both. The surprise ending to the rough draft described in chapter 7 materializes almost literally in chapter 13, not because he so designs it but because he finds himself at the mercy of *both* art and life. He cannot author his story according to a particular plan any more than he can live his life according to one. Indeed, success comes only when he forfeits the role of author and lets the writing—and events—take their own course. Writing, seemingly powerless to address the rift, becomes itself in due time the source of harmony. Thus, *Wakai* itself becomes as much the story of writing as it is the story of reconciliation.

SELF, NATURE, ART, AND BEYOND

With *Wakai* we realize that Shiga, for reasons of discretion and simply of temperament, had little interest in dramatic character interaction. And yet it is no less successful a text for that fact. Excepting such blatant attempts at fictionalization as *Aru otoko, sono ane no shi*, which allow him some freedom in analyzing human relations (although at the cost of forfeiting his hallmark of "sincerity"), Shiga typically dispenses with character analysis in favor of depopulating his stories, entirely. In fact, he seems to feel least constrained, psychologically and artistically, in settings inhabited only by himself, creatures of nature, and characters who appear, if at all, merely as part of the landscape. Only in such settings, virtually devoid of human society, does he seem truly at liberty to depict personal experience without compunction.

---

portance in *Wakai* of the writer trying to write. Ikeuchi Teruo ("*Wakai* ron") suggests that *Wakai* is the fulfillment of Natsume Sōseki's wish (as recorded by Shiga) that Shiga, having failed to compose a work due for serialization in the *Asahi*, at least write about his inability to write. See also the chapter on Shiga in Saeki Shōichi, *Nihon no "watakushi" o motomete*, esp. 199.

Such a strategy may be anathema to narrative fiction; yet it resulted in an important part of the Shiga oeuvre: the *shinkyō shōsetsu*, those (usually) brief sketches in which the author-sage explores his inner landscape in a setting virtually stripped of people and props. No celebration of self emerges from this most introspective of *shishōsetsu* forms, however. Isolated from society, the hero accommodates himself to forces in nature that reduce to insignificance the autonomous, individuated ego. It is ironic yet revealing of the so-called "I-novel" that its acknowledged master should have arrived at such an enigmatic view of self.

"Horibata no sumai" (1925) is typical of the *shinkyō shōsetsu* in that the hero appears on a nearly empty stage, engaging in only one very brief exchange with another character. The story describes an alley cat's raid on a neighbor's chicken coop and the cat's eventual capture and extermination. The narrator-hero sets the stage for solitary meditation in the very first sentence: "I lived alone one summer in Matsue" (*SNZ* 3:191). Exhausted by life in the city and by the constant dealings with people there, the hero resolves to lead an existence, at its most basic level, in the small provincial town of Matsue. Here his companions are "the insects and birds, the fish and the water, the grass and the sky—and, finally, other human beings" (*SNZ* 3:191). Over and above its depiction of a man who shuns active engagement with his surroundings, "Horibata no sumai" can be read as a metaphor for the Shiga hero's reluctance to become a dramatic character in his writing. The author-sage's brief encounter with the neighbor who owns the chicken coop is purely explanatory in function, a mere formal exchange. The chickens and their plight are at issue here, not the two people who converse.

An even purer example of the hero depicted in contemplative isolation is "Kinosaki nite" (At Kinosaki, 1917), which is in its own way a masterpiece. The story chronicles the author's three-week sojourn at a well-known spa on the Japan Sea coast after being hit by a train in Tokyo. During the course of his convalescence, the narrator-hero witnesses all varieties of death—natural, murderous, accidental—that affect the small creatures he happens to see: a bee outside his inn window, a rat in a stream, a water lizard sunning itself on a rock. He communes solely with the natural world, and all other human beings recede into the background.

Identifying to an extraordinary degree with the ego-denying forces of nature, he experiences something akin to total self-dissolution—not in any negative or nihilistic sense but in a very positive one, as several critics have noted, in which life is no longer opposed to death.[36]

Reflecting on his accident while convalescing at Kinosaki, the hero faces an insoluble dilemma: how to cope with his mortality? If the occasion for a life-and-death struggle arises, should he yield to his new-found desire for self-extinction that results from a thoroughgoing identification with nature, or should he follow his animal instinct for self-preservation? The hero faces a dilemma of another sort as well: how to continue writing when recent experience has so wrenched him that he can no longer identify with his heroes' frames of mind? Thus he ponders, in addition to the future of his existence, the future of his attempts at narrative. Having written "Han no hanzai" (Han's crime, 1913), the story of a Chinese juggler's impulsive wife-slaying narrated from the juggler's point of view, he is now seized with the desire to write of the wife, dead and quiet in her grave, from the wife's point of view. "I would call the story 'The Murdered Wife of Han.' I never did write it, but the urge was there. I was dismayed to find, moreover, that my feelings had strayed very far from those of the hero of a long narrative I was writing" (*SNZ* 2:178).

The long narrative, of course, is *Tokitō Kensaku*, the precursor of *An'ya kōro* that Shiga finally abandoned, having found himself no longer in tune with his hero. It comes as no surprise, then, when we learn that Shiga's difficulty writing *Tokitō Kensaku* in fact resulted in the first of several fallow periods, which finally ended three years later with the publication of this very story. Shiga at last regains momentum as a writer by avoiding the familial conflicts that had plagued him and by depicting himself in "Kinosaki nite" as a totally isolated being. When all conflict is erased, the hero is at liberty to engage in the pensive musings that are the *shinkyō shōsetsu's* core. As in "Horibata no sumai," the hero sets the stage for solitary meditation in the very first sentence: "I . . . traveled alone to Kinosaki Hot Spring to convalesce" (*SNZ* 2:175). He is absorbed in himself and his immediate surroundings, his sensibility the mea-

36. See, for example, Sudō Matsuo, "Shiga bungaku no shizen, seimeiryoku," 99.

sure of all things. Only on such a deserted stage, free from external challenges, does the Shiga hero fulfill most completely the role of sage. In a story without dialogue, the hero is already halfway to the world of eternal silence.

"Kinosaki nite" has little of the self-righteous tone that often mars Shiga's first-person narratives, however. One does not get the feeling that the hero has tried to manipulate his material simply to bolster his image as a moral arbiter; on the contrary, he gains credibility by refusing to rationalize his situation. Having quelled the desire to demonstrate his moral authority, he devotes himself to a much profounder exploration of experience, and in doing so emerges as a far more sympathetic character. The author-sage, now a truly noble figure, attains this heightened consciousness with surprising ease in "Kinosaki nite." He attains it with difficulty, but with even greater effect, in Shiga's only extended narrative, *An'ya kōro*.

THE *SHISHŌSETSU* AS NOVEL

An'ya kōro (A dark night's passing, 1921–37), whose hero Tokitō Kensaku discovers that he is the product of his mother's and the victim of his wife's sexual indiscretion, has been variously described as a brilliant romance, as a youth's long and arduous but ultimately successful search for a mate, as one man's quest for happiness in the face of bitter experience and the humanization he undergoes in the process, and as the affirmation of a personal reality over the reality of the family or larger social order.[37] These attempts to describe, as we might a conventional novel, what the text is "about" are misleading, however, for they imply the existence of a well-conceived plot to which all characters and events are related, when in fact nothing could be further from the truth. Both the author's inexperience at writing sustained narrative and the work's composition over a period of many years militate against the narrative consistency we expect in a novel, but there are other reasons as well. This "fictional" *shishōsetsu*, as critics are wont to

---

37. The characterizations are made, respectively, by Kobayashi Hideo, "Shiga Naoya ron," in *Shintei Kobayashi Hideo zenshū* 4:114; Miyoshi Yukio, "Kakō no 'watakushi,'" 147; Nakamura Mitsuo, *Shiga Naoya ron*, 116; and Edwin McClellan, in the preface to his translation of Shiga Naoya, *A Dark Night's Passing*, 10.

call it ("fictional" because a few events and characters have no counterparts in the author's own life, and *shishōsetsu* because of the nonetheless complete identity of hero and author), is at bottom more *shishōsetsu* than fiction in the novelistic sense, as we shall see below.

An'ya kōro grew out of the author's speculation, during a self-imposed exile in western Japan in 1913, that he had been sired by his grandfather and not by his father, toward whom he had long felt great animosity (*SNZ* 8:18). But rather than universalize the hero's predicament through an exploration of the complex ramifications of illegitimacy and infidelity, Shiga insists on turning both text and hero in on themselves. The reader is lead through a series of claustrophobic emotional soundings by a narrator whose range of awareness is virtually coincident with his hero's; at the conclusion he still possesses no insights into the "themes" that superficially inform the text.

It is no wonder, then, that such a starkly self-centered work should have its detractors. Dazai Osamu, himself an egoist of no small proportions, is positively venomous in "Nyoze gamon":

> *A Dark Night's Passing:* what an overblown title this book has! Shiga often accuses other writers of hamming it up, but he should know that he is as guilty as the next fellow. He really plays to the crowd here. This is a fine example of "stacking the cards" in your favor. Where is the Dark Night, anyway, in this insufferable song to the author's ego? What is there to commend in a style so awash in self-conceit? The hero catches a cold; the hero suffers an ear infection—is this the Dark Night? The book left me absolutely stupefied. A piece of juvenile literature this is, fit only for a composition class![38]

Dazai's description is not inaccurate. *An'ya kōro* is indeed a narcissistic exercise brimming with elitism and adolescent conceit, as Nakamura Mitsuo has also argued in his important critical study of Shiga.[39] And yet, for all its eccentricities, it remains a strangely powerful work, containing in its pages some of the most extraordinary and moving passages in all of literature. It is also, ironically, the greatest work of an author who will be remembered primarily

---

38. *Dazai Osamu zenshū* 10:321.
39. *Shiga Naoya ron*, esp. 148–52. Nakamura also writes: "[Shiga's] literature is essentially a young man's literature. It is founded on the dreams and fastidiousness and carnal melancholy of youth" (ibid., 184).

as a short-story writer. Miyoshi Yukio, whose critique of *An'ya kōro*
is much more thoroughgoing than Dazai's casual remarks, nevertheless manages to touch on what makes it a classic: "*An'ya kōro* is
a truly remarkable *shishōsetsu* . . . in which its hero's originality
comes alive as its fictionality withers away. This is not an irony but
a measure of its success. As a novel, it is riddled with contradictions, and yet by that very failure it has achieved its just reputation
as a landmark text in modern Japanese literature."[40]

Miyoshi, then, postulates an inversely proportional relationship, which Dazai understandably overlooks, between the text's
fictionality and the vividness of the hero's presence. Dazai accuses
Shiga of flagrant exhibitionism, but he never questions the propriety of Shiga's retreat from fictionality, as he is no less eager to
produce stories that aim at collapsing the distinctions between author, narrator, and hero. Indeed, Dazai's remarks sound like the
petulant grumblings of a writer unable to market his sincerity as
successfully as Shiga did. Dazai's jealous wrath would have been
mollified, one feels, not by the insertion of a greater distance between author and hero in *An'ya kōro* but rather by a less blatant
display of smug self-confidence, a quality with which Shiga was
prodigiously, and Dazai poorly, endowed. The question of the hero's autonomy as a fictional character is never raised.

Precisely that question, on the other hand, informs Miyoshi's
essay, which lengthily catalogs the contradictions making *An'ya
kōro* a failure as a novel. The catalog is worth reviewing, along with
other commentaries; for the exact nature of the "failure" will help
us determine the ways in which the modern Japanese *shōsetsu* differs from what we would unhesitatingly label a novel, a comparison Miyoshi suggests but does not articulate in any detail.

An'ya kōro is characterized by an identification between author
and hero that is virtually total. It is not so much the text's personalism that undermines its fictionality, however, as its peculiar narrative stance. Shiga's admission that he modeled his hero after himself

---

40. "Kakō no 'watakushi,'" 154. One indication of *An'ya kōro*'s enormous reputation is a poll appearing in *Bungei* 9 (June 1952): 16–69. Of twenty-four writers and
critics asked to name the five best and/or most important works in Japanese fiction
written since the turn of the century, fourteen included it in their lists. Tōson's *Yoake
mae* (chosen by six writers), Tanizaki's *Sasameyuki* (four), and Sōseki's *Meian* (three)
finished a distant second, third, and fourth.

is couched in terms any novelist might use: "The hero Kensaku is myself. [*An'ya kōro*] depicts him doing what I would do, or what I would want to do, or what I have actually done, under the circumstances" (*SNZ* 8:20). But few can be as guilty of such complete confusion between author and hero as Shiga is in part 3, chapter 5, which describes the hero's anxiety about how the circumstances of his birth might affect the courtship of his future bride:

> It occurred to Kensaku that one way of telling the other party about himself was to write a long autobiographical story. But the project came to a stop after he had published the prologue entitled "The Hero's Reminiscences." He decided not to show them even this short piece, so afraid was he of seeming to be inviting their sentimental pity.
>
> (*SNZ* 5:312)[41]

This curious passage makes little sense at first reading. We learn nothing more here about this "long autobiographical story" than the title of its prologue. Its contents are not revealed. We do not find out when or where the prologue was published or the title of the work as a whole or anything else to suggest that Kensaku had actually written a story of this description. There is in fact no other textual information to verify the existence of such a story—none, that is, save the *An'ya kōro* text itself. Nakano Shigeharu, in an extended critique of *An'ya kōro*, puts it this way:

> People will puzzle over this passage—and then again, maybe they will not. . . . They apparently read the phrase "he had published the prologue entitled 'The Hero's Reminiscences'" and link it to *An'ya kōro* itself without giving the matter another thought. *An'ya kōro*, after all, has a "prologue entitled 'The Hero's Reminiscences.'" The prologue to the "long autobiographical story," then, is the prologue to *An'ya kōro*.[42]

41. Shiga Naoya, *A Dark Night's Passing*, 222. McClellan's translation, on which I have relied exclusively for my citations from *An'ya kōro*, actually reads: "It occurred to Kensaku that one way of telling the other party about himself was to write *an* autobiographical story. But the project came to a stop after he had *written* the *preface* entitled 'The Hero's Reminiscences'" (emphases added). However, the original clearly indicates that the story in question was a full-length narrative (*chōhen shōsetsu*) and that the prologue was not only written but saw the light of print (*kakagerareta*). These are important distinctions in view of the following argument. Further, McClellan's choice of the word "preface" in the above passage and "Prologue" for *An'ya kōro*'s opening section appears to be an attempt to transform this self-reflexive passage into something more readily assimilable as fiction to a western audience.

42. "*An'ya kōro* zōdan" (1944), 548.

In other words, the prologue authored by Shiga Naoya meets all the specifications for the one allegedly authored by Tokitō Kensaku, with the result that the reader is encouraged to view the prologue's "I" as synonymous with *both* the narrated "he" *and* the narrating "I" of the main text. As Nakano notes, the reader was in effect reading *An'ya kōro* as a text by Shiga *and* by its hero, Tokitō Kensaku.

This identification of author with hero is of a very different order than of, say, Flaubert with his celebrated heroine ("Madame Bovary—c'est moi"). Nakano emphasizes that Shiga did not become Kensaku—that is, make an emotional investment in a character he could identify with; rather, he made Kensaku over into *himself*, mindless of the implications for the text as an autonomous narrative. "It is understandable that some critics would mistake the hero for his author in this particular text," Nakano writes. "The text itself is written and structured so as to create just such confusion." [43]

Shiga alerts the reader to the author-hero equation at the very beginning. The first chapter opens with Kensaku's reflections on a story just published by a cohort named Sakaguchi that describes a man's affair with his housemaid, which Kensaku believes to be based on Sakaguchi's own experience. Kensaku, exercising the Shiga hero's now-familiar prerogative as moral arbiter, finds the author Sakaguchi *and* his hero equally guilty of indiscretion: "[Kensaku] could have forgiven the facts if he had been allowed to feel some sympathy for the protagonist; but the flippancy, the superciliousness of the protagonist (*and of Sakaguchi*) left no room for such sympathy" (*SNZ* 5:20; trans., 26; emphasis added).

Kensaku's analysis of Sakaguchi's story is a primer for the reading of any *shishōsetsu* (including, of course, *An'ya kōro*), for it at once defines and problematizes the relationship of author to hero. The author is completely accessible through the text, we are made to understand. Once this convention is accepted, hero and author— the former being the *equivalent* and not simply a creation of the latter—become interchangeable; thus, Kensaku cannot talk about Sakaguchi's protagonist without talking about Sakaguchi himself, and vice versa. Because Kensaku's equation applies not only to his adversary in *An'ya kōro* but also to the author himself, Shiga can

43. Ibid., 551.

think of a prologue *to* a text he wrote himself as *part* of the text, a creation of its hero.

Just as conspicuous as the symbiosis of author and hero in *An'ya kōro* is the tenuousness of plot. This derives, no doubt, from the telosless epistemology in the Japanese literary and intellectual tradition, which regarded life as an experience without goal or denouement. But another factor, namely, the circumstances of its composition, is also at work. Twenty-five of the twenty-six installments of *An'ya kōro* were published over the seven-year period from 1921 to 1928, with the final installment (part 4, chapters 16– 20) appearing nine years later. Although an extended composition time need not change the basic plan of a fictional narrative—one thinks, for example, of *À la recherche* or *Finnegans Wake*—it has an unquestionable impact on a *shishōsetsu*, as we noted in the case of Shimazaki Tōson's *Shinsei* in Chapter 5. Embedded in fictional time, a novel easily takes on the quality of a seamless narrative regardless of interruptions in the actual composition. We read it as a unified, monolithic artifact, playing the fictional time scheme against the conventional, temporal organization of the referential world we call chronological time. We read a *shishōsetsu*, however, in a quite different way, for it is very much a product of the writing time—that is, the period or process of textual production and its temporal relationship *to the events recorded.* Any *shishōsetsu*, but in particular one written over a long period, is shaped by the events it describes as much as it gives shape to them. This can be true even of shorter works when events are coincident with the time of writing, as we observed in the case of the "Yamashina" cycle. The composition process's potential for becoming a source of narrative disruption, along with the system of solicitations and deadlines that pressure many writers to rely on (usually) recent experience for textual production, is a principal reason for the form's brevity. In the face of narrative disintegration, short-windedness becomes a mechanism of textual self-defense.

When *An'ya kōro* first appeared in the pages of *Kaizō*, readers were conditioned to regard each installment by this writer, famed for his short stories, as a separate unit. They were not able to examine the installments together as a whole until 1937, sixteen years after the initial publication. Nakano Shigeharu recalls that the individual installments gave the impression of finished stories in the magazine, but they did not give one of completion when they appeared together between the covers of a book.[44] Nakamura Mitsuo likens *An'ya kōro* to a loose set of exquisitely formed pearls that were never strung together into a necklace.[45] Shiga himself had originally thought of writing a series of short stories and later arranging them into a longer narrative. Such was the rationale, he later recalls, behind publishing the prologue and the final chapter of part 2 as separate pieces (*SNZ* 8:19). The discontinuities and inconsistencies between episodes and especially between the first and second halves[46] are legion. The animosity of the hero toward his father and the mystery of his birth, for example, which figure so prominently in the first half, fade into insignificance in the second. Although there are no appreciable gaps in fictional time, the numerous interruptions in publication, especially of the second half, have attenuated the work's thematic and psychological unity, as Miyoshi, Nakano, and a host of other critics have observed.[47]

Perhaps the main reason for this discontinuity is the existence of the unfinished manuscript *Tokitō Kensaku*, which we know from Shiga's own words provided the author with a working draft of *An'ya kōro*'s first half (*SNZ* 8:19). Shiga's initial difficulties with *Tokitō Kensaku* were rooted in his reluctance, which we noted in our discussion of *Wakai*, to express fully the ill feelings he harbored against his father, even though those feelings had played a central role in his writing career. His dilemma as an author could be re-

44. Ibid., 539. The first half of *An'ya kōro* appeared in hardcover as early as 1922 and is generally more familiar to readers than the second half.
45. *Shiga Naoya ron*, 89. *An'ya kōro* might also be compared to an *emakimono*, or picture scroll, in which there is not one but several points of interest that appear and then disappear from view as the scroll is unrolled and rerolled. Each scene and each small, faceless figure in the landscape is important in establishing the mood of the whole without necessarily being related dynamically to other scenes and figures. Linearity in such a scroll, and in texts like *An'ya kōro*, is necessitated by the physical arrangement of scenes/words on the paper/page, but it is not structurally supported by a series of causal relationships.
46. *An'ya kōro* is presently divided into four parts, but it was originally divided into two halves (parts 1 and 2, and parts 3 and 4). Most critical discussions treat *An'ya kōro* as a two-part text.
47. See Miyoshi Yukio, "Kakō no 'watakushi,'" esp. 98–105; Nakano Shigeharu, "*An'ya kōro* zōdan," 550 and passim; and Hirano Ken, "*An'ya kōro* ron," a chapter in *Hirano Ken zenshū*, vol. 4, *Bungaku: Shōwa jūnen zengo*, 236–64, esp. 254–57. See also Akiyama Shun, "Shiga Naoya no 'watakushi' ni tsuite." Akiyama argues that the first half, a tale of "frustrated existence," and the second half, a tale of "fulfillment," are practically unlinkable and that the many interruptions in writing the second half reveal that Shiga himself was aware of the difficulties in linking them.

solved in only one of three ways: he could throw caution to the winds and write about the matter that concerned him most, regardless of the repercussions in private life; he could ignore it and write about something else; or he could stop writing altogether until the matter had resolved itself in such a way that he could resume his career without compunction.

Shiga chose the last, and the result was a silence spanning the years 1914–17. Interruptions in Shiga's writing career sometimes affected the content and even the very existence of a story, as in the case of "Kinosaki nite." Had Shiga successfully completed *Tokitō Kensaku*, he might very well have inserted the incidents "about the bee's death and about the rat that had its neck run through with a bamboo skewer and was then thrown into the stream" that he had witnessed at a Japan Sea spa into the section of this story set on the Inland Sea, as his diary tells us he once planned (*SNZ* 10:721). It was his failure to do so (despite the appeals of Natsume Sōseki, on whose literary page in the *Asahi* the story was to have been serialized after *Kokoro* in 1914) that made it possible for Shiga's famous meditation on death to take form as a separate story, ending the three-year hiatus. The appearance of the bee, the rat, and the water lizard episodes in a context other than the one Shiga had originally intended signaled the ultimate dismantling of *Tokitō Kensaku*. Then, less than half a year later, came the celebrated reconciliation. The "fundamental discord" between father and son having been resolved in private life, Shiga no longer felt the need to deal with it in his professional life. The father-son relationship as a universal question had never interested him; it was enough that his own predicament be resolved. And once he had written what was to be his most thorough account of the relationship with his father in *Aru otoko, sono ane no shi* (1920), which is itself a product of several earlier manuscripts that were probably related to *Tokitō Kensaku*, he "completely lost interest," as he put it, "in themes that had concerned me up to then" (*SNZ* 8:18).[48]

It is thus surely no coincidence that the rift between father and son even in *An'ya kōro*'s first half is depicted only in a most understated way. The real-life clash of wills is transformed into a kind of

48. *An'ya kōro* manuscripts nos. 2, 14, 33 (6:28–33, 248–50, 359) all contain material used in *Aru otoko*. See "Kōki," in *SNZ* 6:373, 404, 425.

natural catastrophe beyond the control of either party: the hero is the illegitimate child of his supposed grandfather. This tragedy, seemingly ordained by fate, effectively neutralizes the hostility of both parties by removing all the blame. The fiction of the hero's birth, as presented in *An'ya kōro*, serves to absolve both father and son of any responsibility for their mutual hatred. And since even these remnants of violent emotion, along with the general atmosphere of discord, are a legacy of the prereconciliation *Tokitō Kensaku* manuscript, they virtually disappear in the second half, which has no antecedent text and was of course begun after the reconciliation.[49]

The hero's attitude toward his father is only one of several problems of discontinuity for which the text seemingly offers no adequate solutions. It is odd, for example, that Shiga would let an earache (the same one that Dazai Osamu satirizes with such venom) determine his hero's movement from Onomichi to Tokyo and even odder that he should dwell at such length on the operation to clear the ear of fluid, until one realizes that Shiga himself suffered an earache while in Onomichi, which forced his return to Tokyo for treatment. The makings of dramatic narrative are here: Kensaku is on the verge of ending his solitary life at Onomichi and proposing to Oei, his maid and grandfather's former mistress. But here, too, because Shiga did not become Kensaku but instead made Kensaku over into himself, he restricts Kensaku's perimeter of actions. And so Kensaku, rather than take destiny into his own hands once he has resolved to propose to Oei, merely tells himself lamely that "even if his ear had not given him trouble, he would probably have not stayed in Onomichi much longer" (*SNZ* 5:217; trans., 158).

Although it is of course hardly unusual for a writer to incorporate his personal life into, or even to make it the exclusive subject of, his work, few writers have done it so seemingly without regard for an overall narrative plan. Shiga appears reluctant to edit out any impressionable personal experience coincident with the hero's actions, regardless of its relevance to the text as a whole. Thus the inclusion of many extraneous scenes throughout *An'ya kōro*, such as the extended description of Kensaku's train journey from Onomichi back to Tokyo in part 2, his visit to a Kyoto museum in

---

49. Miyoshi Yukio, "Kakō no 'watakushi,'" 80–81. Nakamura Mitsuo makes similar observations in his chapter on *An'ya kōro* in *Shiga Naoya ron*.

part 3 and to a temple on the way to Mount Daisen in part 4, and the rather tedious episode in part 1 of Kensaku's vain attempt to nab his sister's would-be suitor. They are examples of the "finished stories," as Nakano calls them, which end up detracting from the completed text. As with the earache episode, the best explanation for their presence in the text is their chance occurrence in the author's life, as we know through Shiga's diary.[50]

Shiga attaches little importance to Kensaku's supporting cast. Characters like Oei, Kensaku's brother Nobuyuki, and Kensaku's grandfather lack the substance to interact with the hero in any significant way. True, these characters have no real-life antecedents: Oei and Nobuyuki are entirely imaginary figures and Shiga was at pains to create a character who bore no resemblance to his real grandfather, for whom he felt great respect (*SNZ* 8:19). But Shiga also fails to bring to life even characters that are clearly modeled on his own acquaintances. They flit across the pages like clouds scudding across the sky. The use of initials for several characters, moreover, seems to confirm Shiga's lack of deep interest in anyone but his hero.

Even Naoko, the most important person in Kensaku's life, is overshadowed by the introspective hero until the curious passage at the end, which views Kensaku from her point of view (see below). The nature of the hero's relationship with Naoko is presaged in Kensaku's first glimpses of his future bride. Unseen by her, Kensaku spies Naoko working gaily in a house facing the street in Kyoto where he takes his morning walks. It is not until much later, when he has already asked his friend Ishimoto to act as go-between and proposed marriage that he exchanges his first words with her. He sees Naoko's seduction by her cousin not as a marital problem that concerns them both but as a riddle he poses to himself in isolation. It is the "emotional reverberations caused by Naoko's indiscretion," as Miyoshi Yukio puts it, rather than the affair itself, that are at issue for Kensaku.[51] Kensaku's reflections, as transmitted by a narrator whose sensibility overlaps his hero's, extend no further than his own mental state. Nowhere is this fact demonstrated more

---

50. Endō Tasuku makes note of this in his annotations of the *An'ya kōro* text. See Shindō Junko and Endō Tasuku, eds., *Shiga Naoya shū*, 232 n. 8.

51. "Kakō no 'watakushi,'" 123.

forcefully than in a scene in part 4, chapter 10, following the episode in which Kensaku, in a "reflex action," pushes his wife Naoko off a train moving slowly away from the station as she tries to step aboard. Later, husband and wife sit alone, face to face. Never before in the work do we encounter such an opportunity for dramatic revelation of character. But when Naoko pressures Kensaku to explain his irrational act, he replies tersely:

> What you have to understand is that, for me, everything is my problem, mine alone, to solve. . . . It's an egotistic way of looking at things, but given my nature, it may also be the most practical for me. You don't have a place in it, I know.
>
> (*SNZ* 5:514; trans., 356)

Here is perhaps the most startling in a text filled with startling illustrations of a character so completely absorbed in his own sensibility that he interacts only very awkwardly with his fellow human beings. No one, not even his wife, has a "place" in his way of looking at things.

Despite such attenuated plotting and characterization, we must not overlook the fact that *An'ya kōro* does possess a certain continuity, as evidenced in the prologue that serves as an overture for the entire narrative and in the numerous foreshadowings of later events. The depiction of Oei in the prologue as a sensual being adumbrates Kensaku's later sexual attraction to her. The mysterious rejection by a prospective bride's family of Kensaku's marriage proposal hints at a blot in the hero's past. The soaring airplane, the object of admiration at the beginning, becomes a symbol of disillusionment at the end of *An'ya kōro*. Kensaku's interest early on in the theatrical confessions of "Omasa the Viper" and in the geisha Eihana's stubborn silence is later linked to his wife's confessions of adultery. The nameless mountain in Hōki casually mentioned during Kensaku's trip to Shikoku in part 2 turns out to be Daisen, on whose slopes he attains a kind of spiritual release in part 4. Ishimoto, a friend of Kensaku's briefly introduced in part 1, chapter 3, reappears in part 3, chapter 5, as the go-between who arranges Kensaku's marriage with Naoko. The seeds of Naoko's adultery—a lewd game called "turtle–snapping turtle" she played with her cousin Kaname in her youth—are metaphorically planted in the very beginning of Kensaku's marriage discussions (part 3, chapter

5), which are held at a restaurant that specializes in, of all things, snapping turtle cuisine. But surely the most impressive evidence of topical continuity are the striking rites of passage in part 2, chapter 1, and part 4, chapter 19. Aboard a steamer bound for Onomichi—and on the slopes of Mount Daisen years later, in the hero's and in the author's life—Kensaku feels himself being absorbed into nature. The imagery in the two scenes, which is unmistakably parallel yet effectively contrasted, signals a crucial transformation in the hero's consciousness. Both episodes commence with the hero's physical debilitation: a spell of seasickness on board ship and a much more serious bout of food poisoning just before the mountain climb. Kensaku compares the steamer to "an enormous, silent monster" and the mountain to "the back of some huge beast" (*SNZ* 5:154, 579; trans., 114, 401). Most significantly, he yields completely to nature's embrace on the mountain slope, whereas before, aboard the steamer, he resisted the feelings of being "swallowed up by the great darkness surrounding him" (*SNZ* 5:154; trans., 115). These and other foreshadowings suggest an overall narrative plan, however loose, that was carried out in spite of the sixteen years it took to complete the text and serves to bind the seemingly "unlinkable" two halves.[52]

Shiga's own insistence in "Zoku sōsaku yodan" (*SNZ* 8:22) that he did not deviate greatly from his initial conception is borne out by an outline (included in the collection of draft manuscripts and documents relating to *An'ya kōro* in *SNZ*, vol. 6) that introduces many episodes that figure prominently in the text: the hero's wrestling match with his "father," his infatuation with his "grandfather's" mistress, his marriage, his journey to Onomichi and efforts to write, his discovery of the secret of his origins, the direction of his attention away from his father to his wife and children, his wife's adultery, his trip to Mount Daisen, his fight for his life at the story's end (*SNZ* 6:558–59). True, the final product diverges in

52. The characterization is Akiyama Shun's. See n. 47. Hiraoka Tokuyoshi is one of the few commentators who stresses the work's continuity. See *"An'ya kōro no sakusha,"* in *Shiga Naoya zenshū geppō*, no. 12:5–6. He cautions elsewhere, however, that the several "epiphanies" (he borrows the term employed by Saeki [*Nihon no "watakushi" o motomete,* 209–16] to describe a Joyce-like aspect of Shiga's fiction) dotting the text with memorable instants lack the Joycean resonances that light up an entire text. *Bungaku no dōki,* 59. Takahashi Hideo also contests the dualistic interpretations of the two halves in his *Shiga Naoya.*

places from the outline. Kensaku marries a woman from a well-to-do provincial family rather than one from a boardinghouse family. He learns the truth about his birth from his brother Nobuyuki rather than his grandfather's former mistress. His last illness is the result of food poisoning rather than an accidental fall. And *An'ya kōro* ends with his life hanging in the balance rather than with his eventual recovery. Several key motifs are missing as well, as Kōno Toshirō, editor of the draft manuscripts, notes. There is no mention of the hero's cohort in dissipation, Sakaguchi, or of the physical and spiritual exhaustion that accompanies his life of debauchery, although both play important roles in the text's first half.[53] Yet it is precisely those unexpected gaps that make this outline so remarkable. Kōno Toshirō dates it sometime between late 1918 and early 1920, or roughly contemporary with the two independently published stories that were later incorporated into *An'ya kōro*: "Aware na otoko" (A man to be pitied, April 1919) and "Kensaku no tsuioku" (Kensaku's reminiscences, January 1920).[54] This means that even though the vast majority of the unpublished material treats incidents (particularly Kensaku's life of dissipation and his sojourn in Onomichi) that appear in the first half of *An'ya kōro* and only the last three unpublished pieces (nos. 34–36) treat incidents appearing in the second half, Shiga clearly knew the direction his story would take long before he published its first installment.

Reading the draft manuscripts as a whole, however, one is left with an overriding impression of the author's uncertainty about the text's composition. Several manuscripts are little more than false starts. It is not simply a problem of the author's treating a great many sporadic (and at the manuscript stage, seemingly unrelated) incidents. He is clearly unsure of how to *present* his story. Interspersed with manuscripts written in third-person narration are those with a first-person narrator-hero (*watakushi*), as well as a first-person narrator (*jibun*) who chronicles the story of an acquaintance identified either by name or simply as "he" (*kare*). The problem of continuity or narrative unity would seem, then, to revolve less around thematic content, as so many critics have suggested, than

53. "Kōki," in *SNZ* 6:426.
54. Ibid. Kuribayashi Hideo dates the outline even earlier, from 1917 or 1918. See "*An'ya kōro sōkō no kentō*," 135.

around the mode of presentation. And it is surely this mode, far more than any mere similarities between author and hero, that invites people to read the text as a *shishōsetsu* despite its several clearly identifiable "fictions."

We have already touched on one crucial problem in presentation that bears further examination: the episode in part 3, chapter 5, describing Kensaku's publication of a first-person prologue ("Shujinkō no tsuioku" [The hero's reminiscences]) to "a long autobiographical story" that we take to be none other than *An'ya kōro* itself. Shiga published the prologue, we also noted, as an independent story one year prior to its inclusion in *An'ya kōro*—except that as a short story it is a third person narrative entitled "*Kensaku no tsuioku*" (Kensaku's reminiscences). That is, what was written *about* Kensaku in the short story becomes Kensaku's own writing in the prologue to *An'ya kōro*. But here we encounter yet another problem. The hero in the prologue can no longer be Kensaku, because it is Kensaku himself, we are told in part 3, chapter 5, who authors the prologue and creates a character who reminisces at the beginning of *An'ya kōro* about that memorable series of events occurring in the hero's distant childhood. Just *who* is writing what? the reader wants to know. A piece composed by Kensaku has somehow been incorporated into a third-person narration. Does Kensaku exist separately from the narrator, or is he one and the same person?

Shiga apparently agonized over his very point in the manuscript stage—thus, his many experiments with both first- and third-person narration. His decision to dismantle *Tokitō Kensaku* seems to have been motivated, perhaps even more than by the reconciliation with his father, by a desire to apply a new, more distant perspective to his material.[55] In draft manuscripts nos. 21 and 29–32, for example, he attempts to separate narrator and hero by making the former an acquaintance of the hero (already dead in nos. 29–30) who chronicles the latter's life. Shiga ultimately felt too constricted by this approach, however. Using this format to distance himself from his hero, he was forced to describe his hero only from

<hr />

55. Such is the argument of Hiraoka Tokuyoshi, "*An'ya kōro* no sakusha." This incisive article, tucked away in an otherwise nondescript collection of memoirs that commonly make up the *geppō* genre, has been the springboard for much of the argument on *An'ya kōro*.

the outside. The narrator could read what the hero had written, but not chronicle his day-to-day thoughts. So great a distance was, in the end, unworkable for a writer like Shiga.

Faced with the contradictory desires of creating an autonomous hero and representing his own mental state, Shiga arrived at a compromise commonly elected by *shishōsetsu* writers. As in the "Yamashina" cycle, he simply transformed the narrating "I" (*watakushi*) into a narrated "he" (*kare*), thus "objectifying" his hero without, however, granting him the true autonomy found in a conventional third-person narrative. How was this possible? The answer lies in the character of the Japanese language, analyzed in Chapters 1 and 2 and again in the discussion of Shūkō in Chapter 7. One cannot narrate the experience of another person in Japanese without fictionalizing or "lying"—that is, without assuming a pose of omniscience that allows access to the minds of others. Telling the "truth" is in effect telling only of one's own direct experience. What we have called the "written reportive style" differentiates between the *relating* of one's own and the *surmising* of another's experience by grammatical distinctions based on this epistemology. True, the narrating "I" as authorial persona is itself a kind of fiction, as we observed in Chapter 3, but no less powerful as a benchmark of authenticity. For a narrator to describe a character other than himself and still use the markers of direct knowledge (e.g., pure adjectives and verbs instead of adjectival and verbal suffixes like *-rashii* and *-garu*) found in the written reportive style means either that he adopt the pose of omniscience and forfeit all claims to personally authenticated truth or that he present an authorial persona clearly understood as such by the reader. The *shishōsetsu* writer, needless to say, consistently chooses the latter alternative. Thus, he has nothing to lose in the way of authenticity by narrating in the third person. When the conventions of the written reportive style are observed, a *kare shōsetsu* is in the end identical to a *watakushi shōsetsu*. The first-person / third-person distinction being negligible in Japanese, Shiga has no need to "become" his protagonist in order to describe the workings of his mind after the manner of Flaubert; he simply makes the latter over into himself, as Nakano Shigeharu suggests.

Nowhere is this interchangeability more clearly demonstrated than in the curious passage in part 3, chapter 5. The prologue itself, as mentioned earlier, was originally published separately as a third-person narrative.[56] Shiga could have avoided altogether the overlap of authors (Shiga/Kensaku) and the resulting circularity had he retained the prologue in its original form, since "Kensaku's Reminiscences" would then not need to be identified strictly with "The Hero's Reminiscences" in part 3, chapter 5. What, then, motivated Shiga to make the switch in narrative person? His aim, it seems clear, was to lend his fiction an otherwise impossible authenticity. The hero's first-person voice in the prologue reverberates throughout the entire text. Even after the narrative switches from the first-person *watakushi* to the third-person *kare* in the main text, the hero continues to monopolize the point of view, and his sensibility infuses the narrative consciousness. We cannot see around him.[57]

Shiga's apparent slip in part 3, chapter 5, then, actually reveals his narrative intent: to lend a fictional character the authenticity of his own consciousness. So absorbed is Shiga in his hero that his own consciousness at the time of writing seems to displace that of Kensaku and determine Kensaku's actions and thinking, even when they contradict the work's internal fictive design. To say that Shiga is his own hero is to express all too inadequately the radical nature of this profoundly antirepresentational act. Skeptical of the power of language to represent another world, he refuses to invest his

---

56. Other than the transformation of *kare* into *watakushi*, the prologue appears virtually unchanged from its original form, with only a few minor revisions, all of a semantical and not a grammatical nature, except for one change of tense. (The prologue does not include the last section of "Kensaku's Reminiscences," which describes a frog-killing expedition.) Compare "Kensaku no tsuioku" in 5:604–11 with the textual revisions to the original magazine version of "Shujinkō no tsuioku," in "Kōki," in *SNZ* 5:648–49. The parenthetical note originally prefacing "Kensaku no tsuikoku" ("Tokitō Kensaku was the illegitimate child of his mother and grandfather. But he did not learn this until he had reached his mid-twenties" [ibid. 5:604].) is deleted in the prologue.

57. One important exception to this monopoly of point of view will be discussed presently. McClellan's translation makes it appear as if the narrating consciousness is more independent of its hero than it actually is. In trans., 43, to take one of several examples, the narrator states flatly that Ishimoto "*was* only *being* polite" with respect to Kensaku's request that he attend a geisha party, when in fact the original says, "Ishimoto wa . . . amari kyōmi wa nai-*rashikatta*" (*SNZ* 5:45). In trans., 93, the narrator notes, "[Kensaku] *did not know it*, but his face still looked cross," whereas the original makes no such assertion of knowledge about the hero: "Kensaku wa . . . mada okotta *yō* na kao o shite-ita" (*SNZ* 5:121). In the prologue, McClellan has the first-person narrator make the kind of judgment about another's feelings that Japanese grammar will not allow. His translation of "Chichi wa itsu ni nai aiso-*rashii* koto o watakushi ni itta" (*SNZ* 5:12) is a much more direct: "[Father] spoke to me *kindly*" (trans., 20). (Emphases added.)

hero with a discrete set of emotions generated by the text itself. Shiga's insistence in this way on the equivalence of, rather than the mere correspondence between, author and hero practically eliminates the fictional autonomy of the text's time-space continuum; at the same time, however, it presents a powerfully persuasive world of higher authenticity, namely, the narrator's own consciousness. Hiraoka Tokuyoshi puts it this way: "It is precisely because the authorial persona is half 'third person' [*kare*] and half 'first person' [*jibun*] that Shiga is able to pass off part of the autobiographical story that his hero Kensaku writes as the prologue to his own text. This became possible, of course, only after he transformed the story 'Kensaku's Reminiscences' into a first-person narration."[58]

This merging of the author and hero's consciousness, which becomes explicit in part 3, chapter 5, is common in the *shishōsetsu* and already familiar to readers of Shiga in such works as *Wakai*. Needless to say, it breaks the rules of conventional, "realistic" fiction. The author who breaks them must therefore ask himself, just where does his narrator fit in the narrative? "In order to see all," Hiraoka argues, "the writer must focus on himself as writer. To do so, however, is to tread the thin line between . . . art and artifice. That Shiga succeeded was due to his discovery in Tokitō Kensaku of a protagonist who enacted the role of both 'other' [*kare*] and 'self' [*jibun*] and yet who was neither a completely third-person 'he' or first-person 'I.'"[59]

So preoccupied is the *An'ya kōro* narrator with the hero's sensibility to the exclusion of all others, so blatantly does this *shōsetsu* call itself into question as a novel, that the western reader is led to reconsider altogether his strategy of classification. Merely to say, however, that *An'ya kōro* differs radically from the fictional norm is, in the words of Kobayashi Hideo, like telling an elephant that its nose is too long—too long, that is, if one is comparing it with, say, a lion's.[60] We must, in other words, refrain from using the conventional novel as a standard of measurement if we are to understand the text's enduring place in modern Japanese literature.

58. "*An'ya kōro* no sakusha," in *Zenshū geppō*, no. 13:5.
59. Ibid., 7.
60. "Shiga Naoya" (1929), in *Shintei Kobayashi Hideo zenshū* 4:16. Kobayashi satirizes those who would compare Shiga with Chekov. Miyoshi Yukio borrows the comparison in his discussion of *An'ya kōro*. See "Kakō no 'watakushi,'" 128.

What, then, is the standard to which we can appeal for an informed assessment? How can we characterize the text in a way that accounts for its extraordinary power? Nearly every commentator has pointed to Shiga's inimitable ability to project his presence on paper. Miyoshi Yukio argues that *An'ya kōro* "works" because it succeeds, as any good *shishōsetsu* does, in communicating the quintessential individuality of its author-hero.[61] Nakano Shigeharu argues that the great attraction of the *An'ya kōro* text lies in the author's fastidious concern with his persona.[62] Nakamura Mitsuo, however, attributes Shiga's appeal to his invention, or at least perfection, of a contentless self: a transparent hero with virtually no distinguishing traits of his own, who gives the reader the illusion that he has actually come in contact with the real author.[63] No matter that Kensaku is a mere "bundle of sensations" living in a hermetic world; it is his virtue that he is utterly reliant on the reader's knowledge of his creator for any specificity of character. The contentless hero becomes a fitting vessel for the author/narrator's presence.[64]

This does not mean, of course, that the reader comes face to face with the author. Yet it is in the nature of Japanese narrative in the written reportive style that the reader identifies with the narrator's voice (whether expressed through the first-person *watakushi* or third-person *kare*) and no other; for it speaks with a directness that allows for no transindividual consciousness. This characteristic is common to first-person narration in any language. But it is common to "third-person" narration as well in Japanese, for as we have seen, the deployment of *kare* in a *shōsetsu* does not itself result in an autonomous third-person narrative. The con-

---

61. "Kakō no 'watakushi,'" 129.
62. "*An'ya kōro* zōdan," 560. One of the decorum-conscious author's techniques, Nakano suggests, is his use of euphemisms in describing the less savory actions of his hero. For example, he employs a phrase like "Shintai dake wa, kare wa masu masu hōtō no fukami e otoshite itta no de aru" ("With every passing day, his self-indulgence became more intense"; *SNZ* 5:133; trans., 101) for what simply means "Kensaku visited the brothels even more frequently."
63. *Shiga Naoya ron*, 20–22; 137ff.
64. Ibid., 90. Saeki Shōichi emphasizes that the very refusal of a *shishōsetsu* writer like Shiga to invest his hero with a plenitude of presence makes it possible for a reader to identify all the more closely with the character in the belief that he is the same authorial persona he has known all along. See *Nihon no "watakushi" o motomete*, 5–25, esp. 10–11.

tentless *kare* is actually the *watakushi* in a disguise every reader recognizes.

The penultimate chapter marks the fruition of Shiga's first-person / third-person collation. The Shiga hero loses his "self" on the slopes of Mount Daisen, holy to the Tendai school. It is here, Hiraoka concludes, that Kensaku ultimately attains to a transcendent, personless (in both ontological *and* grammatical senses, we might add) world where the hero's consciousness is absorbed into nature's vastness.[65] As if to emphasize this melting into the void, the author deletes the hero's name during nearly the entire lengthy passage at the end of part 4, chapter 19, which describes the state of blissful rest on the mountain slope, and instead punctuates the narrative with an occasional *kare*.[66] Kensaku literally disappears during that fleeting, eternal moment of meditation at daybreak. The name reappears only when Kensaku returns to himself at chapter's end and descends the mountain at the beginning of chapter 20.

But what a different character he has become! In *An'ya kōro*'s final chapter, we can see for the first time *around* the hero—that is, view him from a perspective other than the hero's own. In fact, we see the gravely ill Kensaku, delirious from the food poisoning that afflicted him on Mount Daisen, through the eyes of each character appearing in the chapter: Oyoshi and her mother the priest's wife, the doctor, and finally Naoko. Here, at the very end, *An'ya kōro* sheds its *shishōsetsu* skin and emerges as the kind of "realistic" narrative we are accustomed to as readers of western fiction. The authorial persona whom we have come to know so intimately as the Shiga hero fades away and is superseded by a group of characters, with Naoko as the central figure, that comport themselves like characters in a conventional novel. We are party for the first time to information beyond the hero's ken and to conversations out of his earshot. The hero, at the threshold of death, yields his monopolistic point of view to a suddenly omniscient narrator intent on transforming his *shōsetsu* into a novel.

65. "*An'ya kōro no sakusha*," in *Zenshū geppō*, no. 13:7.
66. The passage begins: " . . . finding a suitable resting place in the grass, he sat down with the mountain at his back." (*SNZ* 5:578; trans., 400.) McClellan appears to attach particular importance to this fact, for his translation duplicates Shiga's usage of the proper name in this section even though it varies considerably elsewhere.

With Kensaku no longer at the core of narrative consciousness, *An'ya kōro* begins to operate in a radically new way.[67] Is the hero's sudden exit from center stage simply a fluke? All indications are that it is not. Shiga makes no definitive statement about the reasons behind the abrupt change of narrative focus, but certain peripheral evidence is too suggestive to ignore.

First, there is the rebuttal ("Nakamura Shin'ichirō-kun no gimon ni tsuite" [1948]) to a critique of *An'ya kōro*'s finale, in which Shiga emphasizes that the shift in narrative perspective was no accident and not even unique, referring to the earlier description of Naoko's indiscretion in part 4, chapter 5.[68] He then mounts an attack on those who would scruple over narrative method.

> Fastidious readers may think it odd that the hero suddenly disappears from the scene, but such people are surely in the minority. I think that the general reader, going through the work rapidly, would not be bothered by the passage. It is in any event the product of a calculated risk and not of carelessness. I was fully conscious of what I was doing. I found that this approach best suited my purposes, but I was also motivated by the desire to take a certain risk.
>
> (*SNZ* 8:159)

67. The hero's displacement from the narrative center, and his metamorphosis from actor to acted upon, is nicely realized by the scene that concludes part 4, in which he finds himself in Woman's hands as he lies before Naoko, his hand in her lap. This contrasts vividly with the scene that concludes part 2, in which he literally takes Woman in *his* hands as he fondles a prostitute's "round, heavy breast" (*SNZ* 5:275; trans., 197).

68. Part 4, chap. 5, and part 4, chap. 20, differ substantially in at least one sense, however. The final chapter is an attempt at truly omniscient narrative that adopts several points of view; whereas part 4, chap. 5, which appears in English as omniscient narrative, is best interpreted as hearsay reported through Naoko. (The English translation sometimes moves away from Naoko's point of view, but the original never wavers. For example, the sentence "Kaname *suffered* from extreme stiffness around the neck and shoulders, and *complained* constantly about it" [trans., 256] is a rendering of "Kaname wa kata ya kubi no hageshii kori de, hidoku *kurushigatte-ita*" [*SNZ* 5:482]; emphasis added.) This is Shiga's not altogether felicitous solution to the problem of how to transmit a great deal of information, to which Kensaku has become privy, in a conciser form than dialogue. Evidence for such an interpretation is supplied by a section of the original text (coming between part 4, chap. 5, and part 4, chap. 6) that was deleted when the complete *An'ya kōro* came out in book form. The section begins: "Kensaku did not of course *hear* the story precisely as given here" ("Kensaku wa mochiron, kono hanashi o sono mama kiita no de wa nakkata ga") and continues with Kensaku addressing Naoko: "You have done what you should by *telling* me about the incident" ("Omae wa sore o uchiaketa to iu tokoro de, suru koto wa sunda no da" [*SNZ* 6:614; emphasis added]). The overall impression received from reading this chapter and the one that follows is one of Kensaku remembering what Naoko has told him about the incident. He has internalized her point of view, and that is why he so boldly announces later, part 4, chap. 10, that "everything is my problem, mine alone, to solve."

Shiga never discloses the exact nature of this "risk." But his opinion that the litterateur would stumble over a passage to which the general reader would not give a second thought suggests that he attempted to create a new, truly novelistic, narrative voice even at the risk of distancing himself from his hero's sensibility, which any critic attuned to the world of *junbungaku* aesthetics would be loath to accept. That he made the attempt at all is remarkable, considering what he must have thought to be the limitations of the language, as we can surmise from an essay published two years prior to the one quoted above.

Scarcely six months after Japan surrendered to the Allied Powers, when people were suffering from starvation, disease, and economic collapse in addition to the agony of defeat, Shiga wrote, in an essay entitled "Kokugo mondai," of still another crisis he believed that the people faced. It was one that, although seemingly not as pressing, could prove to be the most perilous of all: the state of the Japanese language.

> Although we may not be sensitive to the fact (since we are accustomed to our own language from childhood), there is in my opinion no language more imperfect or inconvenient than Japanese. Considering how much the language has impeded the nation's cultural advancement, I believe that we should deal at once with the onerous problems it poses.
>
> (*SNZ* 7:339)

Shiga goes on to recount the plan by Mori Arinori, the Meiji government's first minister of education, to adopt English as Japan's national language, and he argues in essence that Japan would have been spared the tragedy of war had Mori's plan been carried out. He then suggests that the time is ripe to adopt French, known for its logical clarity, as the national language, in the same pragmatic spirit that the Japanese showed when they adopted the metric system of weights and measures.

Shiga's belief that the adoption of English in the Meiji period would have resulted in a more civilized and less bellicose nation is laughable, to be sure. It is hard to take seriously (especially in today's economic climate) Shiga's attack on the language as being an impediment to advancement. Japanese may be "imperfect" in that it is constantly undergoing change to meet new conditions, but it is inherently no less perfect than any other language. Yet it will also not do merely to discount the essay as so many cranky remarks uttered in a period of lost national pride or as wholly representative of the stream of tirades against the language and culture that gushed forth at war's end, as some critics suggest.[69] Indeed, if we read this foray into cultural criticism in light of Shiga's calling as a writer of fiction, the words "imperfect" and "inconvenient" take on new meaning.[70] For what was Shiga, as the would-be producer of an omniscient but still "authentic" narrative, to call a language if not imperfect, if that language sounds unnatural when it attempts to incorporate more than a single point of view? And what, if not inconvenient, if that single point of view must merge with the narrator's own? Shiga may have shared his countrymen's postwar frustration when he penned his critique against the native tongue. But his frustration would also seem to stem from a creative malaise. Having exploited the language's genius as fully as any author, was he not perhaps looking wistfully to new horizons that he had glimpsed through translations from western literature?[71] To become an author with all the power that the word implies; to be the mover of his hero, and not be bound by him—was this not the "risk" that Shiga took, the bold experiment he embarked on when penning *An'ya kōro*'s last chapter?

69. Nakamura Mitsuo, for example, suggests the attack is a sign that Shiga's growth as an artist has stopped. See *Shiga Naoya ron*, 9. Kinda'ichi Haruhiko opens his well-known book, *Nihongo*, with a defense of the Japanese language against Shiga's attack. Suzuki Takao refutes Shiga's essay in the first chapter of his *Tozasareta gengo* and insists that the problem of "imperfection" lies in Shiga's imperfect use of the language and not in the language itself (25–26).

70. For a dissenting interpretation, see Roy Andrew Miller, *Japan's Modern Myth*, 109–15. Miller's book, which shows how the Japanese have placed the language at the center of their cultural identity, correctly debunks the notion that any single language is unique by noting that all languages, by their very existence, are "unique" in some way; but it dwells rather excessively on the masochistic pleasure he claims Japanese take in the difficulty, oddity, and "illogicality" of their language. We have noted throughout, meanwhile, not the ontological uniqueness of Japanese but rather certain features that distinguish it in particular from western languages, in the belief that uniqueness and particularity are not the same thing and that the latter can be studied profitably without conceding the former.

71. The question of how a western language translates into Japanese, important though it is, is too complex to go into here. Suffice it to say that it requires a radical transformation, as suggested in our discussion of the Japanese-to-English translation of *Mon* in Chapter 2. To the extent that its omniscient voice prevails in the translation and is not assimilated into the Japanese epistemology, however, a western novel inevitably comes off as a gross "fabrication," as Kume Masao and others have suggested apropos of Balzac, Tolstoy, et al.

This experiment, however, triggers the text's final crisis. Kensaku's critical illness embroils the narrative itself in a life-and-death struggle for survival and eventually deals it a mortal blow. The narrator's particularized voice, wedded to the written reportive style, finally cannot survive, or transcend, the hero's consciousness. When *An'ya kōro* closes with Naoko's silent soliloquy—the first and last uttered by any character other than Kensaku—what we hear is an uncharacteristic, sexually neutral language that sounds uncannily like Kensaku's own speech: "Naoko wa 'tasukaru ni shiro, tasukaranu ni shiro, tonikaku, jibun wa kono hito o hanarezu, doko made mo kono hito ni tsuite iku no da' to iu yō na koto o shikiri ni omoitsuzuketa" ("[Naoko] kept on thinking, 'Whether he lives or not, I shall never leave him, I shall go wherever he goes'" [*SNZ* 5: 589–90; trans., 408]).[72] It is as though Kensaku's soul has taken flight and migrated to the body of Naoko. Or, on second thought, are those words not more appropriately spoken by the narrator of his hero? For when the former parts from the latter, it means the end of them both.[73]

Shiga's narrative experiment signaled not only the end of *An'ya kōro* but for all intents and purposes the end of his writing career. His last three and a half decades, by all accounts, were spent living out contentedly his hyphenated role of author-sage. It was a role more securely played in private life than on paper and one that he played with apparent ease. For Shiga's goal in writing, as Hiraoka Tokuyoshi observes, was always a more satisfactory personal life.[74] Writing, in other words, was a means, not an end—a form of autotherapy, as we noted at the beginning of this chapter, that led to a

---

72. The only commentator to make note of Naoko's decidedly nonfeminine language is Donald Keene. See *Dawn to the West* 1:467.

73. There was of course a more "practical" reason for the text's completion: a plea from Shiga's publisher to finish writing in time for its inclusion in a newly edited *zenshū*. Thus the appearance of the final and longest (part 4, chaps. 16–20) installment in *Kaizō* (Apr. 1937), after a nine-year hiatus. Such pressure (to say nothing of the fact that the work was already quite long) no doubt encouraged Shiga to end his narrative where he did, but that alone does not explain the motivation for his narrative experimentation—*unless*, knowing that he had to finish writing soon, Shiga did not feel obliged to extend his novelistic project. At any rate, it would have been impossible for him to pursue this project and still remain true to the traditional linguistic and narrative rules governing the production of "authentic" fiction in Japanese.

74. "*An'ya kōro* no sakusha," in *Zenshū geppō*, no. 13:6.

fulfilled silence. Dazai's inference in "Nyoze gamon" that Shiga had not written anything significant for two decades (excepting, we would protest, the final chapters of *An'ya kōro*) is correct;[75] but such is hardly grounds for condemnation, since Shiga had passed on to a new stage: from writing to living. Shiga was always more interested in attaining peace with himself than in searching at all costs for the meaning of "self." This very limited and concrete notion of selfhood—true to the traditional epistemology and the product of a particularized narrative voice—is of course what characterizes the *shishōsetsu* in general and so much of Japanese literature. Shiga saw his task as one of resolving the contradiction within himself as observer and as actor, as writer and as private man. "The part of me that observes is completely divorced from the part that acts," Shiga writes angrily in a short piece included in the collection of *An'ya kōro* manuscripts. "I must make myself whole. I must hold onto something, something very basic, something that will form a world all my own. . . . Without it I cannot confront existence, cannot survive. I must find it. But I don't know how. I will go to the mountains and think" (*SNZ* 6:60–61).

The logical conclusion of this train of thought is that literature is subordinate to life, that the goal is to be a content person, not a prolific writer. If we accept Shiga's motive for writing—to bring an emotional crisis to conscious light and liberate oneself from its burden—then we can see that this is precisely the goal that Shiga pursued. One might argue that this is the reason all writers write; but few writers have recognized, as Shiga did, its ramifications: if realized, it leads the writer to silence. For Shiga, literature was useful only insofar as it fulfilled a particular need in his life; once the need was met, he could discard his art as he would an outgrown pair of shoes. For Shiga, silence in the end signified a healthy reintegration into life. Granted, he was a fastidious stylist, intensely concerned with imagery and tone and profoundly aware of the genius—and the limitations—of his language. But looking at matters in the above light, perhaps we can say that his ultimate aim as author-sage was to do what most private citizens do, and that is not to write at all.

75. *Dazai Osamu zenshū* 10:325.

9

Kasai Zenzō:
The Hero as Victim

Having to write this sort of rubbish again for the money
saddens and embarrasses me. Only recently, I published an
identically colorless and uneventful tale of poverty and
aimless wandering—call it the scrap-paper literature of private life; yet here I am about to serve up the same old fare
all over again. I really hate the thought of doing this and I
feel sorry for you, the reader; but circumstances have forced
my hand. I humbly beg your indulgence.

Kasai Zenzō, "Nakama"

For the artist himself art is not necessarily therapeutic; he
is not automatically relieved of his fantasies by expressing
them. Instead, by some perverse logic of creation, the act of
formal expression may simply make the dredged-up material more readily available to him. The result of handling it
in his work may well be that he finds himself living it out.
For the artist, in short, nature often imitates art.

A. Alvarez, *The Savage God*

One is not quite sure whether the opening paragraph in Kasai Zenzō's "Nakama" (In the same boat, 1921), quoted above, is a sincere
apology to readers for the narrator's stated lack of interesting material or a not-so-subtle boast about that lack. And one is no surer
after reading widely in the Kasai oeuvre and encountering many
similar disclaimers. But it is certain that no other modern Japanese
writer, including Shiga and Shūkō, relied so exclusively on the
"scraps" of private life for his literature as Kasai did. Such an extreme reliance on personal experience for one's fictional material
was, however, fraught with risk, not the least of which was running out of things to write about, as the narrator laments that he
has done in this story.

Such risks are, of course, part of the occupational hazard faced by any writer who insists on limiting the scope of his art to his private life. But Kasai often succeeds in turning an apparent liability into an asset: the writer-hero's creative sterility itself becomes the subject of many Kasai stories. The writer who cannot write is the perfect material for an author who, as Yamamoto Kenkichi suggests, is not a storyteller but a soliloquist who deals in cries and whispers, sighs and prayerful supplications.[1] The final motivation in Shiga's literature is the will to silence; in Kasai's it is the will to write when there is in fact nothing to write about, when life itself has reached a seemingly irreparable impasse. Although this reckless borrowing on bankrupt experience sometimes foredooms Kasai's literary experiments, it is at the same time the only possible road to success. For Kasai, the triumph of art over private life is based on a precarious formula that succeeds only to the degree that his life actually threatens to overwhelm his art. Reading through his stories, from the depressing "Kanashiki chichi" (An unhappy father, 1912) to the even more dismal "Imiake" (The end of mourning, 1927), one is struck by the author's obsession with a single vision: the writer on the verge of artistic creation even as he faces imminent physical and/or mental collapse. Kasai's guiding vision is not art fulfilled, but art in the making; his concern is creativity in its potential phase, rather than its final fruition.

If art is forever in the process of becoming but never fully achieved, the artist in Kasai's eyes is a derelict vainly risking body and soul to create. For Kasai, artistic creation is therefore nearly synonymous with self-destruction. The Kasai persona, mired in the grim realities of sickness, alcoholism, and poverty, is a permanent resident in the cirques of a living hell. Kasai's stories are filled with portraits of the hero at a physical and emotional nadir. That these portraits indeed resemble Kasai in private life as well does not make them less viable as fiction: they are a testament, rather, to a consistency of artistic vision that far surpasses that of lived experience. The artistic vision, moreover, usually anticipates the actual circumstances. That is to say, Kasai projects onto his hero his own bleakest fantasies, and the projections are usually prophetic. The hero undergoes first, like a sacrificial lamb, experiences

1. "Kaisetsu," 498.

that the author too will eventually suffer, as if by delayed reaction, in his personal life. In an ironic reversal of roles, the Kasai hero provides a treacherous model for Kasai the man.

Kasai's literary output was meager even for one whose life was cut short by alcoholism, tuberculosis, and numerous other ailments. The entire oeuvre fills only three volumes in the most recent edition of his collected works. (By comparison, the collected works of Akutagawa Ryūnosuke, the famed short-story writer who died at age thirty-five, fills twelve.)[2] Kasai was a notoriously slow writer, a fact to which both he and many of his personal acquaintances attest in numerous anecdotes. It seems that Kasai could produce a maximum of only two or three pages a day, and not infrequently only a few lines. More than one writer, recounting a visit to one of the squalid dwellings Kasai lived in over the years, describes the author kneeling at his desk (often the only piece of furniture he owned, the rest having been pawned) and staring at a sheet of manuscript paper that was blank except for a story title and the author's name.[3]

Even when his popularity grew and literary magazines began soliciting stories from him, Kasai rarely turned in a manuscript on time, and he was continually hounded by editors who dispatched angry letters, angrier telegrams, and finally tenacious messengers who would not let him out of their sight until he had penned the last sentence. Still Kasai would not be hurried. He would stay up all night and sometimes several nights in succession to write a few lines, cross them out in disgust, then write a few more. Dictation, a method Kasai employed increasingly in his later years when his health had declined, did not accelerate the snail's pace of his writing. Kamura Isota, the transcriber of Kasai's last major text, "Suikyōsha no dokuhaku" (A mad drunk's monologue, 1927), and himself a *shishōsetsu* writer of note, recalls that it took Kasai sixty-five days to dictate the seventy-four-page story (thirty-six pages in the modern *zenshū* edition).[4] Kasai was permanently in his cups in

---

2. *Kasai Zenzō zenshū* (*KZZ*; Hirosaki: Tsugaru Shobō, 1974–75) and *Akutagawa Ryūnosuke zenshū* (Iwanami Shoten, 1977–78). *KZZ* has a fourth volume, *Bekkan* (identified as vol. 4 in the citations below), which contains material about, but not by, Kasai.

3. See, for example, Uno Kōji's amusing description in "Kasai Zenzō no isshō," in *Uno Kōji zenshū* 11:418.

4. See "Kaidai," in *KZZ* 2:795.

those last years, it is true, but the deliberate pace of dictation—to say nothing of how these works actually read—suggests that it was not simply the "drunken palaver" many critics assumed it to be.[5]

Despite his notoriously small output, Kasai demanded and often managed to receive advance payments for his manuscripts. But this arrangement only invited more trouble, for it encouraged the author to borrow ever more liberally from his publishers to pay his landlord or his wineseller and in effect mortgage his future literary production to the whim of the bleak fate he had unleashed. Such unenviable circumstances form the "plot" of many Kasai stories: the debt-ridden writer-hero faces eviction from his lodging and a deadline from his publisher with nothing to write about except that very predicament. Dull stuff, one might think, but not in this author's hands. These desperate conditions often brought out the best in Kasai, because they fulfilled his vision of art in its potential and never-to-be-completed stage.

Unquestionably, Kasai's work marks both a crowning achievement and a precarious crossroad in the history of *shishōsetsu*. Never long on story, the *shishōsetsu* in Kasai's hands becomes ever more fragmented the more it is "framed" by various verbal ploys bent on convincing the reader of the narrator's authentic voice. Such a radical undermining of narrative had a mixed reception. Indeed, few writers have inspired such extremes of devotion and repugnance as Kasai. Uno Kōji, for example, claims admiringly that no *honkaku shōsetsu* could measure up to the psychological intensity of Kasai's late stories. Fukuda Kiyoto, on the other hand, cannot conceal his spleen: "With the exception [of two stories], none of Kasai's work even begins to hold my interest. In my boredom I gaze out the window at the blue sky . . . and wonder idly if the true purpose of literature is to make one suffer so."[6]

Even Kasai's strongest supporters would readily admit that their champion is something of an acquired taste. His stories lack the sheer excitement of Shūkō's best work, the crystalline brilliance of Shiga's. Indeed, we shall frequently be asking during the course of

5. Tayama Katai and Chikamatsu Shūkō both use the term (*sake no kuda*) in describing a slightly earlier work, "Ware to asobu ko" (1925), for example, in a panel discussion published in *Shinchō*. See *KZZ* 4:441.

6. Uno's comment can be found in "'Watakushi shōsetsu' shiken" (1925), 65. Fukuda's can be found in "Kasai Zenzō" (1934), 381.

this chapter, how can a story with so many things "wrong" with it still work—that is, still make a powerful claim on our imagination? The fact that it does attests to both the uniqueness of Kasai's style and his understanding, beyond that of most of his contemporaries, of the meaning and destiny of *shishōsetsu*.

Kasai was a native of Tsugaru, a cold, isolated district in northern Honshū that also produced Dazai Osamu. Unlike many authors who hailed from the provinces and were eager to shed their country trappings in order to make a name for themselves in Tokyo (the only large market for writers), Kasai clung to his roots and returned to them frequently, although by necessity as often as inclination. Marriage at the relatively early age of twenty-one forced him to lead a dual existence: one life as a struggling writer in the capital, the other as a husband and provider for a family with whom he could seldom afford to live. Kasai showed no interest in pursuing an agricultural career at home, but it soon became apparent that writing—particularly at his slow pace—would bring him no wealth. His wife's family virtually subsidized his career. Of the several dozen letters to his father-in-law, most are charmingly insistent requests for money.

Kasai lived with his wife and children for brief periods in both Tokyo and Tsugaru; but contented family life, like finished art, seemed to go against his grain. It was much simpler to put his family under the care of his father-in-law and carouse in Tokyo with his literary cohorts, working when he had to and writing home for cash when he ran out. "I am not at all lonely," he writes to a friend. "I'm the sort who can manage quite well by myself. I don't think that I'd feel the least bit lonely even if every last one of my relatives died off. The world is really not such a sad place to be in as long as you can go on loving and tormenting yourself."[7]

This seemingly flippant assessment of his living arrangements sounds a refrain throughout Kasai's literature. No one knew better than Kasai the arts of self-conceit and self-torment; and it is these preoccupations, reminiscent of those found in the Russian literature he loved and bordering at times on megalomania and paranoia, that provide the driving force in his literature.[8] In contrast to

---

7. Quoted from a letter to Mitsumochi Kiyoshi, 17 May 1910, in *KZZ* 3:441. Citations from the *zenshū*, where appropriate, henceforth appear in the body of the text.
8. Ōmori Sumio describes Kasai as an avid reader of Andreyev, Dostoevsky, and Sologub. See "Kasai Zenzō," 156.

Shiga, who employed writing as a means of recovering his emotional equilibrium and stopped writing when he had attained it,
Kasai employed writing to drive himself to the brink of sanity and
stare into the void.

THE MAKING OF A STYLE

Kasai's first serious attempt at writing (or at the very least, at leading the writer's life) came in the summer of 1909, when he was
twenty-two. He had left Tsugaru alone for Tokyo in the previous
year, shortly after his marriage, to attend school and receive the
instruction of Tokuda Shūsei, the prominent naturalist writer. In
May 1909, he traveled to Ōarai, on the Ibaragi Prefecture coast, for
what became a six-month sojourn, in hopes of immersing himself
full-time in writing. The disappointing results hint at the course of
his entire career, for he produced not even a single story. Virtually
the only writing he did was in the form of correspondence, fully
half of which was to his father-in-law asking for money in order
that he might extend his stay. Yet the experience in Ōarai was
clearly a watershed, and its impact is difficult to exaggerate. Shortly
after returning to Tokyo in the fall, he reflects on his experience to
a friend:

> My life as a vagrant this past half year has yielded absolutely noth-
> ing. But in my way of thinking, such a life had its value. This time I
> stopped at nothing to assert myself, to fulfill myself. . . . I feel that
> I've become the master of my own fate. . . . I have become even
> more steadfast in my desire to sacrifice myself and all that is a part
> of me to literature.
>   (*KZZ* 3:429–30)

Kasai soon made good on his pledge of sacrifice. He spent less
than four of the next ten years with his wife and children, and the
rejection of a secure family life in favor of the artist's bohemian
existence becomes the major motif in his early writings. Kasai's first
published work, "Kanashiki chichi," illustrates the dilemma that
plagued his entire career: the choice between the domestic and the
artistic life. One could aspire after paternal satisfaction or poetic
vision, but not both; for Kasai, there was no middle ground. "Kanashiki chichi" is the story of a nameless young poet who lives
alone in the city. He has sent his wife and child back to their home
in a faraway province, being unable to support them and afraid that

their presence will dampen his artistic resolve. (He likens them to germs capable of infecting and ultimately destroying his chosen life.) He lives in a squalid tenement inhabited by a motley array of derelicts who, like himself, are mired in direst poverty. With virtually no dramatic content and reading more like a prose poem, the style of "Kanashiki chichi" foreshadows, in the eyes of at least one critic, the author's entire oeuvre.[9]

Certainly the most important—and problematic—aspect of this style is Kasai's literary version of himself. In addition to the autobiographical link between author and hero observed by members of the coterie magazine *Kiseki*, where the story was first published, and generally assumed by the wider reading audience for the duration of his career, there is a linguistic link to be made as well. The hero is identified from first to last as *kare*. But as we noted in the cases of Shūkō's *Watashi wa ikite kita* and Shiga's "Yamashina" cycle, *kare* has no antecedent; what appears at first glance to be a pronoun ("he"), a placeholder for another signifier, is more correctly thought of as a proper name with all the specificity that term implies. *Kare* refers only to the hero and to no other male character,[10] and his range of perception overlaps that of the story's narrator. Both grammar and epistemology link narrator to hero; the narrating "I" and narrated "he" are interchangeable.[11]

The connection between author and hero is thus easily made. Yet it is ultimately misleading. The regular reader of Kasai, to be sure, recognizing the Kasai persona and noting the continuity of events from story to story, not unnaturally assumed the hero to be the author himself. Yet Kasai was by no means committed to recording the events of his life as they had actually happened. He took an interest only in the events and the part of himself that conformed to his artistic predilections. When they did not conform,

---

9. Uno Kōji, "Kasai Zenzō no isshō," in *Uno Kōji zenshū* 11:416. For an extended analysis of "Kanashiki chichi" as the leitmotiv in the Kasai oeuvre, see Ōmori Sumio, *Kasai Zenzō no kenkyū*, 87–91. My reading of "Kanashiki chichi" has benefited from discussions with Osanai Tokio held in the fall of 1984.

10. The one exception is a reference to the hero's son as *kare* in a dream in which three generations of characters—father [the hero], son, and grandfather—merge in the hero's unconscious.

11. The interchangeability is reinforced by such expressions as "Mata rinshitsu no wakai saikun wa . . . hotondo okite-ita hi ga nai *yō* de atta" (The young housewife who lived next door to him was *apparently* almost never out of her sick bed [*KZZ* 1:14; emphasis added]). The constraint on the narrator to report events within the hero's realm of perception further suggests the identity of narrator with hero.

he would fashion them into an artifact consistent with his vision of physical, and later mental, decay. "Kanashiki chichi" is a case in point. Whereas the author was already the father of two children at the time of writing, the story's hero is the father of only one child. Whereas the author's father had survived his mother (and had re-married), it is the hero's aging mother who is still alive. Whereas the author, so far as we know, was still healthy, the hero shows symptoms of tuberculosis. And finally, whereas the author contin-ued to spend some time with his family, if only for brief periods, the hero, we are given to believe, will never set eyes on them again.

It is not our purpose to dwell on episodes in the story that de-viate from the author's life. We have already seen in our study of Shūkō that any author, no matter how "faithful" his attempt to record life, inevitably focuses on some events and ignores others in a way that produces a picture quite at variance not only with the way another person might look at it but even with the way the author himself might look at it on another occasion. The impor-tance of these examples is rather in the insight they provide into Kasai's literary project. To be sure, Kasai was committed to writing about private life to the virtual exclusion of anything else.[12] But he was aware nonetheless of the subtle yet crucial distinction between literature and experience. "I suppose my stories all look pretty much the same," he says in response to an interviewer's question about the correspondence between his writing and his life, "but the fact is, I cannot write a story unless my objective is one step ahead of—or one rung above—my actual circumstances. That is why it annoys me when people say my writing is at the mercy of my private life. I prefer to think that I'm in complete control of my life—indeed, that this very attitude puts me one step ahead of it. . . . But in the eyes of others, apparently, it looks just the other way around" (KZZ 3:228).

Keeping "one step ahead" of real life is Kasai's way of describing the process of representing personal experience in a manner con-sistent with his artistic objectives, and it is with this understanding

12. A letter to his friend and mentor, Funaki Shigeo (1884–1951), typifies his sentiments. "I feel very strongly about the self-exposé in my writings. I certainly do not intend to dress up my stories with tiresome fabrications after having worked this long and hard creating my own style. . . . If you say that my feelings and my life need embellishing before they can become literature, then writing is not for me. It is simply inconceivable for me to fashion my life into something marketable" (KZZ 3:611–12).

that we can better appreciate this process in "Kanashiki chichi."
Each detail in the story serves to accentuate the conflict between
familial duty and artistic calling, to heighten the mood of hopelessness, and to equate the poet's final choice in favor of the artistic life
with inevitable physical and moral ruin. The author's decision to
make his hero the father of one child rather than two, for example,
makes it possible for him to bring into sharper and more poignant
focus the object of the hero's paternal emotions. And the decision
to replace his living widowed father, who as a man could more
easily fend for himself, with the hero's widowed mother, who becomes helplessness personified, makes the hero's resolve to pursue
a literary career in spite of familial duties appear all the more desperate. Finally, the decision to portray the hero with a terminal
illness makes the commitment to art appear all the more extreme.[13]

Details such as these about health and family composition underscore the incompatibility of artistic aspiration and familial obligation. There are others as well. The story begins, "Once again, almost before he knew it, he found himself driven to the edge of
town" (*KZZ* 1:9). This description seems all the more ominous for
its being followed by a series of warm, pleasant images: tree leaves
glinting in the sunlight outside his room, sparrows incessantly
chirping their mating calls, men calling out rhythmically as they
prepare the ground for construction, presumably of a family dwelling. The dependable cycle of growth in nature and in society alluded to here underscores the hero's pathological state in an otherwise healthy world.

Kasai's idiosyncratic prose itself highlights the hero's sense of
helplessness and persecution in "Kanashiki chichi" and throughout the Kasai oeuvre. Most notable is the unusually high incidence,
on the one hand, of ponderous, double-negative, (*nakereba naranai*)
expressions of obligation and, on the other, of "adversative" and
"spontaneous" passives (to use Samuel E. Martin's terminology).[14]
These two forms of the passive voice in particular are a hallmark of

13. This last point is discussed in detail in Ōmori Sumio, "Kasai Zenzō to watakushi shōsetsu," 183–84. In "Nakama," the hero confesses that the description of
the hero in his first published story ("Kanashiki chichi") coughing blood was a lie
(*KZZ* 2:107–8). If we are to believe the chronology in *KZZ* 4:657–82, however, the
hero's consumptive attack in the latter story (*KZZ* 2:113) is a "lie" as well. Kasai
himself did not cough blood until 1924, three years after he published "Nakama."
14. See *A Reference Grammar of Japanese*, 295, 307.

Kasai's writing. The former (as in the opening to "Kanashiki chichi": "Kare wa mata itsu to naku dan-dan to basue e oiko*marete*-ita") suggests a hero who acts far less than he is acted on, forever at the mercy of his circumstances. The latter (as in his frequent use of *ki ga sareru* in place of *ki ga suru*) makes even the hero's own thoughts appear to be beyond his control, originating, as it were, spontaneously from without.[15]

These subtle linguistic distinctions underwrite Kasai's major fiction: that his hero is purely the victim of circumstance, purely at the mercy of outside forces. We must not forget, Enomoto Takashi suggests with reference to "Kanashiki chichi," that Kasai to a large degree willingly *drove* himself ("onore o . . . oikonda") into the dire straits he describes his alter ego as being *driven* to ("oikomarete-ita"), as if out of a frenzied desire to fulfill his prophecy, made during his six-month stay at Ōarai, of a total and irrevocable self-sacrifice to literature.[16]

"Kanashiki chichi," then, illustrates well Kasai's belief that art begins, and indeed is possible, only when the end of a comfortable existence—and perhaps of life itself—is in sight. For the Kasai persona, art is inextricably entwined with the fragility of the human condition. To engage in art is to accept loneliness, poverty, sickness, and premature death. Tanizaki Seiji, younger brother of the novelist Tanizaki Jun'ichirō and one of Kasai's most perceptive critics, writes, "Kasai saw life only as suffering. . . . There are those who say that Kasai was an unhappy man, and he may have indeed been that; but the fact remains, he had consciously rejected worldly happiness from the start."[17] He also rejected in no uncertain terms, Tanizaki goes on to say, the credo of self-affirmation. "In contrast to personal fiction in the west, which celebrates the individual's awakened self . . . Kasai's objective was not to express the self but to chastise it, to persecute it—indeed, to extinguish it. His 'fiction of the self' [*watakushi shōsetsu*] aimed, in short, at doing away with self."[18] In this respect, of course, Kasai's literary project differed

15. No statistical comparison of writers' usage of these forms is available, but the high incidence in Kasai's case is noticeable on even a casual reading. For a brief comment on Kasai's use of these forms, see Negishi Masazumi, "Watakushi shōsetsu no buntai," 231–32.

16. "'Kanashiki chichi' ron," 214–15.

17. "Kasai Zenzō hyōden" (1957), 524.

18. Ibid., 586.

only in degree from that of other Japanese chroniclers of lived experience.

Such an outlook does not necessarily express itself in somber resignation, however. The relish with which the Kasai hero abandons himself to his ruinous life is vividly illustrated in his next published work, "Akuma" (The devil, 1912). The story's plot is even less substantial than that of "Kanashiki chichi." The hero is involved in the publication of a coterie magazine with his associates (as, indeed, the author was). The bulk of the story consists of the hero's emotional outpouring to a friend. He sings the virtues of sacrificing self to art despite the inevitable havoc it wreaks on one's life:

> We shall be destroyed! Then we shall live anew! . . . Our life is wretched, tormented, miserable. But we are a blessed group because we have our souls and our art. . . . O Lord, O God . . . show us the beauty of total destruction! . . . Destiny is always sad; the spirit, forever alone. And in that sad aloneness resides our art. . . . Let me sing the ballad of Oshiyoro Takashima. Oshiyoro Takashima was my boyhood dream. . . . If I had only died then. . . . Ah, boyhood dream! But I can no longer sing that song. I can sing only the most dissonant of melodies now.
>
> (*KZZ* 1:31–32)

As a story, "Akuma" is a disaster. But as a manifesto it warrants our scrutiny. The contemporary Kasai scholar Ōmori Sumio suggests that the Kasai hero, secure in the knowledge of his superiority as an artist, proudly and defiantly declares his willingness to become an outcast.[19] Indeed, given the adamantly elitist consciousness that prevailed in the Taishō *bundan*, a socially marginal existence was considered a precondition of artistic superiority. The Kasai hero relishes, and not merely endures, his superfluity and isolation. But behind the bravado is a haunting message. "Akuma" celebrates the hero's attempts to fashion an aesthetic out of decay and destruction, as others would out of beauty and harmony. In Kasai's imagination, this stark vision nonetheless takes on the aura of a lofty ideal. To be sure, the promise of a life patterned after an ascetic in "Akuma" is never completely fulfilled; the hero's yearn-

19. *Kasai Zenzō no kenkyū*, 95–96.

ing for family and home continually surfaces in later texts. Yet it remains the keynote of the Kasai oeuvre.[20]

The circumstances of Kasai's private life reflect this vision, as we have seen. His indigence exacerbated by a minimal output, Kasai compounded his difficulties with heavy drinking and, in his later years, by keeping a mistress he could barely support. Real life, in short, provided a seemingly endless supply of episodes of hardship, without his having to invent more. But that is precisely what he did. Kasai's life had more than its share of hopeless moments, but it also had its brighter ones. His biographers have established that he enjoyed periods of relative financial stability, that his friends bent over backward to accommodate him in times of need, and that his health did not deteriorate until the later years.[21] For the Kasai hero, however, the hopelessness has to be total. The crises he faces must be unceasing and overwhelming—familial problems wearing him down, disease eating him away, friends conspiring against him. He is forever the victim of willful persecution or mindless misfortune. The Kasai hero can be nothing but a loser.

It is no wonder, then, that Kasai's family and friends, on whom the author depended for nearly all his character models, often recognized themselves on paper only just well enough to realize that a gross transformation had taken place. Tanizaki Seiji, who figures in several of Kasai's stories, writes that Kasai considered "faithful" depiction merely tedious. He was not satisfied unless he had turned his models into sadistic schemers whose cruel acts of persecution justified the hero's paranoia.[22]

Tanizaki is himself the victim of this sort of distortion in "Ko o tsurete" (With the children in tow, 1918), which firmly established Kasai's reputation when it was published in the widely read *Waseda bungaku*. (Kasai wrote very little between 1913, *Kiseki's* last year of publication, and 1917, when he began contributing to *Waseda bungaku*.) Oda, a destitute writer, has sent his wife home to a faraway

20. Ibid., 124. "Kōhan shuki" is an example of a work in which familial obligation again figures large. See below.
21. Several chronologies detail the author's life. See Ōmori Sumio, "Kasai Zenzō nenpu"; and Osanai Tokio, "Nenpu," in *KZZ* 4:657–82. See also Furui Yoshikichi, *Tōkyō monogatari kō*, 65–94, for a very readable account of Kasai's life.
22. "Kasai Zenzō hyōden," 524.

province to raise money while he remains in Tokyo, cares for his two children, and fends off the landlord's periodic threats of eviction. The story ends at a typically bleak moment. Oda's wife has failed to send word or money, and he is finally evicted from his lodging. Having spent the last of his money on a dinner for his children and a drink for himself, Oda boards an empty train with no place to go.

An early scene vividly illustrates the hero's sense of persecution. We learn that Y, a friend in Oda's literary coterie who recently lost his father, has mailed a canister of choice tea to all those who helped defray funeral expenses, including Oda, although it was actually another friend, K, who contributed money in Oda's name, knowing that Oda was penniless. Oda gleefully unwraps his present only to pull out a dented canister. A few days later, he learns from K that Y dented his canister on purpose, and he is shocked. And so was Tanizaki (Y in the story) when he learned of Kasai's misconstrual of the incident. Kasai later apologized to Tanizaki for assuming him guilty of willful humiliation and for writing the story on the basis of that assumption. The tea canister had actually been dented in the mail. But such motiveless accidents of chance do not make a good story, of course, nor do they conform with Kasai's paranoid world view; and thus the change.[23] Since his "ideal" was the derelict artist, Kasai was forced at times to "distort" lived experience in order that it conform to the ideal. Such distortions would continue to shock his colleagues for the duration of his career.

NARRATIVE FRAMING AND
FRAGMENTATION

Obsessed though Kasai was by a single vision, he showed less and less concern with narrative unity as his career advanced. What we have identified confidently as "themes" in his earlier stories, therefore, are perhaps more properly characterized in his later ones as thematic traces or vestiges left in the wake of radical narrative dis-

23. Ibid., 515.

persal. If "Kanashiki chichi" and "Ko o tsurete" established the Kasai oeuvre's leitmotiv, works like "Nakama" (1921) inaugurated Kasai's subversive presentational scheme. Certain earlier works adumbrate Kasai's strategy. "Kurai heya nite" (In a dark room, 1920), which describes the narrator's life at the great Zen monastery Kenchōji in Kamakura (where Kasai rented a room in a small temple from 1919 to 1923), contains several sudden shifts in time and scene and makes self-conscious references to the story in progress. "Sennin-buro" (The pool-sized bath, 1920), which opens with a comic repartee between the hero and a maid at a spa, breaks off abruptly into an eerie dream sequence, from which the shaken hero awakes a few lines from the end. It is in "Nakama" and works following it, however, that Kasai begins in earnest to foreground the narrative frame. Rather than suppress the process of literary production, he exposes the illusion of the text as spontaneous expression, as an always and already finished form. Paradoxically, such foregrounding does not push the narrative in the direction of the surreal or fantastic; calling more attention to the frame actually heightens the sense of reality. The reader is easily taken in by the narrator's casual self-consciousness: the professed sincerity of the "frame" implies an authenticity of "content." Kasai uses this ploy of disarming candor to gain a foothold into the house of fiction, "shaping" his deceptively ill-wrought narrative into a familiar, if frequently disrupted, tale of a hapless writer who engages life with the best of intentions only to be wronged and humiliated in the end.

"Nakama" is the first of several Kasai texts that begins with either a direct appeal to the reader or a pensive meditation and then drifts into a more dramatic mode in which one or more episodes gain narrative momentum. In some stories, such as "Suikyōsha no dokuhaku" (A mad drunk's monologue; discussed below), the lyric and dramatic modes battle for supremacy throughout the text: the urge to sing a song (or in Kasai's case, a dirge) clashes repeatedly with the urge to spin a yarn. In "Nakama," the narrator interrupts his "story" several times in the first half with anxious reflections on his storytelling. Despite the casual tone, the aim of this narrative fragmenting is far from cavalier; by damming and diverting the linear flow, the narrator calls attention to the act of writing itself. Writing is something that can never be taken for granted by the

Kasai hero. However smooth and seamless the words may appear on the printed page, they are the product, he reminds the reader again and again, of excruciating pauses and silences.

In the opening soliloquy, the writer-hero comments on his recent lapse in production (which, however, is not substantiated by the actual publication record). After the apology that heads this chapter, he continues:

> Thanks to a period of sheer indolence lasting from winter into spring, I was spared my usual asthma attack. I had even thought myself fully recovered. Every day I was out practicing with my air gun. . . . Indeed, I thought my time better spent stalking prey in the temple grounds than trying to pen some poor excuse for fiction, both in the interest of health and out of courtesy to my readers. . . . But with no other source of income, I've had to spend these past several months putting off day by day the several debts I've incurred here. . . . What I lament most are my poverty and the lack of a rich, creative imagination that could overcome it and make me a wealthy man. . . . I might no doubt be censured for having imprudently embarked on such a career as this without money or talent. And yet the fact that I persist in my folly is surely a sign of divine caprice. I have resigned myself to this inescapable fate for the duration of my existence.
>
> I came up to Tokyo from Kamakura 24 May on the 7:00 P.M. train. A party commemorating the publication of an anthology by K. M. [Kume Masao] was being held at the Tōyōken in Shinbashi Station, and I had planned to attend.
>
> (KZZ 2:103–4)

Thus the narrator backs into his "story," in which he recounts his vain efforts to sell the copyrights to some of his other stories to raise money. Halfway into this story he interrupts his narrative to inform the reader that he has not written a word for nearly six weeks owing to a consumptive attack. It is now July, and he is still in Tokyo and still penniless. He cannot return to Kamakura without first selling the very manuscript he is now writing (i.e., "Nakama") in order to pay off his debts. He despairs of his situation and envies the successes of his peers. "I have lost all desire to write this sort of half-serious literature that flatters the likes of Noda [a literary cohort]," he reflects. "But the fact is, I need the money so I can return to the temple as soon as possible and get back to writing, quietly and humbly, my meager autobiographical tales" (KZZ 2:114).

The hero continues his tale of physical and financial woes. Now sick enough to need a doctor, he stays at his brother's home in

Tokyo, working on his manuscript (which is to say, the story we are now reading) whenever he feels up to it. He interrupts his story again to report the receipt of letters from his wife, who lives with her family in a distant province because he cannot support her, and from his son in Kamakura. His guilt and frustration mount. The work concludes with a pathetic yet comic scene in which a fellow writer, who is "in the same boat" because he can no longer support his wife and has to send her back to her family, incites the hero into a drunken brawl. The ailing hero, of course, winds up the loser and fears for his life.

> This time he pinned me against the wall. I fought back, going at his throat with my fists but fearing that I would cough blood any moment.
> "Are you trying to kill me?" I said. "All right, I'm licked. Now let me go!" I detected a murderous gleam in his eyes.
> "The hell I will!" he shouted. "Damn me if I ever let a sickly, good-for-nothing like you go!" He jabbed the bony kneecap of his right leg even harder into my gut.
> "Let me go, you animal! I can't take it any longer! It really hurts! You'll make me cough blood! Look, I'm sorry. I'm sorry!" My voice quavered as I spoke. I continued to clutch at his throat.
> (*KZZ* 2:128)

And so the story ends. Tanizaki Seiji suggests that this scene is yet another of Kasai's "distortions." (Kasai was no crybaby in real life, he insists.)[24] Distortion or no, it is another in a series of vignettes calculated to portray a man oppressed by illness, creditors, friends, and finally his own meager talents—framed by a self-conscious meditation (on the very possibility of continuing the narrative) that anchors the fiction of his persecution in the reality of recording it.

The pull away from narrative closure in "Nakama" is ironically rectified in "Asa mairi" (Morning pilgrimage, 1922), which describes one of the Kasai hero's frequent bouts with writer's block. To treat such a topic, however, is in a sense to "tell" a story that never gets told; the hero, after all, can do no more than relate his failure to write. Thus, the seemingly straightforward "Asa mairi" actually goes one step further than the disjointed "Nakama": whereas the latter occasionally foregrounds the narrative frame in an attempt to authenticate the hero's haltingly recounted story of victimization,

24. Ibid., 535.

the former presumes to do away with story altogether and present nothing but the authenticating mechanism of the frame itself. For what could be more authentic, or more sincere, than the hero's confession of his failure to write? Yet the final irony in "Asa mairi" is that this "storyless" frame exposes the fiction of that very confession.

The motif of composing under the pressure of a deadline is not uncommon in Taishō literature and reflects the journalistic realities of the time. The editor of a major literary magazine like *Kaizō* (which published "Asa mairi"), knowing that readers prized even the most desultory fragments by a popular *bundan* author, would dispatch one or more messengers to hound the author wherever he might be for days or weeks on end. The messenger would at last extract a manuscript (often only a few pages long in Kasai's case),[25] but frequently only after incurring miscellaneous expenses far exceeding the author's fee. Under this sort of pressure, the author found himself yielding to the urge to write about that very pressure being applied to him. The subject was eminently marketable, and no *shishōsetsu* writer exploited it more successfully than Kasai.[26] The motif of a writer who cannot write certainly complements Kasai's vision of life on the skids and of a literary career as the livelihood of last resort. And even though such a motif easily degenerates into tedious grumbling, "Asa mairi" is proof that the story of a failed manuscript need not translate into a failed story.

On one level a lame, five-page apology, "Asa mairi" is representative of Kasai's response to this journalistic pestering. The narrator-hero, who resides in the temple precincts of Kenchō-ji in Kamakura, recounts his futile effort to produce a solicited manuscript. He describes himself as besieged by his editor's messenger, although it is clearly the result of his own delinquence.

---

25. "Saiban" (Year's end, 1923), for example, filling only two pages in *KZZ* (2:285–86), is little more than an apology for the author's inability to meet the repeated demands of his publisher to produce a story for its New Year's issue. Yet it was published in *Shinchō*, one of the major literary magazines. A later example, "Bakasukashi" (1925) was also published in a major magazine, *Kaizō*.

26. "The Taishō period was a curious age," writes Tanizaki Seiji, " . . . in which a story about writer's block was perfectly acceptable. The image of an author bewailing his loss of creativity appealed to readers. . . . *Bundan* writers actually gained in popularity by revealing how difficult it was for them to write" ("Kasai Zenzō hyōden," 547–48.)

The only thing he "produces" in this story after applying himself three nights in succession is the grime he nervously rubs from the palms of his hands while thinking in vain of something to write about.

On another level, "Asa mairi" is a series of narrative deflections. The Kasai hero describes the fruits of his resistance to all the editorial hounding. He leaves his desk, air gun in hand, to do some shooting practice in the temple precincts and presents a dead bird to the messenger when he arrives. The victim of his impulsive shooting spree, he claims, has fallen prey to the "demon literature," that is, the manuscript he has failed to write for want of creativity. He then recalls a brief, year-end jaunt to Tokyo a few weeks before, ultimately ruling it out as a possible subject for the story he must write because of the potential embarrassment it would cause him. He finally lays down his pen for good to contemplate, during a predawn visit to a shrine overlooking the temple, the prospect of his failure. The "story" ends at the bleakest possible moment, with the narrator praying at the shrine and the messenger due to arrive yet a third time for his still unwritten manuscript.

Because the "Asa mairi" narrative frames a continually deflected, "contentless" story, the frame itself, as suggested above, becomes the story by default. Yet the truncated conclusion underscores the distinction that necessarily exists between life and art even in stories claiming to be "true to life." The final scene counters the reader's dramatic expectations and we never learn the hero's fate at the hands of the messenger, due to arrive shortly that very morning. But precisely because the story *is* based on the author's life, Kasai has no intention of letting chronological time overtake story time, for to do so would be to lose what little artistic freedom he has. The hero tells us that he tore up everything he wrote; yet the reader has before him that very story of the hero's struggle to create. Clearly, the author-hero equation will not work here. In order for the hero to "fail" at the task of producing a manuscript, the author must succeed at that very same task. Ironically, success is accomplished through a denial of narrative closure, for only such a denial can preserve the autonomy of a text grounded in private life. "Asa mairi" thus ends where it does in order that the story we hold in our hands can materialize phoenixlike from the blank pages of a "failed" manuscript.

ART WRITES LIFE

Whether by foregrounding the frame to the extent of forfeiting the story, as in "Asa mairi," or by imposing a separate, more "authentic" writing time on the story time, as in "Nakama,"the Kasai hero's preoccupation with the writing process effectively camouflages his wholesale inventions. Many examples of this calculated invention can be found in Kasai's later stories, but perhaps the most striking appear in a series of stories—"Ugomeku mono" (Wriggling creatures, 1924), "Shiji o umu" (A stillbirth, 1925), and "Ware to asobu ko" (A child to play with, 1926)—which dissertate on fetal, and textual, abortions. Each succeeding story refers self-consciously to the preceding one, at once providing a corrective reading and subtly lending credibility to ever more outrageous fictions. In all the stories, art is boldly presented as the only possible solution to real-life problems. Like the Shiga hero in *Wakai,* the Kasai hero believes that literary incantations will somehow enable him to resolve the crises he confronts in his personal life. But whereas the former passively waits for art and life to converge, the latter aggressively applies his incantatory magic. Each new story redefines the earlier text in a continuous process of erasure and rewriting. The reader, confronted with Kasai's contradictory presentations of experience, cannot remain aloof: to accept one story means rejecting the previous one.

"Ugomeku mono" opens with a virtuoso reflection on the hero's recently deceased father, after which he suddenly announces: "Having written this much, I realized with no little embarrassment that I had gotten quite carried away with my own glibness; and so I laid down my pen and went out on my daily constitutional, a practice that I had taken up four or five days before" (*KZZ* 2:425). Here again the Kasai hero interrupts his story with a metafictional ploy to remind the reader that he is *writing*—and thereby authenticating the narrative with his "presence." He is now able to propel his narrative in any number of directions, having assured readers of his "sincerity" by willfully undercutting the story line and implying that he will never again get "carried away."

Yet carried away he becomes indeed in the explosive conclusion, which describes a violent quarrel (one of the most awesome in Taishō literature) with Osei, the daughter of a shop proprietor in the Kenchōji precincts, who brought meals to his room. She has now followed him to Tokyo after the Great Earthquake (September 1923) to make sure, the hero claims, that he does not renege on his debts. That Osei is more than a tenacious creditor, however, is obvious from the fact that she was apparently pregnant with the hero's child—apparently, because she did not tell him directly about her condition. Feeling guilty that Osei has replaced his wife (who still lives in the provinces with the children because he cannot afford to support them in Tokyo) as the object of his affections, he begs her to leave him and return to Kamakura. But she refuses with a vociferous reminder that, having disqualified herself as a candidate for marriage, she has no choice but to become his mistress. She then announces that she has lost her baby and blames his heartless behavior for the miscarriage.

All this is by way of background to "Shiji o umu," a short piece that invokes "Ugomeku mono" so frequently that one scholar suggests that it is impenetrable without a reading of the latter.[27] In fact, Kasai offers a complete rereading of his earlier work that not only calls its "truthfulness" into question but also radically problematizes the whole project of "documenting" one's life. As in "Nakama," the hero deflects his story with a grim reminder of the difficulty he has producing it. "Things just couldn't be worse," he writes. "It has taken me ten whole days to complete just these five pages! The fact is, I simply have nothing to write about. Yet despite the agony this is causing me, the indomitable S shows up every day from the publisher's and plants himself stiffly in front of me . . . and so I am forced to spend an hour or so each day at my desk, inspiration or no. He refuses to leave until I have come up with at least a page" (KZZ 2:563). But in "Shiji o umu," as in "Nakama," the hero's lament over an impoverished imagination merely serves as a cue for the next yarn. The Kasai hero uses such confessions of imaginative bankruptcy to wipe his narrative slate clean; for in reality, there is much to write about, once having negated the truth of what he has written before. He can give birth to a new story, it appears, only by killing off the previous one.

After announcing Osei's pregnancy, the narrator claims that he cannot possibly shoulder the financial and emotional burden of child rearing. He recalls the solution to the problem of Osei's last

27. Ōmori, *Kasai Zenzō no kenkyū*, 164.

pregnancy, as recorded in "Ugomeku mono," which was a miscarriage. His recollection is couched in terms, however, that suggest that the miscarriage never took place. "In 'Ugomeku mono' I write that Osei has a miscarriage," the hero explains. "And I have her accuse me of placing a curse on her unborn child" (*KZZ* 2:565–66). But if Osei's miscarriage in "Ugomeku mono" is a fiction, then so is her pregnancy, we must conclude—and by extension the entire quarrel scene at the story's end.[28] Yet the hero gives us no time to reflect; for immediately after this curious revelation, he goes on to say that he has mulled over the idea of applying a similar solution to the present crisis. "I considered adding a scene, to take place last October, in which I force Osei to get an abortion at a mountain resort, and sat down at my desk toward evening to write" (*KZZ* 2:566).

The Kasai hero seems to be playing a game of wishful thinking in which he attempts to resolve personal crises with his fictional scenarios. But that is not all. For this second curious revelation (which suggests the degree to which the Kasai hero is willing to play the game) is immediately followed by a third: he interrupts his writing to reread a fan letter from a prison inmate who describes the powerful impression that one of the hero's stories has made on him. The story is none other than "Ugomeku mono."

> One cannot be too careful when writing, I exclaimed to myself. The prisoner interpreted my story in a favorable light. One must go on living, if only like a wriggling mole; one must search undauntedly for the light even as one trembles before the gravity of one's crime— this is what he said, and I was deeply impressed by his sincerity. And yet I did not think that my story really measured up to such noble sentiments. To begin with, it is not a factual account; some parts are grossly exaggerated. But it was read by this youthful inmate as the literal truth and gave him a degree of emotional satisfaction that far exceeded the story's worth. My conscience was pricked. . . . I'm hardly in a position to boast to this stranger of a youth that I led a particularly shameless life before "Ugomeku mono"—or after, for that matter.
>
> (*KZZ* 2:568)

The ramifications of this self-deprecating commentary for the Kasai oeuvre and for the *shishōsetsu* in general are clear: the naive prison

---

28. This last point is argued by Tsukagoshi Kazuo. See "'Ugomeku mono' sono ta o megutte," 228.

inmate who misconstrues the Kasai hero's gross exaggerations as factual accounts is also a "prisoner" of his literalist imagination. But there is a metaphorical significance as well; this commentary on the act of reading also applies to the *bundan* audience, which was equally guilty of taking the seemingly factual accounts of the author's private life as literal truth. As if to test his audience's gullibility, the hero concludes "Shiji o umu" with the incredible claim—since the story itself is dated March 1925—that Osei was delivered of a dead fetus on 2 April. Another child is tragically—and another story, safely—aborted.

A stillborn child proves a most convenient denouement for the hero in art as well as in private life, for it avoids a repetition of the "solution" already employed in "Ugomeku mono." Yet the conclusion is a sham. In "Ware to asobu ko," the Kasai hero admits that the earlier story's ending was yet another imaginary construct. The story begins with a footnote to "Shiji o umu," in which the hero proceeds to rewrite his own fiction:

> A certain magazine published a story of mine entitled "Shiji o umu" last April, the month following the birth of my daughter Yumiko. Yumiko was in fact born alive and healthy in a Koishikawa hospital a few days after I had completed the manuscript. Of course I harbored no deep-seated resentment at the prospect of the child's birth. It was just that circumstances had led me to believe that life would bring only sorrow to the child and that it would have been better if it never saw the light of day. But when the boardinghouse maid came into my room one morning and announced to me, still in bed, that the hospital had phoned to report the birth of a baby girl at 2:00 A.M. the night before and that both the baby and Osei were doing fine, I felt only great relief.
>
> That was 19 March. . . . A stillborn child—I never once wished for the baby's death! But how many times I had wished for my own.
>
> (*KZZ* 2:641)

Both "Ware to asobu ko" and "Shiji o umu" are typical in their references to previous texts. Although such allusions doubtlessly blur the boundary between life and art, it is even more important that they reinforce the continuity of Kasai's fictional world and serve warning to zealous critics who would insist on a referential reading of the oeuvre. Such a reading, we have observed, inevitably yields contradictions—on comparison not just with "real life" but among the stories themselves as well. So strong was the convention of the *shishōsetsu* narrator's candor, however, that critics were bewildered by the Kasai hero's blatant "lies," uttered after such disarming protestations of sincerity. The following exchange, excerpted from a roundtable discussion of "Shiji o umu" and other recently published stories, illustrates this sense of betrayal. The participants include Hirotsu Kazuo, Nakamura Murao, and Kanō Sakujirō, all of whom were writers as well as critics.

> HIROTSU: Kasai is obviously writing about himself, and yet here he says that his child was born on 3 April [*sic*] even though the magazine that published the story has a deadline sometime in March.
>
> NAKAMURA: Maybe he means *last* April! (*Laughter*)
>
> HIROTSU: Kasai makes his baby die in "Shiji o umu" and he makes [Osei] get pregnant in "Ugomeku mono." He can't seem to write a story without tacking on this sort of catastrophic ending.
>
> KANŌ: I haven't read this story yet. Did the baby really die?
>
> HIROTSU: No, of course not. After all, he writes that the baby was born on 3 April in a story which had to have been submitted sometime in March. And he's writing about the present. . . . But that Kasai is a strange one, isn't he? He's not happy unless he kills the baby off. . . .
>
> KANŌ He does that sort of thing quite often, doesn't he? Like writing a few years back that he had coughed blood . . . as if he were a consumptive, when in fact nothing was wrong with him.

> (*KZZ* 4:439)

The critics feel duped, of course, because their insistence on connecting events in a *shishōsetsu* to what they know of the author's personal life yields only contradictions. To be sure, they are encouraged to make this connection by the stories themselves, which point so freely to the "real world" and to each other. The settings are invariably specific and familiar to *bundan* readers, and members of the small cast (frequently appearing without introduction) seem to invite comparison with real-life models.[29] Yet even stories that appear when perused in isolation to depend on a referential reading take on new meaning when read together, as one might read a series of poems in which the nuances of each verse are clarified

---

29. "Chi o haku" (Vomiting blood, 1925), for example, begins abruptly, "Osei visited me in the mountains on 1 December" (*KZZ* 2:527), with no explanation anywhere of who Osei is. But regular readers of Kasai from "Kurai heya nite" (1920) on would be familiar with her relationship to the hero.

and amplified only in the context of the overall sequence. Kikuchi Kan suggests as much when he notes, in a panel discussion of one Kasai story: "The *bundan* is a curious institution. Episodes in a writer's daily life eventually become part of a long, continuous work. I'm thinking of something called a 'poetic sequence'—that is what Kasai's style recalls" (*KZZ* 4:434).

This is not to say that Kasai adheres to the strict formal rules and thematic conventions governing the composition of classical poetic sequences like *renga* and *haikai*, nor that the end result is necessarily as felicitous as the best examples of those forms. But the idea of reading the individual stories as segments of a larger sequence does provide an approach to Kasai's texts that frees us from a referential reading and allows us to pay closer attention to narrative strategies. The stories may not be self-contained, because they depend on a reading of other works in the oeuvre; but they are still meaningful lexical units out of which the reader can construct a "grammar" of the author's corpus. Places and characters appearing without introduction become a kind of literary shorthand, then, alluding to circumstances described in previous texts with which the reader is presumed to be familiar. Even contemporary readers had an inkling of this fact. "Kasai's stories are interrelated," Satō Haruo argues in a panel discussion of Kasai's writings, "and they make much better sense when read together. I think we'll get our first clear picture of the author when his works are anthologized, however disconnected they may now seem when read piecemeal" (*KZZ* 4:410–11).

SPEECH, WRITING, AUDIENCE

"Disconnected" is probably a gross understatement when used to describe a text like "Shii no wakaba" (Young pasania leaves, 1924), the "story" (which must be recovered from a noisy background of extraneous discourse) of a quarrel that ensues after the hero visits Kamakura to retrieve Osei, who has been whisked away from him in Tokyo by her father. It is not only difficult but inadvisable to summarize the events of this chaotic tale, for to do so would be to impose on it a narrative order that does not exist. Far from being self-contained, it mentions characters and events as if the audience is already familiar with them (which it would be if it has followed Kasai's earlier writings) and shifts haphazardly from one incompletely told episode to the next. It invokes several other Kasai stories by name as well, as if to remind the audience that it must confront the entire Kasai oeuvre rather than deal singly with each text.[30]

Yet interestingly, the Kasai hero himself attempts the impossible task of imposing order on events by framing them, as he is so often wont to do, with a self-conscious meditation before plunging the reader in medias res. This time, in some of Kasai's best-known lines, the hero contrasts the effulgence of nature in early summer with his own winter-bound body and soul. "Mid-June: I gaze fondly and wistfully at the young pasania leaves that bathe in the morning sunlight during a break in the monsoon," he begins, collecting himself in the wake of the bizarre events he is about to relate. Then, at the end of his frenzied narrative, he reverts to the measured cadence of his original reverie: "O pasania leaves: my own foliage is withering away; bless me with a few rays of your light!" (*KZZ* 2:465, 473).

The hero addresses the trees in his neighbor's garden like a poet calling upon his Muse, using somewhat archaic language to set off the frame from the "body" of the text. The irony is that the entire text, archaic passages and all, is in fact the product of dictation, the first of several that Kasai composed in this way.[31] Kasai was frequently bedridden during his last years, the drinking having finally taken its toll. Although illness had diminished his already-miniscule production, he had no choice but to continue writing, it being his only source of income. (He could no longer even rely on his meager royalties, having already sold off all the copyrights he owned.) When the physical act of writing itself proved too strenu-

---

30. In a panel discussion on recently published fiction in *Shinchō* (Aug. 1924), seven writers gathered all comment on the haphazardness of "Shii no wakaba" and debated whether readers need to know more about Kasai than what is presented in the narrative to understand it. See *KZZ* 4:425–29.

31. The scribe was Koki Tetsutarō, an employee of *Kaizō*. According to Koki, dictation was the method of last resort, as he had already made three or four visits on prescribed due dates and sent innumerable letters and telegrams, all to no avail. The dictation took place over a twelve-hour period, amid a succession of drunken antics—from boisterous singing to mimicking a urinating dog—that brought Kasai no little notoriety. Koki is amused that a story composed under such conditions came to be regarded as a classic. See the chapter on Kasai in his *Taishō no sakka*, 25–31.

ous, his publishers called on their solicitous messengers (the likes of whom we met in "Asa mairi") to take dictation. Kasai interrupted his drinking long enough to produce a few pages—later only a few lines—each night.

On one level, this method of composition reveals the Taishō period's journalistic pressures at their most intense, and perhaps their most insidious. Once a commitment was made to produce a story, the editors spared no effort getting it churned out. Yet on another level, it represents a new phase in Kasai's bid to subvert the *shishōsetsu*'s hallmark of sincerity—the promise to communicate itself, directly and unmediated, to the reader—by positing a double audience (scribe and reader) that is neither fully determinate nor distinguishable. To whom is the Kasai hero really talking? is the question that immediately comes to mind when reading this and later works. For unlike stories by other writers who have had recourse to dictation (Tanizaki Jun'ichirō's *Yume no ukihashi* [The bridge of dreams, 1959] for example), "Shii no wakaba" never hides the fact that the narrator is telling his story, not writing it.

Although the dictation was necessitated by illness, it is also true, as the contemporary writer Furui Yoshikichi (1937–) notes in his meditation on Kasai, that it was in a profound sense a logical consequence of the *shishōsetsu* form.

> One can argue that, in the last analysis, the *shishōsetsu* inevitably approaches an oral telling, one in which the narrator converses with himself. There are certain critical moments when a person can express only right then, and only vocally, his subtle contact, and conflict, with truth. And in fact, the more Kasai is driven, mentally and physically, into such extremities, the more his writing seems to break the narrative mold and speak out loud: speak, plea, cry out, and at times crack a weird joke, before lapsing again into silent monologue. In this way, step by step, his writing approaches an oral telling.[32]

Kasai's dictations are, to be sure, the product of a highly literate mind. Moreover, we read them as words isolated in a text, rather than hear them spoken in the fuller context of an existential present. Yet it is interesting to note that the author's refusal (according to observers) to read over the previous day's production—his refusal, in other words, to treat it as a written text to reflect on and rework—befits a member of an oral more than a typographic culture. Like an oral narrator, Kasai is able to recall what he has said before by thinking only memorable thoughts. His abhorrence of closure, his textual cannibalism, and his excess of self-references, moreover, add an entirely new kind of open-endedness to the non-emplotted *shishōsetsu* form. His increasingly redundant summations, meanwhile, and his frenzied yet almost formulaic musings about insanity in his last stories all sound a refrain that moves the narrative along its fragile track, which is forever in danger of being sabotaged by forgetfulness.[33] And although such an otherwise staunch defender of Kasai's style as Tanizaki Seiji laments its decline in the dictations,[34] it is tempting to say that it undergoes not so much a decline as a kind of regression to an inchoate state between orality and literacy, in which the memory of one and the anticipation of the other incite the narrator alternately to garrulousness and to speechlessness. Straddling the borderline between oral and written narrative, the Kasai hero is more performer than recorder.

Thus, the orality of the presentation asserts itself emphatically and repeatedly. At the same time it never completely succeeds in effacing the text's writtenness. The narrator-hero alternately foregrounds and conceals the text's mediator (i.e., the scribe), and the result is a cacophonous skirmish between the spoken language and the medium in which it is finally inscribed. Traces of that skirmish are littered throughout the text. Although the story is generally narrated in the informal *da* style, it shifts frequently to the polite *desu/masu* style—a reminder that the narrator is addressing a specific audience. Moreover, a closer look at the informal style as it is used here reveals that it too attempts to be audience-specific, mimicking familiar colloquial speech. For example, the contracted form of the explanatory sentence final (*na*) *n da* typically replaces the standard (*na*) *no da,* and sentences are frequently punctuated with the interjectional *na* and *ne*—all elements of the pure "reportive style" we examined in Chapter 2.

---

33. In oral cultures, knowledge of course *is* recollection: what cannot be recollected is forever lost. The ramifications of this fact are explored by Walter J. Ong in his *Orality and Literacy,* a thoughtful synthesis that provides the foundation for my discussion. See esp. 33–40, 101–3, and 132–35.

34. "Kasai Zenzō hyōden," 584–85.

Appealing to a specific audience as any speaker would in the reportive style, however, places the narrator in an inexorable bind. By attempting to "speak" and thus grammatically foregrounding the "hearer" (scribe), he puts the lie to an "unmediated" telling meant solely for the reader. Yet attempting to distance himself from his situation as speaker and reasserting himself as writer only results in an ambivalently self-conscious display of the text's mediation as *both* speech and writing. In addition to "framing" his colloquial monologue with archaic language, the narrator occasionally punctuates it with the written *de aru* style, as if in an effort to transcend his role as speaker. The effort is only halfhearted, however, and lends at times to such incongruous juxtapositions as " . . . Kamakura eki de oriru to dōji ni Tsujidō-yuki no kippu o katta wake *nan de aru*" (. . . and so I proceeded to buy a ticket for Tsujidō as soon as I got off the train at Kamakura); or even more absurdly: "Nani mo kani mo sanjū-hachi nenkan no zaigō kashitsu no zange o shitai tokoro *de aru n da* . . ." (I'd like to confess here and now all the sins and errors of my thirty-seven years; *KZZ* 2:468, 472; emphasis added).[35]

As we observed in Chapter 2 the intimacy between recorder and witness in the written reportive style obtains paradoxically from the positing of an audience without precisely identifying it. Locating the audience too specifically would move the style toward the speaker-hearer paradigm, which (because the latter can never be generalized in Japanese) would in turn have the effect of excluding the reader. The formal *de aru* style was developed as a compromise in the absence of a truly universal colloquial idiom. Although many writers, including Kasai, pushed the *de aru* style into the direction of the informal, personal *da* style, which more closely approximates familiar colloquial speech, neither style could ever attain universal currency, given the degree of specificity demanded by the language's system of honorifics. No single style can mediate with equal authenticity, therefore, between the narrator's specific and general audiences. In "Shii no wakaba," the narrator finds it impossible to address the two—scribe and readers—on exactly the same level. Any attempt to do so, moreover, results in the ludi-

---

35. Similar juxtapositions are to be found in later dictated texts. In "Jakusha," the narrator ends one sentence with *nan de aru* (*KZZ* 2:618), another with *nan de wa aru* (*KZZ* 2:622), and a phrase in yet another with *de aru ga na* (*KZZ* 2:619).

crous juxtapositions noted above, although their very ludicrousness graphically reminds us of the mediative qualities of, and the ambiguities contained in, *both* speech and writing.[36]

The narrator finds himself in a similar bind over the nature of his text. His ambivalence about audience (talking to one while at the same time writing to another) destabilizes his notion of fiction, and he ends up sending mixed signals about the latter in the same way he does about the former. "I don't feel right about using real names, because the story I am telling you is a fictional one," the Kasai hero insists. "But I'm going to use them anyway, because I'm a *shishōsetsu* writer" (*KZZ* 2:466).[37] And he goes on to name "real" names and places, as well as mention his own stories: "Furyōji" (Delinquent child, 1922), "Ugomeku mono," and "Norowareta te" (A cursed hand, 1918). Are we reading fact or fiction? we want to ask. "What is the difference?" would seem to be Kasai's reply. We are, either way, at the mercy of the text. "Drunkards are an impossible lot, you know," the hero reflects half-boastfully, suggesting but refusing to admit outright that his quarrel with Osei's father has gotten violent. "They have a way of *acting* as if they're drunk" (*KZZ* 2:471). Narrators, too, are an impossible lot, is the bittersweet lesson we have learned reading Kasai; they have a way of acting as if they are telling the truth, or lying, or both, or neither. Alternately flaunting and hiding his fictions, the Kasai narrator ac-

36. Ambiguities between speaking and writing and by extension between audiences are certainly not unique to Kasai's work or to Japanese literature. Dorrit Cohn notes in her *Transparent Minds* that Dostoevsky's anonymous narrator in *Notes from Underground* adopts an oratorial stance even as he self-consciously mentions his writing activity; and that Poe's narrator addresses, yet never identifies, a disincarnated "you" in "The Tell-Tale Heart" (pp. 176–78). Next to Kasai's gross contradictions, however, such "ambiguities" seem rather tame. When the narrator in *Notes from Underground* ends an exclamatory passage with "Wait, let me catch my breath," he is under no linguistic constraint (in the English, and presumably in the original Russian) to alter the grammar of his delivery according to the audience (whether real or imagined), as would be the case in Japanese. Yet Kasai does alter it, in midsentence—indeed, in midword—in such a way that reveals the double bind involved in addressing a multiple audience. And when Cohn conjectures whether the listener in Poe's tale is a mute character in the fictional scene or the reader or an imaginary interlocutor present only in the speaker's mind and argues that, depending on how we answer this question, we can interpret the story as a spoken, written, or silent discourse, she intimates that such an interpretation has no specifically linguistic grounding. Yet we must interpret Kasai's story as spoken *and* written *and* silent discourse, as all styles, presented here in a hodgepodge, are gramatically identifiable in a way not possible in the English.

37. Kasai uses the term *jiko* ("self") *shōsetsuka* rather than *watakushi shōsetsuka* for "*shishōsetsu* writer," but the meaning is virtually identical.

knowledges them to be a construct as unstable as the audience he addresses. He can get no closer to the "truth" than he can to his audience. In the end, Kasai "solves" the dilemma of direct communication by forfeiting his authority over meaning and his control over audience. The final stories can be likened to monologues in which the narrator "tells" his stories to no one. But the tellings are at times a mad pursuit that threatens the Kasai's hero's sanity. It is only fitting that Kasai's last major text is entitled "Suikyōsha no dokuhaku" (A mad drunk's monologue).

The motif of escape—from audience and meaning—figures large in Kasai's next major text, "Kohan shuki" (Lakeside notebook, 1924), a story that, although not dictated, was penned under duress in the presence of the same *Kaizō* employee who took down "Shii no wakaba." "I've run as far away as I can, and so here I am" (*KZZ* 2:495), the hero begins. "Here" is a hot spring in the mountains above Nikkō.[38] Despairing of getting any writing done in Tokyo and loathing the sight of his mistress, whose pregnancy (with the child he will later "kill off" in "Shiji o umu") intensifies the guilt he feels toward his separated wife, he flees to this remote spa in hopes of "becoming as indifferent to society, people, and my surroundings as the trees on that mountain, the water in that lake, are to man" (*KZZ* 2:500).

The hero chronicles his withdrawal in a diarylike notebook intended, he claims, for his wife. Halfway through the story, however, the hero's attention moves away from the wife he has abandoned in the provinces to the mistress he has just abandoned in Tokyo. "I curse my liaison with Osei," he declares. "I admit the error of my ways, and I have no desire to continue this loveless and unfulfilling relationship" (*KZZ* 2:510). But what is Osei doing now, he then wonders, while he relaxes in the mountains? "Yes, you are to be pitied. If I had no wife and family, I would never have even thought of treating you so vilely. We could have truly loved each other if I were a free man" (*KZZ* 2:511).

The tirade he has launched against Osei thus turns into professions of concern and finally affection. This solicitous attention moves back and forth between the two women hereafter; the hero

38. Koki Tetsutarō writes that he visited Kasai in Nikkō several times and brought a few pages of the "Kohan shuki" manuscript with him on each return trip to Tokyo. See *Taishō no sakka*, 25–31.

finds that he cannot address one audience without subsequently reckoning with the other. The tension produced by this dual audience is evident throughout. As early as the story's second page, the hero presents two poems—one about his wife and one about Osei—side by side in an effort to bring together in verse the two people he has tried in vain to reconcile in person, as we learn later in the story. The Kasai hero has chosen personal freedom over familial obligation, but he finds that escape from the latter has only led him into another trap; he feels ensnared, not liberated, by his relationship with Osei. Thus, the shift in intended audience does not bring about a change in attitude. Neither the above nor any other passage comes forth with a true apology to his wife or a promise to make amends for his "vile" treatment of Osei. It merely brings home the fact that he has fled from both and taken refuge in words uttered in remotest isolation.

There is of course still another audience to reckon with, the hero realizes—his readers—and their very presence threatens to undermine his entire confessional project. They are consumers, not confessors, and their expectations are naturally at odds with those of his intended audiences.

> It saddens me to think that, although I began writing this notebook intending to make a full apology to my wife about my involvement with Osei, it has turned of its own accord into a fictional story [*shō-setsu*]. Be that as it may, I must convert this manuscript into cash and get down off this mountain as soon as possible. My wife and I have grown even further apart since July. My attempt to bring her and Osei together on the occasion of the second anniversary of my father's death ended in failure—as did my plan to cultivate my wife's understanding with this notebook.
>
> (KZZ 2:521–22)

Such a willing confession has startling ramifications. It is an acknowledgment, first, not simply of a plurality but of an inevitable indeterminacy of audience, once he commits his "apology" to paper. At the same time, it is an acknowledgment of an equally inevitable indeterminacy of intention. However hard the hero tries to contextualize his apology—first in a direct meeting with his wife and now in this "notebook"—he finds it impossible to say what he means or even figure out whom to address. The hero writes his apology/story in the knowledge that he can control neither its intention nor reception. Finally, it is an acknowledgment that such indeterminacy is an integral part of textuality. It cannot simply be attributed to authorial misconstrual or the audience's misinterpretation, moreover: the notebook, insists the hero, "has turned *of its own accord* into a fictional story." Writing has a will of its own, he suggests, which interposes between a writer's conscious intention and any reception of his text. The same holds true, moreover, for speech: the Kasai hero tells us that he is equally and inevitably as unsuccessful at communicating with his wife in person as he is on paper. This loss of control brings with it a paradox. The hero is ironically transformed from chronicler (of a diary) to author (of a fictional text) even as he loses his *author*ity over the writing process and over the meaning of what he has written.[39]

What, then, *is* the meaning of this failed attempt to placate the hero's wife, this "notebook" that has turned into a fictional story? Clearly, the Kasai hero is not interested in the answer. The story's meaning matters less than its production. It is no longer a question of confessing or fictionalizing, but of readying the text for consumption. Throughout the story he reminds himself that he must publish something at all costs simply in order to make ends meet. "This notebook progresses at a damnedly slow pace," the hero laments. "I'm being hounded by the innkeeper for rent, and I want desperately to return to Tokyo and visit the ailing K [a writer friend ill with tuberculosis]; yet I can turn out barely half a page or so a day on the average. It's disgusting" (*KZZ* 2:520). Having forfeited his monopoly on meaning, the hero contents himself with an account of the text's labored production.

His progress thwarted by writer's block and a variety of physical ailments, the hero turns to alcohol and drugs for relief. But these have their own dangers, as the distraught hero himself is well aware. "'K's consumption will no doubt eventually take his life. And what fate awaits me? Madness, at the rate things are going. But how awful that would be! To lose one's mind without being able to lose one's life, to rant in front of my family year after year. Oh, spare me that horror!' These were the thoughts I mumbled after having writhed about in bed until I had fallen into a self-

39. The discussion here is indebted to Antony Easthope, *Poetry as Discourse* (esp. 14–15).

anesthetized stupor" (*KZZ* 2:520). It is bad enough having to utter a confused pastiche of confession and fiction to an ambiguous audience of wife/mistress and confessor/consumer; but to be reduced to blurting out mindless babble—to speak and not to be heard at all—is a fate worse than death.

MADNESS: THE HERO'S FINAL VICTIMIZER

The impending insanity hinted at in "Kohan shuki" becomes an obsession in Kasai's last major stories: "Jakusha" (The oppressed one, 1925) and "Suikyōsha no dokuhaku" (A mad drunk's monologue, 1927). Here the sense of discontinuity is even greater, the events more dismal, the style more diffuse than in any of the previous stories. The obsession parallels a deterioration in Kasai's physical, financial, and emotional well-being. Kasai was now often too sick to write. The sake he loved, which was a source of humor in many of the earlier texts, had now become so ominously central to his life that Tsugawa Take'ichi, a medical doctor who has written extensively on Kasai, calls his last works "the literature of alcoholism."[40]

Contemporary critics were quick to denounce what they interpreted to be nothing more than the author's "drunken palaver."[41] It surely was, although not in the sense it was ordinarily taken to be. Kasai's critics mistake form for content. For just as the verbal construct of literary sincerity provides the *form* that most convincingly packages authorial candor in the *shishōsetsu*, so the patently affected inebriate in Kasai's later stories becomes the most authentic conveyor of honest emotion. Thus, Kasai laughs at his critics, in a dictated "essay" appropriately entitled "Guchi to kuda to iyami" (Grumbling, palaver, sarcasm, 1925): "What is left after you remove the grumbling and the palaver and the sarcasm from my fiction? Why, nothing! . . . If people insist on calling my writing of these last fifteen years drunken palaver, I can't very well protest. Because that's exactly what it is. When I drink, you get the truth (*honne*) in

---

40. *Kasai Zenzō sono bungaku to fūdo*, 33.
41. Kasai did not take such criticism lying down. Responding to indictments by Tayama Katai and Chikamatsu Shūkō (see n. 5), both authors of numerous works with sexually related themes, he facetiously questions the right of "lechers" to condemn the writing of a "drunkard." See "Shōkan," in *KZZ* 3:248–49.

the form of palaver. When I don't, you get it in the form of grumbling. And here and there between the two, a bit of sarcasm, a pinch of spice: that's what my personal fiction is all about" (*KZZ* 3 : 201, 203). To declare so audaciously that "nothing" would be left if all such "drunken" rambling was removed suggests how crucial Kasai believed this mode of discourse was to his strategy of presentation. "Kasai may have been a habitual grumbler," writes Tanizaki Seiji, "but he never lost control of his emotions; that is what lends the texts an element of objectivity. 'Palaver' is the *form* of Kasai's late stories." [42]

Still, it is not a pretty literature. The psychotic Kasai hero strikes a grim contrast indeed with the author-sage that Shiga Naoya portrayed so fastidiously and to such general critical acclaim. Tsugawa remarks with some truth that the stories Kasai wrote after he had become a confirmed alcoholic angered and eventually alienated his readers. [43] The contemporary critic Aeba Takeo typifies the reader who finds the late works quite inaccessible. The redeeming sense of moral anguish that the Kasai hero experiences in such stories as "Ugomeku mono" and "Shii no wakaba" finds its last appealing expression in "Kohan shuki," according to Aeba, whose commentary on Kasai focuses on the author's alleged spiritual aspirations. The texts that follow, lacking this moral appeal, are not worth reading, he declares. [44]

But literature does not have to be pretty or edifying to be of profound import. "Jakusha" and "Suikyōsha no dokuhaku," because of their thematic and narrative turbulence, represent most graphically both the culmination and the limits of the *shishōsetsu* form. Many writers, beginning with Uno Kōji in his 1925 essay "'Watakushi shōsetsu' shiken," have argued that Kasai took the *shishōsetsu* as far as it could go and that writing's task of "plumbing the depths of self" resulted, perhaps inevitably, in the disruption of private life. [45] The disruption of course worked both ways—the relationship between art and life being a particularly symbiotic (or

42. "Kasai Zenzō hyōden," 577. Emphasis added.
43. *Kasai Zenzō sono bungaku to fūdō*, 34.
44. "An'utsu naru musōsha: Kasai Zenzō ron," in *Hihyō to hyōgen*, 148. Matsubara Shin'ichi also writes approvingly of Kasai's "humanity" in *"Gusha" no bungaku*, 64–92. But here, too, a discussion of Kasai's last stories is conspicuous by its absence.
45. In *KBHT* 6 : 65–66. See Chapter 3.

parasitic) one in the *shishōsetsu*'s case. Yet the culmination spoken of here is of another dimension as well: Kasai's method appears to disrupt not just the *shishōsetsu*'s production but also its very mode of presentation.

Throughout this study we have argued that the *shishōsetsu*'s sense of authenticity and reality derives from the presence of an epistemologically nontranscendent narrator in either the first or third person, who observes the written reportive style's speaker-specific grammar. Shunning the "fabrications" of emplotment and omniscient narration, each *shishōsetsu* presents the supposedly inviolable truth of its recorder's own perceptions. It is precisely this truth, however, that comes under attack in Kasai's last stories. Having already undergone a crisis of interpretation in "Ugomeku mono" and "Shiji o umu," which led to an escape from lived experience, and a crisis of expression in "Shii no wakaba" and "Kohan shuki," which led to an escape from audience and meaning, the Kasai hero, in his final extremity, undergoes a crisis of cognition itself in "Jakusha" and "Suikyōsha no dokuhaku," which leads ultimately to the loss of self. This final escape is registered in these texts' very linguistic performance: more than any of his actions or reflections, it is the Kasai hero's use of language that betrays his dementia. No longer trusting even in his own perceptions, the hero finds it increasingly difficult to express himself coherently: he has lost faith in the linguistic ground rules for expression. The result of his rambling outcry is one of the starkest portraits in modern Japanese literature of the psychotic mind, which, at the same time, reveals the fragility of the *shishōsetsu*'s epistemology. The products of dictation like "Shii no wakaba," moreover, these two stories put even greater pressure on the communicative act, constantly problematizing their own status as speech and as writing.

"Jakusha" is the story of the hero's deteriorating physical and mental health, punctuated by melancholy interludes in which the hero reflects on why he must tell his story at all. At first, the interludes are merely cryptic innuendos: "You're probably wondering why I must call this story 'The Oppressed One,'" he tells his scribe, "but please don't ask me to explain." "Oppressed—how I hate that word. . . . To be oppressed is to be a coward. Which is to say, a spineless good-for-nothing, isn't it? That's all there is to it. A good-for-nothing. A weakling. That's what makes things interesting" (*KZZ* 2:617, 618). The motive for these reflections becomes clearer as the story progresses, however; they are cries of angst about the state of his mental well-being. "I just don't want to go mad," the hero suddenly blurts out. "I realize that I will get sick and die sooner or later, but I refuse to die insane. I am very conscious of who I am. Those who have lost their senses seem oblivious to any symptoms of their derangement, but that is not my problem. . . . I may be a nervous wreck, but I'm not crazy" (*KZZ* 2:626).

H, a youthful admirer and apparently this text's scribe,[46] forces the hero into seeing his uncle, a famous doctor, over the hero's protests that nothing is wrong with him other than alcoholism and a case of nerves. The hero's greatest fear is being diagnosed as insane. Yet even as he insists on his sanity, his behavior speaks otherwise. He throws tantrums, becomes increasingly violent, and exhibits extreme paranoia. More significantly, his very manner of speech reveals his instability, most obviously in his subversion of the grammar of the reportive style and in his choice of self-referents. "Jakusha" is filled with sentences that end with -*rashii*, a morpheme that, as we noted in Chapter 2, identifies the speaker's perception of an action or thought as *outside* his own direct experience. The Kasai hero is wary of making definitive statements, however, not just about the actions or thoughts of others but about his own as well. It is not uncommon for a speaker/narrator to distance his present mental state from a state (e.g., drunkenness) that he relates in the interest of objectification, but the narrator-hero in "Jakusha" carries the practice to a new extreme, frequently applying this grammar of indirect perception even to situations where he is by rights in control of his faculties. Thus, the hero describes himself as *appearing* to be disappointed when he fails to see a single firefly while out on a walk (*KZZ* 2:623), and as *appearing* to have ridden on a bus to an *apparently* large house that *appeared* to have stepping stones and a lawn in front (*KZZ* 2:630). In the first instance, the hero is "slightly drunk" and, in the second, overcome with fright as he is dragged by H to the doctor's office. Yet the use

46. This supposition is confirmed in "Suikyōsha no dokuhaku," which contains an extended reflection on the production of "Jakusha" and H's role in taking dictation. See *KZZ* 2:710–15.

of *-rashii* here seems not an exercise in objectification but rather a symptom of the hero's mental collapse.

There are other signs of cracks in the hero's sanity. The hero uses a different self-referent in nearly every sentence, and sometimes several different ones in a single sentence. *Ore*, used in casual speech to denote one's informal or private self, is intermixed freely with *jibun* or *watashi*, normally indicators of the formal, public self. This haphazard use of first-person pronominals in the presence of an unchanging audience (namely, the scribe) is emblematic of the Kasai hero's vain attempt to constitute his self in a world stripped of its referential moorings. The hero can be certain of nothing, because his locus of perception is shattered into fragments: *watashi, wagahai, boku, ore, washi,* and *jibun* are used seemingly at random and without correlation to his audience. "Is this big-shot doctor going to torture me until I [*watashi*] lose my mind? Is he going to bully me [*watashi*] into losing my wits over my repeated protests that I [*ore*] don't want to go mad? I [*boku*] don't care what the diagnosis is. . . . But is he going to put me down as insane when insanity is the one thing I won't accept, when I've said I'll resign myself to any other illness? I [*ore*] really hate that doctor's guts" (*KZZ* 2:634).[47]

The hero's psychosis leads finally to incoherence; his narration breaks off barely a page later. The last section is a brief account by the scribe, who claims to be an "unmitigated apologist" for the hero (A) despite the latter's tantrums and drunken fits. He reports that he has suggested "Kyōsuisha no dokuhaku" (A mad drunk's monologue) as the title for this story, but that A insists on "Jakusha." Thus the narrative ends, as it begins, with a reflection on its title. Even this text, fragmented though its story line and even its narrating subject may be, has a frame.

The title that H suggests to the hero in "Jakusha" is not forgotten: Kasai's next major work is "Suikyōsha no dokuhaku." (*Kyōsuisha* and *suikyōsha* are synonyms, the first two Chinese characters merely being reversed.) It is an even looser, more haphazard production than "Jakusha," straining narrative continuity to the limit as the hero's obsession with the prospect of insanity intensifies. Yet it

47. The first-person singular renderings in English without bracketed original have no equivalents in Japanese.

is also the quintessential articulation of the Kasai hero's most urgent concern: the search for an ultimate point of reference with which to bolster his eroded sense of self. And because it is a dictated text that vigorously asserts its orality, the hero wrestles not only with all the demons that inhabit the Kasai oeuvre but also with the copiously aggregative and iterative marginalia that threaten to crowd out his narrative.

The story revolves around a diagnosis. Is the hero sick, or is he mad? The bedridden, alcoholic narrator-hero believes himself to be ill with tuberculosis, while the two women living with him (his mistress Osei and Tomoko, the daughter of a cousin who died of tuberculosis) insist that excessive drinking is driving him to the lunatic fringe. Far from being dismayed by the onset of a fatal illness, the hero welcomes it; for tuberculosis is a disease of the body, with symptoms as tangible and perceptible to the patient as they are to the observer. The hero declares his "right" to be ill, as it is the surest sign to him that he is still sane. If, as Osei and Tomoko claim, he is "insane" and not merely "sick," the hero fears that he will have lost any chance for self-determination and will be damned to a hellishly ambiguous world in which one's own perceptions have no meaning or bearing. He longs for the security of the unambiguous sign and feels most threatened by a dispersive signifier that disseminates multiple signifieds. He wants coughed blood to *denote* a consumptive fit, for example, and not to be taken for an alcohol-induced stomach ulcer, as Osei suggests. At a time when it was still a sign of, and even a metaphor for, certain death,[48] tuberculosis becomes a kind of salvation for the Kasai hero, a reassuring reminder of the infallibility of individual cognition. In the absence of a clearly defined self, this death warrant is a positive, if morbid, mark of identity.

The story line of "Suikyōsha no dokuhaku" is as elusive as the Kasai hero's romantic quest for absolutes. It wanders haphazardly from topic to topic (from details of his latest eviction to the death

48. Although Susan Sontag argues that illness is *not* a metaphor in her study of cultural responses to illness (which, though making no reference to Japan other than Kurosawa's film *Ikiru* about a cancer patient, could certainly apply to the Japanese case), she has shown that various cultures have viewed such serious diseases as tuberculosis and later cancer punitively—indeed, as irrevocable death sentences ("the germ of death itself"). See *Illness as Metaphor*, 18–19.

of his mentor's wife), each with no apparent connection to the other. Having resigned himself to an early end, the hero looks on his writing as a kind of will or testament—the graffiti of despair scribbled aimlessly on life's confining walls. Such "storytelling" only serves to strengthen the impression of a schizoid narrator, as chatty and personable, however, as he is paranoid. Like so many of Kasai's narratives, the story begins with a self-conscious, meditative introduction, this time on fishing, which soon aborts with the hero's grim realization that writing itself, far from helping him come to grips with what is bothering him, is just one more escape— like a fishing trip. Two pages into his story, he begins again: "It would be ridiculous at this late juncture for me to make a show of calling myself a rogue. Besides, I frankly don't think I'm all that bad, even if other people do. But what others think is their own business, right? It's really odd that I should get all worked up about their opinions" (*KZZ* 2:702).[49]

And yet what others think of the hero, we come to realize during the narrative's twisted course, is indeed the hero's greatest concern. Having lost trust in his own perceptions as the unshakable point of reference, he is at the mercy of what others make of him. He vents his spleen against Osei and Tomoko, who refuse (out of some ulterior motive, he believes) to acknowledge the gravity of his physical illness and wonder aloud about his sanity. He realizes, to his horror, that they are in effect removing the linchpin of his identity; in his defense, he invests his self-diagnosed tuberculosis with absolute value in an otherwise indeterminate world. Should this ever be undermined, he fears that his mind really will slide irrevocably into a truly demented state that knows no certainties.

Even personal sensation and cognition are not safe from this external attack. The hero sees alcohol as a balm for the neuralgia that leaves him bedridden most of the day. Osei, however, sees it

49. The difficulty that the Kasai hero has in beginning his "story" before finally starting, as it were, in the middle of things once again recalls the oral narrative. Walter J. Ong notes in his *Orality and Literacy:* "Oral poets characteristically experience difficulty in getting a song under way: Hesiod's *Theogony,* on the borderline between oral performance and written composition, makes three tries at the same material to get going. Oral poets commonly plunged the reader in medias res not because of any grand design, but perforce. They had no choice, no alternative" (143). Kasai may have had a choice; but not only did he not exercise it, he speaks/ writes as if the choice were nonexistent.

as the poison that produces increasingly erratic behavior. Likewise, the hero regards his having coughed blood as confirming his own diagnosis of tuberculosis; yet Osei insists that it is merely the symptom of a stomach perforated by drink. Faced with such challenges to his cognition, he is forced to question his former conviction about the nature of his illness.

> I wonder if what they [Osei and Tomoko] say is true—that something is wrong with my nerves, that I really don't have TB but some mental illness caused by alcoholism? If that's so, then my life is without hope. TB, stomach ulcers, strokes—they don't frighten me, and they never have. But a nervous disorder—that is the one thing I cannot cope with. I don't want to go mad. I've written time and time again that I don't want to go mad. . . . "Dying is nothing," my mentor once told me, "but not being able to die—to have to stay alive year after year without being able to work—that is something you have to think about. It really happens to people, you know."
>
> (*KZZ* 2:732)

Since mental illness has no tangible symptoms like fever or coughing fits, the hero clings to any symptom capable of demonstrating his illness to be physical and consequently real to the patient, rather than mental and therefore beyond the patient's power to diagnose. Thus, the hero: "I'd feel much better about things knowing that it was the poisons from TB that were aggravating my nerves like this and causing these seizurelike fits. Those two women, knowing full well that the fever alone is proof that I have the disease, still try to get me to work out of sheer meanness and treat me unflinchingly as a simple neurasthenic" (*KZZ* 2:733). Convinced that Osei is actually scheming to hasten his mental demise in order to gain complete control over him, the hero tries to persuade Tomoko, whom he has taken into his home to nurse him through his "final illness," that he indeed has tuberculosis.

> You've got my disease all wrong. . . . Considering the kind of life I've led, it would be odd if I had *failed* to contract the disease. I'm really not surprised at all. People who can vent their fantasies and passions do not suffer. Those who cannot and turn in on themselves—it's those who get TB. . . . I refuse to be treated like a madman![50]
>
> (*KZZ* 2:734–35)

50. In her *Illness as Metaphor*, 20–26, Sontag writes that tuberculosis was once commonly thought to be brought on by the repression and sublimation of feelings

Osei and Tomoko do just that, however. The hero overhears a conversation in which they liken him to a deranged patient they have read about in the newspaper, who shoots his doctor. Instead of nursing him, they refuse even to acknowledge that he is physically ill. In a world characterized by uncertainty and flux—evictions and threats of eviction, poverty, unstable relationships—he feels robbed of his touchstone of identity, the cognition to which he has tied his sense of self. The hero concludes his story with an announcement that he has dismissed Tomoko, who he has decided is a conspirator, not a nurse. He coldly refuses to hear her defense. Indeed, "monologue" that this story is, we hardly hear Tomoko or Osei directly at all. Throughout the entire narrative, the hero allows each to speak only once in her own voice (*KZZ* 2:734, 735). He assumes a virtual monopoly on discourse, as if words alone can argue his case; yet his sense of the women's intimidatingly contradictory perceptions of him has virtually consumed his consciousness. By sending Tomoko away, he attempts, in effect, to banish insanity from his person, as if it were a wholly external threat. He sees physical illness, on the other hand, as internal, his own creation. He believes himself the master of what he can name (i.e., "diagnose"): this disease that, if it is what he says it is, will soon kill him. But no matter. He would rather die from something of his own making.

An eccentric he surely was, but did Kasai actually become the lunatic we see in the late texts? A madman cannot distance himself to the point of depicting the self on paper, Tanizaki Seiji insists, and the fact that Kasai did so proves that he was not insane.[51] Furui Yoshikichi, however, fresh from a reading of "Suikyōsha no dokuhaku," is less certain. "Should we say that one can observe oneself no more dispassionately than when one is mad?" he asks. "Or that such dispassionate self-observation itself is a sign of madness?"[52] Furui provides no answer, and perhaps there is none. What can be said for sure is that in flirting—whether in literature or in life or

---

for which there was no outlet. She also notes the belief that thwarted passions were a cause of the illness (p. 45).

51. "Kasai Zenzō hyōden," 577.
52. *Tōkyō monogatari kō*, 94.

both—with the limits of sanity, Kasai also pressed the *shishōsetsu*, and literature as written artifact, to their limits. Never does one feel so certain as at the end of "Suikyōsha no dokuhaku" that an author has nothing more to *say*. After publishing his final story, "Imiake," three months after "Suikyōsha no dokuhaku," he lapsed into a silence that lasted the remaining fifteen months of his short life. Even if he had not finally run out of things to write about, his fiction had anticipated once again the actual event. In 1928 his health took an ominous turn for the worse. He coughed blood again in March and died three months later. Kasai the author fulfilled the hero's wish: to die of consumption rather than be sentenced to a living death of insanity. For Kasai, madness, like artistic creation, took on the greatest significance in its potential, rather than its fully realized, state.

Epilogue:
The Shishōsetsu Today

No one can reveal oneself completely. Yet writing becomes impossible if one discloses nothing of oneself. Rousseau was enamored of self-exposé; yet he does not reveal himself fully even in his *Confessions*. Mérimée despised confession; yet does not *Columba* reveal something very profound about him? The line between "confessional" and "non-confessional" literature is a hard one indeed to draw.

Akutagawa Ryūnosuke,
"Shuju no kotoba"

This book is not a book of "confessions"; not that it is insincere, but because we have a different knowledge today than yesterday; such knowledge can be summarized as follows: What I write about myself is never *the last word:* the more "sincere" I am, the more interpretable I am . . . my texts are disjointed, no one of them caps any other; the latter is nothing but a *further* text, the last of the series, not the ultimate in meaning: *text upon text*, which never illuminates anything.

Roland Barthes by Roland Barthes

Why end a study of *shishōsetsu* with Kasai Zenzō? It is because, as one writer has remarked, pure literature in Japan met its demise with Kasai's passing.[1] Hyperbole notwithstanding, this opinion expresses a certain truth: Kasai's death did coincide with the end of the *shishōsetsu*'s heyday. After the Taishō period, the *bundan* would never again be as receptive to writers who wrote only about themselves and only in their own voices. By the mid-1920s, the central place of *junbungaku* was being challenged by the first wave of *shi-*

---

1. The writer is anonymous, but the eulogy is frequently cited. Tanizaki Seiji quotes it in "Kasai Zenzō hyōden," 495.

shōsetsu criticism, as we noted in Chapter 3, and by the emergence into the limelight of more aesthetically inclined neo-perceptionist and more socially conscious proletarian literature.

The aftermath of the Pacific War brought with it self-examination on the literary as well as other fronts; postwar critics typically charged the *shishōsetsu* with being a vestige of what was "feudal" and unprogressive. Since the early 1960s, with the rise to prominence of writers like Abe Kōbō (1924–), Ōe Kenzaburō (1935–), and Kurahashi Yumiko (1935–), all of whom are steeped in the western intellectual tradition, Japanese literature has entered into an age of internationalization. *Junbungaku* has lost its strict autobiographical connotation, and both the form and content of "serious" literature have regularly strayed from the *shishōsetsu* mode.

Yet there is no question that the *shishōsetsu* is still deeply entrenched in contemporary literature. Despite the western novel's continued impact on Japanese fiction, the traditional poetics of authorial "presence" has remained largely intact. One of the "attractions" of the *shishōsetsu*, Masamune Hakuchō wrote soon after the war, was its apparent longevity, and this of course is all the more true today. The *shishōsetsu*, like haiku and *waka*, would survive as long as Japanese culture did, he predicted, because it was similarly bound to the native sensibility and observed the same crucial literary convention: the depiction of a particularized, personal, narrowly defined world that was still the most "real" to a Japanese.[2] Literary realism, of course, is "plausible not because it reflects the world but because it is constructed out of what is (discursively) familiar."[3] Our awareness of this fact, however, far from undermining the *shishōsetsu*'s reality, actually helps us better appreciate its persuasiveness, realizing as we do that its sensibility and conventionalism are bolstered by a powerfully supportive epistemology that valorizes lived experience.

This essentially antifictional (which, as we have seen, is not the same as "unimaginative") view of literature has prompted the *shishōsetsu* writer Kanbayashi Akatsuki (1902–80), for example, to remark on numerous occasions that he regarded each of his stories as if it were a final document, that he recorded his life as if leaving

2. "Watakushi shōsetsu no miryoku" (1947), in *Masamune Hakuchō zenshū* 7:380.
3. Catherine Belsey, *Critical Practice*, 47.

a testament. "I write in the *shishōsetsu* mode not because I believe it to be the greatest literary form," he reflected early in his career, "but because I feel that I have no choice. . . . I acknowledge the worth of the more 'objective' kind of fiction . . . but I cannot write unless I have a great personal stake in the material."[4] We can easily recognize in Kanbayashi's words, written just before the beginning of the Pacific War, the same underlying view of literature that we noted in Yasuoka Shōtarō's remarks three decades later: "Truly creative writing involves . . . discovering something in yourself, not dreaming up some formally satisfying story."

Few critics would deny the *shishōsetsu*'s continued prominence, but most argue that it has undergone a transformation, in the decades following the period we have studied, that has been variously described as a "fictionalizing" or "distorting" of the form. Nishida Masayoshi's (1931–) observations typify this view. The *shishōsetsu* entered into a period of decline soon after the early years of Shōwa, Nishida observes. With the exception of a handful of "dispassionate," "life-affirming" authors like Kanbayashi and Ozaki Kazuo, most later writers are prone to exaggeration or idle reverie. Thus, Makino Shin'ichi's (1896–1936) writing is characterized as "hallucinatory," Kajii Motojirō's (1901–32) as "undisciplined," Kawasaki Chōtarō's (1901–85) as "decadent," Dazai Osamu's as "nihilistic," and Shimao Toshio's (1917–86) as "fantastic."[5]

What Nishida and many others see as a decline, however, can more profitably be regarded as a sign of the form's diversification, something that, moreover, has been apparent from the beginning. If our study of three *shishōsetsu* authors has taught us anything, it is that their common struggles with "authentic" narrative representation were resolved in various ways that, for all their supposed fidelity to lived experience, reveal considerable editorial license and imagination. Hiraoka Tokuyoshi (1929–) notes that the *shishōsetsu*'s seemingly most logical and comfortable definition—that it is a first-person (or third-person) narration about the author's own experience, with no fictional embellishment—quickly reaches an impasse over the meaning of "experience." One might of course

4. "Watakushi shōsetsu shikan" (1941), quoted in Matsubara Shin'ichi, *"Gusha" no bungaku*, 227–28. Kanbayashi expresses similar sentiments in "Watakushi shōsetsu no unmei" (1947), in *Kanbayashi Akatsuki zenshū* 15:285–91.
5. *Watakushi shōsetsu saihakken*, 243–77.

argue that it includes such everyday activities as eating, sleeping, and walking; but a case could easily be made as well for including what the author sees or hears or reads. And in fact an author like Shiga—not to mention other writers like Takii Kōsaku (1894–1984), Nagai Tatsuo (1904–), and Shōno Junzō (1921–)—typically writes about the latter as much as the former. The very recording, however "faithful," of these acts, surely requires no little creativity, Hiraoka suggests. But if what the writer has seen or heard or read is part of his personal experience, Hiraoka argues further, then is not also what he himself has imagined? In that case, is not an ostensibly "fictional" story like "Kamisori" (or like "Kozō no kamisama," we might add), in which the author *faithfully* records the experience of his imagination, just as much a *shishōsetsu* as any of Shiga's other works? And if so, then are not all *shōsetsu* actually *shishōsetsu?*[6]

Hiraoka's rather facetious complication nevertheless exposes the fragility of conventional wisdom about the *shishōsetsu:* that it depicts, with greater accuracy and authenticity than any other form, life as it is really lived. Still, the myth of sincerity dies hard. Kanbayashi Akatsuki, the self-styled writer of testaments, for example, tells fellow participants at a roundtable discussion in amazement that he received a letter inquiring about the health of a character in one of his stories. Such an inquirer obviously does not know how to read fiction, he concludes.[7] Yet he then goes on to defend his habit of neglecting to describe characters and narrative situations because, he claims, they are bothersome and redundant, as readers would be familiar with them anyway—clearly a move by the author to link his writing unequivocally to the referential world.[8]

This example is hardly unusual. In 1981 Matsubara Toshio (1905–86) published a story in which the narrator reminisces about his visit as a boy to Kinosaki, the spa made famous by Shiga Naoya's story. He describes a chance meeting with a man whom he later deduces to have been Shiga himself at a Kinosaki bathhouse and

6. *Bungaku no dōki,* 44–45.
7. Kanbayashi Akatsuki et al., " 'Watakushi shōsetsu' ron," 42.
8. Ibid., 50. We have noted, of course, that the author's previous texts themselves provide the necessary "background" information (thus suggesting a tradition or convention of reading, as opposed to a "simply" referential reading) but this is certainly not what Kanbayashi means here.

recalls the scene in Shiga's story, which he witnessed, that depicts a rat struggling in a stream running through town to escape a crowd bent on killing it.[9] We learn in a sequel published two years later, however, that this experience is not only untrue but also that its untruth, which he finally confesses to a Shiga disciple out of good conscience, greatly annoys the disciple and other Shiga admirers, who have read the first story as nonfiction and invited the author to a reception commemorating the tenth anniversary of Shiga's death. The author is told by one acquaintance that never again will he be able to believe what the author has written.[10]

The very massiveness of Matsubara's attack on referentiality in his second story would seem to privilege it as a "truthful" account. But might not this, too, be a trap? We cannot help wondering whether we are really being told the whole truth even here, in a story that rewrites (after the manner of Kasai Zenzō) the earlier story in a way that alters forever our reading of it. Just as we now reject the first story as a true account, might not the appearance of a third story later on make us reject the second? Matsubara is able to "deceive" his readers not because he is the first *shishōsetsu* writer to try it (we have learned in this study that deception—in the guise of "sincerity"—is in the nature of the form) but because of the powerfully persuasive rhetorical apparatus that still binds the *shishōsetsu* narrator "inside" a text to the author "outside" it.

The attraction of the *shishōsetsu*'s rhetoric is so great, in fact, that it continues to win converts from among its opponents. Akutagawa Ryūnosuke, the frequent critic, as we noted in Chapter 3, of the *junbungaku* chroniclers of personal experience, took to writing *shishōsetsu* himself late in life. Of his posthumous "Haguruma" (Cogwheel, 1927), Kasai Zenzō is reported to have said, "At last Akutagawa has written a true *shōsetsu*."[11] For Kasai, being "true" to the word *shōsetsu* of course meant rejecting the transcendent grammar of fabrication. More recently, Ōe Kenzaburō, once the literary world's enfant terrible whose distinctly alien prose style shocked his elders into stern remonstrances about the limits of the language's resiliency, has become a *shishōsetsu* writer of note, al-

9. "Hanasanakatta hanashi."
10. "Kutsu."
11. Yamamoto Kenkichi, *Watakushi shōsetsu sakka ron*, 28.

though he himself would no doubt recoil at the characterization. Ōe expressed his defiance of the form as early as 1961, when he set forth a manifesto of his goals as a writer: "Kobayashi Hideo wrote, in the very year I was born, 'The *shishōsetsu* is dead, but have people vanquished the self? The *shishōsetsu* will doubtlessly reappear in new forms, so long as Flaubert's celebrated formula, "Madame Bovary—c'est moi," lives on.' But I believe otherwise. The *shishō-setsu* is *not* dead. People have *not* vanquished the self. And the *shishōsetsu* has *not* appeared in new forms."[12] Indeed, the *shishō-setsu* seems a poor vehicle, he concludes, in which to embark on his own admittedly personal yet at the same time highly imaginative and metaphoric journey of self-exploration.[13]

Beginning perhaps with his "Rain Tree" series, however, which appeared in the early 1980s, Ōe presents a new kind of narrating voice. The first-person *boku*, modeled clearly as never before after the author himself, serves as a thoroughly accessible and concrete locus of perception, guiding his readers through a world that is both linguistically and epistemologically "authentic." To be sure, this seeming authenticity, which pays its respects repeatedly to the referential world, actually provides a springboard to an often densely allegorical realm. But Ōe has succeeded in putting his new wine in an old bottle and showing them both off to good advantage. One of the *shishōsetsu* tradition's most vociferous rebels has come nearly full circle, using Japanese literature's most realistic discursive mode to push realism to its limits. In an interview following his receipt of the Yomiuri Prize for his *"Rein tsurii" o kiku onnatachi* (Women who listen to the "rain tree," 1982), Ōe denies that his work is a *shishōsetsu* and emphasizes the process of fictive reconstruction to which he subjects personal experience, while adding demurely that he has given more direct expression to his thoughts than ever before.[14] Yet it is not his "thoughts," somehow more directly expressed, that lead us to label this and much of his recent writing as *shishōsetsu*; rather, it is the specifically located narrating voice, which fairly exudes authenticity by its apparent denial of fictive imagination. Ōe presents a narrator who relates only what he can

---

12. "Watakushi shōsetsu ni tsuite," 192.
13. Ibid., 197.
14. *Yomiuri Shinbun* (evening edition), 2 Feb. 1983, p. 5.

see or hear himself. Whether or not this nontranscendent narrator tells us the "truth" about Ōe's lived experience is not our concern; he presents his story *as if* to chronicle that experience and nothing else. Thus, Ōe, like Kasai and other writers before him, has found a way to transcend lived experience by paradoxically forfeiting all pretensions to transcendence.

Ōe is not alone in pushing the "realism" generated by Japanese literature's most trusted mode of narrative representation to its limits. Fujieda Shizuo (1908–), a disciple of Shiga Naoya, adamantly maintains a nontranscendent stance even as he explores manifestly transcendent realms. At the conclusion of *Gongu jōdo* (In search of the Pure Land, 1970), for example, the narrating "I" dies and rejoins his deceased relatives in the family grave. Confronted with so blatant a transgression of "reality," even as it is told in the quintessentially authentic *shishōsetsu* voice, the reader is forced to question the truth of all details in this story, which has seemed to correspond so faithfully to the referential world.[15]

To say that the *shishōsetsu* is being exploited to suit the contemporary writer's idiosyncratic needs and that "fantasy" cannot be separated from "truth," however, is merely to say that it is business as usual with this deceptively straightforward form. Hiraoka Tokuyoshi, one of the more sensitive *shishōsetsu* readers, notes in a suggestive essay that the *shishōsetsu*, having now become so well established, has broadened its discursive perimeters. Today's *shishōsetsu* no longer needs a first-person narrator, he argues; a third-person narrator will do just as well. Nor does it need to be based strictly on the author's own experience; it need only give the impression that it does.[16] The argument is true as far as it goes, of course, but we have learned from our survey of the Taishō *shishōsetsu* that it has in fact *always* been true. Indeed the difference from author to author or from generation to generation in the amount of narrative "deception" is of little significance, as the potential for it is always there. We have seen that a wide range of

15. Ironically, Fujieda is the model for the character (identified by an initial) in Matsubara's story, cited above, who is offended by the author's "untruth." This lack of sympathy for another writer's "fabrications" has informed the consumption (as opposed to the production) of *shishōsetsu* throughout the history of the form—a sign, no doubt, of the myth of sincerity's unwaning power.

16. "Watakushi shōsetsu no suitai to tensei," 154.

morally and artistically disparate writers have all found a common ground of expression in the *shishōsetsu*—not because they were equally motivated to tell the truth but because they found in it a readily available medium for marketing their candor.

The *shishōsetsu* seems quite capable, therefore, of thriving in an age of "internationalization." For what marks this form as tradition-bound is not its thematic content, as is often suggested, but its mode of discourse, which is by no means intrinsically ill-suited to the contemporary scene. That is why the critic Isoda Kōichi's (1931–87) argument that the *shishōsetsu* is an expression of an era that now belongs to the past, is problematic. "In my own view," he writes, "the style of the I-novel is closely associated with the traditional Japanese way of life; the world portrayed by Shiga Naoya and Ozaki Kazuo belonged to the Japanese-style dwelling with its tatami, its shoji, and its back garden. As a literary form, it was ill suited to life in high-rise, reinforced-concrete apartment houses." [17] On the contrary: the *shishōsetsu* is very much at home with "modern" life in Japan and will continue to be as long as its epistemological base remains intact. The presence of so many major *shishōsetsu* writers of both sexes active today—Yasuoka Shōtarō, Irokawa Budai (1929–), Miura Tetsurō (1931–), Abe Akira (1934–), Setouchi Harumi (1922–), Hayashi Kyōko (1930–), and Tsushima Yūko (1947–), to name just a few—moreover, belies the form's alleged affinity with a bygone world.

The history of narrative in Japan that produced the *shishōsetsu* is a long one, but the relatively brief history of the modern *shishōsetsu* itself is still unfolding. Now that the first generation of *shishōsetsu* writers are in their graves and their works have achieved the status of classics, they will surely be reread by those with far less to invest in the writers' private lives. Shiga Naoya's wishful comparison of the writer's anonymity with that of the Kannon goddess's sculptor may yet become a reality. The evolution in language necessary for a clean break between narrating subject and narrated object, however, will not take place overnight. Readings of the narrated object in *shishōsetsu* will no doubt continue to be constrained by the subject—the particularized voice that refuses to assume a presence independent of the author-hero, regardless of the narrative person. We confuse

17. "The Historical Context of Postwar Japanese Literature," 8. See also Isoda's discussion in *Sengoshi no kūkan* (from which the article cited here is adapted), 197–99.

watakushi—which Kobayashi Hideo erroneously equates with Flaubert's *je* in his famous essay—with first-person pronouns in any western language, at our peril. As long as that difference remains, the *shishōsetsu*'s nontranscendent, communal narrating voice will overlap its principal actor and even you, the reader. And as long as narrator continues to merge with actor—*watakushi/boku/ore*, etc., with *kare* or *kanojo* or even *anata*—*shishōsetsu* will always occupy the heartland of language and literature in Japan.

Bibliography

WORKS CITED IN JAPANESE

All books were published in Tokyo unless otherwise indicated. The English translations in brackets are to be considered only as rough guides for those not literate in Japanese. For abbreviations, see page xiv.

Aeba Takao. *Hihyō to hyōgen: kindai Nihon bungaku no "watakushi"* [Criticism and expression: the "self" in modern Japanese literature]. Bungei Shunjū, 1979.

Akiyama Shun. "Shiga Naoya no 'watakushi' ni tsuite" [On the self of Shiga Naoya]. *KKKK* 21, no. 4 (Mar. 1976): 64–68.

Akutagawa Ryūnosuke. *Akutagawa Ryūnosuke zenshū* [Akutagawa Ryūnosuke: collected works]. 12 vols. Iwanami Shoten, 1977–78.

Chikamatsu Shūkō. *Bundan sanjū nen* [My thirty years in the *bundan*]. Chikuma Shobō, 1931.

———. "Bungei hyaku hōmen: komamono ten" [One hundred aspects of literature: bric-a-brac shop]. Part 3. *Yomiuri shinbun*, 4 Apr. 1910, p. 5.

———. *Chikamatsu Shūkō shū* [Chikamatsu Shūkō: an anthology]. Hirano Ken, ed. Vol. 14 of *Nihon bungaku zenshu*. Shūeisha, 1974. (*CSS*)

———. "Hakken ka sōsaku ka" [Discovery? Creativity?]. Part 1. *Yomiuri shinbun*, 13 Mar. 1909, p. 15.

———. "Honrai no negai" [My most fervent wish]. *Shinchō* 23 (June 1926): 14–16.

———. *Keien* [A lover's lament]. Uetake Shoin, 1915.

———. *Koi kara ai e* [From infatuation to love]. Shun'yōdō, 1925.

———. "Koi o enagara no shitsuren" [Winning love and losing it]. *Bunshō sekai* 3, no. 9 (July 1908): 40–43.

———. "*Kyōran* gakuyabanashi" [The origins of my story *Kyōran*]. *Yomiuri shinbun*, 1, 2, and 4 Apr. 1922, all p. 7.

———. "Omotta mama" [As the thoughts come to me]. *Yomiuri shinbun*, 13 May 1910, p. 4.

———. *Shinsen Chikamatsu Shūkō shū* [Chikamatsu Shūkō: a new anthology]. Kaizōsha, 1928.

———. "Sono ato" [Aftermath]. *Shin Nippon* 4 (June 1914): 163–74.

———. "*Wakareta tsuma* o kaita jidai no bungakuteki haikei" [The literary background to *Wakareta tsuma*]. *Waseda bungaku*, no. 257 (June 1927): 12–19.

Chikamatsu Shūkō and Uno Kōji. *Chikamatsu Shūkō, Uno Kōji*. Vol. 42 of *Meiji Taishō bungaku zenshū* [Meiji and Taishō literature: an anthology]. Shun'yōdō, 1929.

Dazai Osamu. *Dazai Osamu zenshū* [Dazai Osamu: collected works]. 13 vols. Chikuma Shobō, 1971–72.

Dōmeki Kyōsaburō. *Shinchōsha hachijū nen shōshi* [Shinchōsha's first eighty years: a brief history]. Shinchōsha, 1976.

Endō Hideo. "Chikamatsu Shūkō *Kurokami* ron" [On Chikamatsu Shūkō's *Kurokami*]. *Nihon bungaku kenkyū* (Daitō Bunka Daigaku Nihon Bungakukai), no. 21 (Jan. 1982): 106–15.

———. "Chikamatsu Shūkō shoki sakuhin kenkyū: 'Shokugo' o chūshin ni" [A study of Chikamatsu Shūkō's early writings, with a focus on "Shokugo"]. *Nihon bungaku kenkyū* (Daitō Bunka Daigaku Nihon Bungakukai), no. 17 (Jan. 1978): 82–88.

———. "*Giwaku* ron" [On *Giwaku*]. *Nihon bungaku* 27 (Sept. 1978): 81–82.

Enomoto Takashi. "'Kanashiki chichi' ron" [On "Kanashiki chichi"]. In Nihon Bungaku Kenkyū Shiryō Kankōkai, ed., *Taishō no bungaku* [Literature of the Taishō period], 207–19. Yūseidō, 1981.

Fukuda Kiyoto. "Kasai Zenzō." In *Kasai Zenzō, Sōma Taizō, Miyaji Karoku, Kamura Isota, Kawasaki Chōtarō, Kiyama Shōhei shū* [Kasai Zenzō . . . : an anthology], 381–85. Vol. 49 of *Gendai Nihon bungaku taikei*. Chikuma Shobō, 1973.

Fukuda Kiyoto and Kuribayashi Hideo. *Shiga Naoya: hito to sakuhin* [Shiga Naoya: the man and his works]. Shimizu Shoin, 1968.

Furui Yoshikichi. *Tōkyō monogatari kō* [Tales of Tokyo]. Iwanami Shoten, 1984.

Futabatei Shimei. *Futabatei Shimei zenshū* [Futabatei Shimei: collected works]. 9 vols. Iwanami Shoten, 1964–65.

Hasegawa Komako. "Higeki no jiden" [My tragic life]. Parts 1, 2. *Fujinkōron* 22, no. 5 (May 1937): 282–90; no. 6 (June 1937): 200–210.

Hasegawa Tenkei. "Genmetsu jidai no geijutsu" [Art in an age of disillusionment]. In *KBHT* 3:43–49.

———. "Jiko bunretsu to seikan" [Self-dissolution and serene contemplation]. In *MBZ* 43:207–9.

Hashimoto Yoshi. "*Futon* ni kansuru memo" [Notes on *Futon*]. *Jinbun gakuhō* (Tōkyō Toritsu Daigaku Jinbungakukai), no. 19 (Mar.1959): 58–71.

Hirano Ken. *Geijutsu to jisseikatsu* [Art and private life]. Shinchō Bunko, 1964.

———. *Hirano Ken zenshū* [Hirano Ken: collected works]. 13 vols. Shinchōsha, 1975.

———. "Sakuhin to sakka: Chikamatsu Shūkō" [Chikamatsu Shūkō: The man and his works]. In *CSS*, 400–430.

———, ed. *Mayama Seika, Chikamatsu Shūkō shū* [Mayama Seika and Chikamatsu Shūkō: an anthology]. Vol. 70 of *MBZ*. Chikuma Shobō, 1973.

Hirano Ken et al., eds. *Gendai Nihon bungaku ronsōshi* [A history of literary disputes during the modern period in Japan]. 3 vols. Miraisha, 1956–57.

Hirano Ken and Matsumoto Seichō. "Watakushi shōsetsu to honkaku shōsetsu" [*Watakushi shōsetsu* and true novels]. *Gunzō* 17 (June 1962): 132–45.

Hirano Ken, Takeuchi Yoshimi, and Takami Jun. "Bundan" [The *bundan*]. *Gunzō* 16 (Feb. 1961): 138–54.

Hiraoka Tokuyoshi. "*An'ya kōro* no sakusha" [The author of *An'ya kōro*]. In *Shiga Naoya zenshū geppō* [Newsletter to *Shiga Naoya: collected works*], no. 12:5–8; no. 13:4–7. In vols. 8 and 13 of *Shiga Naoya zenshū*.

———. *Bungaku no dōki* [Motivations for literature]. Kawade Shobō Shinsha, 1979.

———. *Meiro no shōsetsu ron* [On fiction of the labyrinth]. Kawade Shobō Shinsha, 1974.

———. "Watakushi shōsetsu no suitai to tensei" [*Watakushi shōsetsu*: its decline and transformation]. *KKKK* 20, no. 9 (July 1975): 149–55.

Hiraoka Toshio. *Nihon kindai bungaku no shuppatsu* [The beginnings of modern Japanese literature]. Kinokuniya Shoten, 1973.

Hirotsu Kazuo. *Hirotsu Kazuo zenshū* [Hirotsu Kazuo: collected works]. 13 vols. Chūōkōronsha, 1974.

Honda Shūgo. "Jigazō sakka e no michi" [Becoming a writer of the self]. *Gunzō* 38 (July 1983): 244–57.

———. "Kaisetsu" [Commentary]. In *Nakamura Mitsuo zenshū* [Nakamura Mitsuo: collected works] 7:619–34. Chikuma Shobō, 1972.

———. "*Shirakaba*" ha no bungaku [The literature of the "shirakaba" school]. Shinchō Bunko, 1960.

———. "Wakai ron" [On *Wakai*]. *Subaru* 32 (Dec. 1977): 220–34.

Ibuse Masuji. "Dōjin zasshi no koro" [When I wrote for coterie magazines]. *Shinchō* 81 (Oct. 1984): 222–24.

Ikegami Kenji. "*Yomiuri shinbun* to Tayama Katai" [Tayama Katai and the *Yomiuri shinbun*]. *Nishō Gakusha Daigaku jinbun ronsō*, no. 24 (Mar. 1983): 28–37.

Ikeuchi Teruo. "Naoya no riarizumu" [The realism of Shiga Naoya]. In Miyoshi Yukio and Takemori Ten'yū, eds., *Taishō bungaku no shosō* [Various aspects of Taishō literature], 45–54. Vol. 4 of *Kindai bungaku* [Modern (Japanese) literature]. Yūhikaku, 1977.

———. "*Wakai* ron" [On *Wakai*]. *KKKK* 21, no. 4 (Mar. 1976): 150–54.

Ikukata Toshio. "Bundan no suhinkusu Tokuda Shūkō" [Sphinx of the *bundan*: Tokuda Shūkō]. In *KBHT* 4:147–57.

Ikuta Chōkō. "Nichijō seikatsu o henchō suru akukeikō" [A nefarious literary trend that distorts daily life]. In Hirano Ken et al., eds., *Gendai Nihon bungaku ronsōshi* [A history of literary disputes during the modern period in Japan] 1:97–108. Miraisha, 1956.

Inagaki Tatsurō et al., eds. *Kindai bungaku hyōron taikei* [A collection of critical essays on modern (Japanese) literature]. 10 vols. Kadokawa Shoten, 1971–75. (*KBHT*)

Ino Kenji. *Meiji no sakka* [Writers of the Meiji period]. Iwanami Shoten, 1966.

Isoda Kōichi. *Sengoshi no kūkan* [The space of postwar history]. Shinchōsha, 1983.

Itō Sei. *Itō Sei zenshū* [Itō Sei: collected works]. 24 vols. Shinchōsha, 1972–73.

————. "Kindai bungaku no shutai" [Identity in modern (Japanese) literature]. In *MBZ* 29:344–48. Chikuma Shobō, 1976.

————. *Shōsetsu no hōhō* [The method of fiction]. Shinchō Bunko, 1958.

Itō Sei et al., eds. *Shinchō Nihon bungaku shōjiten* [The Shinchō compact encyclopedia of Japanese literature]. Shinchōsha, 1968.

Iwagiri Keiichi. "*Wakaretaru tsuma ni okuru tegami* ron" [On *Wakaretaru tsuma ni okuru tegami*]. In *Pamphlet Chikamatsu Shūkō* 1 (Apr. 1983): 1–14.

————. "'Yuki no hi' no teiryū ni aru mono: 'rei naru ai' no kikyū" [An undercurrent in "Yuki no hi": the desire for a spiritual love]. In *CSK*, 76–98.

Iwanaga Yutaka. *Shizenshugi bungaku ni okeru kyokō no kanōsei* [On the fictive potential of naturalist literature]. Ōfūsha, 1968.

Iwano Hōmei. *Hōmei zenshū* [Iwano Hōmei: collected works]. 18 vols. Kōbunko, 1971–72.

Kanbayashi Akatsuki. *Kanbayashi Akatsuki zenshū* [Kanbayashi Akatsuki: collected works]. 15 vols. Chikuma Shobō, 1966–67.

Kanbayashi Akatsuki et al. "'Watakushi shōsetsu' ron" [On the *watakushi shōsetsu*]. *Shinchō* 39 (May 1942): 40–51.

Kasai Zenzō. *Kasai Zenzō zenshū* [Kasai Zenzō: collected works]. Ed. Osanai Tokio. 4 vols. Hirosaki: Tsugaru Shobō, 1974–75. (*KZZ*)

Katsuyama Isao. *Taishō, watakushi shōsetsu kenkyū* [A study of Taishō literature and the *watakushi shōsetsu*]. Meiji Shoin, 1980.

Kawakami Tetsutarō. *Nihon no autosaidā* [Outsiders in Japan]. Shinchō Bunko, 1965.

Kikuchi Kan. "Bun wa hito nari" [Writing is the man]. *Bunshō kurabu* 4 (Apr. 1919): 10–11.

————. *Kikuchi Kan zenshū* [Kikuchi Kan: collected works]. 12 vols. Heibonsha, 1929–30.

————. *Kikuchi Kan: tanpen sanjū-san to Han jijoden* [Kikuchi Kan: Thirty-three stories and the autobiography]. Bungei Shunjū, 1977.

Kimura Ki. *Watakushi no bungaku kaiko roku* [My literary memoirs]. Seiadō, 1979.

Kinda'ichi Haruhiko. *Nihongo* [The Japanese language]. Iwanami Shoten, 1957.

Kitamura Tōkoku. *Kitamura Tōkoku shū* [Kitamura Tōkoku: an anthology]. Ed. Odagiri Hideo. Vol. 29 of *MBZ*. Chikuma Shobō, 1976.

Kobayashi Hideo. *Shintei Kobayashi Hideo zenshū* [Kobayashi Hideo: collected works (new edition)]. 15 vols. Shinchōsha, 1978–79.

————. "Watakushi shōsetsu ron" [On the *watakushi shōsetsu*]. In *KBHT* 7:181–202.

Koki Tetsutarō. *Taishō no sakka* [Writers of the Taishō period]. Ōfūsha, 1966.

Kokubo Atsumu. "*Kurokami* no seiritsu: Shūkō bungaku no tenkai" [The writing of *Kurokami* and the development of Chikamatsu Shūkō's literature]. *Hanyūya kokubun*, no. 6 (Feb. 1976): 57–65.

————. "Shūkō bungaku no ichimen" [An aspect of Chikamatsu Shūkō's literature]. *Shitennōji Joshi Daigaku kiyō*, no. 9 (December 1970): 43–56.

Kōno Kensuke. "*Kurokami* ron josetsu: 'kurido' no sekai" [A preparatory study of *Kurokami:* the world behind the "sliding door"]. In *CSK*, 278–302.

Konō Toshirō. "*Kiseki* kaisetsu" [*Kiseki:* commentary]. In Odagiri Susumu, ed., *Kiseki fukkoku-ban bessatsu* [*Kiseki* reissue: supplement], 9–16. Nihon Kindai Bungakukan, 1970.

————, ed. *Chikamatsu Shūkō kenkyū* [A study of Chikamatsu Shūkō]. Gakushū Kenkyūsha, 1980. (*CSK*)

Konō Toshirō et al., eds. *Iwano Hōmei, Chikamatsu Shūkō, Masamune Hakuchō shū* [Iwano Hōmei, Chikamatsu Shūkō, and Masamune Hakuchō: an anthology]. Vol. 22 of *NKBT*. Kadokawa Shoten, 1974.

Kosugi Tengai. "*Hayari uta* jo" [Preface to *Hayari uta*]. In *KBHT* 2:418.

Kumakura Chiyuki. "Nihongo no shukansei ni tsuite: Ōe Kenzaburō no *Kaba ni kamareru* o yominagara" [On the subjectivity of Japanese: reading Ōe Kenzaburō's *Kaba ni kamareru*]. In Imada Shigeko, ed., *Bulletin of the ICU Summer Program in Japanese* 1:142–51. International Christian University Summer Program in Japanese, 1984.

Kume Masao. "Junbungaku yogi setsu" [*Junbungaku* as an avocation]. In Itō Sei et al., eds., *Kikuchi Kan, Kume Masao shū*, 411–13. Vol. 57 of *Nihon gendai bungaku zenshū* [Contemporary Japanese literature: an anthology]. Kōdansha, 1967.

————. "'Watakushi' shōsetsu to 'shinkyō' shōsetsu" [*Watakushi shōsetsu* and *shinkyō shōsetsu*]. In *KBHT* 6:50–57.

Kunikida Doppo. *Kunikida Doppo zenshū* [Kunikida Doppo: collected works]. 10 vols. Gakushū Kenkyūsha, 1978.

Kunimatsu Akira. "'Yamashina' mono ni tsuite" [On the "Yamashina" series]. In Issatsu no kōza Henshūbu, ed., *Issatsu no kōza: Shiga Naoya* [One-volume course: Shiga Naoya], 113–24. Yūseidō, 1982.

Kuribayashi Hideo. "*An'ya kōro* sōkō no kentō" [A study of the *An'ya kōro* manuscripts]. In Issatsu no kōza Henshūbu, ed., *Issatsu no kōza: Shiga Naoya* [One-volume course: Shiga Naoya], 125–37. Yūseidō, 1982.

————. "Chikamatsu Shūkō nōto: sono shoki sakuhin ni tsuite" [Notes on Chikamatsu Shūkō: the early writings]. In *Nihon bungaku kenkyū* (Daitō Bunka Daigaku Nihon Bungakukai), no. 18 (Jan. 1979): 86–93.

Maeda Ai. *Kindai dokusha no seiritsu* [The growth of a modern readership]. Yūseidō, 1973.

Masamune Hakuchō. *Masamune Hakuchō zenshū* [Masamune Hakuchō: collected works]. 13 vols. Shinchōsha, 1966–68.

Matsubara Shin'ichi. "*Gusha*" *no bungaku* [The literature of fools]. Tōjusha, 1974.

Matsubara Toshio. "Hanasanakatta hanashi" [An untold story]. *Furate*, no. 30 (Aug. 1981): 12–19.

————. "Kutsu" [Shoes]. *Furate*, no. 33 (Sept. 1983): 12–22.

Matsuoka Yuzuru. *Sōseki no inzei chō* [Sōseki's royalty ledgers]. Asahi Shinbunsha, 1955.

Miyoshi Yukio. "Kakō no 'watakushi': *An'ya kōro*—Shiga Naoya" [The fictive self: *An'ya kōro* and Shiga Naoya]. In *Sakuhin ron no kokoromi* [An
attempt at textual analysis]. Shibundō, 1978.

Mori Atsushi and Takano Etsuko. "Taidan: bungaku to eiga" [Dialogue:
literature and film]. *Shinkan nyūsu*, no. 401 (Dec. 1983): 8–17.

Mori Masamichi, ed. *Shinbun hanbai gaishi* [An unofficial history of newspaper sales]. Nihon Shinbun Hanbai Kyōkai, 1979.

Nagata Mikihiko. *Bungō no sugao* [Literary giants unmasked]. Kaname
Shobō, 1953.

Nagayo Michiyo [Okada Michiyo]. "*Futon, En,* oyobi watakushi" [*Futon,
En,* and me]. In Yoshida Seiichi et al., eds., *Toson, Katai* [Shimazaki Tōson and Tayama Katai], 264–72. Vol. 13 of *Kokugo kokubungaku kenkyū
taisei.* Sanseidō, 1960.

Nakajima Kunihiko. "Chikamatsu Shūkō ni okeru sakuhin keiretsu no
mondai: 'Wakareta tsuma mono' o megutte no danshō" [The problem
of Chikamatsu Shūkō's textual lineages: notes on the "Wakareta tsuma"
series]. *Kokubungaku kenkyū*, no. 68 (June 1979): 12–20.

———. "Kyakkan shōsetsu e no yume: *Maizuru shinjū* zengo no Chikamatsu Shūkō" [Aspiring toward objective fiction: Chikamatsu Shūkō
around the time of *Maizuru shinjū*]. *Bungei to hihyō* 4 (Jan. 1976): 47–58.

———. "*Shūjaku, Giwaku* o sasaeru mono: Shūkō sakuhin seiritsu no sho-
jōken" [The supports of *Shūjaku* and *Giwaku*: the development of Chikamatsu Shūkō's texts]. In Kawazoe Kunimoto, ed., *Bungaku 1910 nen-
dai* [Literature in the 1910s], 99–109. Meiji Shoin, 1979.

———. "Tōsui to ninshiki: Chikamatsu Shūkō 'Ōsaka no yūjo mono' no
sekai" [Rapture and awareness: the world of the "Osaka courtesan"
series]. *Nihon bungaku* 24 (Sept. 1975): 36–45.

———. "Yuki no hi no gensō: Meiji yonjū-san nen fuyu no Chikamatsu
Shūkō" [The fantasy in "Yuki no hi": Chikamatsu Shūkō in the winter
of 1910]. In *CKS*, 33–58.

Nakamura Mitsuo. *Fūzoku shōsetsu ron* [On the novel of manners]. Shinchō
Bunko, 1958.

———. *Nakamura Mitsuo zenshū* [Nakamura Mitsuo: collected works]. 16
vols. Chikuma Shobō, 1971–73.

———. *Shiga Naoya ron* [On Shiga Naoya]. Chikuma Shobō, 1966.

Nakamura Murao. *Bundan zuihitsu* [Essays on the *bundan*]. Shinchōsha,
1925.

———. "Honkaku shōsetsu to shinkyō shōsetsu to" [True novels and the
shinkyō shōsetsu]. In *KBHT* 6:11–16.

———. "Junbungaku to shite no watakushi shōsetsu" [The *watakushi shōsetsu* as *junbungaku*]. *Shinchō* 32 (Oct. 1935): 5–7.

———. *Meiji Taishō no bungakusha* [Literary figures of Meiji and Taishō Ja-
pan]. Rume Shoten, 1949.

Nakano Shigeharu. "*An'ya kōro* zōdan" [Topics in *An'ya kōro*]. In *Nakano Shigeharu zenshū* [Nakano Shigeharu: collected works] 8:536–70. Chikuma Shobō, 1960.

Nakano Yoshio, ed. *Gendai no sakka* [Contemporary writers]. Iwanami Shoten, 1955.

Natsume Sōseki. *Sōseki zenshū* [Natsume Sōseki: collected works]. 16 vols. Iwanami Shoten, 1965–67.

Negishi Masazumi. "Watakushi shōsetsu no buntai: Kasai Zenzō o chūshin ni" [Style in *watakushi shōsetsu*, with a focus on Kasai Zenzō]. In Nihon Bungaku Kenkyū Shiryō Kankōkai, ed., *Watakushi shōsetsu*, 224–33. Yūseidō, 1983.

Nihon Daijiten Kankōkai, ed. *Nihon kokugo daijiten* [Dictionary of the Japanese national language]. 20 vols. Shōgakukan, 1972–76. (*NKD*)

Nihon Kindai Bungakukan, ed. *Nihon kindai bungaku daijiten* [Encyclopedia of modern Japanese literature]. 6 vols. Kōdansha, 1977–78. (*NKBD*)

Nishida Masayoshi. *Watakushi shōsetsu saihakken* [The *watakushi shōsetsu* rediscovered]. Ōfūsha, 1973.

Noguchi Takehiko. *Shōsetsu no Nihongo* [The Japanese language in fiction]. Vol. 13 of *Nihongo no sekai*. Chūōkōronsha, 1980.

Ōe Kenzaburō. "Chūnen no kiki o egaku" [Writing about the mid-life crisis] (interview). *Yomiuri Shinbun* (evening edition), 2 Feb. 1983, p. 5.

———. "Watakushi shōsetsu ni tsuite: jiko tanken no bunshō" [On *watakushi shōsetsu:* writing in search of self]. *Gunzō* 16 (Sept. 1961): 192–97.

Ogasawara Masaru. "Watakushi shōsetsu ron no seiritsu o megutte" [On the origins of *watakushi shōsetsu* criticism]. *Gunzō* 17 (May 1962): 42–56.

Ogata Akiko. "*Futon* zen'ya: *Onna kyōshi* kara 'Shōjo byō' made" [The advent of *Futon*: from *Onna kyōshi* to "Shōjo byō"]. *Bungei to hihyō* 4 (July 1976): 43–52.

Ōi Zetsu. See Ogasawara Masaru.

Oka Yoshitake. "Nichiro sensō-go ni okeru atarashii sedai no seichō" [The post-Russo-Japanese War generation grows up], Part 1. *Shisō*, no. 512 (Feb. 1967): 1–13.

Okada Michiyo. See Nagayo Michiyo.

Ōkubo Fusao. *Bunshi to bundan* [Literati and the *bundan*]. Kōdansha, 1970.

Ōmori Sumio. "Kasai Zenzō." In Shibundō Henshūbu, ed., *Sakka to kyōki* [Writers and insanity], 153–60. Shibundō, 1973.

———. "Kasai Zenzō nenpu" [Kasai Zenzō: a chronology]. *Tōyō Daigaku Tanki Daigaku kiyō*, no. 16 (Mar. 1985): 125–46.

———. *Kasai Zenzō no kenkyū* [A study of Kasai Zenzō]. Ōfūsha, 1970.

———. "Kasai Zenzō to watakushi shōsetsu" [Kasai Zenzō and *watakushi shōsetsu*]. In Nihon Bungaku Kenkyū Shiryō Kankōkai, ed., *Watakushi shōsetsu*, 181–90. Yūseidō, 1983.

———. "'Watakushi shōsetsu ron' mokuroku" [A bibliography of articles on *watakushi shōsetsu*]. *Watakushi shōsetsu kenkyū*, no. 1 (May 1972): 25–49.

Ono Hideo. *Nihon shinbun hattatsu shi* [The development of newspapers in Japan: a history]. Osaka: Ōsaka Mainichi Shinbunsha, 1922.

Ozaki Kazuo. *Ano hi kono hi* [That day, this day]. 2 vols. Kōdansha, 1975.

———. "Shiga Naoya no koto" [On Shiga Naoya]. In *Saru no koshikake* [A monkey's chair], 298–307. Takayama Shoin, 1940.

Saeki Shōichi. *Nihon no "watakushi" o motomete* [In search of the Japanese "self"]. Kawade Shobō Shinsha, 1974.

Satō Kōichi. "Ihi roman" [The *Ich-Roman*]. *KKK* 12, no. 14 (Dec. 1962): 10–14.

Sawa Toyohiko. "*Wakaretaru tsuma* to sono hen'yō: Chikamatsu Shūkō to watakushi shōsetsu no mondai ni tsuite" [The transformation of *Wakaretaru tsuma*: on Chikamatsu Shūkō and *watakushi shōsetsu*]. *Shura* 20 (Aug. 1984): 41–48.

Senuma Shigeki. *Hon no hyaku nen shi: besuto serā no konjaku* [A hundred years of books: best sellers yesterday and today]. Shuppan Nyūsusha, 1965.

Shashi Hensan Iinkai, ed. *Mainichi shinbun nanajū nen* [*Mainichi shinbun*: the first seventy years]. Mainichi Shinbunsha, 1952.

Shiga Naoya. "Satoko no shi" [Satoko's death]. In Shirakaba Dōjin, ed., *Shirakaba no sono* [A garden of white birches], 31–53. Shun'yōdō, 1919.

———. *Shiga Naoya* [Shiga Naoya: an anthology], vol. 1. Vol. 21 of Tanizaki Jun'ichirō et al., eds., *Nihon no bungaku* [Literature of Japan]. Chūōkōronsha, 1972.

———. *Shiga Naoya zenshū* [Shiga Naoya: collected works]. Ed. Mushanokōji Saneatsu et al. 15 vols. Iwanami Shoten, 1973–74. (*SNZ*)

Shimada Akio. "Chikamatsu Shūkō shiron" [A study of Chikamatsu Shūkō]. Part 7. *Bungei nenshi* 7 (Spring 1984): 14–24.

Shimamura Hōgetsu. "Bungeijō no shizenshugi" [Naturalism in literature]. In *KBHT* 3:100–117.

———. "*Futon* gappyō" [A multiple critique of *Futon*]. In *KBHT* 3:430–32.

———. "Jo ni kaete jinseikanjō no shizenshugi o ronzu" [By way of a preface: on naturalism and my weltanschauung]. In *KBHT* 3:253–58.

———. "Kaigi to kokuhaku" [Skepticism and confession]. In *KBHT* 3:274–82.

———. "Kanshō soku jinsei no tame nari" [Contemplation for the sake of one's life]. In *KBHT* 3:247–48.

———. "Shizenshugi no kachi" [The value of naturalism]. In *KBHT* 3:200–215.

Shimazaki Tōson. *Tōson zenshū* [Shimazaki Tōson: collected works]. 18 vols. Chikuma Shobō, 1966–71.

Shindō Junkō and Endō Tasuku, eds. *Shiga Naoya shū* [Shiga Naoya: an anthology]. Vol. 31 of *NKBT*. Kadokawa Shoten, 1971.

Shirai Kōji. "Roman perusoneru ni tsuite" [On *le roman personnel*]. *KKK* 27, no. 14 (Dec. 1962): 15–19.

Sōma Motoi. *Tōnichi nanajū nen shi* [*Tōkyō Nichi Nichi Shinbun*: the first seventy years]. Tōkyō Nichi Nichi Shinbunsha, 1941.

Sudō Matsuo. "Shiga bungaku no shizen, seimeiryoku" [Nature and life-force in Shiga Naoya's literature]. In *Bungei tokuhon Shiga Naoya* [A Shiga Naoya reader], 98–107. Kawade Shobō Shinsha, 1976.

―――. *Shiga Naoya no bungaku* [The literature of Shiga Naoya]. Ōfūsha, 1963.

Sugiura Seiichirō et al., eds. *Bashō bunshū* [The prose writings of Bashō: an anthology]. Vol. 46 of *Nihon koten bungaku taikei* [A collection of classical Japanese literature]. Iwanami Shoten, 1959.

Suzuki Haruo. "Enpon to bungaku zenshū" [One-yen books and literary anthologies]. *KKK* 37, no. 9 (July 1972): 100–101.

Suzuki Takao. *Tozasareta gengo: Nihongo no sekai* [A closed-off language: the world of Japanese]. Shinchōsha, 1975.

Takada Mizuho. *Shiga Naoya*. Gakutōsha, 1955.

Takahashi Hideo. *Genso to shite no "watakushi": watakushi shōsetsu sakka ron* [The "self" as an element: on writers of *watakushi shōsetsu*]. Kōdansha, 1976.

―――. *Shiga Naoya: kindai to shinwa* [Shiga Naoya: modernity and mythology]. Bungei Shunjū, 1981.

Takahashi Hiromitsu. "'Wakareta tsuma' mono o megutte: gaikaku to naijitsu" [On the "Wakareta tsuma" series: outer world and inner truth]. In *CSK*, 99–122.

Takemori Ten'yū. "*Giwaku* no sekai" [The world of *Giwaku*]. In *CSK*, 7–32.

Takeyama Michio. "Honkaku shōsetsu no umarenu wake" [Why we don't have true novels]. *Bungei shunjū* 25 (Jan. 1947): 96–100.

Tanizaki Jun'ichirō. *Tanizaki Jun'ichirō zenshū* [Tanizaki Jun'ichirō: collected works]. Chūōkōronsha, 1968.

Tanizaki Seiji. "Kasai Zenzō hyōden" [Kasai Zenzō: a biography]. In *Tanizaki Seiji senshū* [Tanizaki Seiji: selected works], 495–600. Azekura Shobō, 1960.

Tayama Katai. *Tayama Katai zenshū* [Tayama Katai: collected works]. 17 vols. Bunsendō Shoten, 1973–74.

Tayama Katai et al. "Shinchō gappyōkai" [Shinchō critics' circle]. *Shinchō* 42 (Mar. 1925): 49–85.

Tazawa Motohisa. "Hōhō no mosaku: *Giwaku* seiritsu no dōtei" [Groping for a technique: the writing of *Giwaku*]. *Bungei to hihyō* 5 (July 1982): 24–35.

Terada Tōru. "Shinkyō shōsetsu, watakushi shōsetsu." In *Bungaku sono naimen to gaikai* [Literature: its interior and exterior world], 140–53. Shimizu Kōbundō Shobō, 1970.

Tosa Tōru. "Futon no nioi: hikaku bungakuteki nōto" [The quilt's scent: a comparative literary analysis]. *Kokugo kokubungaku hō* (Aichi Kyōiku Daigaku), no. 42 (Mar. 1985): 111–22.

Tsubouchi Shōyō. *Shōsetsu shinzui* [The essence of the novel]. In *MBZ* 16:3–58.

Tsugawa Take'ichi. *Kasai Zenzō sono bungaku to fūdo* [Kasai Zenzō: his land and his literature]. Tsugaru Shobō, 1971.

Tsukagoshi Kazuo. "'Ugomeku mono' sono ta o megutte" [On "Ugomeku mono" and other works]. In Nihon Bungaku Kenkyū Shiryō Kankōkai, ed., *Taishō no bungaku* [Literature of the Taishō period], 220–26. Yūseidō, 1981.

Uno Kōji. *Uno Kōji zenshū* [Uno Kōji: collected works]. 12 vols. Chūōkōronsha, 1972.

———. "'Watakushi shōsetsu' shiken" ["Watakushi shōsetsu": a personal view]. In *KBHT* 6:61–66.

Wada Kingo. *Byōsha no jidai* [The age of depiction]. Sapporo: Hokkaidō Daigaku Tosho Kankōkai, 1975.

Wada Kingo and Sōma Tsuneo, eds. *Tayama Katai shū* [Tayama Katai: an anthology]. Vol. 19 of *NKBT*.

Yamada Akio. "Watakushi shōsetsu no mondai" [Issues concerning *watakushi shōsetsu*]. *KKK* 30, no. 1 (Jan. 1965): 43–47.

Yamamoto Fumio. *Nihon shinbun hattatsu shi* [The development of newspapers in Japan: a history]. Itō Shoten, 1944.

Yamamoto Kenkichi. "Dōjin zasshi hyō" [The coterie magazine corner]. *Bungakukai* 6 (June 1952): 177–80.

———. "Kaisetsu" [Commentary]. In *Uno Kōji, Kasai Zenzō, Kamura Isota*, 492–505. Vol. 33 of Tanizaki Jun'ichirō et al., eds., *Nihon no bungaku* [Literature of Japan]. Chūōkōronsha, 1974.

———. *Watakushi shōsetsu sakka ron* [A study of *watakushi shōsetsu* writers]. Chinbisha, 1966.

Yamamoto Taketoshi. *Kindai Nihon no shinbun dokusha sō* [The readership of the modern Japanese newspaper]. Hōsei Daigaku Shuppankyoku, 1981.

Yamamuro Shizuka. "*An'ya kōro* o chūshin ni: Shiga Naoya ni okeru geijutsu to morarisuto no kankei" [Art and morality in Shiga Naoya's literature: a look at *An'ya kōro*]. In Taishō Bungaku Kenkyūkai, ed., *Shiga Naoya kenkyū* [Studies of Shiga Naoya], 342–53. Kawade Shobō, 1944.

———. "Kasai Zenzō to watakushi shōsetsu" [Kasai Zenzō and *watakushi shōsetsu*]. *Waseda Bungaku* 6 (Jan. 1939): 40–44.

Yamazaki Masakazu. *Fukigen no jidai* [The age of ill humor]. Shinchōsha, 1976.

Yanabu Akira. "*An'ya kōro* ni okeru 'kare'" ["Kare" in *An'ya kōro*]. *Nihon kindai bungaku*, no. 30 (Oct. 1983): 155–59.

Yasaki Dan. "Jiga no hatten ni okeru Nihonteki seikaku" [The development of self in Japan]. In Itō Sei et al., eds., *Gendai bungei hyōronshū* [Modern literary criticism: an anthology], 312–17. Vol. 107 of *Nihon gendai bungaku zenshū* [Modern Japanese literature: an anthology]. Kōdansha, 1969.

Yasuoka Shōtarō. "Gendai ni okeru watakushi shōsetsu" [*Watakushi shōsetsu* in the contemporary age]. *Mita bungaku* 8 (Oct. 1971): 28–34.

Yokomitsu Riichi. "Junsui shōsetsu ron" [On pure fiction]. In *KBHT* 7: 143–54.

Yokoyama Haruichi. *Kaizō mokuji sōran sōmokuji* [A listing of tables of contents to *Kaizō*]. Shin'yaku Shobō, 1966.

Yokozeki Aizō. *Omoide no sakkatachi* [Writers I remember]. Hōsei Daigaku Shuppankyoku, 1956.

――――. *Watakushi no zakki chō* [My personal notebook]. Kaizō no Kai, 1970.

Yomiuri Shinbun Hyaku Nen Shi Henshū Iinkai, ed. *Yomiuri shinbun hyaku nen shi bessatsu* [Supplement to *Yomiuri Shinbun: the first hundred years*]. Yomiuri Shinbunsha, 1976.

Yoshida Seiichi. *Shizenshugi no kenkyū* [A study of naturalism]. 2 vols. Tōkyōdō, 1955–58.

――――. "Watakushi shōsetsu no mondai ni tsuite" [Issues concerning the *watakushi shōsetsu*]. *KKK* 12 (July 1947): 19–24.

Yoshida Seiichi et al., eds. *Tōson Katai* [Shimazaki Tōson and Tayama Katai]. Vol. 13 of *Kokugo kokubungaku kenkyū shi taikei*. Sanseidō, 1960.

WORKS CITED IN ENGLISH

Ackroyd, Joyce. *Told Round a Brushwood Fire: The Autobiography of Arai Hakuseki*. Princeton: Princeton University Press, 1979; Tokyo: Tokyo University Press, 1979.

Auerbach, Erich. *Mimesis: The Representation of Reality in Western Literature*. Trans. Willard R. Trask. Princeton: Princeton University Press, 1968.

Banfield, Ann. *Unspeakable Sentences: Narration and Representation in the Language of Fiction*. Boston: Routledge and Kegan Paul, 1982.

Barthes, Roland. *Writing Degree Zero*. Trans. Annette Lavers and Colin Smith. New York: Hill and Wang, 1968.

――――. *Image, Music, Text*. Trans. Stephen Heath. New York: Hill and Wang, 1977.

Becker, George J., ed. *Documents of Modern Literary Realism*. Princeton: Princeton University Press, 1967.

Bellah, Robert N. "Continuity and Change in Japanese Society." In Bernard Barber and Alex Inkeles, eds., *Stability and Social Change*, 377–404. Boston: Little, Brown and Co., 1971.

――――. *Tokugawa Religion*. Boston: Beacon Press, 1970.

――――. "Values and Social Change in Modern Japan." *Asian Cultural Studies* (International Christian University) 3 (1962): 13–56.

Belsey, Catherine. *Critical Practice*. London: Methuen, 1980.

Bowring, Richard John. *Mori Ōgai and the Modernization of Japanese Culture*. Cambridge: Cambridge University Press, 1979.

Brandon, James R. *Kabuki: Five Classic Plays*. Cambridge, Mass.: Harvard University Press, 1975.

Burch, Noël. *To the Distant Observer: Form and Meaning in the Japanese Cinema*. Berkeley and Los Angeles: University of California Press, 1979.

Chatman, Seymour. *Story and Discourse: Narrative Structure in Fiction and Film*. Ithaca: Cornell University Press, 1978.

Cohn, Dorrit. *Transparent Minds: Narrative Modes for Presenting Consciousness in Fiction*. Princeton: Princeton University Press, 1978.

Cooke, Miriam. *The Anatomy of an Egyptian Intellectual: Yahya Haqqi*. Washington, D.C.: Three Continents Press, 1984.

Dick, Kay. *Writers at Work: The* Paris Review *Interviews.* Harmondsworth, England: Penguin Books, 1972.

Easthope, Antony. *Poetry as Discourse.* London: Methuen, 1983.

Eco, Umberto. *The Role of the Reader: Explorations in the Semiotics of Texts.* Bloomington: Indiana University Press, 1979.

Fowles, John. *The French Lieutenant's Woman.* New York: New American Library, 1970.

Freedman, Ralph. *The Lyrical Novel: Studies in Hermann Hesse, Andre Gide, and Virginia Woolf.* Princeton: Princeton University Press, 1970.

Genette, Gérard. *Figures of Literary Discourse.* Trans. Alan Sheridan. New York: Columbia University Press, 1982.

———. *Narrative Discourse: An Essay in Method.* Trans. Jane E. Lewin. Ithaca: Cornell University Press, 1980.

Gombrich, E. H. *Art and Illusion.* New York: Pantheon Books, 1960.

Grant, Richard B. *The Goncourt Brothers.* New York: Twayne Publishers, 1972.

Harootunian, H[arry] D. "Between Politics and Culture: Authority and the Ambiguities of Intellectual Choice in Imperial Japan." In Bernard S. Silberman and H. D. Harootunian, eds., *Japan in Crisis,* 110–55. Princeton: Princeton University Press, 1974.

———. "Introduction: A Sense of an Ending and the Problem of Taishō." In Bernard S. Silberman and H. D. Harootunian, eds., *Japan in Crisis,* 3–28. Princeton: Princeton University Press, 1974.

Hauptmann, Gerhart. *Lonely Lives: A Drama.* Trans. Mary Morrison. London: William Heinemann, 1898.

Hibbett, Howard. "The Portrait of the Artist in Japanese Fiction." *Far Eastern Quarterly* 14 (May 1955): 347–54.

Hsia, C. T. *The Classic Chinese Novel: A Critical Introduction.* New York: Columbia University Press, 1968.

Hutcheon, Linda. *Narcissistic Narrative: The Metafictional Paradox.* Waterloo, Ontario: Wilfrid Laurier University Press, 1980.

Isoda Kōichi. "The Historical Context of Postwar Japanese Literature." Trans. Lynne E. Riggs. *The Japan Foundation Newsletter* 12 (June 1984): 1–9.

Katō Shūichi. *A History of Japanese Literature.* Vol. 2, *The Years of Isolation.* Tokyo: Kodansha International, 1983.

Keene, Dennis. *Yokomitsu Riichi: Modernist.* New York: Columbia University Press, 1980.

Keene, Donald. *Dawn to the West: Japanese Literature in the Modern Era.* Vol. 1, *Fiction.* New York: Holt, Rinehart and Winston, 1984.

Kellman, Stephen G. *The Self-begetting Novel.* New York: Columbia University Press, 1980.

Kermode, Frank. *The Sense of an Ending: Studies in the Theory of Fiction.* London: Oxford University Press, 1975.

Kinmouth, Earl. *The Self-made Man in Meiji Japanese Thought: From Samurai to Salary Man.* Berkeley and Los Angeles: University of California Press, 1981.

Kuroda, S.-Y. "Reflections on the Foundations of Narrative Theory from a Linguistic Point of View," In Teun A. van Dijk, ed., *Pragmatics of Language and Literature*, 107–40. Amsterdam: North-Holland Publishing Co., 1976. Also in *The (W)hole of the Doughnut*, 185–203.

———. "Where Epistemology, Style, and Grammar Meet: A Case Study from Japanese." In Stephen R. Anderson and Paul Kiparsky, eds., *A Festschrift for Morris Halle*, 377–91. New York: Holt, Rinehart and Winston, 1973. Also in *The (W)hole of the Doughnut*, 205–31.

———. *The (W)hole of the Doughnut: Syntax and Its Boundaries.* Ghent: E. Story-Scientia P.V.B.A., 1979.

LaFleur, William. *The Karma of Words: Buddhism and the Literary Arts in Medieval Japan.* Berkeley: University of California Press, 1983.

Levin, Harry. *The Gates of Horn: A Study of Five French Realists.* New York: Oxford University Press, 1966.

Levine, George. "Realism Reconsidered." In John Halperin, ed., *The Theory of the Novel: New Essays*, 233–56. New York: Oxford University Press, 1974.

Liu, Wu-chi. *An Introduction to Chinese Literature.* Bloomington: Indiana University Press 1966.

Lukács, Georg. *Writer and Critic and Other Essays.* Ed. and trans. Arthur D. Kahn. New York: Grosset and Dunlap, 1971.

McClellan, Edwin. "Tōson and the Autobiographical Novel." In Donald H. Shively, ed., *Tradition and Modernization in Japanese Culture*, 347–78. Princeton: Princeton University Press, 1971.

Martin, Samuel E. *A Reference Grammar of Japanese.* New Haven: Yale University Press, 1975.

Maruyama, Masao. "From Carnal Literature to Carnal Politics." Trans. Barbara Ruch. In Ivan Morris, ed., *Thought and Behaviour in Modern Japanese Politics*, 245–67. London: Oxford University Press, 1963.

Mathy, Francis, S.J. "Kitamura Tōkoku: The Early Years." *Monumenta Nipponica* 18 (1963): 1–44.

———. "Kitamura Tōkoku: Essays on the Inner Life." *Monumenta Nipponica* 19 (1964): 66–110.

———. "Kitamura Tōkoku: Final Essays." *Monumenta Nipponica* 20 (1965): 41–63.

Miller, Roy Andrew. *Japan's Modern Myth: The Language and Beyond.* Tokyo: Weatherhill, 1982.

Miyoshi, Masao. *Accomplices of Silence: The Modern Japanese Novel.* Berkeley: University of California Press, 1974.

———. "Against the Native Grain: Reading the Japanese Novel in America." In *Critical Issues in East Asian Literature: Report on an International Conference on East Asian Literature*, 221–48. Seoul: International Cultural Society of Korea, 1983.

Morris, Mark. "Sei Shōgagon's Poetic Categories." *Harvard Journal of Asiatic Studies* 40 (June 1980): 5–54.

Murasaki Shikibu. *The Tale of Genji.* Trans. Edward G. Seidensticker. New York: Alfred A. Knopf, 1976.

Najita, Tetsuo. *Japan*. Englewood Cliffs, N.J.: Prentice-Hall, 1974.

Nakane Chie. *Japanese Society*. Berkeley: University of California Press, 1970.

Natsume Sōseki. *Mon*. Trans. Francis Mathy. London: Peter Owen, 1972.

Nishida Kitarō. *The Problem of Japanese Culture* (excerpts). In Ryusaku Tsunoda, Wm. Theodore de Bary, and Donald Keene, eds., *Sources of the Japanese Tradition*, 857–72. New York: Columbia University Press, 1958.

Okada, Richard Hideki. "Unbound Texts: Narrative Discourse in Heian Japan." Ph.D. diss., University of California, Berkeley, 1985.

Ong, Walter J., S.J. *Orality and Literacy: The Technologizing of the Word*. London: Methuen, 1982.

———. "The Writer's Audience Is Always a Fiction." *PMLA* 90 (Jan. 1975): 9–21.

Peyre, Henri. *Literature and Sincerity*. New Haven: Yale University Press, 1963.

Plato. *The Republic*. Trans. H. D. P. Lee. Harmondsworth, England: Penguin Books, 1955.

Pyle, Kenneth B. *The New Generation in Meiji Japan*. Stanford: Stanford University Press, 1969.

Rubin, Jay. *Injurious to Public Morals: Writers and the Meiji State*. Seattle: University of Washington Press, 1984.

———. "Kunikida Doppo." Ph.D. diss., University of Chicago, 1970.

Said, Edward W. *Beginnings: Intention and Method*. New York: Basic Books, 1975.

———. "The Text, the World, the Critic." In Josué V. Harari, ed., *Textual Strategies*, 161–88. Ithaca: Cornell University Press, 1979.

Sansom, George B. *The Western World and Japan*. New York: Alfred A. Knopf, 1950.

Scholes, Robert, and Robert Kellogg. *The Nature of Narrative*. London: Oxford University Press, 1966.

Seidensticker, Edward G. *Kafū the Scribbler*. Stanford: Stanford University Press, 1965.

Shiga Naoya. *A Dark Night's Passing*. Trans. Edwin McClellan. Tokyo: Kodansha International, 1976.

Sibley, William F. "Naturalism in Japanese Literature." *Harvard Journal of Asiatic Studies* 28 (1968): 157–69.

———. "Review Article: Tatsuo Arima, *The Failure of Freedom*." *Harvard Journal of Asiatic Studies* 31 (1971): 247–85.

———. *The Shiga Hero*. Chicago: University of Chicago Press, 1979.

Sontag, Susan. *Illness as Metaphor*. New York: Farrar, Straus and Giroux, 1978.

Stevick, Philip. *The Theory of the Novel*. New York: Free Press, 1967.

Strong, Kenneth L. C. "Downgrading the 'Kindai Jiga': Reflections on Tōson's *Hakai* and Subsequent Trends in Modern Literature." In Japan P.E.N. Club, ed., *Studies in Japanese Culture* 1:406–11. Tokyo: Japan P.E.N. Club, 1973.

Tayama Katai. *The Quilt and Other Stories by Tayama Katai.* Trans. Kenneth G. Henshall. Tokyo: University of Tokyo Press, 1981.

Thornbury, Barbara E. *Sukeroku's Double Identity: The Dramatic Structure of Edo Kabuki.* Ann Arbor: University of Michigan Center for Japanese Studies, 1982.

Todorov, Tzvetan. *The Poetics of Prose.* Trans. Richard Howard. Ithaca: Cornell University Press, 1977.

Tokutomi Roka [Kenjirō]. *Footprints in the Snow.* Trans. Kenneth Strong. New York: Pegasus, 1970.

Walker, Janet A. *The Japanese Novel of the Meiji Period and the Ideal of Individualism.* Princeton: Princeton University Press, 1979.

Watson, Burton. *Early Chinese Literature.* New York: Columbia University Press, 1962.

Watt, Ian. *The Rise of the Novel.* Berkeley: University of California Press, 1957.

Waugh, Patricia. *Metafiction: The Theory and Practice of Self-conscious Fiction.* London: Methuen, 1984.

White, Hayden. "Fictions of Factual Representation." In *Tropics of Discourse,* 121–34. Baltimore: Johns Hopkins University Press, 1978.

———. *Metahistory.* Baltimore: Johns Hopkins University Press, 1973.

Zola, Émile. *Thérèse Raquin.* Trans. L. W. Tancock. Harmondsworth, England: Penguin Books, 1962.

Index

Abe Akira, 297
Abe Kōbō, 291
Abiko, as setting in Shiga Naoya's fiction, 209
Ackroyd, Joyce, 192n, 199n
Activism, political, 78, 83, 96
Actor-audience relationship, xxv
Adolphe (Constant), 121n
Adversative passive, 256
Aeba Takeo, 211n, 281
Akagi Kōhei, 149, 152, 185
Akiyama Shun, 230n, 235n
Akutagawa Ryūnosuke, xvi, 69; on Chikamatsu Shūkō, 182–83; on confessional literature, 290; death of, 188; elitism of, 137–38; Kasai Zenzō on, 294; literary output of, 250; on Shiga Naoya, 187–88, 196; on Shimazaki Tōson, 111; on *shishōsetsu*, 50; *shishōsetsu* by, 294.
    Texts: *Bungeiteki na, amari ni bungeiteki na*, 187; *Haguruma*, 187n, 294; "Shuju no kotoba," 52n, 290; "'Watakushi' shōsetsu shōken," 50n
Alcoholism, Kasai Zenzō and, 249, 250–51, 276, 280–81, 285
Alexandria Quartet (Durrell), 164
Alienation, 13n, 81, 151
Alvarez, A., 248
Anata (pronominal), 175, 298
Andreyev, Leonid, 252n
Anonymity: of Chinese fiction writers, 21; of Japanese writers, 55; Shiga Naoya's urge toward, 190; of western writers, 55
An'ta (pronominal), use of, 175
An'ya kōro (Shiga Naoya), 14, 132, 184, 190n, 224–46, 247; author-hero identification in, 226–29, 238–40; characterization in, 233–34; childhood memories in, 237; completion of, 246; continuity in, 234–36; critical studies of, 224–46; drafts of, 230–31, 235–39; hero's self-absorption in, 233–34; Edwin McClellan's translation of, xi,

227n, 239n, 242n, 243n; narrative change in, 242–43, 246; point of view in, 242–43; as primer for reading *shishōsetsu*, 228–29; as "realistic" novel, 242–46; Shiga Naoya on, 243; structure of, 229, 230, 235; tenuousness of plot in, 229–33; textual history of, 225, 229–32; themes in, 224, 225, 233, 234; time in, 229
    Criticism: Dazai Osamu on, 225, 226, 232; Hirano Ken on, 230n; Hiraoka Tokuyoshi on, 235n, 237n, 240; Kobayashi Hideo on, 190n, 224, 240; Kōno Toshirō on, 236; Edwin McClellan on, 224; Miyoshi Yukio on, 224, 226, 230, 232n, 233, 241; Nakamura Mitsuo on, 224, 225, 230, 232n, 241; Nakano Shigeharu on, 227–28, 229–30, 238, 241
Arab writers, xxviii
Arai Hakuseki, 191, 192n, 199
Archaic language, use of, 272. *See also* Colloquial style
Arishima, Takeo, 132, 149, 191
Aristotle, on imitation, xxiiin
Art: Akutagawa Ryūnosuke on, 50; experience and, 144; Kunikida Doppo on, 90; morality and, 48; private life and, 54–55, 193; reality and, 18n, religion and, 94; Tayama Katai on, 107–8; truth and, 25, 50, 93; unity of life and, 213
Asahi (newspaper), 110, 130, 134, 135t, 140, 221n, 231
Audience, xxv, 38, 93; Chikamatsu Shūkō and, 160–62, 167; interpretation and, xvii–xviii, xxviii, 192, 273, 275–79; reading and, xvii. *See also* Reader
Auerbach, Erich, 19n
Authenticity, x, 10, 108, 238–39, 245, 292; of text, 7, 261; of unmediated transcription, 65–66, 261, 282, 295. *See also* Sincerity; Written reportive style

315

Confucianism, 21, 22, 79, 83–84, 86, 90,
130, 190, 192; didacticism and, 83–84
Contentless hero, 241
Contentless story, 265
Cooke, Miriam, xxviii n
Coterie magazines. See *Dōjin zasshi*
Creativity in Japan, xxvi
Crémieux, Benjamin, 66
Criticism, Japanese, xxii. See also *specific writers*

Da style, 274. See also Colloquial style
Daisen, Mount, as setting in Shiga
Naoya's fiction, 233, 234, 235, 242
Dark Night's Passing, A. See *An'ya kōro*
David Copperfield (Dickens), xix n
Dazai Osamu, 144, 225; death of, 188;
personal style, 189; on Shiga Naoya,
187–88, 225, 226, 232, 247, 252; *Nyoze
gamon*, 187, 188 n, 225, 247
De aru style, 275. See also Colloquial
style
Death: identity and, 285; Shiga Naoya
on, 218, 222. See also Suicide
Defoe, Daniel, 15
Desu/masu style, 274
Diaries, xvi, xxviii, 16, 82, 279. See also
Kana nikki
Dick, Kay, 156 n
Dictation, Kasai Zenzō and, 250, 272–
74, 283
Didacticism, 86–87, 93, 191; in Chinese
literature, 21–22; Confucianism and,
83–84; Kitamura Tōkoku and, 80;
Kunikida Doppo and, 91; Tsubouchi
Shōyō and, 87
Documentation, *shishōsetsu* as, xix
Dōjin (dōnin) zasshi, 131–32
Dōmeki Kyōsaburō, 133 n
Doppo. See Kunikida Doppo
Dostoevsky, Fyodor, 47, 52, 276 n;
Crime and Punishment, 13 n, 47; *Notes
from Underground*, 276 n
Double negatives, 256

Easthope, Antony, 279 n
Eco, Umberto, 31 n
Edo fiction, xxii, xxv, 16 n, 22, 79, 87,
121
Edo period, 15, 22–23, 25, 83, 87, 130,
191
Eguchi Kan, 210 n
Eliot, George, 29–30; *Adam Bede*, 29
Emakimono, 230 n
Emerson, Ralph Waldo, 82

Emma (Austen), 13
Emotion: Chikamatsu Shūkō's conversion of into language, 156, 158; depersonalized, 85; distancing of, 121 n,
155, 203; jealousy, 116, 152, 158–62;
lack of in *Ken'yūsha* school, 89; writ-
ing and, 198. See also Love affairs;
specific authors
Emplotment: artificiality of, 48, 282;
Chikamatsu Shūkō on, 154; Christianity and, 83; Japanese literature
and, 19–20; in narrative, xx, xxviii,
19 n, 73, 87
Endō Hideo, 153 n, 157 n
Endō Tasuku, 197 n, 233 n
English language, adoption by Japanese, 244
Enlightenment (European), 10, 12, 73
Enomoto Takashi, 257
Enpon (one-yen books), importance of
to *bundan*, 141
Epiphanies, 235 n
Episteme, medieval, 84 n
Epistemology, 101, 126, 181, 194, 282;
experience and, 39; grammar and,
31, 94, 238, 254; *ichigen byōsha* and,
124; Japanese language and, 30–31,
183, 238; narrative and, 53, 58; omniscience and, 181–83, 238; sensation
words and, 31 n, 32; *shishōsetsu* and,
181–82, 185, 229, 297, translation
and, 245 n. See also Grammar; Mediation, of reality; Omniscience; Reportive style; Truth
Erlebte Rede. See Represented speech
and thought
Essay form, xx, xxviii, 16, 63, 75, 86
Estang, Luc, 69
Ethnology, xv
European literature. See Western
literature
Experience, 117; consistency of, 152;
dictated by writing, 202; different
tellings of, 178, 257–58; epistemology
and, 39; fabrication and, 92; *Futon*
and, 117–18; as history, 18; meaning
of, 292; mystical, 242; nature and,
108; realism and, xxiii–xxiv; recording of, 108; *shishōsetsu* and, 14; transformation of into art, 144–45. See also
Epistemology; Truth; Realism

Fabrication, in narrative, 7, 26, 47, 84,
92, 107–8, 181, 207–8. See also Fiction
Family: conflicts in, 202, 205, 223; ex-

tended, 98; in fiction of Tayama Katai, Tokuda Shūsei, and Shimazaki
Tōson, 150. *See also* Society
Father-son relation, Shiga Naoya and,
204–21, 224, 231. See also *An'ya kōro;
Wakai*
Federman, Raymond, 42
Fiction, xxvii, xxviii; in age of disillusionment, 101n; autobiography and,
xx, xxvi; confession and, 101, 279–80;
definition of, 10; family resistance to
writing of, 191; Fowles on, 10; history and, 18–19, 87; in Japanese
literature, 16–27; Japanese writers'
distrust of, 46, 107; narrative and, xx;
nonfiction and, xviii; as nonliterature, 22–25, 79, 102; notions of, 10–
11; positive connotations of, 11; reality and, 7, 11, 18; "refined" vs. "vulgar," 22–23, 86; serialized, 134, 135,
138, 231; society's use of, 11; truth
and, 19, 25. *See also* Autobiography;
Epistemology; Fabrication; Mediation; Narrative; *Shishōsetsu; Shōsetsu;
specific authors and texts*
Fielding, Henry, 15, 18, 29, 196n; *Tom
Jones*, 13, 18, 196n
Film, Japanese, xxin
First-person narration, x, xxvii, 28–29,
35–36, 39, 64n, 107, 171–72, 184,
200, 236–37, 240, 241, 282, 296; merging with third-person narration, 53,
171–72. *See also* Third-person
narration
First-person pronominals, 5, 28, 31n,
184, 207. See also *specific pronominals*
Flaubert, Gustave, 47, 49, 53, 54–55,
228, 238, 295, 298; *Madame Bovary*,
13, 47
Fourth-person, 53
Fowles, John, 10, 29, 198n; *The French
Lieutenant's Woman*, 10n, 198n
Fragmentation of narrative, 260–63,
284
Framing of narrative, 263–65, 272, 275,
284
Freedman, Ralph, xxviin
French language, adoption of in Japan,
244
Fujieda Shizuo, 296; *Gongu jōdo*, 296
Fukuda Kiyoto, 207n, 251
Fukunaga Takehiko, *Shi no shima*, 220n
Funaki Shigeo, 255n
Furui Yoshikichi, 259n, 273, 288
Futabatei Shimei, xviin, 3, 23–24, 76,

87, 113, 183; on fiction writing as a
career, 24; on narrative perspective,
183; Tsubouchi Shōyō and, 87
  Texts: *Heibon*, 113, 122, 183–84;
Sono omokage, 183n; *Ukigumo*, 23,
183n; "Watakushi wa kaigi-ha da," 3,
24n
Futon (Tayama Katai), xvi, 59, 103, 139;
as autobiography, 109–23; comic
scenes in, 116, 121; confession in ,
111, 113, 115, 117; familial obligation
in, 122; feminine ideal in, 104, 117,
120; *Hakai* and, 59, 117; importance
of, 60–61; individualism and, 112,
jealousy in, 116; use of *kare* in, 36n;
Katai's earlier fiction and, 117–21;
Katai's later fiction and, 123; literary
sources of, 117–19; naturalism and,
117; parody in, 116, 121–22; privatization and, 103; as prototypical
shishōsetsu, xvi, 53, 104, 123; referential reading of, 113–18; sales of,
139; *shishōsetsu* and, 123, summary
of, 104; success of, 107, 112, 122;
Thérèse Raquin and, 118–19; as turning point in literature, 61
  Criticism: Chikamatsu Shūkō on,
112–13; Hirano Ken on, 114–15;
Nakamura Mitsuo on, 59–61, 113–
14, 121n; Okada Michiyo on, 115–17;
Shimamura Hōgetsu on, 99. *See also*
Tayama Katai

Gakushūin University, 129
Gender, of authors, xxix
Genesis, as an emplotted narrative,
19n
Genette, Gérard, 8n, 9, 34n, 177
Genre. See *specific writing modes and
styles*
Gesaku (playful composition), 23, 24,
87, 129
Gide, André, 9, 52, 54
God, in Japanese tradition, ix, 83
Goethe, Johann Wolfgang von, 54,
121n; *Werther*, 13, 121n; *Wilhelm
Meister*, 13
Gombrich, E. H., 18
Goncourt brothers, 123, 123n–124n
Grammar: epistemology and, 31n, 94,
183, 238, 254, 283; textual trans-
parency and, 205; thought and, 194.
See also *Da* style; *De-aru* style; *Desu/
masu* style; Double negatives; Epis-
temology; Honorifics; Interjectionals;